Nuthatch County

Steven Popkes

Nuthatch County

Steven Popkes

A Howard Cycle Novel

Walking Rocks /Book View Café

Cover design by Wendy Zimmerman
Cover illustration © 2023 by Wendy Zimmerman
Published by Walking Rock Publications in association with
Book View Café Publishing Cooperative
www.bookviewcafe.com

ISBN: 978-1-63632-170-7

Dedicated to the State of Missouri

Table of Contents

"Nuthatch County is a rough 10 by 20 mile rectangle on the Missouri side of the Mississippi. The White Bluffs and the Bittersweet Ridge form its northern and western border. The southwest corner of the county is occupied by the Bluewater Indian Reservation, home to branches of the Choctaw and the Osage tribes.

The county's highest point is Little Mountain, a limestone knoll barely a hundred feet above the surrounding ridges and bluffs and only six hundred feet higher than the river. Situated at the base of Little Mountain, Fox Park, the county's sole public park, is barely more than a parking lot and a picnic table. A switchback trail proceeds up the side of Little Mountain to a flat unmarked ledge called Table Rock.

Nuthatch County has two towns, Pilate and Ridgeville. Pilate is the county seat with a population of perhaps six hundred.
There is no clear record of how the town of Pilate got its name. Pilate, as you'll recall, washed his hands of the matter."
—Missouri: A Guide to the "Show Me" State, WPA, 1941

"A common feeder bird with clean black, gray, and white markings, White-breasted Nuthatches are active, agile little birds with an appetite for insects and large, meaty seeds. They get their common name from their habit of jamming large nuts and acorns into tree bark, then whacking them with their sharp bill to 'hatch' out the seed from the inside. White-breasted Nuthatches may be small but their voices are loud, and often their insistent nasal yammering will lead you right to them."
—All About Birds, Cornell Lab of Ornithology

"Watch, watch, watch, for you never know when the dark is coming."
—The Passion of St. Mark

Prologue

February 19, 2001

Betty DaFoe rolled over in her sleep. She laid one arm across Jeremy's side of the bed. Jeremy wasn't there and she woke up briefly and looked at the clock. 3:00 AM. She wasn't surprised. She rarely woke up when Jeremy paced the County but nearly always awakened when he returned. This was one of the rare nights where she roused in between.

The sheet was cold to the touch. He'd been gone for some time. For a moment she was wide awake, as calm and quiet as the winter night. She patted his pillow and hoped his walk went well. Sometimes things didn't and he came home sad.

The edge of her dream caught at her attention. Betty had been pregnant. Something she had given up as impossible the day she married Jeremy since he could not father children. Betty could still remember how the baby felt: the heavy weight. The sense of warmth. The feeling of being lit from within. She felt a sudden pang of loss and drew her hand over her flat stomach. After being married for ten years you'd think she would have accepted the way things were.

Betty rolled back to her side of the bed and snuggled the pillow as if it were Jeremy. The thought of him made her happy and she found herself still surprised to be here. She smiled to herself. She was only thirty. She had years to live. Years to be with Jeremy. Something else you would think she'd accept after a while. She buried her face in the pillow until she caught the smell of him.

Betty fell easily back to sleep.

As Jeremy walked along the frozen Mississippi the air was sharp and dry, cleared of moisture by a month of unseasonable cold. The river was broad here and rarely froze but this winter had stilled it. But it was no flat icy stream. As the waters had frozen, broken free, and frozen together again, the violence of the collisions had been preserved. Jeremy looked out over an icy field of broken boulders that glittered in the moonlight.

He was tall and very thin so that in the pale light his bones seemed to show. He wore an old broad-brimmed hat. His skin was stretched over high cheekbones and unshaven with a day's worth of stubble. He wore a cloth coat and thin cloth gloves.

Jeremy stopped and stared across the river. Nothing stirred. He pulled off the glove from his right hand, squatted down, and rested his fingertips on a sheet of limestone sticking up through the ice. He could feel the faint tremble as the water moved past. A frown crossed his face and he shook his head.

Jeremy stood up and looked across the water again, turned, and walked across the frozen bottomland road west of Pilate, passing miles of fertile bottomland on the way.

Jenny and Glenn Waxman were sitting up with the twins. Both twins had croup. It wasn't clear if they were sick enough for Glenn to drive into town and rouse Doctor Faraday and have him open the clinic—if the clinic wasn't already open. They had no phone to call ahead. Glenn was trying to ease their coughing by boiling water on the little stove and filling the trailer with steam. Each time the tub ran dry he refilled it from a pickle barrel. When the barrel ran dry he dressed up against the cold and walked the fifty yards to the well-house next to the ruins of his grandfather's house. There, he cracked the ice off the pump with a hammer and pumped the water by hand until the barrel was full and then carried forty pounds of water back to the trailer.

Jeremy skirted the east end of the Bluewater Reservation along the river bottom road and walked past the well house while Glenn was pumping furiously. Glenn never saw him. When Glenn returned to the trailer, Jenny was sitting next to the twins on the bed, relief plain on her face. Both children were asleep and breathing easily.

County Commissioner Pam Small didn't stir when Jeremy walked past her house on the outskirts of Pilate. Sheriff Grace Cox fretted in her sleep but only for a moment. Grace's old redbone hound, Paley, woke up from his bed on the porch. Paley joined Jeremy on the main road as it turned away from town. Jeremy squatted down and rubbed the dog's ears as Paley shivered both from the cold and the joy of companionship. Jeremy smiled and rubbed Paley's neck and back and then his legs. As he did, the stiffness melted away and Paley jumped like a puppy.

Paley walked with Jeremy out of town as far as the old and abandoned bottling plant and then left him, baying as he chased a fox. In her sleep, Grace heard him and smiled.

Jeremy turned north off the main road onto County Road 2 towards Blue Pond. A mile further a dirt driveway split off the road and rounded the pond, making a loop before an old Victorian house. The front porch of the house was so designed it could look straight down the main road toward town. On a clear day, the top of the First Baptist Church could be seen.

Jeremy didn't turn with the road but instead went straight over the frozen water to the front porch of the house. The ice vibrated and rang like a bell. Jeremy stopped in the middle of the lake and listened. He continued across the lake to the beach on the other side, past the privacy signs, and up the slope to the porch.

Deacon Williams rolled over in his sleep. The movement triggered a deep coughing fit that did not cease when he awoke but went deeper each time until it took a major effort to keep from vomiting. Things came up anyway and he was conscious of nothing but the effort to breathe. When the fit eased, he found himself leaning over the edge of his ancient brass bed staring at a pool of blood on the floor. Someone held his head and eased him onto his back.

He looked up in the dimness left by the kitchen light.

"Shit," he said. "Jeremy DaFoe." He closed his eyes wearily. "Shit. Haven't you got anything better to do than this?"

Jeremy sat in the chair next to the bed. He pulled off his hat. "No."

"Only vultures and Jeremy DaFoe know when somebody's going to die." He stuck out his hand. "Help me up. If I'm going to die I'm damned if I'm going to do it lying down like this."

Jeremy helped him to sit up.

The old man breathed hoarsely, shallowly, for a long time. "Have I got any lungs left?"

Jeremy shook his head. "Not really."

"Christ." Williams shook his head. "Don't you get tired of this? Can't you leave me alone?"

Jeremy shook his head slowly.

"You son-of-a-bitch," Williams said without heat. "I've hated you since I knew what you were. You know that, don't you?"

Jeremy nodded.

"The very idea that you keep on living past the death of better men. Myself included." Williams lifted his hand and dropped it in resignation. "But you're not a man, are you?"

Jeremy didn't answer.

"You could heal me in a moment, if you wanted." Williams rubbed his hands on his withered thighs. "But you won't."

"No, I won't."

"I didn't think so. I don't even have the satisfaction of thinking it's revenge. Tornadoes don't exact revenge. Floods don't exact revenge. Nor does Jeremy DaFoe. You'll die, too, someday."

"Yes."

"I live in hope." He cleared his throat experimentally. "What do you do on these visits, anyway?" Deacon Williams asked. "Gloat? Tell me what I missed? How happy I could have been?"

Jeremy shook his head. "I've come to keep you company."

Williams chuckled and almost coughed but caught himself. "I'm not proud enough to turn you away. Help me into the kitchen so I can have a drink. Do you want a drink?"

"Sure."

Jeremy sat with Deacon Williams for almost two hours. After the old man died, he carried Williams back to his bed. Then, he picked up the phone. Carter Faraday's voice was tinny on the other side of the line. Carter agreed to call Jake Withers to pick up the body. The state would need a death certificate.

Afterward, Jeremy walked around the house three times, watching the windows. Then, he crossed the lake again going south.

Clouds came in from Arkansas and mixed with the cold clear air over the County. The resulting snow, as hard and round as pearls, rattled as it struck Jeremy's hat.

The ground was slippery here, and steep. He walked carefully.

A deer came out of the woods and walked beside him. Every now and then, Jeremy slipped and steadied himself against the deer. Near the last hundred feet or so of the ridge when the scrub soil turned to rock and even the grass disappeared, he stopped and nodded to the deer. The deer watched him for a moment and then bounded down the slope into the forest.

Jeremy walked along the bare ridge until he reached Table Rock. He brushed the accumulated snow from his hat and looked around. He shook his head and frowned. Jeremy leaned against the rock and removed his boots and socks, then his gloves. With bare fingers and toes, he inched his way up the side of Little Mountain. This high and unimpeded, the wind grew fierce. The top was no more than six feet across. He stood up gingerly. The wind nearly took his hat off and he held it down with one hand. The snow was turning to mist and freezing rain now and visibility was no more than forty feet. Jeremy turned this way and that, staring through the darkness.

After a while, he worked his way back. He rubbed and blew on his feet for several minutes, then pulled on his socks and shoes. He descended a different way, westerly, and in a few minutes, the rain began in earnest. He stumbled through the slush until he came to the southern part of Ridgeville and walked, south now, past the storefronts and the gas station, across the bridge over Bluegill Creek, into Ashby.

Buddy Parker knew it was late. He sat up on the edge of his bed and looked out and saw a tall man standing on his porch staring up at the sky.

Buddy picked up his robe and winced. He rubbed the swollen joints of his arthritic hands, looked at them, and felt embarrassed. Once, he had been proud of his hands: black as pecans, black as the rich earth, imbued with such strength that it seemed his muscles and tendons danced. His palms were pale and he remembered how graceful his hands had been, like birds with dark back and light breast.

A knocking brought him back to himself and he hurried to the door. Buddy was still half asleep in his reverie. Jeremy's face, backlit by the streetlight, startled him.

"Papa Jeremy?" he asked.

Jeremy came in, smiling. He removed his hat. "You haven't called me that since you were four."

"I'm sorry." Buddy stopped and collected himself. "I was startled." He looked closer at Jeremy. "Good God. You're wet clear through."

Buddy turned to the hall closet and pulled out tall, thin clothes to match him. As Jeremy undressed, Buddy took each article, pants, shirt, socks, and carefully put them in the hamper to be washed and stored back in the closet.

While Jeremy dressed, Buddy went into the kitchen and put on the kettle.

Jeremy came in and sat at the table just as Buddy poured out instant coffee into a mug and put it in front of him.

"Thanks," said Jeremy and sipped it.

"What are you out for on a night like this?"

"Deacon Williams died."

"May God have mercy on his soul," said Buddy automatically. Then: "Oh."

Jeremy nodded. "You're the Eldest, now." He drained the mug and stood. "It's good to have an Eldest that doesn't hate me."

"Did the Deacon always hate you?"

Jeremy shrugged. "Pretty much. He got that from his father, I think. Or maybe his grandfather." Jeremy rose. "Got to get going. I thought you'd like it if I was the one to tell you."

"Yes," said Buddy absently. "Thanks."

"Good night," said Jeremy and started for the front hallway.

"Wait." Buddy followed him to the door. "Is that all?" He had a vague feeling of unease.

Jeremy didn't answer for a moment. "No," he said, and went outside.

Jeremy walked west out of Ashby and along a back road going towards the White Bluffs. The road rose until it hugged the limestone and looked down the seventy feet or so to Sandy Creek. He heard drunken voices ahead of him. He walked noiselessly but the effort was wasted on the high school kids ahead of him in the turnout. Two boys shoved each other and one lost his balance. Jeremy reached out and steadied him before he fell over the cliff.

"Evening, Cooper," he said to the boy.

"Jesus. It's Jeremy." Cooper turned and threw up on the dirt.

The other boys fell silent when they saw him.

Jeremy didn't speak immediately. "Anybody sober enough to drive?"

They looked at one another, then at the ground.

Jeremy nodded. "Leave the car here. Go back into town. Keller's mother is still up so you would have gotten into trouble anyhow. Call her to come pick you up. The car will be safe." He looked at each of them in turn. "Don't come up here drunk anymore. Next time I won't catch you."

He walked past them and went on down the road.

Cooper didn't want to leave the car. The others crowded around him.

"Are you nuts?" one said. "That was *Jeremy*."

That was enough to convince him and they descended the road suddenly sober.

Walking back east now, the road dropped back down to the bridge over Sandy Creek but Jeremy turned away from it into the shadow of the woods.

The Pilate Clinic was small: six beds and space in the emergency room for four patients if everybody knew one another well enough. A small surgical suite. A waiting room that could hold perhaps a dozen people sitting and reading out-of-date magazines. Carter Faraday was the only doctor and Peggy Small, one of two nurses. Tonight only Peggy and Carter were on duty and it had been a long night so far.

Three hours ago, Emmet Posey had managed to get drunk enough to slice off two fingers with a straight razor—at least, that was Posey's story and his wife backed him up. It didn't help that both of them had been drunk on Porter hooch and had driven their car into the loading dock getting Emmet to the clinic. While Faraday had been making sure the stumps were stable enough for Emmet to be taken to the hospital in Cape Girardeau, Peggy Small had searched the wrecked car for the Styrofoam cup containing Emmet's fingers. By the time she had found the cup, Carter had woken up Sheriff Cox. The Sheriff took Emmett Posey, Emmet's fingers, and Loretta Posey north to Southeast Hospital. An hour after that, Jeremy had called him and told him Deacon Williams had died. That meant another call, this one to Jake Withers, Nuthatch County's only mortician.

Meanwhile, Mary Jo Pedersen had decided to come in

because she was feeling "poorly." Mary Jo weighed in at three hundred and seventy-five pounds so any examination was an exercise in patience. "Poorly" was soon redefined to be "in labor," which came as a surprise to Carter since Mary Jo had not informed him she was pregnant. It came as a surprise to Mary Jo, as well, since she hadn't thought she was able to get pregnant as she'd been living with Sidney Robinson for the last twelve years without using any birth control in all that time. Mary Jo had only been out of town once in the last year, for two weeks back in May, when she'd gone up to Cairo to visit her great Aunt. There she'd only done it once standing up with "a friend of the family." You couldn't get pregnant that way, could you?

Mary Jo's labor slowed somewhat after Carter had administered the epidural and he took the opportunity to flee here to the loading dock, huddling deep in his coat and contemplating the stars above him and the wreck of Emmett Posey's car below. Someday soon he'd get back to someplace warm. Someplace where he could be part of a real hospital staff in a real hospital with real hospital equipment. Carter Faraday had been working in the Nuthatch County Clinic for nine years.

"Evening, Carter," said Jeremy as he stepped out of the shadows.

Faraday cried out. "You scared the shit out of me," he accused.

"Sorry."

"Jake hasn't brought the Deacon in yet. I think he's going to wait until morning."

Jeremy took off his hat. "I'm not here about that. Thought I'd look in on Mary Jo." Jeremy walked into the clinic.

Faraday followed him anxiously. "Is there something I should know about?"

Jeremy didn't answer and stopped just short of Mary Jo's room. "How are you at C-sections?"

Carter blanched and called out to Peggy, then entered the examination room. Jeremy followed him in. Mary Jo smiled at him.

"Hi, Papa Jeremy," she said sweetly. "Did you come to meet my baby?"

"She'll be a lively one, Mary," he said. "She's going to give you plenty of trouble."

Mary Jo nodded. "I expect so."

"Fetal heartbeat's good," Carter said, looking up at Jeremy.

Jeremy nodded and stepped back outside the room. "You'll do fine. But the baby's going to have to go to Southeast. The heart's not closing right."

"Sheriff Cox already went to Southeast."

"Call up Lenny Cooper. He'll be awake by now. He'll be happy to take the ambulance and get the extra pay. You go with them."

"What if somebody comes in tonight?"

Jeremy smiled at Carter. "Don't worry. Nobody else will come in tonight."

Jeremy left the clinic while Carter was on the phone.

Betty awoke as Jeremy came into their room. He sat down on the bed and looked out the window in silence.

"Honey?" she said. "Was it a tough night?"

Jeremy shook his head. "Not really."

"What's wrong?"

Jeremy shook his head again. "Nothing." But his face looked worried.

Betty rubbed his shoulders until he sighed.

He took her hands. "Play for me, would you?"

The piano was in the front room. She padded softly across the cold hardwood floors and turned on the music light. For a moment, she looked over the music and selected one of the Hungarian Dances by Liszt. She knew her own ability: an amateur of little talent but great enthusiasm. She had to regularly pause and work out the notes measure by measure. Often, she wondered why Jeremy liked her to play for him. Perhaps, she thought, he can hear the same music I can hear inside.

Betty raised her hands over the keyboard. The room was hushed in the early dawn light as in a great concert hall. She brought her hands down and began to play.

Part 1

Chapter 1: The February Briefing

Luke Prescott walked three miles every day.

It didn't matter if the weather was bitter or sunny, rainy or covered with snow. If a blizzard kept him in his Georgetown apartment, he paced the length of the hallway outside. Three miles. No more. No less. Thus are rituals conserved.

Luke had always liked to walk. One of the first problems he'd had when he moved to Washington was not being able to walk. It was during the Kennedy administration and automobiles could do no wrong. Catherine had taken his growing frustration and anger for nearly a year before she had forced him outside: "Go walk some place, damn it."

That day he'd walked clear down to the Lincoln Memorial before he felt like he could sit down. There, on the steps, looking across the spring green flanking the reflecting pool, he felt comfortable again. He was Jeremy DaFoe's liaison with the United States. He could speak with the President whenever he needed to—which, he fervently hoped, would never happen on his watch. His little girl was thirteen and getting as difficult as any teenager. But he loved both little Nadine and Catherine more than he ever thought he could love anything or anyone. Life was actually pretty good if he could keep walking. He was twenty-nine years old.

The liaison he'd replaced had been named John Bitters, as pleasant and happy a man Luke had ever met. John had a round, pink face as if he lived on a diet of donuts and happy thoughts and he seemed to bubble when he spoke.

"Let me tell you how Washington works," John said over lunch the day Luke met him. "All problems devolve until they can fit on a single desk. If a problem is too big or too important, there will magically appear enough desks to support it. If a problem is too small or nobody cares about it, desks will come together until the number of desks matches the problem. Each desk will eventually have its set of problems that fit perfectly. It's a natural evolution. The Democritan atom of Washington is a desk." He pointed at Luke. "*You* are the Nuthatch County Desk. We represent a single desk problem. It's too important to add onto someone else's desk and too small to warrant more than one."

"It's an awesome responsibility," said Luke hollowly. "I don't know if I'm up to it."

"Hush puppies," said John happily. "Balderdash and other like sentiments. You're young—Jeremy always likes to start them young so he'll have the same person in the same place for a long time. I started at thirty-two. You have a young wife and daughter to keep you company. You're reasonably handsome and your wife is wonderful. Jeremy will tell you what he needs. You tell the President. The President does what he can do. You tell Jeremy. Jeremy nods and says, 'Okay, Luke'. Your job is to help the President interpret what Jeremy needs into things the President can do."

John waved at him. "It's not hard. Look, conversations with the President will go something like this: 'Mister President, Jeremy needs a bridge across Sandy Creek.'" His voice took on a credible Boston accent. "'Is that so? Dean: could you do something with that?' Secretary Rusk and you will figure out what's involved so that Rusk can hand it off to Luther in Commerce. Luther, who knows nothing of Jeremy, will make sure the money gets into a grant fund. You will call Edith Orville, as long as she's Eldest, and tell her the grant information and where to send the application. She will tell County Commissioner Potter who will delegate out that job. A few weeks later the grant comes through and some months after that the money is sent. That's the way things are done."

"That's it?"

"Brief the President every February and make sure you're available to the Pentagon in case they get nervous. That's it."

Luke shook his head. "You make it sound easy."

"It is easy." John's face clouded. "Well, mostly."

"Uh oh."

John looked a little perplexed and embarrassed. "You're never quite sure that you're accomplishing anything. That you're doing enough. It seems a small thing to bend the President's ear for a bridge over Sandy Creek."

Luke nodded. "Couldn't you contact the governor or something? It's a state road—"

John shook his finger at him. "Never," he said. "Never. Never. Never. The fewer tongues the better. How else would you keep Jeremy a secret? Who else could you trust?"

Bitters retired in June of 1963. The traditional February time had been put in place during Madison's term but Luke's first solo briefing had been to Lyndon Johnson that terrible December after the assassination. He'd been disorganized and scared and it had taken far too long. Johnson very nearly threw him out of the Oval Office—would have if it hadn't been for Rusk. The next one, in February of 1964, had been better. LBJ had barely looked up from his desk. Luke had been in and out in ten minutes. Now he stood outside the Executive Building and stared up at the corner window of his office. The ground was bare of snow and in the wind, he could smell spring preparing its assault. He was seventy-one years old. John Bitters died after Nixon had resigned. Catherine had passed on during the last summer of the elder Bush administration. Luke's brother, John, had been buried for eight years. Nadine and her husband, Joseph Durant, were living back in the County. Joanie, his granddaughter, drank far more than she should but neither Nadine nor Joanie would ever speak of it. Both girls took after their mother that way. He didn't even know exactly where Joanie was living these days. Where's the sense in that? Somewhere in Baltimore. An artist in an art school.

Luke had been liaison for thirty-nine years. He felt surrounded by ghosts.

He went up to his office and put down his briefcase and gym bag. He went down the hall and showered. After he changed clothes he returned to his office, opened his briefcase, and pulled out his notes for the briefing. They were thicker than usual since this was President Bush the younger's first briefing. Luke packed up his briefcase, checked his watch, and walked outside and down the street. He reached the White House exactly twenty minutes early.

Thirty-five minutes later he was ushered into the Oval Office by the Chief of Staff. He opened his briefcase and pulled out his notes—though he probably had this particular briefing memorized through sheer repetition. He sat down on the sofa and waited.

Half an hour later President Bush came in flanked by Colin Powell and Dick Cheney. Luke rose. They shook hands and Bush sat down and gestured for Luke to proceed.

"Thank you," said Luke. "First a quick history lesson. In the winter of 1803, Lewis and Clark spent the winter camped where the Missouri and Mississippi rivers joined north of Saint Louis.

Lewis was especially interested in local folklore and wrote some of them down. One story was of a spirit that lived further south on the banks of the Mississippi. The spirit always appeared in the shape of a man. He tilled the soil, hunted, and took wives like any normal man but he was tied to his place and had great power. What intrigued Lewis about the story was the detail of where this spirit lived, near the town of New Madrid. He noted similar stories from both French and Spanish settlers and from this material Lewis drew a map in his journals.

"In 1807 Lewis was made Governor of the Upper Louisiana Territory. In 1809 there was a controversy over finances and Lewis decided to go to Washington to straighten them out. He remembered the story and on the way he made a side trip down the Mississippi to this place." Luke handed the President a reproduction of an ancient map. Bush looked confused. Luke sighed. The first presidential briefing was always the worst. There was a long list of things any new President discovered that completely contradicted the candidate's impression of the office. Jeremy was just one of many.

"Not much is known about his trip but he did manage to send a long letter to President Jefferson saying, essentially, that the story was true. Lewis died in a Tennessee roadhouse two weeks later. Benjamin Howard replaced him. Later, Clark replaced Howard in 1813.

"Jefferson didn't think much of it but to be on the safe side, some projects he had in mind for the region were either moved to different sites or canceled.

"In 1809, James Madison, Secretary of State under Jefferson, took office as President. One of Jefferson's canceled projects was a thorough survey of the area where this 'spirit' lived. Madison decided to go ahead with the project and sent surveyors to the area. This was in October of 1811. On November first of that year, Madison received a letter signed by a man named Bill Pratt. In very polite language, Pratt asked Madison to stop the survey or there would be consequences. If the survey was not stopped the nature of these consequences would be revealed before the end of the year."

Luke picked up and gave a copy of an ancient letter to the President. "This is a page from the diary of Zacharia Williams, a resident of the area. Let me read it to you. 'This morning, Bill and I walked south over the creek and up into the hills. I walked with him for several hours as he searched for something, staring at the ground and here and there digging with his foot. Finally, in the evening, he seemed satisfied and we had a nice rabbit dinner. At about two in the morning, Bill returned to the spot he had chosen and raised his foot as high as he could and stamped the ground.'"

Luke took a deep breath. This was the hard part.

"The New Madrid Earthquake struck at 2:15 AM on the night of December 16, 1811. The quake rang church bells in New York City. It caused damage as far away as Washington, D.C., and Charleston, South Carolina. It made the Mississippi river run backward to Saint Louis and changed its course and created Reelfoot Lake in Tennessee. Survivors of the quake said the ground cracked open and rolled in waves like the ocean."

"What the Hell are you trying to tell me?" said Bush.

"Bear with me, sir. Madison took it seriously and so should you. Madison sent a representative on a secret mission to speak with Pratt. This is a sketch of Pratt and the representative." Luke handed a copy of an old drawing to Bush.

Bush glanced at the gaunt face. "Who's that standing next to him?"

"William Clark."

"Of Lewis and Clark?"

"Yes."

"This is nuts."

"Many people have thought so, sir. President Madison established my office to act as a liaison with Pratt." Luke gave the President another picture. "In 1820, Missouri became a state, and Nuthatch County, where William Pratt lived, was created." He handed a modern photograph to Bush.

Bush held up the drawing and the photograph together. "They look alike."

"The man in the photograph is called Jeremy DaFoe. Before that, he was known as Nathan Collins. Before that, he was known as Bill Pratt."

"You're trying to tell me this man is two hundred years old?" shouted Bush.

"No, sir," said Luke calmly. "Jeremy DaFoe is not a man and he is considerably older than two hundred years old. He is a being of unknown power that has lived in Nuthatch County since long before historical times."

Bush looked at Cheney. Cheney looked as if he didn't know what to do. Powell looked strained.

"I haven't got time for this." Bush started to rise.

"Mister President," said Powell softly. "You should listen to this briefing."

"You don't tell me you *believe* this crap do you?" Bush shook his head in disbelief.

"The Pentagon has known about Jeremy DaFoe for some time."

Bush stared at Powell, then at Luke. "You mean this is *true?*"

Luke nodded. "Every word of it."

"Every word of what?" Bush waved it away with his hand. "You say there's this witch doctor in Missouri that's hundreds of years old. Maybe so. But what do you really know about him? President Madison thought he caused an earthquake by stamping his foot. It certainly was a heck of a big earthquake but maybe this DaFoe character just knew when it was going to happen and took advantage. What do we actually know about him?"

Luke spoke slowly. "I have evidence he can be in more than

one place at a time and that he has some knowledge of the future. He knows when people are going to die. He can kill from a distance."

"You've *seen* this?"

"Yes. Jeremy sat on my porch one afternoon and later I found he had been sitting up with Edith Orville at the same time." Luke hesitated. "Sir, if I may—"

"What's this Nut County like, anyway?"

"Sir?" Luke blinked. "I just said—"

"You just told me what it looked like. What do the people do there? What's under the ground? What do they grow?"

Luke stopped. He'd fallen into speaking from rote by habit and it took him a moment to find his footing. "Corn and soybeans, mostly. Some have jobs in Sikeston or Cairo. Jefferson believed there were diamonds there. That was the reason for the survey—"

"Diamonds?" asked Cheney. "In America?"

Luke nodded. "There's lamproite breccia under Nuthatch County like Diamond Crater in Arkansas—both are geologically similar to the diamond country of South Africa. No jewel quality diamonds have ever been reported in Arkansas but many people have tried."

"Oh." Bush sounded disappointed. "So it's just a story."

Luke watched Bush for a long silent minute. "No, sir. Clark's survey was quite clear. It was kept secret, of course. I lived in Nuthatch County for several years before I came here. Jeremy was my friend. I was a civil engineer at the time and looked for diamonds myself. I never found any but the Clark survey is quite clear: Little Mountain sits right on top of the largest jewel quality diamond deposit in the New World."

Bush looked thoughtful. Cheney looked speculative.

"How old is he?" asked Bush.

"Beg pardon?"

"You have records that go back a couple of hundred years.

But you say he's older than that. How old?"

"I'm not sure," Luke said slowly. "Perhaps long before Columbus."

"Hundreds of years? Thousands of years?"

Luke shook his head, not sure how much of his thoughts he should reveal. "Back in the thirties, my grandfather, Norton Parker, considered himself the amateur archeologist in the County, said he found evidence in Mound Builder artifacts suggesting Jeremy lived in Cahokia twelve hundred years ago."

Bush studied him for a moment. "But that's not what you think."

"No, sir." Luke took a deep breath. "I think Parker found evidence of Jeremy's *influence* in Mound Builder culture but I don't think Jeremy ever made it that far north. He is tied to the earth of Nuthatch County. There's nothing special about that land except Little Mountain, the gem deposit. I think Jeremy was there waiting for the first Clovis hunters when they showed up. I think he watched the glaciers roll back and forth. He's been there for thousands of years."

Cheney blanched but Powell didn't look surprised. The Pentagon must have come to similar conclusions. It came to Luke that they must have been studying Jeremy for decades.

Bush's gaze didn't waver. "You think this Jeremy was born in the age of the cavemen?"

"I have no idea, Mister President. I'm just saying I think he must be older than we imagine."

Bush crossed his arms across his chest. "Do you know your Bible, Mister Prescott?"

"No, sir."

"After Cain slew Able he went out of Eden and went to the land of Nod where he took a wife. Some say Cain's children were demons. Is that what you think this Jeremy is?"

Luke looked at Cheney and Powell. Both faces were non-committal.

"I don't know what Jeremy is," said Luke slowly.

"I'm not a Bible literalist myself. But there is insight there if you're willing to look." Bush considered Luke for a minute. "You're not a God-fearing man," Bush said, smiling. "That's all right. There's room in my administration for many kinds of good people. And I can tell you are good people." Bush's stare turned hard. "But you're no friend of this Jeremy DaFoe. You hate him from the very depths of your heart."

Luke closed his eyes a moment. The President guessed right. Luke knew when he realized it but not when it started. When Catherine died? His nephew? His brother? He opened them and met Bush's eyes. "Yes, sir. For years."

Luke Prescott met Catherine Meyers because he wanted to see the ocean.

He was fifteen and Perdoux, Missouri was seven hundred and forty-two miles from the closest point in the Gulf of Mexico—which, as far as Luke was concerned, constituted the sea.

Luke had never seen the sea. He'd never smelled the ocean or dipped into any salt water save the salt lick discovered by Daniel Boone a hundred and fifty miles west. His mother had relatives in Booneville and the salt lick was its sole unique attraction.

Luke was the third generation of Prescotts on that Perdoux farm so he felt some connection to it. Land connections are important in such a transient nation as America. In England, folks can boast of their ancestors being in the same place for a thousand years, fighting at the Battle of Hastings or with Oliver Cromwell. But in America, only the east coast settlers and the western sons and daughters of the Conquistadors could look back even a few hundred years, much less a millennium.

Natives had been here longer but since they predated America they often weren't considered true Americans anyway.

Of course, the Natives were newcomers, too. Where Europe could boast of Neanderthal settlements older than two hundred thousand years, the ancient Clovis people couldn't look back in anger to much more than a fraction of that amount. America has always been the place immigrants can finally call home.

Luke's great-grandparents, Norris and Dolly Prescott, were lured from their warm Pennsylvania farm to Nebraska by the promise of cheap and productive land. The promise was true, too. It was also so damned cold neither could stand to change their underwear from October to April. By Christmas the cloth had adhered to Norris' skin, sealing in all manner and sorts of things. When Norris and Dolly became amorous and the seal was broken, the smell was such that Dolly could not bring herself to perform her wifely duties, regardless of how much she loved her husband. Norris loved her just as much and did not press the matter.

Still, there is power in biology. On the first day the temperature strayed above freezing more than an hour, they broke the ice on the pond and scrubbed each other hard with homemade lye soap. The soap was so strong that cleanliness wasn't so much next to godliness as next to a snake shedding its skin. That evening, they cuddled together, naked and sinless, and Luke's grandfather was conceived.

In the morning, Norris watched the spring grass ignore the remaining snow and erupt right out of the earth. He decided this was God's Country. Or at least, he decided, God could have it. They were going south.

They followed the old roads, down through Iowa and into Missouri, until they reached the Missouri River. They turned east, as the Nebraska west retained unpleasant memories. Until, lying in the wagon one night, in the farm country north of Saint Louis, the two of them watched fireflies wheel over them. The fireflies lit on the sides of the wagon, on the edge of Dolly's bonnet, the tip of Norris' hat, walked the country to and fro between the horse's ears and tail and investigated the growing continent of Abel Prescott growing deep inside of Dolly.

"Right here's pretty nice," commented Dolly.

"All right," said Norris, resting his hand comfortably on Dolly's swelling abdomen.

Good farmers as they were, the Prescotts never seemed to manage a bumper crop of children. Norris and Dolly had a son, Abel who begat on little Ethel Biers after a revival meeting and had to marry her before she began to show. But little Ethel couldn't hold him and Abel abandoned her for parts unknown. Ethel named the baby Righteous in revenge.

Ethel told Righteous over and over and with hearty relish the burdens of marriage and sin. A gentle soul, Righteous determined never to marry. He was happy enough to run the farm. But Opal Givens, a young woman living down the road, had other ideas. Righteous found himself, surprised and befuddled, waiting for her to walk down the aisle when he was thirty-five and she a young twenty-two. They had one son, John, and, after a few years of trying, never expected to have another. But on a hot summer night in 1930 when Righteous was fifty, he held a tiny baby in his hands. Luke's older brother John was fifteen. The windows were open and the fireflies came in of a cluster and landed on Opal's bed, Righteous' hands, and John's arms. One lit on Luke's sleeping head and stayed there, still, blinking on, then off. On, then off.

In 1946 the harvest was in. The war had been over for a year and fifteen-year-old Luke felt he could be reasonably spared for a couple of weeks. School held little attraction for him but Luke was big for his age and helped keep the more rambunctious

Tamarlane and Marquis boys in check. Mrs. Patterson was willing to let him go if he *promised* to get back no later than Thanksgiving.

As the two brothers forked hay down from the loft, Luke told John of his plans. John didn't say much but gave him a half grin—the other half of John's face being permanently immobile. At Anzio, John had negotiated a settlement with an exploding M-1. The M-1 took his right eye, part of his right hand, and the use of all of his right facial muscles from eyebrow to chin. In return, John was allowed to keep his life. Every time Luke was struck by what had happened to his brother John invariably caught it on Luke's face. "Better'n the alternative," John always said, chuckling out of one side of his mouth.

Luke planned to hitchhike if he could and jump trains if he had to. John didn't say much but he looked thoughtful. "Can you wait until Sunday?"

Luke allowed that he could wait until Sunday and packed and repacked what he would take with him.

That morning he woke before anyone else and stole downstairs with a bindle. It didn't quite set well with him, leaving in secret on a Sunday. It smacked of lying. Luke was a good, God-fearing boy. What would his father think? Righteous Prescott was big in the church—hadn't missed a Sunday except the time Gramma Ethel had died.

Righteous Prescott, gray hair slicked back and smoking a Chesterfield, was in front of the house, sitting at the wheel of the family's Model A Ford. Waiting for him.

Righteous tapped the wheel and said casually, "Think she'll make it to Texas?"

It was Luke's turn to be thoughtful. He went to the barn and grabbed an assortment of tools from the shop and threw them into a canvas bag along with some cans of oil. He put the lot in the trunk. He saw John watching him from the upstairs window, half-grinning.

"We better hope so," Luke said as he tossed the bindle in the back seat and got in on the passenger side.

They never made it to Texas. In those days roads were poorly marked and maps unreliable, pointing to distant, unimaginable countries like Memphis, Paris, and Versailles. Somewhere near Pulaski—somewhere being as close as they could reckon—Righteous declared that Columbus himself had better directions than either of them could ever find in Tennessee. They didn't truly determine where they were until they found themselves in Decatur, Alabama.

"Could be worse," observed Righteous. "Could be Illinois." They gave up on Texas and settled for the panhandle of Florida.

Righteous pulled over in the middle of red dirt hills and ordered Luke into the driver's seat. He trusted to the Good Lord, and good Detroit steel, to get them through the ordeal ahead. Luke surprised him and drove tolerably well, leaving only a small piece of bumper and a bit of taillight glass on the road to Dothan.

Then, they descended the Alabama hills towards the Gulf. The red dirt turned darker, blacker, as they neared Mobile. They stopped in the middle of the road. The red dust they'd brought with them down from Birmingham swirled, eddied, and settled down on the gray dirt road like cleansing smoke. Below them at the mouth of the river lay Mobile.

Roosevelt's war was over. No longer were battleships or destroyers being built near the water but the scaffolding and shipyards remained. The river, flat as rolled brown glass, emptied into the bay. Luke felt like the whole world was opening up to him. Like God himself spoke through the landscape. *Luke? You can do anything. You can go anywhere.*

Righteous, older, and mortal, knew better.

They spent the night at an old hotel that smelled of salt and tidal flats. In the morning, they both rose at dawn like farm animals and ate breakfast in the diner next door. Neither of them liked grits but they liked the way the waitress spoke with a mix of soft vowels and nasal twang. Luke thought she was beautiful. Righteous thought Luke had only two reasons for that opinion.

But it was the broad Gulf that held them now: a gentle surf beating with a rhythm that came to them from beyond the great blue horizon. Luke had never realized there were so many different variations of color between blue and green.

Opal, his mother, had brought a small set of precious books to her marriage. Righteous was indifferent to them but Luke had noticed she often opened them and looked at the careful plates: paintings or landscapes or people dressed in ancient ruffles and Errol Flynn tights. When Opal had lived in more civilized Saint Louis, her father had taken his little girl to the 1906 World's Fair. There, impressed by the elegance of that Art Museum, he'd purchased a book of expensive chromolithographs. Young Opal had been delighted and the aged corners of the pages were worn by her gentle fingertips.

When she wasn't around, Luke brought them down and examined them. He didn't see the sense of it.

But now, driving along, struck by the bending and weaving of the light by grass and sea, he thought he might understand it a little bit. The urge to capture what he was seeing, to be able to make a picture, tell a story, or sing a song about it was overwhelming. Able to do none of these things, he listened to the radio, joining together in his mind forever the sound of Harry Truman, radio crooners, and the brushing whisper of the sea.

They rented a cabin on the beach in Panacea, Florida—so named for the sulfur springs thought to have powerful healing properties. September was neither summer nor winter and there was a shortage of customers so they were able to get a good deal.

By morning, Luke's reverence had turned to excitement and

he ran down to the water's edge.

Righteous followed more sedately, smoothed the crease of his pants, and sat down on a cedar chair. He lit a cigarette and watched Luke. This was, he thought, one of those moments where he had to let the little boy go. After all, Luke was fifteen. He could marry if he wanted—Opal's brother had married a girl at that age, though the wedding was quick and uncomfortable. Every child takes nine months but the first, as the saying goes. But now, he had to watch and see where Luke's judgment took him. After all, Luke could swim. Righteous could not.

Luke ran into the water and swam out in a straight line. The water was warm as blood. The sun was hot. He was young. The combination held true until he was treading water and looked back and saw how awfully *far* his father was back at the beach. Luke was not as good a swimmer as Righteous thought he was.

There was an old truck inner tube floating in the water some distance away. Luke decided that he'd rest there for a minute. As he approached, the tire turned and he saw a girl holding on to it. Automatically, he looked around for a father or a brother. She appeared to be by herself.

"Hey there," Luke called out.

The girl looked at him speculatively. She was younger than he was, with a fierce, concentrated expression on her face. "Yeah?"

"Could I hold on for a minute?"

The girl shrugged. "Suit yourself."

"Luke," he said once he'd grabbed and managed to hold onto the slippery rubber. "I'm Luke Prescott."

"Catherine Meyers."

"Do you live around here?"

She snorted. "I'm traveling down here same as you. My folks brought me down for the waters. I'm from Missouri."

Luke smiled. "Me, too. From Perdoux, north of Saint Louis."

She nodded slightly. "I'm from Pilate."

"Where is that?"

"Across the river from Cairo."

Luke couldn't place it but didn't try terribly hard. Missouri was a big state with lots of tiny towns.

Catherine didn't say anything further. She just looked tense and angry—or maybe upset. Luke couldn't tell which. For a moment, he thought to just leave her there, swim back to shore. He was rested enough. But he couldn't get it out of his mind that he was obligated to help if he could. Wasn't that what he had been taught every Sunday of his life? Wasn't that what Jesus would do?

Finally, shyly, he said, "What's wrong?"

She shrugged. "Nothing much."

"Really. You look like something's bothering you." He felt suffused in the glow of Christian goodness.

She didn't say anything. Luke held back. She would talk or she wouldn't.

Finally, she looked at him. "I'm thinking of the last four men I've slept with."

There was a roaring in Luke's ears and all that Christian goodness was swept away by an older and more primitive emotion.

"Really?" he squeaked.

Catherine might have been born wild. It's hard to tell such things in a young child. Toddlers are wild by nature. Parents learn to accommodate the sudden appearance of a cruel savage where their sweet cooing baby used to be. A playful slap becomes a sock in the eye. An aimless, twitching kick gets aimed at the balls. It's the way nature prepares parents for adolescence.

But when Catherine was four, polio blighted Nuthatch County. Her right arm and leg withered into useless sticks and seemingly overnight she developed a tilt to her spine.

It took two years for her to relearn how to walk. Her case wasn't the worst. Etta Franklin ended up in an iron lung at Barnes Hospital and died there the day she turned seven. Arah Blackbird was pregnant and lost her unborn baby and three-year-old daughter. Her husband just wasted away in front of her eyes until she had to bury the twig he'd become. Arah didn't get over the loss until she remarried after the war.

Papa Jeremy walked the County a lot that year. Many children ended up in Saint Louis and Kansas City hospitals. Etta even made a long and fruitless trip to Chicago before she came back to die in Saint Louis.

At the age of six, when it was clear she was going to be able to walk again, Catherine decided there was no point in being fearful. What more could happen to her? When the girls started smoking during the war, it was Catherine that snuck off to find cigarettes. It was Catherine who stuck with it, through vomiting and diarrhea, until, pale and proud, she could smoke just like Alice Faye in *Fallen Angel*.

It was twelve-year-old Catherine that figured there must be *something* good going on in her parents' bed a few times a month. Though her father grunted and her mother moaned, they kept at it as if it were important. She snuck out of bed one night and watched through the doorway. Catherine couldn't see enough to figure out *all* of the mechanics but she saw enough to determine the general region of activity.

Catherine returned to her room and poked and prodded herself in various ways as she tried to figure it out. Some things hurt. Most things didn't feel like much of anything. More or less by chance, she found one or two spots that did feel sort of pleasant. As she concentrated on those her body handed her a treat for which she was unprepared.

Wow, she thought, warmly surprised. *That works.*

Catherine experimented with a neighbor named Lee Thomas. She couldn't figure out quite how something as big as Lee's penis could fit in there but Lee was more than willing to demonstrate.

It hurt but not as much as relearning how to walk. With practice, she got an inkling of what was in store. But Lee was just as inexperienced as she was. While it got so it didn't hurt it still wasn't much fun. She dumped Lee and kept to her own devices for the next couple of years.

But things changed when she grew from a flat-chested and crippled twelve to a limping, C-cupped fourteen. Her mother told her about pregnancy and condoms—Catherine wondered if her broken body was incapable of bearing children or if she and Lee had just been lucky.

Catherine also discovered that boys of fifteen were much more interesting than boys of twelve. Seventeen was more interesting yet. One young man of twenty who should have known better was positively fascinating.

As terrific as sex was, it palled. Catherine wanted to go out and have a soda as much as any other girl. But it seemed to her, that she had become the best-kept secret in Pilate. *That Meyers girl is a lot of fun in the sack but who wants to be seen with a cripple?*

Catherine decided she'd had enough and swore off sex— even with her pet twenty-year-old.

Clearly, she had to rethink things.

Her parents had taken her to Panacea every year since she was seven in a vain attempt to improve things. Catherine liked the trip even if it didn't change anything in her broken body. The warm water felt good.

The Papa Jeremy stories told by Nuthatch County children were distorted by legend and whispered folklore. Papa Jeremy dragged out an eight-hundred-pound catfish from under the bluffs south of town with his bare hands. Papa Jeremy didn't like the set of Deacon Williams' face at church and hexed him, which was the real reason the Deacon didn't like Jeremy. Papa Jeremy fought the devil for Etta Franklin's life. The devil only won by trickery.

Every myth carries within it its own best age to be punctured. The Easter Bunny: seven or so. Santa Clause: nine to eleven. It was the custom in Nuthatch County to tell the kids about Papa Jeremy when they were fourteen. Younger than that and it was hard to separate fact from childish mythology. Older than that and the child felt as if they'd been lied to all their life. Fourteen was the age when the real world began to shyly show itself. Selma and Patrick Meyers decided on the way down that now was as good a time as any.

"You mean," Catherine said slowly when they were done. "Papa Jeremy's an angel?"

"I didn't say that," Patrick said uneasily.

"He's a devil, then."

"No," Selma said in a nervous voice. "That is, I don't *think* he's a devil. Or an angel."

"Then, what *is* he?"

Patrick took his hands off the wheel briefly to shrug. "He's Papa Jeremy. He's just… what he is."

Catherine mulled over that one. "Can he raise the dead? You know, like Jesus did?"

Patrick thought for a minute. "I've never *heard* of him doing it."

Selma broke in. "He might have brought Billy Lightfeather back from the dead," Selma said suddenly.

Patrick nodded. "Maybe. God knows why."

"Who's Billy Lightfeather?"

Selma turned in her seat to see Catherine. "Billy Lightfeather used to be the oldest woman in the County when I was your age. She must have been born right after the Civil War. Wouldn't you say, Pat?"

"Close to it. She sure was the meanest woman in the County, oldest or not."

"Hush." Selma turned back to Catherine. "Anyway, when she was a little girl she fell into the Bittersweet and was swept under the ice. Everybody thought she was dead for sure but Papa Jeremy walked the entire length of the river, right down to the Mississippi, and found her still and cold in one of the pools. He brought her out of the water and she started breathing right there. Wasn't long before she woke up—though I always heard that she didn't talk so well after that."

"She talked just fine," said Patrick. "It's just she was so cold-hearted that what came out was pure spite."

"Don't speak ill of the dead."

"Why not? Do you think Papa Jeremy will bring her back to life *again?*" Patrick laughed.

"What about Mrs. DaFoe? Is *she* an angel?"

Patrick and Selma fell silent a moment.

"No," said Selma. "Charity DaFoe is just like you or me."

"So, she'll die and Jeremy won't?" Catherine wasn't surprised. Mrs. DaFoe looked old.

"Right," said Patrick. "After Charity passes on, we will have to find Jeremy another wife." He grinned at his wife. "This is America where any girl can grow up to be married to Jeremy DaFoe."

Selma slapped his hand. "Don't be vulgar."

"I wasn't!"

"Why does he get married at all?" Catherine watched her father's face in the rearview mirror.

Patrick looked at her, his face suddenly serious. "It wouldn't do for Jeremy to be alone."

"Why not?"

"It just wouldn't do."

Catherine thought about that. "How many wives has he *had?*"

Selma looked at Patrick. Patrick shrugged again.

"I don't know," said Patrick finally. "As long as he's been alive, I suppose."

"How long is that?"

"Nobody knows, sweetheart." Selma patted her arm. "Nobody knows."

Angel, she decided. The alternative made no sense.

All this was rolling through Catherine's mind as she held onto the tire tube with her good arm. Maybe *she* would marry Jeremy. After all, what did Jeremy care if she were crippled or if she'd fooled around? Nobody would *dare* make fun of her then. Maybe he could even fix her.

But then, she'd get old and die and Jeremy would just go on and on. Catherine found the idea intolerable. Better to marry someone like herself. Someone, well, *human*. So they'd grow old together.

Besides, there had to be more to sex than fun and babies. She had seen her mother look at her father and put her hand on his shoulder out of pure affection. Somewhere that had to figure in. So far it hadn't.

Then this *boy* appeared.

A big boy. Handsome enough. Religious, too, by the way he talked. But kind—*really* kind, since she knew he couldn't see much—not in *that* bathing suit. Her father had made sure of it. And innocent—barely been kissed as far as she could tell. So, she told him and it tickled her the way all that religion just melted away. Then, the look on his face didn't change at all when they reached the shore and he could see her arm and leg. She could have had him right then and there just for that.

That night, they snuck out of the cabins and lay on the beach under the moon and the stars and ignored the sand and the sand fleas. She looked up into his face, opened and took him in, nothing to separate them at all.

Right now. Right here, she thought. I'm an angel, too.

Luke was in love.

In love with the sun and the sky, in love with the sunburn on his back and the sand flea bites, in love with the small girl he had just met. In love with the phosphorescent fire in the water when they swam. In love with the waves and the fish and the water, always the water. He was in love with the musky salt of it, the white crystals dried on his skin, the faint dry wrinkles on Catherine's face.

Catherine and the sea were mixed together in his mind, their salty liquid warmth swirling together.

Righteous smiled tolerantly and smoked his cigarettes in the warm evening on the steps of their cabin. He enjoyed Patrick and Selma's blissful ignorance of what was happening right under their very noses. They remained convinced of the chaste puppy dog nature of a summer romance. Righteous could see two young animals, all right. But this was anything but chaste.

Under other circumstances, Righteous might have stepped in and stopped what was going on. Or at least insisted on an honorable resolution. Now, watching Luke unconsciously care for his little crippled girlfriend, he held back. Let things be. They would be leaving by the end of the week and after that, who knew?

Friday came and they packed up the cars. Luke and Catherine exchanged addresses—they weren't far apart at all.

All the way out of Florida, Luke babbled about Catherine, the sea, the birds. Righteous waited until they were miles from the sea and the land had turned from beach plum and scrub to honest oaks and chestnuts.

Then, Righteous told Luke he was dying.

Catherine knew she was pregnant the day after Luke and his father left. Thought about it constantly all the way home. She burned Luke's address and insisted the baby was hers and hers alone. Luke had been fun but no Missouri farm boy was wanted or needed. This was her baby, thank you very much. She'd raise it by herself.

Nadine's birth nearly killed Catherine. The baby was turned upside down and sideways and Catherine's womb was nearly as contorted and damaged as her limbs. The pain was liked ripping muscle from bone. Catherine endured it—she didn't know how not to—until the last resort of surgery was decided upon. Blessed ether delivered her and when she awoke, aching and drunk, Papa Jeremy was sitting next to her bed.

She watched him a moment.

He was reading a thick and heavy book, his angular face calm and his eyes darting over the page. Everything went loose and gelid and she slipped away but a moment later she could focus again. Jeremy was still reading the same book so she knew it hadn't been for long.

He gently laid the book mark between the pages, closed the book, and placed it on the stand.

"How are you feeling?" he said quietly.

Papa Jeremy was always quiet, she thought, surprised she'd never noticed it before.

"Am I dying?" she asked.

Jeremy shook his head.

"What about my baby?"

"She's fine. She's sleeping in the other room. So are Selma and Patrick. I said I'd watch you so they could get some rest."

She sleepily pondered why someone who was not a demon and not an angel would take an interest in her. "Why?"

"I like you."

"You like everybody. Same as Jesus."

He chuckled. "Just the same, I wanted to be here."

"Why?"

Jeremy smiled. "Don't you give up on Luke just yet."

It didn't surprise her that Papa Jeremy knew his name. "I don't love him."

"Honey, you don't know what love is. You might surprise yourself someday."

"Do you like him, Papa Jeremy?"

"He'll be a good man, I expect. By and by."

"I liked him okay." Not enough to tell him about the baby, she thought. *My* baby.

"Do you still?"

She nodded, feeling suddenly shy as a little girl.

"Good," said Jeremy. "You go back to sleep and we'll see what happens."

Catherine realized then her eyes were already closed. Jeremy's voice just drifted away.

It took four years for Righteous to die. Luke, John, and Opal buried him on Luke's nineteenth birthday. Nobody had planned it that way. It was just that in the shock of Righteous' final weeks Luke's birthday was forgotten even by Luke. When it was remembered the plans were already in place.

Opal gave the farm to the two brothers and let them fight it out amongst themselves. There was no fight in either of them. John had the farm appraised and offered to buy out Luke's share. Luke took a few hundred dollars and the Model A. He gave John the rest.

John looked away for a moment and rubbed his remaining eye. "Thanks," he said. "What are you going to do?"

"Wait to get drafted. Drive." Luke waved west. "Go see the world. Get laid."

"That happened the last time you left." John laughed.

"Dad told you about that?"

"Sure. What? Did you think he didn't know?"

Luke had believed exactly that but never said it. "Of course not. I'm just surprised he told *you*."

It was July of 1950 and the heat was brutal in the sunlight and barely tolerable in the shadow. Luke drove south. He had returned to Perdoux with a strong intention to write Catherine but the address had mysteriously disappeared. (Less mysterious now, since he knew that Righteous had figured out what was going on.) He waited for Catherine to write him but she never did. Finally, he concluded that whatever had happened that week had meant more to him than to her.

Therefore, when he decided to drive to Texas (For real this time. No detours to Florida.) he deliberately drove over bad roads to the west of Perdoux to make an intentional detour away from Nuthatch Country.

Southern Missouri was even hotter than Perdoux and when he saw the Johnson Shut-Ins Park, he decided to stop for a dip in the river.

The Shut-Ins were a minor miracle. The Ozarks were a lifted seabed underlain by billion-and-a-half-year-old Saint Francois Mountain granite. The Black River wore straight through the rotten Ozark limestone but became downright artistic when it reached the granite. Smooth chutes and slides, holes, and falls were all over the bottom of the gorge. The water was low and cooler than the air. It made the dry air blow a delicious winter chill across the bones. The sound of the river was only matched by the whoops and yells of those playing in the water.

Luke watched more than he swam. Playing takes companionship and he was alone. He crawled up on a rock overlooking the river and enjoyed the sun baking him dry. Until he noticed a young woman playing with a little girl. A woman with a withered arm and leg.

Luke's first inclination was to climb down, get in his car, and run away. Then, he wondered if the baby was his. What should he do? Go down and confront her? Maybe it wasn't Catherine at all. Polio hit hard before the war. Maybe it was just someone who looked like her.

Luke didn't believe it. Something in the way she moved, the cant of her neck, and the way she held her right hand and her left leg cried out Catherine.

He sat there feeling foolish. Go down and talk to her, turn and leave or stay there and stew. Take your pick of options.

Catherine gathered the child (maybe she's just taking care of it?) and half-carried, half-led her down to the tiny beach. Luke climbed down from the rock and walked over to her.

Four years had burned away any remaining baby fat. She had that odd motherly figure Luke had seen in farm women all his life: strong shoulders and breasts over baby-broadened hips.

Catherine was busy dressing the child and didn't see him at first. She glanced up and then back down at the child. She stopped for a moment and then resumed buttoning the bathing suit. Done, the little girl jumped to her feet and ran to the water.

"Stay nearby," Catherine called, then laboriously drew her stick-and-string body erect.

"Catherine?" asked Luke.

"Yes," she said shortly.

Luke wanted to shout at her or beg for understanding but neither could penetrate the way she watched the little girl.

"What's her name?" he said at last.

"Nadine." She looked at him briefly and then turned her scrutiny back to her daughter. "You didn't write."

"Neither did you."

"True." She fell silent for a moment. "She's vaccinated, you know. One of the first."

"Good." He thought a moment. "I'm not surprised."

Catherine shook her head slowly. "How did you find me? For that matter, why didn't you look for me back in the

County?"

"I wasn't looking."

"Pull the other one."

"Honest. I was on my way to Texas and it was hot."

"This is out of the way for Texas."

"Not if you're trying to miss Nuthatch County and got lost."

Catherine looked at him again. "Well, now." She stopped, gathering her thoughts. "Well, now. That explains some things."

"I'm glad they explain things to *you*. They don't do much for me."

"*I'm* not surprised." She laughed softly. "Nadine?" she called softly.

The child perked up out of the water.

"Come here and meet your Daddy."

Washington weather in February was bipolar: a depressing gray freezing rain with a bone-breaking wet, bitter cold alternating with clear and manic sunshine that thawed the snow and melted the ice, hinting, suggesting, and downright promising an impending spring.

Luke had lived in Washington so long he was inured to false promises from all venues, both political and meteorological. Bush had made no promises. He hadn't even suggested rocking the boat. But he was the first president who ever showed a hint of dissatisfaction with the status quo. Even so and despite bitter experience, he returned from the Bush briefing cautiously hopeful. Optimistic would have been far too strong a word.

Luke had a locked drawer in his desk. He opened it on the rare occasion he had something new to record or had forgotten some small piece of information. Reading the drawer's contents was rare because there was little there Luke couldn't easily recall. Recall was easy because he thought about the drawer all the time.

The drawer contained everything he knew, and everything Deacon Williams knew, about Jeremy DaFoe. Luke thought about Jeremy DaFoe continually because he was convinced there must be a way to get rid of him.

Deacon Williams had been sure Jeremy was a demon. Three times in the last five years Deacon and Jeremy had tried different kinds of exorcisms. Deacon believed they failed because they were never attempted in Jeremy's actual presence but instead relied on bits of hair or cloth.

Luke was not convinced. He believed that Jeremy's nature had little to do with religion. Luke knew only three certain things about Jeremy: Jeremy was not human. He had been in Nuthatch Country for an incredibly long time. And he was locked there for reasons unknown.

Luke didn't *know* Jeremy wasn't God or some other supernatural creature. If there were a God, some of His qualities would likely resemble Jeremy's. Luke might have been a church believer once but decades of interacting with Jeremy had washed him clean of it.

How do you kill something like a deity?

The Deacon and Luke had both come to the same conclusion: you can't.

Well, then, how can you persuade something like a deity to leave? *That* had possibilities.

Patience, Luke, he told himself. Deacon has been plotting against Jeremy most of his life. Compared to that you've only scratched the surface.

Luke measured time in presidents. Johnson, Nixon, and Ford weren't interested since Jeremy was benign. Jimmy Carter had only considered Jeremy *metaphysically*. Reagan appeared to fall asleep through both briefings but Haig had paid attention enough to say it was clearly a problem for the Democrats. Big

Bush already knew about Jeremy from his CIA days and had long since decided to let sleeping dogs lie.

But that long blighted summer when Catherine died overshadowed everything. Even Nadine, her husband Joseph, and his granddaughter Joanie, newly admitted to the Art Institute of Chicago, were unable to penetrate the dark clouds surrounding him. Not that it would have made any difference. His doubts about Jeremy had begun there. The following first briefing with Clinton had been a disaster. Even so, Clinton said this was clearly a problem for the Republicans.

After he and Catherine married he briefly lived in Pilate with Catherine's family. Then they moved to Columbia where he studied Civil Engineering while Catherine worked in the hospital kitchen. Back to the County where he repaired roads, built bridges, and designed tiny municipal buildings. He had Catherine. He had Nadine. He was as happy as he'd ever thought he could be. In a place where he had no roots of his own, he was content to adopt those of his wife. Then, almost a decade later, Jeremy sent all three of them to Washington where no one had any roots at all.

Luke's brother John was of a different sort. He had stayed after Righteous had died, married Eva, sired Roger and Dinah. Dinah took after her Uncle Luke and moved away to Texas to become a chemical engineer. Roger, though, had stayed on the farm, married, and raised a son, David. David remained on the farm. John, Roger, and David. Three living generations of Prescotts farming the same land at the same time. Other men had Jesus or believed in smoky spirits to console themselves. John had his family, right there in front of him, to keep him going.

God willing and the creek don't rise.

In the summer of 1993, Clinton's first term and about a year after Catherine died, came the floods. Like most tributaries of the Missouri, the Perdoux River broke through all manner of banks, levies, and sandbags in its blind, urgent thrust home. It ground down the Prescott land and left behind stinking, contaminated mud. The Prescott homes were transformed into soft, wet reservoirs of frogs, mosquitoes, and snakes. The lower farm buildings sank into the mud and fell over. The fine tractors and combines became so much incipient rust. The animals were dead or lost. The land itself was ruined.

No farm operates on anything more than borrowed time and the Prescotts had no flood insurance. The whole of the Prescott clan couldn't cover the note. Luke tried to steer them into grants and loans. Tried to at least get the land purchased under FEMA buyouts. He failed. The Prescott land didn't qualify. The unquenchable largesse of the United States Government extended to Nuthatch County but not to the liaison's relatives that did not live there.

Roger fell off a sandbank under mysterious circumstances into the still-raging Perdoux River. He wasn't found until he washed up in Saint Louis. John had a heart attack at Roger's funeral, fell into a coma, and died three weeks later. Now, they stood around John's grave, David, Roger's wife, Nan, John's daughter, Dinah, and John's wife, Eva

First, Catherine. Then Roger. Then John. This is too much, Luke thought. He remembered when he and John had buried Righteous. John had held him, a strapping nineteen-year-old kid bawling like a toddler. He had felt like dying when he'd buried Catherine—John had been there, too, crooked face solemn, arm around him. Later, cracking jokes, the two of them drinking cheap rye. It seemed the right thing to do. Catherine would have smiled and drank right along with them. Catherine, Roger, and John. He didn't feel a thing. Was this what age did to you? Burn everything out so there's nothing left but a husk?

He looked around for Nadine and her family, remembered he'd told her to stay home out of some misguided idea of protecting her. Silly. Nadine was a grown woman with a grown daughter. Joanie was half a world away studying in Japan. He wished she was here.

Luke wiped his face. It was, of course, raining. It seemed like it had always rained. Coming off the plane he had smelled the wet mud, the rot. He glanced over at John's wife, Eva. She stood ramrod straight. The rain plastered her gray hair flat to her skull, ran down her face, but she wasn't having any of it. She stared straight ahead until the preacher finished his benediction. Then, she picked up a rock, tossed it into the hole, and turned away.

Luke tossed in his own clod. The slimy feel of the dirt felt offensive. He put his dirty hand in his pocket and rubbed the mud off against the cloth.

Eva stopped at the car. "Are you staying here in town?"

"I haven't decided. If you need me."

Eva shook her head. "You can stay if you want to. I've had it. Dinah's going to sell the place. I've got everything I want packed up back at Dinah's hotel. Soon as we leave here, I'm flying to Arizona with Dinah. You come down and see me in the fall. Or Christmas—Christmas would be nice." She looked back at the open grave for a moment. "I hope I never see rain again." She leaned forward and kissed him on the cheek. "John was always proud of you. You remember that."

With that, she folded herself into the car with her daughter and they left the graveyard.

Luke drove north to the Prescott farm. Along the way, there were vast ponds where there had been cattle. The houses had been flooded out, the windows broken and dark, shadowed as if burned. Bits of debris, plastic, a strip of police tape, and broken scraps of wood showed the high water mark in the trees. Luke felt as if he was standing in the middle of a disaster in Mexico or Indonesia or Peru—any place other than the United States of America.

There's nothing here for me, he thought. Everyone he still

knew was down in Nuthatch County.

He drove back to the County and slept on Buddy's couch. Staying with Nadine and seeing in her face a mirror of Catherine's would have been intolerable. Jeremy came to visit. Luke would have put up with Death himself if it could distract him from what he was feeling.

They were drinking Porter's Piss, the local County distilled product. Jeremy sat in the corner chair. Buddy fell asleep, his head thrown back on the sofa as if he were laughing. Luke stared at the floor through a long wavering tube.

"I'm sorry about your family," said Jeremy softly.

Luke could hear the sympathy in his voice. He could feel the tug of it. "Things happen."

"Yes."

Luke picked up the bottle and leaned his forehead against it. It felt cool and smooth. *I'm made of glass,* he thought.

"Jeremy?" he asked suddenly. "Did you know the floods were coming?"

"Pretty much."

Luke felt cold. "When?"

"Around last Christmas."

"Why didn't you tell me?"

Jeremy shrugged. "These things happen all the time, Luke."

"Jeremy—" Luke started and then stopped. Jeremy? Are you trying to tell me that you chose for some reason of your own not to warn me so I couldn't protect my brother? Couldn't protect my nephew? He looked at Jeremy. Thin face. A couple of days of stubble. Drinking whisky just as if he were a man. Could you have saved Catherine? He remembered something Deacon Williams had said: Only vultures and Jeremy DaFoe know when somebody's going to die.

That was when it struck Luke. He'd had known before but at that moment he could *see* it: Jeremy wasn't human. All of the customs of Nuthatch County depended on thinking of Jeremy as human. The politeness. The nods and conversations. The ritual and mythology. All of it based on a lie.

"Why are you even here?" Luke felt so tired.

Jeremy looked surprised. "Where else should I be?"

"I mean here. In the County. Why not just go? Move on?" He leaned forward on his knees. "If I just asked you to leave the County, could you do it?"

Jeremy gave him a deeply sad look. "You're not the right person to ask, Luke."

Luke closed his eyes. *Okay, then,* he thought. Maybe Jeremy could read his mind right now. Read this. *I'm going to kill you, Jeremy.* Or, he thought, since he always tried to be honest, the next best thing.

But now—eight years later—*now,* he had the sympathy of the President. Maybe. A little.

Sitting there in his office, he let himself dream a moment. With the Pentagon's resources, Powell must have cubic yards of material. Ideas, scenarios, straw men—things neither he nor the Deacon would have ever considered possible. There must be white papers, trade studies, and hypothetical plans about getting rid of Jeremy. Nobody at the Pentagon would sit back and just wonder. They might conclude there was nothing to be done but they'd reach that point of view after filling a train car full of documentation.

Luke wished he had those sorts of resources. Instead, he and the Deacon stumbled along at their own pace, only making the most clandestine of overtures lest they risk the only leverage they had: Luke as liaison. Trying one thing—like the exorcisms—then another. Now that there was the slimmest of possibilities, he wasn't sure what to do next. It's the Nuthatch County mentality, Luke decided. When the whole world revolves around a little piece of land, it was easy to think small. To see only barriers. Even now, sitting at this desk, he'd been an extension of that mentality, a colony of Nuthatch County in greater Washington.

He needed to call Deacon Williams and tell him. It was only a hint. A bare possibility. But if something came through — surely between the two of them they could come up with something.

The phone rang.

He picked it up, still thinking about Deacon Williams. "Luke Prescott."

"Luke?" came a thin and ancient voice. "This is Buddy Parker."

"Hello." Luke shook his head. This wasn't right. Buddy didn't talk to him; they hadn't spoken in years. Not since that night. Luke had never said a word to either of them about how he felt but Buddy knew. Luke didn't know how but Buddy had carefully quit speaking with him unless he had to. Didn't call him. Politely cut short calls Luke had made to him. Buddy had been so polite and reserved that Luke hadn't realized what had happened for months.

Why call now? Did Jeremy put him up to it? Was Buddy trying for some kind of reconciliation? Was it Nuthatch County business? Only the Eldest was supposed to call Luke and that was the Deacon.

Crap.

"I have sad news for you, Luke," Buddy said in a soft, distant, formal voice. "Deacon Williams died early this morning. "

"You're the Eldest now?"

"I'm the Eldest."

Every insular culture develops its own jokes, traditions and customs, explanatory stories, and trickster tales. In this way, Nuthatch County was no different from the Anasazi, the

Mayans, or the French. The difference was that Nuthatch County was isolated from the rest of the world not by geographic barriers, linguistic divergences, or political decisions but by its secret.

Some customs were so old that to the locals they had always been done and were now performed by mere rote. Such as the custom of giving the first deer of the season to Jeremy, or never swatting a firefly if you could help it.

Others were pragmatic, decided upon purely as the best choice of bad methods. Like choosing Jeremy's wife by lot.

In religion, the maintenance of custom falls to the priest to represent the church. In government, it falls to the politician to represent the state. The lawyer and the judge represent the law.

In the matter of Jeremy DaFoe, it fell to the oldest competent resident of the County.

Buddy Parker was seventy-seven years old the night Deacon Williams died. The Deacon died at eighty-nine. There were older folks in the County—three senile centenarians in a home in Pilate and ninety-year-old June Platte, paralyzed on her right side and cared for by her daughter, Jane. Both of them were looking forward to the day that June would need for nothing ever again.

These days Buddy was about the right age, as Eldests go. In earlier years he might have been thought extremely old. In some generations, he would have been considered young.

Buddy's first act as Eldest was to call Luke in Washington and tell him. That tradition predated phones. He picked up the hand set and hesitated. Buddy had known the Deacon all his life. He had known Luke for most of Luke's life. Deacon had lived in Pilate and Buddy in Ashby. Buddy had never understood what made them so different. Why would one turn towards Jeremy and the other turn away? Buddy was the oldest living male Parker since long before the Civil War—the Parkers tended to small families and died young. Buddy was the very first Parker Eldest.

He nerved himself and called Luke. Since Luke had thrown in with the Deacon, Buddy hadn't had much to say to him. But now they would have to talk.

It was a short conversation, a simple transmission of information. But afterward, Buddy felt better. Things would get better. How could they not?

Luke felt bereft as if he'd lost a friend. Though he would never have considered Deacon Williams a friend. Together, they had been trying to solve the problem of Jeremy DaFoe for eight years. Alone, he felt drifting and rudderless in a dark and mysterious sea.

Luke looked up as the door of his office opened. A young man wearing a crisp Army uniform looked in. "Luke Prescott?"

"Yes."

"Captain Joel Rosen, US Army." Rosen stepped in and held out his hand. "Secretary Powell sent me."

Luke took Rosen's hand, shook it, and gestured to his seat. He felt breathless. "What can I do for you?"

Rosen carefully set his briefcase down next to the chair, sat down, and straightened out the creases of his pants. "I'm to be your connection between Secretary Powell and... everyone else in the Nuthatch County matter."

Luke leaned back in his chair. "You have some credentials."

"Here's a note from Secretary Powell." Rosen pulled out an envelope and handed it to Luke.

Luke pulled out his reading glasses and read it. According to Powell's letter, Joel Rosen was a competent assistant in anything Luke might conceivably want to do. He looked at Rosen across the top of his glasses. "This says nothing about Nuthatch County."

"Nor should it. As far as Secretary Powell is concerned that has nothing to do with why I'm here."

"I don't understand."

"Back at DOD, Nuthatch County is our department—our team, actually. We're not big enough to rate a department." He looked around Luke's office.

Luke felt vaguely annoyed. After all, Rosen may have a room dedicated to Jeremy DaFoe, but Luke's desk had existed for nearly two hundred years. "Yes?"

Rosen settled himself. "As you know, Secretary Powell's movements are always under scrutiny. If he were to come to the Executive Building to see some obscure civil servant, that bureaucrat is going to get attention. But no one is tracking an equally obscure and comparatively low-ranking captain. If Secretary Powell goes over to the Pentagon for a regularly scheduled meeting and happens to step into an office for a quick briefing, no one will be the wiser."

Luke nodded. "The Pentagon is still relatively free from journalistic observation."

Rosen shook his head. "Journalism has nothing to do with it. The problem is other members of the staff. Jeremy has been a thorn in the side of the military since we found out about him. Imagine, the equivalent of an undetermined number of hydrogen bombs living in an obscure county in Missouri and out of our control. Our country continues to exist as we know it on his whim. He has to go."

"Did you ever ask him to leave?"

"Did you?"

"Yes," said Luke. "Once. When I was drunk. He said I wasn't the right person to ask." Luke pointed at Rosen. "You might be. Or Powell. Or the President."

"Ah." Rosen grinned at him. "But we *won't*." Rosen smiled at him. "Did you know Eisenhower asked Jeremy for help after Pearl Harbor?"

Luke stared at him. He racked his brains. Like every liaison, he'd kept notes on what he did and had read the notes of previous liaisons. "There's no record of that."

"Eisenhower didn't go through a liaison. He went out to talk to Jeremy directly."

Luke didn't know what to say.

Rosen leaned back in his chair. He glanced out the window. "Back in Lincoln's day, the military didn't know about Jeremy—Nathan Collins, then. But there are some hints in Lincoln's journal that his Secretary of State, William Seward, tried to pressure Lincoln to ask Collins for help. Lincoln didn't but he must have been sorely tempted."

"Why didn't he?"

Rosen spread his hands. "No one knows for sure, of course. Lincoln didn't say. Maybe it was because Nuthatch County was in the middle of a war zone—though I think Lincoln could have managed an emissary if he'd wanted to. I'm guessing he was scared of what might happen if the genie was released. Deals with the devil rarely go well. The same sort of thing happened with Wilson in World War I. It was FDR that let the military in on the secret."

"I know about that." It was all in Rutherford's notes. "What did Jeremy say to Eisenhower?"

"Well, 'no', of course. Eisenhower recorded the conversation in one of his notebooks—one *not* in the presidential library. Jeremy said, 'You'll have to manage.'"

"That sounds like him."

"And we did. That's why we'll never ask him to leave. He's the last possible trick we have in our back pocket."

"Even though he's never said yes?"

"He's never said he would *never* help. He just refused help at that *time*. Some believe he would say yes and help us if we really needed him." Rosen spread his hands. "I do not agree with that position."

Luke chewed over that. "Does the President intend for us to try to get rid of Jeremy?"

Rosen made a steeple of his fingers. "Interesting question. Secretary Powell suggested that is the President's intention."

"You said 'suggested.'"

"Exactly." Rosen fell silent.

"So we're on our own." Great. Just like me and the Deacon for the last eight years.

"No. Powell has given us some resources. Agents on the ground in the County. Data gathered about Jeremy. If things go wrong, we've gone rogue. If they go right, we'll never get the credit. But we can proceed. If we can do it without consequences."

"Nothing happens without consequences."

"Without *significant* consequences. There are also many at DOD who would like to see Jeremy gone. Did you and the Deacon have a plan?"

"The Deacon is dead."

"I know."

"Of course you do." Luke closed his eyes and rubbed his nose. "We didn't have a plan. He schemed for years before I came along and all he had to show for it were some ideas. I came on board and eight years later we have... some ideas."

"What were they?"

"Jeremy is held to the County by something we don't understand. So our idea was first to find out what's holding him and release him. Jeremy is intrinsically alienated from the rest of the world. The people of Nuthatch County have bonded with him. For reasons we don't understand, he's accepted that bond. If we could weaken that bond and at the same time enable him to leave he might just go on his own."

"That's pretty feeble."

"We realized that."

Rosen opened his briefcase and pulled out a map. "This is a

deep radar image laid over a topographic map of Nuthatch County. What do you see?"

Luke stared at the paper. It was a splash of reds and greens with a bright magenta spot near the middle. He pointed to it. "That's Little Mountain."

"Correct. That magenta indicates an abnormal density there. Little Mountain is on top of an isolated kimberlite pipe—the source of the diamonds found in Madison's survey. There are no kimberlite pipes anywhere around the area. The kimberlite structures in Arkansas are not geologically related."

"I figured the diamonds and Jeremy were connected."

Rosen pulled out another sheet and lay it on top of the map. "Here's a gravity variation graph of the area of Little Mountain taken about three weeks ago." He grinned. "NASA has its uses."

The graph showed small peaks and dips but directly under Little Mountain was a sharp, high spike. "What's that?"

"Something geologically impossible. It's about the mass of Everest, fifty feet down and embedded in the middle of the kimberlite. Right on top of the Cretaceous Missouri Embayment at the edge of the K-T boundary. It's resting just below a layer of iridium. "

"How could you possibly know that?"

Rosen grinned and didn't answer. "It's about two feet in diameter. Add that to the mystery. If something is keeping Jeremy in Nuthatch County, that's a pretty likely candidate."

"Three weeks ago?"

Rosen smiled thinly. "We knew your feelings on the matter of Jeremy DaFoe. Secretary Powell wanted to have the work completed before the briefing."

Luke felt hollow. He'd been witness to a larger, secret world for most of his adult life. Now, he had a sense of that world's true scope and it was much bigger than he had imagined.

Rosen pulled out a thick pamphlet. "You and the Deacon

were right on the money regarding Jeremy's attachment to people. Our research indicates Jeremy is becoming *more* attached over time. So even if you were able to blast out whatever that thing is, and it was the key to what kept him there, it's fairly likely he wouldn't want to leave."

"What do you think it is? Or Jeremy for that matter?"

Rosen chuckled. "That's the question, isn't it? What is Jeremy? What's that thing under Little Mountain?"

"He's been around thousands of years—"

"Millions."

Luke closed his eyes for a moment. He felt like he was being hit repeatedly in the head. "Millions. You know this how?"

"The anomaly is about fifty feet down. Core samples indicate—"

"You took core samples on Little Mountain? Didn't you think Jeremy would *notice?*"

"That's how we determined it's resting on an iridium boundary." Rosen shrugged. "We had a cover story. Besides, we didn't drill down to it. We drilled close to it. Seamless sedimentation all the way down to it. That thing has been there for sixty-five million years."

"He could have masked it. Made it look as if it were that old."

"But why would he? Surrounded, until only recently, by primitives? It makes more sense that it's *been* there. All this time."

Suddenly, Luke wanted a drink. Something bitter and strong that would explode all through him. "Maybe he's too much for us."

It was like Rosen read his mind. Rosen pulled a flask out of his briefcase and two silver cups. He set them down on Luke's desk and poured. Whisky by the smell of it. Did military men always drink whisky?

"What about your nephew?" Rosen said as he poured. "What about your brother? What about your *wife?*" Rosen pointed outside. "Every day we have problems he could fix. But he won't. Every day he could destroy us. And we don't know why he doesn't. No. We can't live with that kind of uncertainty. No country can." He handed one cup to Luke, tapped it to his own.

Luke drank it down. Coughed. Felt better. He stared at the map.

Rosen considered his cup. "Our group thinks he's trapped. His life in Nuthatch County is the best he's been able to make of a bad deal."

Luke nodded, the warm glow of the whisky radiating through him. "Does the Pentagon have any idea what's under Little Mountain?"

Rosen hesitated. "Just speculation. The mass/volume ration doesn't make any sense. Too dense for normal matter but not dense enough for anything exotic like neutronium." Rosen chuckled. "I didn't even know what neutronium was before I took this job."

Things began to penetrate Luke's mind. Sixty-five million years. Iridium. "What? You think he rode down with the Chicxulub Meteor? Jeremy is an *alien?*"

Rosen shrugged. "Perhaps *it* rode down with the Chicxulub Meteor and the explosion tore it in two: one part Jeremy, one part thing under Little Mountain. Perhaps it *was* the meteor. Perhaps it collided with it and fell nearby. Perhaps it crashed right before."

Luke looked at the map again. Something nagged at him and then he saw it. "Look. The Bittersweet Range and White Bluffs."

Rosen leaned forward and stared at the map. "Yes."

"They look like rings. Rings in a pond. After a rock hit the water."

Rosen stared at the map for a long time. "Yes," he said slowly. "It's not a crater. I had people look for a crater."

"No." Luke traced it with his finger. "Compression waves? Like tectonic stress is being held back?"

"Or maybe whatever's under Little Mountain is stretching the rock like taffy." Rosen rubbed his forehead. "Speculation. I'll have someone look at it."

Luke stared at the map and had a sudden image of slow and tidal geological processes breaking against Jeremy DaFoe like water against a wall. "They're connected. Little Mountain and Jeremy DaFoe," he said softly.

"I think so, too. It's a safe bet that Jeremy, for all his power, can't reach it."

"Why not?"

Rosen spread his hands. "We don't know. But if he could reach it and leave, sometime in the last sixty-five million years he'd have found a way."

Luke thought for a moment. It was heady excitement thinking this way. Thinking this was *possible*. "Or he saw the meteor strike and decided to stay. Or the Little Mountain object *created* Jeremy. We have no idea."

"Yes."

Luke picked up the whisky cup and held it out to Rosen. Rosen refilled it. "That's a lot of guesses."

"It is. But if we play this right, Jeremy will tell us himself what he needs to leave."

Luke sipped his whisky, speculating. "We have to persuade him. We have to intervene for him. We have to be *enablers*. It's a risk."

Rosen nodded. "It's a great risk. But we have agents on the ground in Nuthatch County. We have the Jeremy DaFoe Liaison on our side. We have the backing of the President of the United States—sort of. With our intelligence and resources and your knowledge and position, we can make it work."

They drained the whisky and slapped down the glasses together.

"Another," cried Luke.

"Another," echoed Rosen.

On through the night.

Chapter 2: Funereal Encounters

Joanie Durant pulled off her welding mask. The air was thick with the stink of iron. She inhaled deeply. It burned all the way through her considerable nose.

Joanie looked more Italian than Choctaw. Though her father was pure through and through, her mother had donated a leavening German and English effect, changing the luster of Joanie's hair subtly to suggest Rome or Sicily instead of the Trail of Tears. Her skin was dark and her eyes black. She kept her hair short so that her nose stood out like the bent prow on an old ship. An ex-boyfriend had likened her to Anjelica Huston, if Anjelica were darker, shorter, and a complete bitch. Joanie was breaking up with him at the time and so considered it a compliment.

Marilyn had started life as a discarded iron fence, a collection of pill bottles, the head and left breast of a Barbie doll, an etched drawing of a human fetus, a single baseball cleat, the preserved hoof of an Arabian horse, and a pair of bronze baby shoes.

Marilyn was what Joanie had come to call a *surround* piece. Joanie planned for the viewer to approach from one side and walk around it. The individual items would remain discreet until, at one point, a fully three-dimensional image of Marilyn

Monroe would spring suddenly from the found objects. A moment later it would dissolve again into its component parts.

Joanie viewed the work critically. Maybe it would be better to put *Marilyn* on a rotating table. Have her appear and disappear into a cloud of accouterments.

Joanie shook her head. Better this way. Any viewer coming into the room with a rotating *Marilyn* had about a one in four chance of seeing the face first. The integration and disintegration effect would be lost.

She had the urge to fiddle with it some more and suppressed it. Better to think about it.

Joanie's studio was a rented storage bay on the outskirts of Baltimore. She grabbed a bottle of wine from an ancient dresser drawer, opened the door, and stood just under the eaves, watching the rain.

The mist was a haze over the mercury lights and she could hear the angry hornet buzz of a dying transformer. The world looked as if there were a mischievous face hidden beneath it, aching to be seen.

Ooo, she thought. How about *Jeremy's* face? Make it a triptych so that one of three images could be seen at any given vantage point. One point of view could be the river—say down by Collins' Landing. The other could be a storm over Little Mountain. In the middle could be a portrait. No, wait. Something better. Another debris painting but one that showed the river, Little Mountain, and—something else. Not sure but it had to come in threes. As you walked around it, each of the images turned into Jeremy. For a moment she wrestled with having the three images simultaneously turn into a single Jeremy, or each image transform into a different Jeremy so that at any given moment a Jeremy was watching. Watching what? The landscape images or the viewer? Need to make some experimental sketches first, *then* decide.

Now, wouldn't that give somebody back in the County

heartburn?

Never mind. It was idle speculation. Around here, Jeremy had meaning for no one but Joanie Durant. It wasn't a tractable symbol—never use symbols that aren't universally determined. Marilyn Monroe, JFK, the Empire State Building, the Spirit of Saint Louis. Jeremy had meaning only in Nuthatch County.

Her cell rang. She pulled it out and glanced down. It was her mother. She briefly debated whether or not to answer. Joanie's relationship with her mother was complex.

"Hey, Nadine."

"Hello, Joan."

Bad news. Nadine only developed that Vincent Price hollowness upon personal discovery of one of the four horsemen.

Joanie downed a good swallow of wine. This might be rough.

"A good friend of your grandfather is dead."

"Who?"

"Deacon Williams."

"Jesus. I thought he was dead already."

"Joan—"

"Okay. I'm sorry. Where should I send the flowers?"

"The funeral is on Saturday and I think you should accompany your grandfather."

Could this be *good* news? Joanie liked Grampy. "Well, Mom. I don't know. I've got a show coming up. The school doesn't pay that well and things haven't been exactly selling—"

"You won't have to pay for a ticket."

"Okay," Joanie said sweetly. "I'll see if I can get off work."

After she hung up, Joanie called the head of the Brodeur Art School.

"Yes?"

"Aaron? It's me, Joanie."

"Ah. How long will you be gone?"

"I didn't even ask yet!"

"You only call me at night at home when you want me to come out to a club or when you want time off."

"I *could* be asking you out to a club."

"And you only do that when you're drunk."

"I *could* be drunk."

"You only call me Aaron when you're sober."

"What do I call you when I'm drunk?"

"Mister Principal Schmaltz."

"Aaron, I've never called you Principal Schmaltz."

"You mispronounce 'Schmidt' when you're drunk."

"I didn't know you were observing me quite so closely. I'm embarrassed."

"Not likely. What's up?"

"A good friend of my grandfather died back home. He wants me to take him back there."

"No doubt your Grandfather is feeble and requires your care."

"Heck, no. Grampy's tough as they come. It's Mom's idea that he'll crack under the strain. Or maybe she wants some help with him. Who knows how a mother thinks?"

"How long?"

Joanie took a long pull of the bottle. "Friday at the latest. Maybe Monday. Lenny can take the casting class—it's just introductory this session. But tell the welding students we'll do double time next week. I want them for myself."

"Maybe I'll take the welding class. I can inoculate them against you."

"Fat chance."

"I'll see you in a week."

"Good bye and thank you, Mister Principal Schmaltz."

Then, she took a deep breath and called her grandfather.

"Hello?" said Luke.

"Hey, Grampy."

"Hello, Joanie."

"Mom told me you're going back home for Deacon Williams' funeral."

A pause. "Yes."

"I wanted to know if I could hitch a ride."

Another pause. "I haven't purchased tickets, yet."

"I can do it for you if you send me your account information."

"Will there be anything left in the account?"

"You mean *after* I buy that plasma cutter I've been lusting after?"

"I'll buy the tickets. I'll email you the schedule."

She hung up. Not bad. With the schedule, she could get the invoice. Nadine would pony up when Joanie gave her the invoice. That plasma cutter was half bought already.

When they left the plane in Saint Louis, Joanie was cold-stone sober. She never liked to be drunk or even tipsy around Luke. Joanie knew that Luke's position, while not powerful in and of itself, still allowed him to rub shoulders with some very interesting people. No doubt enshrined in some FBI office there was a thick folder containing every youthful indiscretion she'd ever committed and some she hadn't—or at least would never admit to. Joanie had no idea what Luke knew about her and had no desire to find out.

A normal person reaches Nuthatch County from Lambert Field by driving towards Sikeston then, south of Cairo, hanging a left onto the County main road. It takes well over an hour to cover the old switch-backed track over the Bittersweet Ridge into Pilate even in good weather. Total time: four hours plus. But Luke preferred his own way to the County. He and Joanie drove over the Mississippi River and down to Cairo in a rented Neon. Then, Luke called up Bob Sheffield. Bob warmed up his ancient ferry, the *New Madrid Fault*, boarded the car, and pulled out of the slip into the river. The current was so strong that all Bob had to do was angle the ferry north west and hold the throttle. The river pushed the boat over to the Missouri side.

It was a clear day and the ferry was just north of where the Ohio River poured into the Mississippi. Luke and Joanie stood outside in the cold and watched the ripping, churning water. Occasional ice chunks rolled past. One struck the side of the *New Madrid Fault* and the hull rang like a bell. Joanie gripped the rail tightly, shivering. Pieces of the scene struck her: the shapeless liquid glitter of the water. A gull, as still as if painted, hovered, over them, then slanted away from them in effortless grace. The eastern sun breaking over them in a clear brilliance, backlighting the Illinois shore into obsidian black. She glanced at her grandfather. Luke stared ahead as if made of stone.

"Did you know Deacon Williams?" Luke asked suddenly.

Joanie shook her head. "I could pick him out of a crowd because he was the Eldest. I never met him."

Luke nodded to show he'd heard her but said nothing.

Joanie looked at him sideways. He looked sad but stoic. Joanie had a sudden vision of that face broken and carved out of bronze—like one of Rodin's *Burghers of Calais*. The scarred bronze showing the tortured soul underneath. She looked away again, wondering if she could get her grandfather to pose for her. Or if she could at least get a picture of him.

"Did you ever hear how Deacon got his name?" Luke said suddenly.

"No." Joanie was still thinking of how she'd carve the wax for a mold.

"None of the ministers like to talk about Jeremy. Religion has an uneasy time in Nuthatch County with Jeremy being who he is. Voids like that have a way of filling themselves. Around 1900 there were two secret Jeremy cults. They had long names but we can call them the Jeremy Cult and the No-Jeremy Cult. As you'd expect, the Jeremy Cult declared that Jeremy was the one true deity and the No-Jeremy Cult adamantly opposed his divinity but embraced his supernatural qualities."

Joanie shook her head. "I had no idea."

"They're still around. Bill Keller runs the Organization for Nuthatch County Progress—today's Jeremy Cult. The No Jeremy Cult calls itself the Nuthatch County Self Actualization Committee. There have probably been Jeremy cults as long as Jeremy's been around. It's something people do." Luke looked out over the water. "Anyway, the Williams family have been anti-Jeremy since before the Civil War so they've been in one or the other No Jeremy Cults pretty much the whole time. But despite declaring Jeremy a bona fide supernatural being, they were still good, God-fearing Christians." Luke leaned towards Joanie. "This didn't set well with the ministers. Maybe it's a 'no man can serve two masters' problem. Or maybe they didn't want to rock the Jeremy boat. Or it could be ministers like to have full control of your spiritual life and didn't want somebody in the church working for the competition." Luke chuckled. "Anyway, Deacon's father, Carl Williams, declared he'd start a church of his own and named his first born and only son 'Deacon.' Then he up and died and Deacon was stuck with the name."

"He must have been a good friend of yours." Jeremy cults? How had she never known about Jeremy cults?

"Deacon Williams was a cantankerous, vindictive, bile-filled old man. He held on to a grudge like it was something precious. There was some talk of him getting a heart transplant when he was in his sixties. It would have been the first time he'd ever had one." Luke spit into the water.

Joanie stared at him. "Then why are you going to his funeral?"

"Well, he's the Eldest." He looked at her. "I'm going to give the eulogy."

"Are you going to say *that?*"

Luke chuckled. "Get a rise out of people, wouldn't it?"

"I think the Williams family would have you shot."

Luke shrugged. "Likely I wouldn't be saying anything that they haven't all thought one time or another. No. I'll think of something nice. It's a funeral of the Eldest. Attention must be paid."

Joanie thought for a moment. "That's not the only reason."

"Eh?"

"You didn't give the eulogy for June Pederson, did you? Or Opal Campbell. This isn't one of the County traditions. What's special about Deacon Williams?"

Luke half grinned at her but it didn't come off. "Let's say he was a business partner of sorts."

"What sort of business?"

Luke leaned heavily on the railing. "The sort of business that makes you work with someone like Deacon Williams."

Under the terms of the Missouri Compromise, Missouri was admitted to the union as a slave state. Deacon Williams' family had owned slaves back then. Buddy's family *were* slaves.

At the time, Jeremy was known as Nathan Collins for reasons known only to himself. Jeremy (or Nathan) changed names when it suited him. In those days, there were two or three villages along the river catering to the steamships. All are now absorbed into the town of Pilate, the only remnants of their existence embedded in street names. Nathan was living in a small house in the village of Picket. Later, the name 'Picket' would be lost and the area known as "Collins' Landing." Nathan ran a store and sometimes rented a room or two.

Twenty-five years after the Compromise, in the spring of 1845, a Williams slave named Parker ran off. Nathan found him hiding behind the wood pile and brought him into the house and fed him.

The dogs caught Parker's scent near the edge of the river and tracked him to Nathan's store.

Lyle Williams found Nathan sorting through stock in his barn. Lyle stood in the doorway and called out to him. "We've tracked a runaway slave here, Nathan."

Nathan nodded and continued sorting through canned goods and flour. He finished and walked outside to talk with Lyle.

"He's inside your house," Lyle repeated.

"Parker is certainly in there, Lyle," Nathan confirmed.

"I mean to take him back."

"Parker says you'll whip him if you do." Nathan said it in the same voice he might say, 'Here's your pound of coffee.'

Lyle was taller than Jeremy but he didn't feel like he was looking down at a smaller man. "I might," said Lyle, eyeing Nathan with some nervousness. "It's no more than he deserves. There are those who'd do worse."

"True enough."

"I'll just go inside and fetch him."

Nathan looked at him. He spoke slowly and clearly. "You mean to go into my house where sleeps my wife and dog, lay hands on my guest, and drag him out by his neck?"

"Of course not," said Lyle hastily. "Not if you don't want me to. But he's not a guest, is he? He's a runaway nigger."

They were standing in the middle of the yard between the barn and the store. Two men Lyle had brought with him were sitting there on horses, trying to look as small as possible.

"You go on home, Lyle," said Nathan quietly. "I'll figure out what to do with Parker." Nathan turned back to the barn.

That was too much for Lyle. "He's my *property*, Nathan. You can't just take my *property*." He grabbed Nathan's arm.

Accounts differ on what happened next, though they agree

on Lyle's statement about Parker being his property. Some said there was a lightning bolt and others just talk about a flash. But when the light died away there was nothing left of Lyle Williams but a soot streak on the ground.

That was enough for Lyle's men. They galloped away. One of them moved to Illinois.

The Eldest that year was a sixty-year-old woman named Abigail Meyers Ferber. Nathan sent word to her to gather all the slaves and bring them down to the store that night. The slaves were not to be bothered or hindered in any way. The story of Lyle's passing had made the rounds and none of the slave owners were of a mind to argue.

That evening, a hundred or more slaves stood in front of Nathan's store. Nathan climbed up on the roof of his porch to talk to them. "Parker tells me you want to be free."

There was a cry among the slaves that it was so.

"You're sure?"

The cry was loud.

Nathan seemed to think a minute. "I say you're free." It's said the cheers could be heard clear to Cairo.

Nathan quieted them down. "There's still work that's got to be done. Money to be paid. Owners to be reimbursed. Families to be brought together. There will be no bloodshed or revenge. Abigail will sort this all out. You listen to her like you would to me."

Nathan sold his store to Lyle's brother, Bill Williams, and moved to a farm north of Ridgeville in the small valley that would one day become Ashby. Parker moved nearby where he worked around town as a carpenter. He took the name Collins Parker. He and his wife were legally married. When the war broke out, Parker left and fought for the Union. County folks fought for the North. County folks fought for the South. But they all had to leave the County to do it.

Nathan allowed no fighting in Nuthatch County. Invaders

coming up on trails that led into the County found themselves inexplicably diverted west into the White Bluffs or north into the Bittersweet. Eddies that previously allowed boats to dock disappeared and were replaced by strong currents and treacherous whirlpools that denied anchorage. Collins's Landing was abandoned. Nathan Collins changed his name, for no reason anyone knew, to Jeremy DaFoe.

After the war, the Parkers considered it their own personal burden to make sure Jeremy was well cared for. While there was little they could do for Jeremy himself, they were always bringing food over to his house, making sure his horses were curried or roof repaired. Later, when the transition was made from horse to horseless carriage, it was Buddy's father who tuned Jeremy's engine and Buddy's uncle that adjusted his brakes.

Bob pulled into the tiny concrete slip. Luke carefully drove the Neon over the edge of the *New Madrid Fault's* deck. The car dropped what felt like four feet and banged the tail pipe. Luke stopped the car and went to inspect the damage.

Joanie remained in the passenger seat, desperate for a drink. She looked at the clock on the dash: just after eleven. It was only ten o'clock back in Baltimore but, hey, it's always afternoon somewhere. She reached into her coat and brought out a flask, looked at it and thought about her grandfather, put it away again. After the funeral. Nadine would be proud of her restraint right up to the point she realized its motivation. Joanie calculated logistics: it was a Saturday. The funeral would be at one. That would take two hours. Then the obligatory visitation to the decaying Williams family homestead. Another two hours. Then dinner. Check into the room at the Taverton Hotel in Pilate—which had a bar that didn't count for much—then sweet freedom and a roaring trip to Atkinson's Road House. If she could get the car. Or grab a cab from the hotel and trust to fate for a ride back.

She remembered closing down Atkinson's while tripping on acid and getting lost after walking for miles on the unbranched two-lane road. Joanie had seen a glow over the bluff and was convinced it was the Emerald City. She climbed the frozen and muddy dirt and found the bright cheery neon sign declaring the sanctity of the Ridgeville U-Storage for the entire world to see. Joanie had sat on the wet grass and laughed until she nearly pissed her pants.

Luke returned to the car and they drove down into Pilate to meet those that cluster around the dead.

Deacon Williams had no children. His wife, Pearl Hatcomb Williams, had been a thin razor of a woman who would never let anything as common as a child violate the sanctity of her body. Pearl had only occasionally let Deacon manage violations of his own all the years they were married—which no doubt contributed to his general disposition. She had contrived to die before the older Deacon needed her to care for him—Deacon remained convinced the timing was intentional. Clean up after you? I'd rather die. And she did.

Thus his part of the Williams blood line came to rest. The ideas of men live after them whether or not those ideas are any good.

Deacon Williams' views on Jeremy DaFoe were well known but few shared them. Few shared Buddy Parker's uncritical approval of Jeremy, either. The storm brought tornadoes and rain. The river brought water and flood. The land brought times of plenty and times of drought. Jeremy was considered by most in this same light. Mythology attempts to put a human face on random fate. Folklore in Nuthatch County did the same: it painted the face of the man next door across a natural power.

Jeremy DaFoe was a personable man to know. You could fool yourself he was just like anybody else. Except, of course, those times you couldn't. But Deacon Williams with his squat spider look, high-pitched nasal voice, and arrogant manner rubbed people the wrong way. It didn't help that the Deacon's family had historically owned much of the County's property worth owning, regardless of the Williams' paltry current holdings. For a lot of people, just knowing that the Deacon didn't like Jeremy was enough reason to make them feel well-disposed towards Jeremy. For others, the same knowledge made them feel good about the Deacon.

The crowd that showed up for Deacon's funeral at the First Baptist Church of Pilate had few genuine mourners. The majority were people who just wanted to make sure Deacon was dead.

Nadine and Joseph were waiting for them at the church. Nadine's stocky presence contrasted with Joseph's ghost-like thinness. Seeing her father made Joanie especially glad she hadn't drunk anything. Not that Joseph would have been offended. He would have likely asked for a hit off the flask and, when it was empty, passed over one of his own. But Joanie had never been able to fathom whatever passed for a relationship between her parents. An alcohol glow just made things more confusing.

Sometimes Joseph was there. Sometimes not. He'd come home affable and pleasant, working around the house or taking odd jobs in Pilate. This might last a week, a month, or a year. Then, for a week or so, he'd stare out the window from the front room. Joanie had a sudden memory of sitting on the floor next to his chair, snuggled next to his leg, the fabric of the chair rasping her cheek, smelling the earth on the stained knees of his jeans. He must have been gardening—Joseph always liked to garden. How old was she? Eight? Nine? Holding on to his leg and repeating fiercely to herself, *you're not going to leave! You're not going to leave!* While he absently patted her head.

Without any effect. A few days later he was gone. Back to the reservation in South County or hitchhiking on the road. Then back again a week, a month, or a year later, no explanation. No response given when Joanie shouted at him. Her mother silently opened the door for him as if he'd never been gone, or there, at all.

Nadine gave Joanie a quick hug, then turned to Luke and kissed him on the cheek.

Joseph shook Luke's hand. He nodded toward Joanie without saying a word.

Dark anger and a darker feeling of helplessness filled her. She went inside the church and sat down next to the first open spot she could find. One with no more room for anybody else to sit next to her.

"Joanie?" came a soft voice next to her.

She turned and Carter Faraday was searching her face.

Carter watched her. His eyes seemed soft. "It is you, isn't it?"

"Carter?" She clapped her hands in relief and joy. Someone she knew and *was not* related to! "I haven't seen you since—" And stopped. Her grandmother's funeral. She had been sixteen and in Japan when the stroke happened, and she'd managed to return just after Catherine died. The funeral had been held on a dismal, cold day even in late summer. The rain seemed to wash the color out of everything. Jackets were blue, gray, or black. People's faces were faded pale. Carter Faraday's bright yellow umbrella had been the only color around the grave and, in its reflection, he was the best-looking man she'd ever seen. Thus are crushes born.

"Yeah." Carter grimaced. "We have to stop meeting at funerals. People are going to talk."

Joanie chuckled. "How about a better class of funeral?"

Carter gestured to the crowd. "How could it be better than this?"

Joanie watched him levelly. "We could meet at Atkinson's. Later."

"Ah," said Carter, looking away for a moment. "Can't drink, you know. Saturday night's all right for fighting here in Nuthatch County. The clinic has to be ready." He looked at her blankly. "Are you even old enough to drink?"

"I'm asking you out for dinner and a soda. Maybe later we can go to the prom." His hand rested on the pew in front of him. She slapped it lightly. "I'm twenty-five, Carter. They barely card me anymore."

Carter stared at his hand where she had touched him. "Why the hell not? After the interment. But we'll have to take two cars." He glanced at her. "I might get paged."

Joanie smiled at him sweetly. "No need. If you do, I'll even drive you to work."

The team had been meeting for cards Saturday afternoon every week for nearly thirty years. Some members had dropped out because of retirement, disease, or death. It was an informal gathering—their superiors would have been cross if they knew. After all, fraternization was discouraged.

Undercover agents of the federal government had been in Nuthatch County since Madison. In the modern course of events, such agents would represent organizations like the CIA or the NSA or the FBI. But since spying on Jeremy long predated any of those organizations, the agents were associated with other, older, agencies.

This year the Post Office was represented by Arnie Herman, the meter reader for Nuthatch County Power and Light. Nate Guilder stood in for the US Geological Survey via the NSA with a day job as a telephone line repair man. Harry Carr manned the helm for the Bureau of Weights and Measures and ran power equipment for the County Highway Maintenance Office. He used to work for the CIA. Tonight they were abusing the hospitality of Weights and Measures.

"Any food, Spooky?" asked the Post Office.

Harry checked the refrigerator. "Just some meatloaf."

Nate/USGS chuckled. "Go ahead, Arnie. Harry's a hell of a cook. Come the day he'll make some guy a terrific wife."

"Shut up," said Harry.

"I need some cards," said Nate plaintively. "At least wait until the hand's over."

Harry ignored the USGS. He pulled out the meatloaf and sliced it carefully. From the cupboard of his trailer, he brought down three small plates with a flower design off to one side. He placed each slice to partially obscure the flower pattern and garnished it with a slice of onion and a small radish. A fork crossed the plate at a perfect thirty-degree angle. He brought the plates to the table and set them next to each spot.

Nate watched him. "Three cards."

Harry dealt them out and then took a bite of the meatloaf. Nice. Needed a bit more rosemary.

The phone rang behind him. Harry reached back and picked it up. He listened for a moment then put it back.

"Who was that?" asked Arnie/Post Office.

"Department of Defense rep," said Harry as he dealt himself a single card. An ace! Excellent. "We have marching orders."

"Pull the other one," said Nate.

"It's for real. Had the right passwords and everything. Could be Presidential for all I know. He said you'll all be getting calls. We'll be working under him."

"No *shit!*" yelled Arnie. "The DOD has a rep out here? Who is it? Who the *hell* is it?"

Harry gave him a mild look. "The guy we'll be working under. Come on, Arnie. After what's been happening at the Pentagon in the last twenty years, are you really that surprised?"

Arnie sat back. "I guess not. Who is it?"

Harry shrugged. "We'll know soon enough."

Nate considered his cards. "What's the gig?"

Harry looked over his hand carefully. "Dealer takes two. We're going to discredit Jeremy DaFoe."

Arnie put down his cards. "Years we've been watching him."

"Years," agreed Harry."

"And *now* they want to do something about him?"

Nate anted in with a small pile of pennies. "I wonder how many agents there are in the County."

Arnie placed a pile of pennies next to Nate's. "The Nuthatch County nuclear family: one mother, one father, one child, two agents of the federal government."

"That's the gig," said Harry. He matched the piles in the pot and added five more. "I raise."

"Any ideas?" said Nate. "I'll match that."

Arnie examined his cards and put some pennies in the pot. "How about a sex scandal? You can't go wrong with a good sex scandal."

Harry laughed. "With Jeremy? He's the closest thing this place has to a celebrity. Half the women in the County would sleep with him in a New York minute. The other half are trying to figure out how to marry him. The remainder is crippled or dead."

"I don't know how he does it," said Nate morosely.

"Status," said Arnie. "Like cops. Or generals. Or actors. Celebrity culture, man. The whole country is going to the dogs."

Harry examined his cards. "Did I ever tell you how we got

rid of the mayor of this little town down in Guatemala?"

"Again with the CIA stories," groaned Nate.

"I tell you a sex scandal would work." Arnie leaned forward earnestly. "It doesn't *matter* how many people want to sleep with him. The thing is he's not sleeping with *you* or with his wife. It's envy. Pure and simple."

Harry ignored him. "We had this guy, Valencia, down in the sticks making trouble for the provincial governor—a guy we liked. We wanted to make an impression so we decided to get rid of him. A sex scandal wouldn't work—"

"Says you!"

"Says me. We had to get him deposed by his own party. Quick. Clean. Non-violent. So we started rumors that he was going to electrify the dam on the local lake." He thought a moment. "I'll raise a nickel."

Arnie and Nate stared at him.

"Okay," said Nate. "I'll bite. How did that work?"

"Cost you a nickel to find out."

Silently, Nate and Arnie each pushed forward a nickel into the pot.

Harry examined his cards again. "Everybody wanted electricity, see? But the dam was just a six-foot wall of dirt. Couldn't get electricity from it since it was so low. Even if you *could* it would never be enough to electrify the village. But we pushed it hard enough that Valencia had to respond. He said it was a false rumor planted by his enemies. The dam couldn't be electrified. But we kept pushing the rumor and now we added that he didn't *want* to electrify the dam. Pretty soon one of his opponents picked up the rumor and started asking *why* Valencia didn't want to electrify the dam. Was it because he wanted the population ignorant and in hovels? Or had he spent all the money on his cronies? We didn't let it die. Inside of a year, he retired."

"You're saying we need to make electricity?" Arnie shook his head. "The Post Office—meaning me—says that's nuts."

"No," said Harry patiently. "I'm saying you put something on the table that everyone wants and push it until everyone thinks they need it and then put Jeremy in the position of refusing it. It'll cause a lot of bad blood. Then, you fan the bad blood."

"What sort of 'something?'" asked Nate.

"Don't know. We'll have to think about that."

"I think I'll call," said Arnie. "Pair of twos."

"I got nothing," said Nate. He tossed his cards on the table in disgust.

"Full house," said Harry and pulled in the pot.

Luke left his seat and moved up the aisle towards the lectern. The First Baptist Church of Pilate was quiet and crowded. All eyes followed Luke as he walked up the steps. Luke felt their pressure. He could feel the twelve-foot cross behind him, the expectancy from the audience, and the presence of the County outside, so pregnant with possibilities. He looked down for a moment as he pulled the speech out of his jacket pocket.

He and Rosen had worked on that speech for hours. Then, Rosen had turned one of DOD's Nuthatch County Group writers on it. *Writers?* What *other* capabilities did Nuthatch County Group have? Rosen was vague. After the nameless writers were done, Luke and Rosen attacked it again to make sure it sounded just as if Luke had written it himself and not like the propaganda it was.

Luke pressed the paper on the lectern. Distant praise for the deceased. Acknowledgment of his place in the history of his family, his town, his country. Brief allusions to the County itself that sounded like praise but was really critical. Reluctant allocation of blame disguised as joining together. All designed to sow doubt about the County's role which was tantamount to laying it on Jeremy DaFoe.

He looked up. Jeremy was in the back sitting next to Betty. He saw Carter sitting next to Joanie, furtively trying to keep himself separate from the attractive woman next to him. Luke understood the meaning of Joanie's barely suppressed glee and wondered if Carter knew what he was getting into.

Two rows behind them sat Nadine and Joseph, both expressionless. Faces carved from rock—he had a brief memory of seeing Catherine that time at Johnson Shut-ins, where the river wore away the veneer of limestone to expose the hard granite beneath.

Buddy Parker sat in the front row looking up at him. Proud, scared, and embarrassed to be the Eldest. Luke had seen that same expression on every Eldest he'd ever met.

He knew them all. Pam Small. Grace Cox. Jake Withers stood in the back overseeing everything but, as an undertaker should, not truly participating.

Here I begin, he thought. Thus I make war upon giants.

Luke cleared his throat and began to speak.

Chapter 3: On the Road

Rosen had brought up to Luke the idea of setting Jeremy up with something desired by the County that Jeremy could never allow. He said it had been suggested to him but wouldn't say by whom. They had thrown various ideas back and forth over a long weekend after Luke had returned from the funeral. Rosen met him in his office.

"How about a Wal-Mart?" suggested Rosen. "Doesn't everybody out there love Wal-Mart?"

"People use Wal-Mart out of desperate necessity. Love has nothing to do with it," said Luke owlishly. He looked into his drink. He never drank this much when Catherine was alive. Hell, he thought. He never drank this much *ever*. Of course, that's a low bar if the extent of drinking is a beer once or twice a week and a glass of wine on weekends. "How about a bridge over the Mississippi? That would be appreciated."

Rosen shook his head. "Take too long. Bridges have to be planned years in advance. We'd have to get legislation through congress."

"I've been waiting eight years. I can wait a little more." Luke chuckled. "Not a lot more. I'm not getting any younger."

"Not my point." Rosen poured a finger full into his glass.

"We need something we can keep control of. It's *hard* to keep Jeremy a secret. Getting harder every year."

"What do you mean? He's been a secret for nearly two centuries."

"People talk—"

"They always talk. I've been watching this for forty years. Bitters saw it in the Eisenhower administration. People leave Nuthatch County and they talk about Jeremy. But nobody believes them. Or, at least, nobody worth a damn. It's like the Roswell kooks. Nobody believes them either."

Rosen watched Luke for a moment. "The internet has changed the definition of kook. But that's not what I'm talking about. I'm talking about the observable facts that surround Jeremy. Take the geology of the region, for example. It's strange. It makes scientists curious. We've headed off a few grants for research in the area. God forbid if the diamonds got out. Back in the eighties, we sent a Delta force team in the dead of night to scoop out anything loose. Not because it was an important military operation but because you can trust those guys to keep their mouths shut about *anything*. Then, there's this guy, Brietenbach, at the university who likes to study plants all over Missouri. He just drives around. Well, he drove through Nuthatch County—God knows why—and found a couple of flowers there previously considered extinct. As soon as we heard about *that* we had to send another team to transplant a whole shitload of the little flowers. They had to be far away from the County to be distinct but near enough so Brietenbach would find them. He's *still* trying to figure that out. Add to that, sociologists studying rural settlement patterns. Psychologists studying folk tales. Medical statisticians poring over census data. Satellite feeds. To the modern scientific world, Jeremy DaFoe's little corner would stand out if we let it. There's a whole group on our team that does nothing but put out disinformation surrounding Nuthatch County—all without anybody knowing where the PR came from. You can't believe what a headache it all is." Rosen ran his hands through his hair. "You know there's an upcoming mission out of NASA to measure gravity all over the earth? Little Mountain's going to show up like a bright red flag. I don't know how we're going to manage that one."

Luke stared at him. He had never heard a hint of any of this. No liaison had. "When did DOD start helping keep this secret?"

"The Viet Nam War," Rosen said. "Right after your second briefing, Nixon said, 'This is too important to leave to some flunky from Missouri.'"

"Meaning me." Luke had never liked Nixon.

"Yeah." Rosen met his eyes and looked away. "It was before I was born. I just read the files. Westmoreland persuaded him the best place to keep a lid on was the Pentagon. Nixon was up to his eyeballs in leaks and didn't trust anybody on his own staff. Didn't trust us, either. He just mistrusted us *less,* if you know what I mean."

"I'm surprised it didn't happen under Eisenhower," Luke said mildly.

"Maybe it did. How does the left hand know what the right hand is doing? There could have been a few unscheduled U-2 flights over Missouri. We'll never know."

"The road." It came to him in a flash.

"Road?"

"The main road. Comes in off the Interstate, meanders around the County, and dumps out on a dirt path next to the airport outside the County. Nobody takes that road unless they're going to the County and nobody goes to the County that hasn't got business there." Luke sat up. "We straighten that road. Make it beautiful and bring it back around to the Interstate. Really put Nuthatch County on the map. Literally."

Rosen's eyes lit up. "No need for legislation. We can use the existing rights of way. At least until we start moving the south end towards the Interstate."

Luke spread his hands. "Who cares? That can happen later. The important thing is we can move forward with the project without congressional approval. Get enough started to bring it on the table in time for the Spring County Meeting. We confront Jeremy in May." He looked at Rosen. "Which side should I come out on? For or against?"

Rosen gave him a long look. "Depends on whether Jeremy DaFoe can read minds."

Luke stared at him. "Everything you know about him and you don't know that?"

Rosen looked away. "Opinions are… mixed."

"What do *you* think?"

"I don't know." Rosen slapped the papers on the table. "Sometimes I think he can. Sometimes I think he can't. Who the hell can say *what* he can do and what he can't?|"

"I don't think he can."

"Why not?"

"Deacon watched him since before I was born. That was one of the things he looked for. He never saw it."

"That's not much proof," Rosen said doubtfully.

"True enough." Luke leaned forward. "Maybe we're predictable if you watch us for centuries."

"Millennia."

"Yeah. But I've still seen him surprised. If he read minds he'd never show that."

"Maybe he wants you to think that."

"Why should he? For *fun?* As far as we know there's no way to hurt him. If we're going to get all paranoid because we think he's screwing with us, we're done for."

Rosen sipped his glass. "Or maybe he could but doesn't bother because he doesn't care." He shook his head and shoulders like a dog shaking off water. "Take the high road. You want this because it's good for Nuthatch County. Then you can reluctantly endorse Jeremy when he cans it. Be a good guy all around."

Luke tapped Rosen's glass and drank off some whisky. "Here's to being a good guy."

Imagine a stone cast into a lake. It's a small stone. The lake is still. The ripples spread far and wide. They're not large but they are visible. When the stone's ripples reach shallow water, they disturb complacent frogs. The frogs jump into the lake. More ripples. A deer and a hare at opposite sides can't see the stone or the frogs; they just know something isn't quite right. Millions of years of evolution have made it clear: it's better to react to something that might be there and isn't than to get caught by something that shouldn't be there and is. They run away from the lake. The movement and scent of them wake up a dog pleasantly sleeping. The same impulses that drive the deer and the hare lie inside that dog but chained to a new purpose: better alert the authorities. The dog begins barking, and a befuddled and angry Hugh Utterback yells at that damned dog to *shut the hell up!*

That, metaphorically, was the plan.

Harry had experience in toppling governments and changing administrations. It's always the accumulation of little things that wears down a great stone. When the idea of the road was communicated to him as if it wasn't his own idea he was unsurprised. Surprise was reserved for the decision the DOD rep had made to keep his identity secret. Harry thoughtfully considered ways and means to discover the agent's identity. Not with any malicious intent, mind you. Just to keep his hand in.

All three agents were well placed to start rumors, though Arnie was perhaps in the best position. Meter reading was still a hands-on job in the County. Each house and business had to be counted. In point of fact, Arnie loved his day job. Sure, the weather sucked in the winter but Arnie had been born and raised in Chicago and measured all weather against that refrigerated morgue next to the lake. Nuthatch County in February was a breeze by comparison. And in the summer people were looser here. Sometimes they were downright frivolous. Arnie always tried to be efficient and come around the corner of the house as fast as possible, sometimes surprising a private sun worshipper. The swearing and screaming did his soul good.

Nate did nearly as well. That winter there were enough line checks that Nate was called in regularly. The recalcitrant phones became mysteriously operational after Nate had time to share nice gossip and a cup or two of coffee.

Harry was probably the least equipped rumor-monger of the three of them. He didn't have many opportunities while manning the snow plow or clearing the storm drains. But he managed to warm his toes in Atkinson's where those who didn't have (or didn't want) a home-cooked meal could always get one.

Harry, Nate, and Arnie were like tiny grains of sand in an oyster, orchestrating excitement, apprehension, and confusion into a pearl-making irritant.

Once tapped, Eldests, like Supreme Court Justices, served until death or retirement.

The actual duties of the Eldest grew out of the needs of the current culture and ranged from determining Osage planting times three hundred years ago to making sure everybody bought as many war bonds as possible when the Battle of the Bulge filled the newsreels.

The sudden influx of newly freed slaves created Abigail

Myers Ferber's outsized role. Managing that salient event occupied her for the remaining twelve years of her life. The day South Carolina seceded from the Union, she died and left the whole mess in the hands of John Jacob Hartwell. County government cracked and fell apart under the strain. For five years of war and two years after, John Hartwell had real power and authority to exercise high and low justice. It killed him. The first thing his successor, Michael Elk-Adams, did was to reinstate the County government and create a benevolent, genial, and largely symbolic role for the Eldest. Being king had killed Hartwell. It was not going to kill *him*.

Moses Blumenthal, the one and only Jewish Eldest so far in the history of the County, had to work closely with the liaison all through the Great Depression to make sure the residents of Nuthatch County did not starve. He became an insidious master of the art of bureaucratic paperwork—a role carefully avoided by all other holders of the office before and since. The String of Women that followed, starting just before World War II and not broken until Deacon Williams in 1988, felt that they must lead by example. Volunteerism was never so completely in style as it was in those years. Until it was his turn, Deacon Williams considered being Eldest an opportunity to get rid of Jeremy DaFoe once and for all. He was disappointed. Once he ascended to the role, its limited utility became clear to him. Opinions of the Eldest, like Supreme Court Justices, ranged from outright dislike to tepid acceptance.

Buddy Parker thought it might be a change to just be *nice* for a while.

Joanie woke up when it was still dark. There wasn't even a hint of light out the window. She started to sit up but, next to her, Carter Faraday stirred in his sleep. She stopped and he went back to sleep.

The clock said four-thirty. The plane back to Baltimore left at eleven. It was easily four hours to Lambert: an hour or more over the Bittersweet, across the bridge to Illinois, and then north and back across the bridge at Saint Louis. If she left in an hour she'd still have an hour to drop off the rental car and check in. Time enough for a hot shower and a nice breakfast. After a weekend with Carter, a hot shower and calorie restoration were necessities.

She turned on the dim light and found a robe.

Carter turned and reached for her sleepily. "You don't have to leave yet."

She danced back. "Not this morning, love. I have a plane to catch."

"I'll drive you." He grabbed for her again.

She dodged and he rolled back onto the bed.

Joanie was smiling as she got in the shower. *Never* expected this. She'd been here practically every weekend since the funeral. Been a month—*Christ!* The credit card bill would be coming this week. Kiss that plasma cutter good-bye.

The curtains parted. "I need a shower, too," Carter said as he got in with her.

As he drew his soapy hands along her sides and down her hips she shivered and bit her lip. *Ah, well, maybe I can catch a later flight.*

Buddy Parker first heard about the proposed new highway from County Commissioner Pam Small.

Government in Nuthatch County, like most things, bent around Jeremy DaFoe. In the state of Missouri power evolved up from municipalities. Power not directly delegated by the state or abrogated by the feds automatically fell to the counties and municipalities. Pilate and Ridgeville were both incorporated and, under normal circumstances, would have been independent of the County since County government concerned itself exclusively with unincorporated land. But Jeremy DaFoe was the responsibility of everyone. The role of a County Meeting and its presiding County Commissioner existed long before there ever was County or Commissioner. Thus, in practice, the town governments of Pilate and Ridgeville were limited to the naming of streets and zoning of pets. Public decisions happened in the County Meetings. The spring meeting came in early May and the fall meeting in late October.

Pam stood fuming on Buddy's front porch. She pushed past him into the room as soon as he opened the door.

Buddy closed the door hastily. Though she was smaller by a foot and tiny in frame, Pam flickered with energy like heat lightning. Buddy was always a little scared of her.

Pam threw her jacket on the sofa, turned, and faced him, hands on her hips. "This is not a good way to start being Eldest, Buddy."

"Beg pardon?"

"You need to *work* with me here. Tell me what you want. You don't just go to the liaison and say this is how it's going to be."

"How what's going to be?"

"The new highway."

"*What* new highway?"

"The replacement for the main road." She watched him for a moment. "You know nothing about this."

Buddy shook his head mutely. Oh, he wished yet once again, if only his wife, Arista, was still among the living. She could manage this tiny storm in his living room.

Pam sat down on the sofa. "Just this morning I have had phone calls from—" She ticked off her fingers. "Both druggists. Two used car salesmen, one from Pilate and one from Ridgeville. Three real estate salesmen. Who knew we had three realtors? And, apparently, the manager of the last remaining Woolworth in the country."

"That would be Ray."

"Ray?"

"Ray Bakerman. My brother."

"Different father?"

"Same father. They had a falling out and Ray took my mother's name—something she was not terribly happy about. Anyway, he's the only used car salesman in Ridgeville." Buddy thought a moment. "He's probably one of the realtors, too. I'm certain he's the Woolworth man."

Pam looked confused. "Woolworths doesn't even exist anymore."

Buddy took a deep breath. "You remember the old Haywood building where the machine shop used to be? On Fifth Street in Ridgeville?"

"Yes."

"It used to have a Woolworth's advertisement on it? For the store in Sikeston?"

Light dawned on Pam's face. "It's the Woolworth *building*."

"Yeah," said Buddy sourly. "That's Ray. Pick a new angle and chances are Ray's already checked it out."

"He's a realtor, too? And sells used cars?"

"He probably has a real estate license," admitted Buddy. "I'm sure he has managed to palm off a couple of old cars on people who didn't know any better."

"Okay," said Pam and took a deep breath. "That means I have *two* realtors and *two* druggists, one *actual* used car salesman and one used-car-salesman-realtor-Woolworthian talking my ear off about a new road that neither of us has ever heard of."

Buddy shook his head. "Replace the main road?"

"Upgrade it. Straighten it over the Bittersweet Ridge. Instead of it dumping onto the back entrance of the Mississippi County

Airport have it loop around and back up to Interstate 57."

"Why would we want to do that?"

Pam snorted. "I can think of fifty reasons. It would cut the travel time to Sikeston or Cairo. That would mean we can develop part of the County as a bedroom community. Tourist revenue. Maybe some small factories. Tax revenue. Carter would love to have an ambulance that could make it to Southeast in an hour instead of three. With enough money, we could even set up that medflight he's been asking for. Maybe afford a real community hospital of our own."

"If we want those things we can always ask the liaison—"

"*And* we wouldn't have to beg at the knees of the feds every time we want to do something!" interrupted Pam savagely. "Sure, we can get money anytime we ask. But we have to *ask*. It keeps us the richest poor county in the state."

Buddy blinked at stared at her. "I didn't know you felt that way."

Pam made a quick sharp motion with her shoulders as if deflecting thrown water. "Would Jeremy support it? Would he *block* it? Stand up in meeting and squash it?"

"I don't know."

She stood up and pulled on her jacket. "Spring county meeting is in six weeks—May first. It's going to come up. You know it is. I'm not going to move on it until then." She gave him a sour look. "I'll just smile sweetly when *everybody* asks and say let's talk about it at the meeting."

"The building has caught fire. We should probably evacuate."

"What?" Joanie looked up.

Aaron was watching her with a weary, patient expression.

"Sorry," she said and shook her head. "Thinking about

something."

"What's his name?"

"What are you talking about?"

Aaron sighed. "I've known you for seven years. Every affair—"

"It's not an affair. He's not married."

Aaron nodded slightly. "Every liaison, tryst, peccadillo, and escapade has started the same way: three months of meditations on the perfection of the new love. Swooning over puppies and kittens. And making diabetically sweet and otherwise execrable artistic objects."

Joanie smiled at him. "Aw, Aaron. You think my stuff is artistic."

Aaron's lips were thin. "*Quite.* I understand you like the live fast, die young, and leave a beautiful corpse approach to life. I can tolerate phases of bad art. But your main duty here is to teach and I'm not going to go through another year of you happily telling every student that they're geniuses, followed by bitter and destructive criticisms, followed by not showing up for days at a time because you're at home in a morose drunken stupor."

"Have I been neglecting my students?"

"Not yet. And I want to keep it that way."

"Then don't—"

"Joanie, *stop!*" Aaron leaned forward. "Don't. I was there last time, holding your head when you puked. I was the one covering for you and teaching your classes. *You owe me.* And what you owe me is to keep working regardless of what happens outside of this school. Am I clear?"

Joanie stared at him. He'd never spoken to her like this before. "I guess last time was pretty bad."

"You threw up on my shoes."

"Really?"

"You think I would lie about *that?*"

"No, no." Joanie waved the image away. "Of course not. I understand, Aaron. I really do." Joanie took a deep breath. "His name is Carter Faraday. He's a doctor. He lives back home. I met him at the funeral of a friend of my grandfather. I like him a lot and I've been spending a lot of money I don't have flying out to spend time with him."

Aaron nodded and gave her a slight smile. "If I were your father I would congratulate you for landing a doctor."

"No. If you were *my* father you'd wonder out loud what you did wrong that all the men I find are white devils. At that point, I'd blame you right back for marrying one."

Aaron chuckled. "I see." He considered her thoughtfully for a moment. "Do you know why I hired you for the school?"

"I'm a great teacher?"

"No. That turned out to be a surprise. There's a terrific portrait in Naples by Titian of Pope Paul III and his grandsons. Have you ever seen it?"

"No."

"You should. Naples is lovely. All of the pain, distrust, scheming, and love are clear on their faces. The Pope is bent forward with age. He's sick. He's old. He's dying. One grandson is looking on, conflicted. Is he eager? Is he sad? The other is making a perfunctory bow—there's nothing of importance to him in the old man. Better he die and quickly. The Pope is watching the bow. His face is wrought with regret, fear, failure, and the closeness of death—but still vital. He's not dead *yet*. Their lives, for good and ill, are captured in the painting." He paused a moment. "It reminds me of your work. You're not Titian and maybe you never will be. But every sketch you make of a person captures some spark of them. True, your technique is primitive and clumsy—"

"Hey!"

"—but I had hopes it could improve in time. And I *definitely* wanted that spark around here to rub off on the students. So I hired you."

Joanie didn't know what to say. "Thanks."

"You should check your own sketches. Possibly you'll see something."

"I have some of him here—"

"Oh, please don't. I have no interest in examining your love-sick drawings for traces of character." Aaron shuddered. "I don't begrudge you any happiness, Joanie. I hope things work out for you. When are you going back out there?"

"Not for a couple of weeks." She gave him a rueful smile. "No money. My grandfather is going out in May for... a meeting. I can probably tag along. Until then I'll have to manage with artificial stimulation."

Aaron gave her a pained look. "You had to say that. An image I could have lived without for the rest of my life."

"Hey. Another opportunity for good judgment narrowly averted."

Buddy called Luke and asked him what he knew about the road. Luke sounded surprised to hear about it but said he'd make a point to attend the County Meeting. Buddy was reluctant to call on Jeremy just yet. Instead, he took his ancient Buick Electra from the garage and shepherded its wheezing hulk up the main road east. He passed Harry Carr filling a pothole just outside of Pilate, skipped the turn into town, and worked up the switchbacks toward the interstate. The Buick had no suspension to speak of and its tires were designed for fair weather in some beautiful mythical place like California. As the road rose, the March crusts of snow crept from the trees and naked rock towards the asphalt. By the time Buddy reached the overlook turnoff at the top of the ridge, the frost had turned a marginal two-lane road to a bit more marginal one-lane road. It was near dark.

He stepped out of the car and drew his coat close. He felt old these days. Arthur and Leticia had visited him just before Thanksgiving. Leticia had remarked how the house was *so* hot. How could Buddy stand it? He forgave her for this (and many other) transgressions because of her singular act of producing the perfect grandson. Franklin had the virtue of being not only the best boy that ever lived but also the spitting image of Arista. Every time he looked down into Franklin's face and saw her beloved face looking back he thought he could forgive anyone anything anytime.

But Leticia's comment was just one of many indicators. He was getting *old.* How did that happen?

The land fell away below him and he could see the lights of Pilate, bright and twinkling, and the further lights of Ridgeville. Dimmer, he thought. But somehow warmer. From here he could even see the street layout that showed where Ashby had been before it had been surrounded and absorbed by the Ridgeville amoeba.

He didn't want to face the trip back down the ridge. But if not he'd have to go up to the interstate, loop around and south to the airport, and come back up on the gravel road through the White Bluffs. That was no better and it would be late when he got home. He'd be tired. Buddy leaned against the car.

He loved this car. To Buddy, all cars were composed of memories. This Electra he'd purchased in the seventies when he finally bought out the Ridgeville machine shop from Paulie Harrison. Not that it was much of a shop: three machinists, a lathe, and a mill. All to rebore tractor engines and reproduce parts for equipment that had been obsolete long before Buddy had been born. But the shop was his. Before the Electra, he'd driven a 1952 Buick into the ground. Buddy kept his cars like he kept his memories: purring on the inside and a little shabby on the outside. A little rust gave a car character, but an engine knock was sacrilege.

Before that, a Chevrolet and a Ford, and then his first car, a beat to Hell 1938 Hudson Terraplane with mechanical brakes and wooden brake pads—a sudden locking stop always brought out the smell of burning cedar. The steering required both hands and a commitment of will. The car always felt as if it were rolling in all directions. But when he'd come back from the war, amazed that he was whole and untorn after all that death, he'd taken little Arista Hart out driving in that car. Out to park in long-dead Tom Sutter's bottomland cornfield, when the spring rain had softened the ground. The air smelled of earth and river, simultaneously rank and fresh. On that long bench seat (no bucket seats back then!) she had lifted her dress and he'd dropped his pants and they'd had each other and lay afterward in each other's arms, spent and sweetly aching, listening to the late-night rushing water.

Buddy laughed. From here, he could see right where Sutter's farm had been, just a little south of Collins' Landing. Nothing left of the landing but a collection of dim and distant lights. He remembered when they pulled their clothes back together—failed and had at each other again. Then, clothed and with her hand resting on his thigh, he'd tried to turn out of the field, spun the car, and stuck it tight in the gumbo dirt. No phone for miles. No *house* for miles—Sutter lived in town. They'd trekked to the woods at the edge of the field, sunk to their knees, and brought back branches and logs. He'd been covered with spun and spattered mud and she'd been not much better when they finally forced the Hudson to firmer ground.

Buddy had been mortally afraid that was the end of it: one beautiful night ended in disaster. But when he brought Arista back to her family's house she'd given him a lingering kiss. "Thanks for the adventure," she whispered in his ear.

Buddy had kept that car in the garage long after the engine had seized and then rusted out. Kept it up on blocks until after

Arista died and he couldn't stand to look at it anymore and sold it to some collector he'd found on the internet. A hired man came down from Saint Louis, pulled it onto a flatbed, and took it away and there was nothing left in the garage but four concrete blocks and empty space.

He leaned on the fender of the Buick. If he waited much longer, the damp on the road from the day's frost melt would crystallize into ice, and that marginal one lane would be gone until morning. He got back inside the car, backed it out of the overlook parking, and worked his way down the road toward town.

Yeah, he thought with unaccustomed bitterness as he inched toward Pilate, straightening this damned road would probably be a good idea.

Betty was in the kitchen making a pie and a batch of cookies when Pam Small dropped by after dinner to ask him what he thought about the road. Betty was the school nurse and, like all those in such roles, had a great deal of knowledge and little freedom to apply it. Each day she saw sick, injured, or merely sad children for whom she could call parents, administer first aid or ibuprofen, and offer consolation. A slice of pie or a cookie was often the best (and possibly only) medicine she was allowed to dispense.

Jeremy had left on a walk early in the evening but Pam stayed anyway.

"You know about the road, right?" said Pam.

Betty thought for a moment. Betty was anything but stupid — you don't ace four years of nursing school being a dunce. But being Jeremy's wife had its limitations. People didn't talk to her as they otherwise might. Jeremy was the center of the County: things revolved around him. Confiding in Betty was the same thing as confiding in Jeremy and people confided different things to Jeremy than they did to each other. Betty imagined it was like being a minister's wife, though none of the minister's wives she knew would confide enough in her to confirm it.

"Which road?" Betty said brightly as she trimmed the edges of a peach pie. The peaches had been a fall gift from a stuttering high school student smitten by her kindness and figure. She had waited until now to thaw them. Peaches reminded people of summer. Interminable March was when that memory was needed most. She added a hint of cloves to make the peach flavor smoky and mysterious. Betty was an excellent cook. Deep in her basement freezer slept the harvest of her truck garden: strawberries, grapes, beans—her occupation when school was out and she wasn't on call to the clinic.

"The *main* road. The talk about the replacement road. Straightening the switchbacks. Surely you've heard about it— seems like everyone has and can't remember how."

"No," she said. She picked up the pie and put it in the oven. "Not a word." She looked at Pam. "Is that such a surprise?" Pam Small was one of the few people who understood the situation. Sure, she tried to get to Jeremy through Betty, but everybody tried to do that one way or the other. At least Pam was honest about it.

Pam shook her head. "Long story short. There's a rumor going around that we might straighten the main road. Make it into a real loop from fifty-seven down through town and back out to the interstate by way of the airport."

"You think that's a good idea?"

"*Hell*, yes."

"You want me to talk about it to Jeremy?"

Pam nodded. "It would be good for the town."

Betty checked the time. Forty-five minutes in this oven for a peach pie. No more. No less. "I'll think about it."

"That's all I can ask." Pam rose. "Got to get going. I need to go over the budget."

After she left, Betty sat at the table. She wished she had a cigarette and thought better of it. She'd quit when she married Jeremy but had never quite given up the desire. She put her hand on her belly. For a moment she imagined a child quickening there.

Betty shook her head and threw it out of her mind. She brought her attention back to Pam and the main road. Would it make any difference to her? In the summer she took whatever excess came from her garden and sold it in the farmer's market in Sikeston. She liked going there. It was an event of sorts and the curly road through the White Bluffs gave it the illusion of adventure. A road that ran straight and sure to the heart of Sikeston would diminish that.

She liked the County the way it was. Of course, Betty was honest enough to realize that she was in a privileged position. Other people might want change. Being with Jeremy had changed her point of view on many things. After all, he'd seen all sorts of changes and managed them. He'd done all manner of jobs. He was a person who stretched indefinitely backward in time. Knowing that had an effect.

These days Jeremy was a farmer. Their house was on the edge of what used to be the farms of abandoned Ashby and fronted about a hundred acres. In the sixties, Jeremy had run a gas station in Pilate and gave that up in the early seventies. He'd sold the station and turned to farming before Betty was born— pure organic. He'd gotten the idea from some traveler named Roessler. Jeremy grew organic soybeans, field corn, and sweet corn on about a third of it, selling the harvest through the Co-Op, which, in turn, sold the County agricultural product in Sikeston or Cairo.

Every year Jeremy's crop was just about the same as most— not much better, not much worse. He never mentioned it, but Betty watched him. If it looked like his crop was going to be much better than his neighbors he withdrew irrigation or water. If it looked like it was going to be much worse, he walked through the fields and the withering crops brightened.

Betty did not doubt that if Jeremy wanted he could make the earth bloom. If he chose not to do so, it was probably for the best. She believed that Jeremy could do anything. He was a miracle walking the earth. He had *chosen* to ground himself. To be one with his neighbors. It was one of the things she loved about him.

Even as a child Betty had believed Jeremy must have qualities no one but his wives saw — confirmed to some extent now that she was one of them. Even so, she wished she could talk about it with any of his previous wives. But Jeremy had always (in living memory at least) married until death they did part. Any relationship Jeremy had with someone previous could only be suggested by speculation and historical reconstruction.

To most in the County, Jeremy was enigmatic and quiet — nearly taciturn. But Betty knew he had a dry humor, and now and then he made a remark or observation that showed a deep context, a historical perspective, beneath what others saw. It gave him an odd and almost circumspect charity. It was as if he had seen a quality in humans that he liked — that kindness, maybe? — and had decided to emulate it. Sometimes clumsily. Other times with deft grace. Betty wondered if he'd tried all sorts of different ways to be human, failing miserably over and over until he'd finally hammered together something that sort of worked and stuck with it. She had a sudden vision of Jeremy presiding over an Aztec human sacrifice, thinking, *well, that didn't work. What should I try next?* Jeremy attempting to be like everyone else was clearly impossible.

Betty giggled. She had always found attempting the impossible wonderfully attractive.

It didn't hurt that she liked the way he looked. The way he

felt. The way he smelled. It made up for not being able to have children with him. It had to.

The kitchen had several drawers but there were two private ones: Jeremy's drawer and her drawer. On impulse, Betty rummaged in her drawer and pulled out the paper she'd written the first month she was married.

10 things I like about Jeremy

1. His smell.
2. His lean body.
3. He's not scared of anybody. Of course, that comes from who he is. But so many men have fear at the root of them—fear of their peers, their bosses, their fate. Jeremy has none of that.
4. Jeremy has nothing to prove. Probably comes from lack of fear.
5. He is kind. He doesn't have to be. It wouldn't change anything in the County. People would still try to get on his good side. Lots of times I've seen him do some small kindness or put in a good word when he doesn't have to.
6. He does what he says. He doesn't bluff. He doesn't argue. He said "I do" knowing what it meant— probably more than I did. And his eyes have never strayed. Not once. I was watching.
7. He's the most honest person I've ever met. He will answer every question I ask him except for those he doesn't. There's a strong barrier between what he will talk about and what he won't. The barrier hurts, of course. But except for the things he won't talk about, he'll talk about everything else.
8. There's a mystery to him. Where did he come from? Where is he going? I don't know and he won't tell me. Maybe he doesn't know. Every marriage should have a little mystery.

9. He's not always perfect or even right. Now and then I can tell he's not a human being like I know human beings. He's older. Stronger. Different. Trying to work out this puzzle of being human. Sometimes he fails at it. He just picks up and keeps trying.

10. He loves me. I don't know why. How could somebody who's lived so long and seen so much love me? How could it happen from a lottery? I don't know. But he does. And he will for the rest of my life. It means something to be loved by someone like that.

They were still true.

Young Betty Thomas was certain she'd be too old for the lottery. Amy Pollock DaFoe was still a young fifty-seven when Betty turned eighteen. Unattainable love only makes love sweeter and Betty had crushed on Jeremy when she was still a girl. Amy was vital. Amy was lively. She even managed to drag Jeremy to dances—something no one had imagined could ever happen. Jeremy didn't even look uncomfortable. Betty hung out at the DaFoe house as much as she could. Amy didn't mind. She liked company. But there was always hushed privacy surrounding Amy and Jeremy. A bubble of comfort. It wasn't how Betty thought of love but it was still something she envied.

So Betty gave up on Jeremy and went off to nursing school in Columbia, fell in love with a doctor, lost her virginity and distaste for oral sex. Her doctor moved to New Mexico and she spent the summer with him fully expecting to marry when she finished school if not sooner. But Amy Pollock DaFoe died that July of an unexpected heart attack. The lottery was suddenly open to her, though no one knew when it would occur. Never less than a year of mourning and often more. It all depended on Jeremy.

Betty stayed in nursing school and put off her pet doctor. She spent a nervous senior year waiting for the lottery and keeping her doctor happy by regular visits until he was so smitten by flesh he wanted to move back to Columbia just to be near her. Betty gently discouraged him. She felt no guilt keeping her doctor as a plan B. Marrying Jeremy was like the distant possibility of becoming queen, an opportunity neither to be denied nor depended upon. If she lost the lottery (the most likely scenario) she'd make the best of it with her pet doctor. But if she won... The worst possibility was that the lottery wouldn't happen before she graduated and her pet doctor would insist on finalizing their arrangement.

Nineteen months after Amy died the lottery was held. By custom, the lottery had to be drawn in person, so Betty tore down to the County through a deep February snowstorm and sat nervously in the First Baptist Church, ice melting and pooling around her boots. The motivations of the women in that church were as individual as snowflakes. Some wanted status. Some wanted miracles. Some loved Jeremy. Some hated him. Some were put there by parents against their will. Some had snuck out against parental wishes.

The names were mixed in a drum and called out in three drawings and a runoff. When it was finally her name standing alone she burst into joyous tears and wet her pants. She was not the first ever to do this and, that night, not the only woman in the church to do so.

Betty went home to her parent's house and took a long shower. Then, after a good nap, she formally called on Jeremy to get his final approval. Jeremy had not rejected a lottery winner in a century but it had happened. He formally kissed her forehead in blessing and less formally kissed her lips in a way that gave her a deep down tingle.

With that, she drove to Saint Louis, maxed out her credit cards on an emergency flight to Albuquerque. There, she kissed (and more than kissed) her pet doctor good-bye and returned the next night. Pleasantly tired, and sore, she resumed her studies. That spring she gave up smoking, visited the County on weekends to plan the wedding, and spent time getting to know her future husband.

She graduated in May and got her nursing license, barely managing a June ceremony. Her wedding night was all she had hoped for and then some, and magnificently dispersed any lingering doubts she might have had.

Betty imagined herself sitting there, holding a cigarette, inhaling, and watching the smoke twist and curl around the kitchen light. A timer rang in her head: forty-five minutes. She put out her imaginary cigarette and found the hot pads. As she pulled out the pie she thought that if people wanted a straight road then, fine. Let them have it.

Samuel and Tyson Porter had been born into slaveholder families. That way of life stopped on October 21, 1845, when Nathan Collins freed all the slaves in Nuthatch County. This didn't make the Porters poor but it was a blow. The Porter family did the best they could by paying as little as possible and charging their former slaves all the traffic would bear for food or lodging. Assured by Eldest Ferber there would be no retaliation, the former slaves voted with their feet and ran off to other former slave owners who paid better. The Porters were left to fend for themselves.

In the present day, County discussion of populations usually referred to Pilate or Ridgeville and occasionally the last relics of Ashby. The Bittersweet Ridge and the White Bluffs were treated as if they were uninhabited. This was not true. The Ridge was always been dotted with little farms and families that lived on the barest of margins. As poor as the Ridge was, they liked to look down on the Bluffs.

The White Bluffs held the families that were the poorest, least educated, and proudest of marginally true or downright fictional heritage. There were kind people in the Bluffs. Pleasant people. People who wanted the best for their kids. There were also bitter people. Resentful. It showed in their recreational drug use. The folks on the Ridge drank moonshine. The people of the Bluffs preferred meth and heroin.

Using a map of the County as a reference, it's not so obvious how this came to be. After all, though both lands were hard to farm, the Bluffs were lower, flatter, the soil a little bit better. The water more plentiful and access to the outside world by the main road easier. The Bluffs were even close to the regional airport.

But if you observe the geography, you can see how the Civil War broke on the White Bluffs like the sea on rocks. Most of the County was untouched by the war, protected as it was by Nathan Collins. The edge of the County served as the interface, the border, the osmotic membrane where Nuthatch County and the War mingled.

The Ridge lay to the east side of the County, protected by a ridge of steep limestone. The lower White Bluffs formed its southern edge. Confederate invasion of Missouri came from the south. Those that lived on the Ridge hunkered down on the southern side and listened while the War battered itself senseless against the Bittersweet cliffs. Those that lived in the White Bluffs had no such protection. They had to defend their homes against the vicious bands of marauders that comprised the outer edge of all armies.

The Porter family lived far from the main road, deep in a southwestern pocket. The Bluewater Reservation blocked any escape to the east. Any Confederate advance crossed here. Any Confederate retreat crossed it again on the return trip. Each time, the area was struck twice. Union then Confederate on the advance. Confederate then Union on the retreat. Thus, most of the Porter family was massacred one early night in 1862 when a spur of Pope's Union Army of the Mississippi dropped in as an afterthought on their way to the Battle of Island Number Ten down near New Madrid. The remaining Porter brothers, Samuel and Tyson, blamed Nathan Collins since he had clearly protected the rest of the County and neglected them.

A year later, Sterling Price raised thousands of rag-tag Confederate men and called them the Army of Missouri. They moved north out of Batesville, Arkansas, avoiding the iron-clad Union boats in the Mississippi River, and moved in a rough line towards Saint Louis.

When the Army of Missouri passed nearby, the Porter brothers left with them. Samuel and Tyson fought in Sterling Price's little piece of the war from Poplar Bluff all the way to Booneville. The following October, when Bloody Bill Anderson arrived in Booneville, the Porters left Price to join Quantrill's Raiders.

Killing and robbing being to their taste, they stayed with the raiders for three more years, long after the end of the war. The ambush in Russellville killed many of the remaining bushwhackers. At this point it was clear they were no longer part of Quantrill's Raiders but the Younger-James Gang. The Porter brothers left and made their way back to Nuthatch County.

The two brothers rebuilt the ruins of their farm on the profits of a particularly cheap, powerful, and repellent form of moonshine dubbed "Porter's Piss" from a comment made by a client: "I'd piss in that stuff if it would only make it taste better."

There, they founded the Nuthatch County Vigilance Committee.

This year the Nuthatch County Vigilance Committee had the smallest membership of any time since its founding in 1870. The

Porter family had always been central to it and now made up the majority.

In fact, except for Glenn Waxman, the Vigilance Committee was *all* Porters. Since Glenn was employed by Robert Porter to run his two meth labs this might be considered a distinction without a difference. There used to be three labs but one exploded. Since they'd built the third lab on the reservation, the Tribal Council had investigated it themselves and declared it a natural gas explosion. Ed Porter grinned. If there was anything left after the fire, *somebody* made use of it.

Ed loaded his Marlin. He liked 30-30s. Enough stopping power for a deer at close quarters without the bullet traveling across the County. He glanced over towards his cousin Robert. Robert favored a .222. Enough stopping power for an elk but it could bounce off a leaf and end up in Saint Louis. Ed wondered if he slept with the damned thing.

Ed shook his head. He and his cousin had gone rabbit hunting last fall. Ed had taken a .22 pistol. Robert had brought his .222. They had flushed a rabbit and Robert had fired a shot. They knew he was the one that'd hit it since all that remained was one ear and one leg.

But today was a bright and early April morning. The weather had cleared enough that they didn't have to oil the guns just to do some target shooting. Which, Ed thought ruefully, is pretty much all the Vigilance Committee did these days. Get together to drink and shoot. And discuss their businesses.

When the Tyson Porter side of the family had bought out the Samuel Porter share of the White Bluffs farm, Samuel's newly moneyed family had moved over to the Bittersweet Ridge. There they continued brewing and distilling "Porter's Piss" for a hundred years. The White Bluff side of the family tried to make a competing product and failed. The farm was not a good investment, and they floundered for decades until the Marihuana Stamp Act. This gave them an illegal activity in which they could succeed. They had started with growing marijuana and later branched into refining heroin from imported Mexican opium with enough success to keep hand and mouth together. The rise of the cartels made the heroin dangerous and competition from the local Missouri hippie trade threatened to make marijuana production uneconomical. Then, in the eighties, they discovered methamphetamine. The Bittersweet branch of the family looked down on the meth *nouveau riche*. The White Bluffs branch resented it.

Robert pulled up his rifle, sighted, and fired at one of the targets.

Ed winced. The .222 had a sharp crack that hurt the ears. He sighted along the Marlin and squeezed, levered to reload, and fired again. Three nice holes appeared in the circle.

Robert sat down and picked up a beer, sipped it. Ed saw him signal Glenn. Waxman approached Ed.

"How're the kids, Glenn?" Ed spoke first to derail the conversation.

"Better. They got pretty sick in February."

"So I hear. You ought to take all that money you and Robert are making and put it into a new trailer. Something with running water."

Glenn shook his head and grinned. Ed looked at his teeth critically. No evidence of meth-mouth. He kept an eye on Glenn and Robert. No telling what might happen to the Committee— or the Porter family—if either of them became meth-heads.

"You know what I'm saving up for, Ed," Glenn said amicably but with a slight reproof. "Going to rebuild the old Waxman house. One of these days my kids are going to live in it. Big rooms. Lots of light."

Ed nodded and reloaded the Marlin.

Glenn loaded his own Winchester. Ed approved of a Winchester—not all that much difference from the Marlin, really. Same caliber. Straight stock instead of a slight curve to the grip.

"Robert and I have an idea," Glenn said as he sighted the target and fired three quick shots.

"Yeah?" Ed had a sour feeling in his stomach. He wondered if anything good had ever come from those words.

"Do you know what ecstasy is?"

"Like the ecstasy of the Lord?"

Glenn chucked. "No. The drug. MMDA."

"I've heard of it."

Glenn reloaded the Winchester. "Turns out MMDA is chemically similar to meth. There's a big demand for it. We can use a lot of the same equipment. Same skills. Might be a good fit."

"So?"

"So we'd like to replace that third trailer with one that can make both meth and MMDA. A bigger trailer. We have a site at the southwest corner of the County—"

"Porter land?"

"No. Not sure who it belongs to."

"As long as it's somebody else. Why are you telling me this?"

"We want you to invest in it with us. We expect to have profits showing before fall."

Ed picked up his Marlin and aimed at the target. Holding that stance he glanced over to Robert. Robert was attaching a telescopic sight to the .222 but he was listening carefully. Ed emptied the Marlin at the target to give him some time to think.

Ed reached into his pocket, pulled out shells, and started reloading the Marlin. "Where are you going to sell the MMDA? Not exactly the normal meth market."

"There's some overlap. We have a contact up at Carbondale that can move as much as we make. Big market up at the university. Maybe even move some as far as Chicago."

Ed lowered his rifle and turned to Glenn. He stared hard at the two of them. "You stay the *fuck* out of Chicago. For that matter, you stay the fuck out of Saint Louis. You've got a nice little racket here selling in the Ozarks and Southern Illinois. Arkansas, too. Even Carbondale. You go up into the cities and you'll bring down that whole damned machine on our heads. You remember how Amy Pollock brought all those city goons down here for parties? Papa had to shut down for six *years*. And that was just for moonshine. Then, he and Robert's dad tried to sell up there and came home in boxes. You go to the cities and you'll bring the feds, the mafia, and everything else down on us."

"We were thinking Jeremy would never let that happen."

"*Fuck* Jeremy DaFoe." Ed felt like slamming the stock of the Marlin across Glenn's face for such stupidity. He looked at Robert. *Now* he understood why Robert had Glenn make the pitch. Ed might have taken a swing at Robert for such an idea but Glenn had no idea of the history here. "Do you know why the Vigilance Committee was formed? Why it's lasted over a hundred years?"

"I figured it was a Porter thing."

"It's a Porter *responsibility*." Ed took a deep breath. "Jeremy DaFoe has been around too long. He's fucked with the natural order. His *very presence* changes the land. This is what the Porter brothers knew when they rode with Price and then took up with Bloody Bill Anderson. This is why they came back to Nuthatch County and founded the Committee. This is why we've been patiently waiting ever since. DaFoe has to die and someday we're going to find out a way to make him do just that. You don't *depend* on Jeremy DaFoe. You *murder* him."

Glenn held up his hands in surrender. "Okay. Okay. We were just thinking that Jeremy's special relationship with the feds might give us some protection. We don't need it. We'll just be careful."

"And stay out of the cities."

"And stay out of the cities. Good advice. Does that mean

you're interested?"

Ed didn't speak for a moment. Let them stew. But the opportunity was good. He wanted little Sterling out of here. Out of the County. For all that the Committee was dedicated to the destruction of Jeremy DaFoe, Ed had no faith it would ever happen, Bloody Bill Anderson or not. "Yeah. I'm interested."

Glenn clapped his hands. "Good!"

"Got something for you," said Robert quietly. He went to his truck and brought out a package of paper. "New targets." He handed a sheet of paper to Ed.

It was a picture of Jeremy DaFoe with target markings over his face.

Ed laughed. "It's not even my birthday."

"We can't spend all day in bed," Joanie said in a teasing voice. She put cheese and bread in the small backpack on the table.

"Why not?" Carter stood behind her kissing her neck and she felt her resolve weakening. "It's so *early*. Look it's not even light out."

"Best to be there before sunrise." She danced away. "Get some water bottles. There's not any water on the trail."

Carter sighed. "After a weekend with you, I'm not sure I can walk."

"*You're* not sure? Try it from my side."

"Interesting idea." Carter found some bottled water in the refrigerator. He held it up for her inspection.

"Perfect."

Joanie was not a confident driver. *Especially* since he had let her drive *his* car. Both hands white-knuckled on the steering wheel. Check. "I can't believe you've been in the County this long and never walked up to Fox's Chimney."

"Believe it," he said contentedly, watching the scenery pass. "What's so special about Fox's Chimney?"

"It's the best place to look at Little Mountain."

"At sunrise."

"That's right."

It was hinting at light when they reached the tiny Fox Park lot. Joanie parked the car, hurrying Carter out onto the gravel. Carter grinned at her sleepily.

"Go on!" She grabbed the pack and pushed him in front of her. "It's not far."

The trail was made up of flint, flat in spots, turned and pointed up so that in some places they had to move carefully lest they slip between two intransigent rocks and break an ankle.

Joanie led here with assurance. She remembered being brought here first by Grandmother Jean and later bringing boys here. She could always tell who was a keeper by how they reacted to the Fox's Chimney. Just being here was a point in Carter's favor.

The trail split from the parking lot in two directions. One went up to Table Rock. Joanie went the other way where the trail followed the ridge and led down towards Turkey Creek. Opposite them was the first ridge that led to Little Mountain, though the Mountain was hidden by pines. The pre-dawn hush infected them both, and they were silent as they walked and stumbled down towards the creek.

From there the trail followed the creek until it opened into a large meadow. In the middle of the meadow was a narrow boulder set improbably on its end.

"A stile?" said Carter, startled. "That's Fox's Chimney?"

"Yeah. Somebody told me once it was left by the same people who built the mounds up by Cahokia. Don't look back. Wait."

They reached Fox's Chimney and stood in front of it.

"What else is around here?" Carter started to look around.

"I *said* don't look back." She slapped his jacket. "A bunch of things. Over at the base of the Mountain is Fox Cave. It has an underground lake."

"Really?"

"Really. Cold as hell, too. Every few years somebody drowns."

"Great."

"The other trail goes up to Table Rock. You can see nearly the whole county from there."

"But we're standing here."

"That's right." Joanie looked at the angle of the shadows. "Ready?"

"Ready for what?"

"We turn on the count of three." She counted carefully and they turned as one.

Little Mountain reared six hundred feet above them. The sun was shining just over its low east shoulder, brilliant in the empty sky. The contrast made the Mountain look a thousand feet tall.

"Wow," breathed Carter.

You pass, she thought. After a few moments, she put down the pack, touched her hand to her lips, and touched the rock. The smooth flint face showed that her hand was far from the first.

"Why did you do that?" asked Carter.

"For luck. Fox's blessing."

"Fox?"

Joanie squatted down and opened the pack. "This place is named for the warrior Faster-Than-Fox. It's an old Osage story—or at least the Choctaw say it is. The Osage don't claim it but they don't discourage the idea either. Anyway, Faster-Than-Fox was friends with Itsike—"

"Itsike?"

"Trickster figure. Like Coyote in some other stories.

Anyway, but Itsike messed Fox up. Fox was going to offer some good food to Male Puma—something about cozying up to a pretty girl, I think. But Itsike was hungry, ate it, and left a vile, thin gruel as a substitute. Male Puma was mistakenly angry at Fox. He asked for justice from the Thunder Bird. Thunder Bird reluctantly agreed. No matter how fast Fox ran, he couldn't outrun the lightning."

Carter looked up to Little Mountain. He grinned. "I thought all the stories in the County had something to with Jeremy."

Joanie shrugged. "Grandmother Jean said she'd heard a different story when she was growing up. In this version, Faster-Than-Fox was known for his quickness. He was a friend of Jeremy's. He bet Jeremy there was a deer not even Jeremy could take. He made it a wager. Then, Faster-Than-Fox disguised himself as a deer and Jeremy killed him. That's why Jeremy never goes deer hunting. The question the story poses and doesn't answer is whether or not Jeremy knew who it was under that deerskin."

"That's not creepy or anything."

"Yeah. I like the Itsike story better." Joanie sat down and watched the mountain.

Carter sat beside her and leaned against Fox's rock. The sun had risen while they were talking, and what had been a pleasantly cool April morning was turning into a hot April day. "Let's move into the shade."

"It'll be cold."

"What? It's got to be seventy degrees."

"You sit in the shade." Joanie chuckled and dragged the pack to the south side of the rock and out of the glare. "I'm sitting here."

Resolutely, Carter moved to the shady side of the stile. He leaned against the rock and then sat bolt upright. "See it's not that bad," He said stiffly.

"Suit yourself." She pulled out a sandwich and passed it to

him.

After a moment he stood up and brushed his backside. "I stand corrected. It's cold as hell in the shade. And besides, my ass is wet."

"Sit over here. The grass is already dry."

He sat next to her, watching Little Mountain as he ate. "Thanks for bringing me."

"It's a test," she said. "I bring all my boyfriends here. The ones that count anyway."

"So I'm a boyfriend now?"

"You can use any term you want."

"Boyfriend is okay."

They continued to eat in easy silence. Joanie drank deeply from one of the water bottles, put it back, and lay with her head on his shoulder.

"Did I pass?" he asked quietly.

"Yes," she said. "You definitely did."

Chapter 4: County Meeting

The State of Missouri had training books for Town Meetings, City Councils, Mayors, Boards of Selectmen. There were rules for County Commissioners, County Elections, County Judges. Nuthatch County had a single County Judge: Hugh Utterback. There were no Missouri governmental guidelines for County Meeting.

But since the County Meeting—or its equivalent—long predated the creation of Nuthatch County (or the State of Missouri, for that matter) it had its own rules.

How the Mississippian Culture or the Clovis People made decisions regarding Jeremy was lost, whatever he might have been called back then. Only small customs remained, such as how people in Nuthatch County always said *missed me* whenever there was a lightning strike nearby.

When the Osage had been the dominant force in the County the meeting had been moderated by a local shaman who always clothed himself in yellow. If things didn't go well he was prepared for impending death. The Choctaws, fleeing the Trail of Tears, had a healthy dose of Christianity and sided with the burgeoning white population that felt a minister should preside. The Civil War changed all that—as it changed most things. No one minister could be agreed upon, since one side said slavery was well founded in the Bible and the other said the Bible found it to be an abomination. This led the majority of the County residents to the conclusion that administration of the County was far too important to be left to religion. A more secular approach prevailed. Before the Civil War, the County Meeting was run by the County Commissioner—always a minister. After the Civil War, the Commissioner was an officer of the meeting independent of religion like the Eldest or the County Judge. The meeting itself was run by the County Moderator—a role wholly created by, and limited to, Nuthatch County.

It always made sense to Pam Small that the County Moderator was also the County Coroner and an undertaker. Death seemed to tie things back to the Osage shamans.

Luke had made a point of attending County Meetings until Catherine died. She had enjoyed them, and seeing Catherine enjoy something was reason enough. After that, he hadn't cared much. Attendance seemed only empty ritual.

Even so, he took the meeting seriously. Most of the important decisions happened there. It was important to Luke that he not influence what the County (i.e., Jeremy) wanted. He should be receptive to their needs and not dictate them.

Of course, that was the opposite of what he hoped for *this* County Meeting.

"Our agents will be in the meeting," Rosen assured him as he was packing things up in his office.

"Who are they?"

"We're happier if you don't know." Rosen shrugged. "We figure they've been hiding under DaFoe's radar all these years. If you know who they are, you might give them away."

Luke gave him a heavy stare. "What I don't know I can't reveal."

"Right."

"Of course, if I fail, what I reveal won't make much difference. You said the secret's going to be out in a couple of years anyway."

Rosen smiled at him. "Not quite that quickly."

"Doesn't matter," Luke said as he resumed packing. "You think Jeremy doesn't know who they are?"

"He hasn't done anything about it."

"That would be presuming that he cares." Luke waved at his papers. "That this might have any effect whatsoever. Could be we're just whacking off."

Rosen pursed his lips and didn't answer.

Luke closed his briefcase. "I've got to go. I'm meeting Joanie at the airport."

Rosen glanced out the window and back again.

"What?" Luke felt tired.

"Do you know she's been sleeping with Carter Faraday?"

"I figured. I saw them at the funeral." Luke took a deep breath. "Good for her. Catherine would be happy she landed a doctor." He saw Rosen's face. "*What?*"

"Nothing." Rosen put out his hand. "Good luck."

As County Clerk, Nadine Prescott Durant was responsible for making sure any materials necessary for discussion were available. Nadine checked her notes. Missouri rules and regulations on roads? Check. EPA regulations? Check. List of known County complaints? Check. She booted up her laptop. After a moment a picture of her, Joseph, and an eighteen-year-old Joanie appeared. She looked at Joseph a moment before she signed on. There was email in her inbox. She didn't bring it up.

She had already seen it. It seemed to shine through the screen without being visible. Nadine looked around the auditorium. She was early. It was empty save for Harry Carr performing mysterious activities by the breaker box. Lights went on. Lights went off.

Nadine was mindful that Joseph had stayed nearly three months. It wasn't lost on her that she had a slight spring in her step and a soft smile because of it. Neither was the knowledge that three months was about average for a stay.

Their relationship was... complicated. But as Nadine thought about it, there wasn't much in her life that wasn't complicated. Let's see. Lesbian? Check—she'd known that since she was eight. In love with a man? Check—ever since she met him at the American Indian Movement protest in Washington, D.C. She'd heard about cross-orientation relationships but dismissed them. Either the women were never really lesbians in the first place or they were pretending to get by in a sexist, patriarchal society. It was obvious.

Until it happened to her on a clear October day in the middle of the National Mall when the attorneys in her office were mobilized to defend AIM for occupying the Bureau of Indian Affairs. Roberts and Flack was a nice little partnership. Full of fun and misplaced ideology: we *can* make scads of money and *be* socially responsible. They had dispatched their junior attorneys to aid and protect the demonstrators. It made them feel better about representing and lobbying for all those companies destroying the reservation land back home.

Nadine crossed the mall to meet with AIM attorneys and representatives in front of the AIM occupation outpost previously known as the Bureau of Indian Affairs.

She never made it.

Cutting across the mall and thinking of possible assault charges that could be levied on the clients and the associated strategies for handling them, she ran smack into a dark man and knocked him down.

Bewildered she'd looked down at him.

Nadine was not a small woman. The man she had knocked down was thin. He sat up and brushed the dirt off his hands. She reached down to help him. He reached up and when they touched and she had a sudden flash through her, a vision of every possibility that could ever happen to them spread out before her in a blink so fast and natural that she had enough time to think, *well, that makes sense*, before it was gone.

She pulled him to his feet. "I'm Nadine Prescott."

"Joseph Durant." He scratched the back of his head. "You want to go for coffee or something?"

"Absolutely."

It was as simple (and complicated: *Check!*) as that.

It was no surprise to either of them that they were both from the County. County people were always running into other County people. It was a fact of life.

Once Nadine and Joe were married, Nadine cycled back and forth between the County and her work in D.C. Joanie's birth barely slowed her down. Often, Joseph was there when Nadine got home. Often, he wasn't. Joanie learned to live with Grandma Catherine or Grandmother Jean. Joanie was grown up and gone when Catherine had gotten sick.

Nadine had come west to help, abandoning a promised appointment in the incoming Clinton administration. Then, Catherine died. After the funeral, Luke and Joanie returned east. Nadine remained where she was.

Nine years later she was County Clerk. Her mouth quirked in a smile. Few had risen so far and so fast. In another nine years she might be… County Clerk. *Check.*

The County Meeting took place in the Regional High School gymnasium. Overflow went to the cafeteria. Only registered voters could vote — another innovation that followed the Civil War. Before that, any adult male resident had the privilege.

Voter registration in Nuthatch County was the highest in the state.

Nadine sat in her seat on the stage and tapped her finger on the table. Nine years she'd been here. Catherine was gone. Joanie was gone. Luke was gone. Joseph spent about half his time with her—more than when she lived back in Washington. But not *that* much more. What the hell was she still doing here? Marking time? Time for *what* exactly?

She brought up the email again. Matt Tibbett was one of the ancillary attorneys at Roberts and Flack. He was consulting for various leftist groups. After the Gore/Bush fiasco last year, the Left was mobilizing. Not *well*, mind you. Lefties were much harder to herd than cats. It wasn't surprising. Your average right-wing activist studied things like business or law or marketing. Your average left-wing activist studied things like sociology or psychology or philosophy. Guess which one is the better political organizer and which is the better dinner companion? Roberts and Flack could use someone with her skills. They could use *her*.

Finish what you're doing and come out here, he said.

What was she doing, exactly?

Shepherding a road through Nuthatch County, apparently. According to Matt getting the road through had become (how?) visible in Washington and was being used as an example of her community (read, "political") management skills. Think of it as proving you still have the chops.

When she was thirteen she realized how much her parents loved her. Lay down their lives for her without consideration? *Check.* Willing to battle schools, boyfriends, girlfriends, government agencies, and the Army of Sumatra on her behalf? *Check.* But love like that (or of a child or of a husband) was a trap. It embedded you in the past. In the nine years of living back here in Nuthatch County, she had seen firsthand how the past can rule the present. It ruled her as much as it ruled anyone and for a long time, she had wrapped herself in its comfort without realizing how tightly wrapped she was. Matt's email had broken loose something in her. She found herself ready to put down her notes and laptop, get in her car, and *go*, whether the main road out of town was straight or not.

Which brought her back to Matt's offer. Did she want the job because it promised freedom and escape? Or did she want the work? She wasn't sure.

Nadine was torn. She loved Joseph—she'd made her peace with the conflict between body and heart years ago. She also missed the action in D.C. Nine *years* missing it to the point that the thought of taking on a worthy opponent was like fire in the loins. Here was the chance. Joseph could come visit her there like he had before. Or not.

She returned to her notes. Nadine had a meeting to prepare for.

Joanie had more or less planned on skipping the meeting in favor of pinning Carter down on the floor and having her way with him. She craved devouring him with every part of her body, leaving nothing left but smoke and ash—an image she'd wanted to sculpt for years. She'd even got to the point of making a wax study. Aaron had made her hide it, horrified that a student might see his gleeful and lusty teacher consuming a hapless (but happy!) man with her woman parts.

But Carter wanted to be at the meeting.

Joanie filed into the auditorium just behind him, irritated and unsatisfied. Only the image of Aaron shaking his head at her, and the certain knowledge that angry, make-up sex was rarely as good as its reputation, had kept her from fighting about it. Instead, she'd shaken her head, closed her eyes, and calmed herself. Much more attractive than holding her breath until her face turned blue.

But much less satisfying.

Luke was on the stage sitting next to Pam Small. Nadine sat at the other end of the table. Judge Utterback and Amos Durant sat in the middle. Grandfather Amos glanced over the crowd and saw her, nodded slightly so she'd know he saw her. Moderator Withers sat at an adjacent table showing common ground but no solidarity with the official County powers. A further table had the County acolytes: County counsel, finance officer, and Sheriff Cox, among others. The first row had the lesser powers: the mayor of Pilate, town council of Ridgeville, and like folks.

The room filled according to constituents. The white Ridgeville people hung mostly together, separate from but near the Ashby residents, confirming their geographic solidarity but preserving ancient status. Lee Thomas sat down next to his son and grandson in the middle of the Ridgeville group. Lee was the head of the Nuthatch County chapter of the Ku Klux Klan. It had no power. Jeremy wouldn't allow it. Instead, Lee ran a racist sort of social club.

Ashby was well turned out. Those who could afford it dressed in suits and ties. But even those who had little more than the clothes on their back wore clean jeans and a newly washed shirt. Jean saw Roy Bakerman, Buddy's brother, sitting up straight and attentive.

Those representing Pilate were mixed by race but Joanie could still tell riverfront from town center, south side from north side. Next to them were various factions, families, and embedded conflicts, close enough to the Pilate section to gain status but not of them. On one side were the Pollocks and on the other side were what was left of the Chases, all that remained of a long standing feud over a small and unimportant piece of farmland now owned by Milt Cleary.

The small groups that had come down from the Bittersweet

Ridge or the White Bluffs sat together. Three generations and two sides of the Porter family—kids, sisters, cousins—sprawled in the middle section of the auditorium, a loud and defiant presence. Only Ed was missing. Joanie thought for a moment. She'd been to many County Meetings over the years, first with Luke and now with Carter, and she didn't recall *ever* seeing Ed. She wondered where he was when his whole clan was present and accounted for.

She glanced at Carter. He leaned forward in his chair, watching the stage intently as they waited for the meeting to start. He hadn't grown up with the County but he paid attention. All he ever did was good work. Joanie shook her head and felt small and petty. She reached over and rubbed his back. When her hand reached his neck he reached back and gently held it.

At that moment the sounds in the room changed. Jeremy came in the back and sat in the last seat next to the windows on the west side—where Joanie had seen him sit her whole life. Betty sat next to him.

Joanie turned towards the stage. Now the meeting could start.

Transcript, County Meeting, Tuesday, May 1, 2001. 7:43 PM.
<Audience>: What about the damned road?
Moderator: Topics have to be dealt with in the order of the warrant. Article 4 is next.
H. Chase: Herbert Chase, twenty-one Forrest Drive, Ridgeville. I have a gripe about the way Pilate water is better than Ridgeville water. We need to get some new wells dug.
Moderator: Frank Ropert? You want to reply to that?
H. Chase: Seems like you never actually come out and check on things, Frank. What? Do you have to sit on your fat ass *all* day? Can't you come out and check on things every *now* and then?

Moderator:	Please address comments and questions to the Moderator. Frank?
F. Ropert:	I think Herb is a fine one to talk. Seems like he hasn't been out of his trailer since the Carter administration. Except to peek through Annie White's windows.
H. Chase:	You take that back!
Moderator:	Did you want to answer Mister Chase's question?
H. Chase:	She just leaves those damned curtains up! What's a man to do?
F. Ropert:	Yeah. I'll answer it. A *man* stays home with his fucking wife instead of mooning over a waitress half his age.
H. Chase:	I ain't fucking married!
F. Ropert:	What a fucking surprise that is.
Moderator:	I mean about the water.
F. Ropert:	The reason Ridgeville water tastes like crap is we're getting it from the new wells we dug last year. We're doing *that* because the old wells weren't pumping out enough to fill *somebody's* new swimming pool.
H. Chase:	I ain't got a swimming pool!
Moderator:	Please address comments and questions—
F. Ropert:	No but your brother has *two*. One for him and one for the house he's building for Annie White!

(Howie Chase in Audience) That's a damned lie!
(Sound of scuffling.)

Moderator:	Officer Price will escort the Chase brothers out of the auditorium to the parking lot where they can settle their differences without permanent injury or death. Sergeant Moon will remain here.

Jeremy, in all his named incarnations, had never said that anything he was capable of could ever be called magic. For that matter, Jeremy maintained a discreet silence as to what he could do and what he actually did. The stories, legends, and accounts came from witnesses and not from Jeremy. Consequently, except for Jeremy himself, there was no scientific evidence of anything remotely magical in Nuthatch County. Since County belief in such things was not remotely based on science, this made little difference. For those willing to pay, there are always those willing to sell talismans, spells, charms, fortunes, and amulets. After all, Jeremy was right there across the aisle in the church. If *he's* around, something magical was just *bound* to rub off.

Jean Durant was the chief purveyor of fortunes and objects of great magical power. In her shop and brochures, she spelled "magic" with a "k" to give it more cachet. Jean had absolute belief in what she sold. If it worked she had gotten it right. If it didn't either she'd misunderstood the signs or the effort had been foiled by capricious spirits. Jean was an Osage and it was not lost to her that most of her clients were white.

After all, the Christians had tried to convert the Osage with the magic of salvation and resurrection. Their magic didn't work any better than any other. All magic, therefore, had equal standing. It worked or it didn't.

She applied this principle to her own life. The Osage and Choctaw of the Bluewater Reservation had been in a state of subdued conflict ever since Jeremy had allowed a band of refugees from Andrew Jackson's relocation experiment to settle in Nuthatch County. The Osage, the Natives of record in the County, resented it. No one in their right mind went against a Jeremy (then Collins) decision and so began the Little War. Fights, thefts, and occasional murders had been the norm until, after World War II, Jeremy lost patience and told the tribes to manage themselves or leave.

Shakespeare had been taught in the Reservation schools that year and they decided the Bard had the perfect solution in Romeo and Juliet: the tribes would marry Jean Blackbird, an Osage, to Amos Durant, a Choctaw. That would show Jeremy they had buried the hatchet. Thus life is forced, bent and shaking, to imitate art.

Ever eclectic in her methods, Jean read the entrails of a rabbit on the eve of her wedding night. She would birth a girl who would win the lottery and become Jeremy's wife as soon as Amy Pollock DaFoe had the grace to die. Jean would wield influence over her daughter and make great things happen.

Joseph Durant was born nine months later.

The magic either worked or it didn't.

In the last week before this meeting, she had been employed to perform three spells in favor of the road, two against, and one to keep anything regarding Annie White from coming up.

She carefully wrapped up a doll with a lock of Annie's hair and put it in her purse. At least that part of her evening was over.

Transcript, County Meeting, Tuesday, May 1, 2001. 9:22 PM.

Moderator:	Article 19 is next. Commissioner Small has asked to speak first.
Small:	Article 19 involves straightening and widening the main road. The idea is to get rid of the switchbacks and connect the road directly to Interstate 57 at the north end. The west end has to be paved and widened and will connect to the main access road of the airport.
\<Audience\>	I'm against it.
\<Audience\>	Shut up, Froley.
Moderator:	Anybody who wants to comment on the article must come to one of the microphones in the aisle and address the moderator.
\<Audience\>	Yeah, Froley. Wait your turn.
R. Porter:	Robert Porter, number four, County Road 7. How much is this mess going to cost us? Two years ago the County bought three new snow plows. Three! Cost us a hundred thousand dollars! And we didn't even have any snow. Where's it going to end?
Moderator:	That's not really—

P. Small:	I'll respond. If you'll recall, Mister Porter, the County at that time had *no* snow plows. We had a 1948 Chevy dump truck with a snow plow attachment. The truck is now serving as a wildlife shelter beside County Road 3. Both the rusted engine and transmission fell out at the same time while it was carrying gravel to resurface the road. Fortunately, since all the fluid had leaked out before its collapse, cleaning up the spill was negligible. When I last had a report from County Forest Agent Nicholson the truck housed several squirrels, two families of quail, a bobolink nest, and a new fawn. We replaced the truck with a road grader, front loader, and a new dump truck—with a snow plow attachment—all purchased used from the town of Cairo. And while last winter was mild, *this* winter has had its share of snow.
Moderator:	Mister Porter was referring to the cost of the road.
P. Small:	We're expecting a federal grant to cover the majority of the work.
L. Prescott:	That's correct. We'll get that going as soon as we get approval from the County.
D. Froley:	Dan Froley, number six, County Road 7. It's going to change the character of the County. We're going to have every sort of character passing through. You mark my words, there's going to be nigras from East Saint Louis coming down here to steal anything not nailed down.
Moderator:	That language will not be tolerated.
D. Froley:	Then they'll come back with claw hammers to take what's left!
Moderator:	Is Officer Price back yet?
<Audience>	Drop Froley off in Ashby. We'll take care of him for you.
D. Froley:	I got a right to be heard!
Moderator:	Officer Price, have the Chase brothers ironed out their differences?
O. Price:	Sort of. We were hoping to borrow Doctor Faraday.
Moderator:	Doctor Faraday: Can you accompany Officer Price? Mister Froley: Can you present your views without being offensive?

D. Froley: I got a right to be heard.
Moderator: I'll take that as a no. Sergeant Moon will escort—
D. Froley: I'll be good.

Without Carter's distracting presence, Joanie paid attention to the proceedings. The familiarity gave her a warm feeling of comfort. These were family squabbles and dank provincial attitudes made public. The Chase brothers needed no excuse for a fight. Dan Froley's tirade against the population of East Saint Louis only required the merest of triggers. Nuthatch County was like a pot on a long simmer. These little events were just lazy bubbles making their tired way into the air.

But Dan Froley looked old. His hair was completely white. Joanie remembered slipping away from her mother and talking to him when she was—what? Seven? Eight?—smelling his whisky and mint-scented breath as he gave her a horehound candy and a John Birch tract. He must have been in his sixties back then. Now his hands shook a little when he sat down and he looked sad. The chair next to him was empty—Joanie remembered he'd always sat next to the stern and rocky presence of his wife. Froley glanced at the empty chair and rested his hand on the raised seat.

Joanie looked around the room. There weren't all that many people here younger than forty. A few families. The Porter clan. But they were the minority in a sea of white hair.

Where did they all go? She split her time as a child between Grammy Catherine and Grandmother Jean. Back then it seemed there were kids around all the time. Jimmy Roark who had a crush on her when she was nine. Rhonda Page, who was her best friend in the entire world from the time she was six until the inexplicable day when she was eleven when they became implacable enemies. You couldn't throw a rock without hitting a kid. They'd all be her age now.

Where were they?

Joanie realized they were the same place she was: somewhere else.

Luke listened patiently. Gripes came first—that was always the way of it in these meetings. The article might contain something as innocuous and positive as a Methodist hymn and there would still be vitriol and bile thrown back and forth across the hall. Luke hoped the quarrels were the tip of a conflicted iceberg but wondered if they were really just small-town entertainment.

At some point, the dark fluids seemed to exhaust themselves. Someone brought up how much easier it would be to go to the Sikeston or Cairo hospital. Luke remembered Ben Philby when he stood up. Ben had babysat Nadine a few times before Luke had moved to Washington. Ben talked about how the new road would make it a whole lot easier for him to get to Barnes for his regular chemo. Belinda Charles brought up how her weekly dialysis might be less torturous if she could get to the center at Cape Girardeau in less than two hours. Carter returned to the hall after he'd stitched up the Chase brothers and spoke at length about a real ambulance service.

Luke wondered if Pam had primed these people or if they came to these conclusions on their own.

Transcript, County Meeting, Tuesday, May 1, 2001. 10:40 PM.
P. Small: I've been counting. You might have seen it, too.
                  There are not many kids here. Just the few the Porters
                  brought. Not many young families here, either. I see

just half a dozen in their twenties. Most of this crowd starts in their forties and march upwards. You know why. For every three children born here, two of them move away before they're twenty. No community can sustain that. With real access beyond the County, we can do something about it. Build attractions. Maybe get in some small factories or office parks. Otherwise, we might as well invest in one big old folks' home because that's all who's going to be left.

R. Porter: Robert Porter, number four, County Road Seven. My family has been here since before Missouri became a state. You can see us here. We work. We got kids. We're not going anywhere. Dan Froley didn't say it the way you'd like to hear it but he did bring up a truth: Nuthatch County is the way it is because it is isolated. It's a rough world out there. Here, we're protected.

P. Small: I know exactly where you're coming from, Mister Porter.

R. Porter: What's that supposed to mean?

P. Small: Changing the main access road to Nuthatch County does mean a change to the County. There's no way around it. Change to the County is a good thing. Back in the courthouse, we've been talking about all sorts of different things to help us. Everybody has made suggestions. Even Deacon Williams stopped by my office last year. His idea was to get a Wal-Mart here.

<Audience> Great idea!

<Audience> Screw Wal-Mart!

P. Small: It's a good idea but Wal-Mart wouldn't put a store here *without* changing the road. We thought about putting up a park or a monument—

R. Porter: How about one to William Quantrill or Bill Anderson? We've been petitioning for that for years.

P. Small: And the twenty-five signatures on every one of them have been counted by my office. My point is *it doesn't matter* what we build if no one can get to it. We need that road.

Heads were nodding in the audience. Luke could tell which way the vote was going from years of watching County Meetings. Pam would get her road. He kept his face neutral but inside he felt nothing but ashes.

Then, Jeremy got up, moved to the microphone, and handed it all back to him.

Transcript, County Meeting, Tuesday, May 1, 2001. 11:10 PM.
J. DaFoe: Jeremy DaFoe. Number 4 Blue Pond Road. I'm sorry to disappoint you. The change in the road is too big. You'll have to think of something else.

The motivations of those in the past rarely transmit forward.

Certainly, people often think they act for the past when they think about parents or grandparents or even earlier. This is illusion. The man that thinks he is carrying out his father's wishes might well be doing exactly that but the motivations behind those wishes were his father's and the son is following his own, entirely different reasons that would no doubt bewilder the father. But, then, few things obscure the intellect more than family emotions.

Ed Porter watched Jeremy through the telescopic sight. Robert's .222 was placed in a weighted tripod securely anchored to an ancient granite boulder, a good two hundred yards up the ridge from the school. The tripod was a beautiful creation. He had put it together from a telescope mount. Tiny stepper motors were able to move the rifle in increments no wider than the antenna of a fly. He had carefully mounted a CCD camera to the scope. Both the controls to the motors and the output of the camera were connected to a laptop. He'd managed to redirect the camera controls to operate a tiny screw motor fit into the trigger guard. The whole assembly could be taken apart or put together in minutes. It was an assassin's wet dream.

Screw hunting *rabbit* with a .222. *This* was what it was for.

When he'd started stalking Jeremy twenty years ago it had been with a target .22 and an iron sight. Now, look at what he had.

Every man needs a hobby.

He watched Jeremy's face on the laptop. Inching the cross hairs up or down a few millimeters, keeping the center of the shot directly on his head. Ed wondered what would stop him if he pressed the firing key. Would a sudden bird or deer deflect the shot? Would it bounce off his head? Would he catch it with his hand? Perhaps the gun would simply misfire or the laptop crash.

Twenty years. In freak snow and bitter rain. More often the air was like tonight, wet, heavy, and miserable with mosquitoes. What's a Missouri spring without mosquitos? He listened to the crickets. He'd brought a radio to listen to the meeting on the community station but had turned it off.

Something small and hard struck the side of his neck and reflexively he started to slap at it. But the weight of it stopped him and he carefully pulled it off. He looked at his hand. A narrow beetle crawled over his fingers—a firefly not yet ready to flash. There were eight or ten species that lived in the County, each with a different time to light. Every week or two over the summer the dark of the night came alive, glittering like the cold and drifting embers of fireworks. Ed smiled at it, happy he hadn't killed it. Funny the things that knit the County together. The County farmers were some of the first to move away from insecticides when they realized it was killing fireflies along with aphids—seemed like every farmer he knew was organic these days. Not that they could avoid fireflies all the time. Sometimes during the middle of the night, you couldn't drive the main road without creating a thick, glowing paste on the windshield. Made you sick to see it.

Ed suddenly remembered when he was a kid—eight? Nine? He and his brother and a mess of kids out in the woods dodging mosquitoes and catching fireflies in the jar. A boy—Jeff Schmidt? Stevens? He couldn't remember his name. Must have been fourteen. Big kid—pulled the glowing abdomens off the beetles and put them on his fingers. "Look, I've got rings on my fingers!" Ed had looked at Robert and unspoken agreement sparked between them. They tackled Jeff and beat the crap out of him. Funny how the past flashes at you.

The beetle reached the tips of his fingers, spread carapace and wings, and gently flew up into the night.

When Ed had started this vigil he thought it was because of those long-dead Porter brothers returning from the Civil War with a mission: to get rid of Jeremy however they could. But that was their motivation, not his. Every generation came to its own conclusion. Ed's was simple: Jeremy was too powerful to live. Ed did not know that the United States Government had come to a similar point of view; he didn't think the government could ever be that smart.

He moved the crosshairs slightly. The shot would hit Jeremy just above the ear. He had gauged the powder in the shells and the weight of the bullet carefully. The bullet should stay rattling around inside Jeremy's skull, turning it into hamburger and injuring no one else. Not Betty who was sitting next to him or old Frankie Paris sitting in front. Of course, a vagary of wind or leaf or the unexpected movement of a bystander could change that in a heartbeat. Would that be how Jeremy avoided the shot? By deflecting the bullet into a bystander or the bystander into the bullet? Ed wouldn't put it past him.

Jeremy got up and left the window. Ed clicked on the safety. He turned up the radio quick enough to hear the words "something else" but no more than that. Jeremy returned to his seat.

Jeremy didn't sit down immediately. Instead, he looked outside and up the ridge. He looked right at Ed.

Without thinking, Ed flicked off the safety and centered the crosshairs on Jeremy's right eye.

Then, for a long minute, Ed stared back, convinced deep in his heart that Jeremy could see right through him.

It was now or never. Ed pressed the laptop's return key that fired the rifle.

Nothing happened.

Ed couldn't breathe as long as Jeremy watched him.

Jeremy turned away from the window and sat down.

Ed flipped the safety back on, lest whatever alchemy that had stopped the shot suddenly release and, like a snake, the gun killed someone it shouldn't.

Part 2

Chapter 5: Changeability

Many of our primary metaphors are geographical. A *close* friend. A *distant* relative. Wouldn't want to be anything other than American. Be damned if I lived outside of Missouri. Nuthatch County is where I'm from. Pilate's better than Ridgeville. Rather be outside of the town than inside. What the hell does it matter as long as it's on the reservation?

While Jeremy knew everybody, not everybody knew Jeremy. That is, though every person living in Nuthatch County could count on at least one visit from Jeremy, not everybody in the County saw him more than once. Those who saw Jeremy regularly were few.

Among those few were Jeremy's two neighbors.

Jeremy's hundred acres were irregular and abutted seven other parcels. Dan Froley and Glenn Waxman lived on two of them. Three of them were covered in woods and owned by land trusts purchased in the vain hope that someday somehow they would be worth something. These trusts had changed hands twenty times since the Reagan administration, each time grasped in a desperate hunger for property and given up in a fierce joy that there was a sucker down the road just a little bit more gullible. Thus, capitalism resembles a game of musical chairs. Two of those parcels, owned by a man named Milt Cleary, were rented and farmed by Dan Froley—or were. Since Edna had died that winter Dan had been approached by the Pollock family. He'd rented both his own land and the subrented Cleary land to them.

The day after the County Meeting, Dan enjoyed his new spring afternoon ritual: sitting on the porch fuming about his tenants. He was convinced he could do a better job plowing blind, deaf, and left leg amputated. Since Froley was half blind, hard of hearing, and limped, he might have been able to prove his point if his tenants had been willing to trust their tractor to that crazy old fart.

The Pollocks were three blond-haired, blue-eyed giants who would stop the tractor and talk to Dan if they couldn't politely pretend not to see him. Froley thought he knew Roger and Dean by sight. He didn't think he'd ever met Robert Earl. He couldn't keep any of them straight anyway. Not one of them could plow straight to save his life. The other day Dean—Roger? Could it have been Robert Earl after all?—had admitted that it would be nice if Dan would mark the ends of the rows so he could make straight turns. Dan had hustled eagerly down to the end of the field, pulling over one waist-high stalk after another.

Dan shielded his eyes. Was that Robert Earl? Or Roger? Or Dean? If he went down there would they let him mark the rows again?

The road was the farthest thing from his mind.

Dawn sent up its hot rosy appendages while Glenn Waxman was filling his water buckets. The night coolness of early May had evaporated and been replaced by the rising miasma of wet heat and roiling mosquitoes. Glenn wondered why the hell they were so fierce *now* when they had a whole ahead summer to consume him. "Fuck off!" he said and waved his hand through the air made viscous by insects. "You want to have something left in August!"

Ten five-gallon pickle barrels—one after another, filled from the hand pump between moments of open-handed, bloody, ineffectual mosquito vengeance—capped and put on the cart. Two would go into the hot water tub on the wood stove. Two would fill the gravity tank that fed the sink and the tiny toilet. Four would be left for later. He'd have to come back in the afternoon. Jenny couldn't manage to lift the buckets high enough to fill the gravity tank on her own.

Glen Waxman lived on ten acres of good farmland gradually turning into ten acres of good woodlot. Of the two hundred acres his grandfather had owned, Glenn had only managed to buy back the land under his grandfather's house. The house was a magnificent ruin. Two stories with a cupola on one side. A broad veranda on a rise that looked down into Froley's fields. Cedar clapboards that had weathered over the years until, in the late afternoon sun, they shone like silver. Inside, a broad stairway dominated the entryway and seemed made for a grand entrance to a party.

There wasn't an intact window in the house. A family of skunks lived in the basement. The floorboards were weather-stained and turned up at the corners from leaks in the roof. The steps of the stairway were split. Two had broken through outright, making a journey to the second floor less a chore and more an adventure.

Glenn had managed to drag a Fleetwood double-wide and an Airstream onto the property and rig a drafty connection between the two. The twins slept in the Airstream when they didn't sneak into Glenn and Jenny's bed for warmth and comfort. There had been more than one embarrassing coital moment, but the twins, not quite four, had managed to conceal their own certain knowledge of parental activities and protect

Glenn and Jenny's fragile egos from harm.

Glenn hooked up electricity from the pole without getting himself killed. Drinking water was hand-cranked from the century-old well. It wasn't much but it was worlds better than the chicken house they had lived in before. Back then, the twins' cribs were two polyethylene barrels Glenn had managed to snag from a car wash and soak in the creek until they no longer stank of industrial soap. In the Airstream the twins even had their own beds.

He hauled the last barrel to the cart and pushed it over the gravel towards the Fleetwood. He went over what he had to do today. Ed had given tacit permission to build lab number three. They still had to find a trailer and haul it to the location. That was item number one. There was a beat-up old Jayco he knew of on the reservation. He needed to find out who claimed it — you did *not* want to get on the bad side of the Natives. Then they'd have to find new equipment — Robert wanted to keep the other two trailers pumping out meth. That meant keeping the Harris sisters, Delmar and Katie, running trailers one and two. Delmar ran the one in the clearing off of County Road 4. Katie ran the one back in the woods off County Road 2. Trailer number three had employed Doug and Ralph Froley. They hadn't been seen since the explosion and no bodies had been found. Glenn wondered if they had managed to make it into the reservation woods, only to die lonely and undiscovered. Or maybe they'd seen the light and skipped town forever. Neither brother was much missed.

Glenn didn't like the Harris sisters. He didn't like how they had nursed some unknown past slight into a frothing mutual hatred and now refused to speak of or to one another. He didn't like their toothless grins, their beehive hairdo, their bright red dagger nails, their emaciated bodies that would have meant a fatal meth addiction except neither imbibed and were active in the same church — Glenn shuddered to think what *that* was like.

He pitied the pastor. How two seventy-year-old twins with barely an eighth-grade education between them had become accomplished recreational chemists was beyond him. But they were and they creeped him out.

Since the Harris sisters were otherwise occupied, that probably meant that Glenn would have to run the new trailer himself.

Every day he worked for Robert he thanked him in his mind. Without the money from the labs, he would never have been able to afford to buy the land or the junked trailers, or the unreliable Ford truck. And every day he racked his brains for some other way to make a living. Not only were the trailers explosions waiting to happen, they were *illegal*. Someday the DEA would find them and Glenn would rot in Fulton—no. Fulton was state. He'd be locked up in Leavenworth. Or shot so Robert wouldn't be implicated—Glenn had no illusions about the nature of their relationship. Glenn had some money saved but he couldn't spend it. It would lead back to him. Back to the labs. Back to Robert. He ached to have a checking account instead of a hidden cache of money. A charge card. A mortgage.

Glenn was torn over the new road. On the one hand, a good road might mean a factory right here in the County. A straight road that lined up with the airport would turn a ninety-minute trip to Sikeston into half an hour. He could get a job at the plastics factory there. Or maybe get a job as a night watchman. He could even (*maybe!*) get a job at the prison down in Charleston. Real money.

Not as good as he got through the lab, of course. Especially with the new trailer making Ecstasy. Glenn had run the numbers on the library computer in Pilate.

He shook his head. More money he would have to hide in the old house. Jenny didn't ask what he did for Robert, and Glenn didn't tell. She didn't know about the money in the old house: second-floor cupola, false bottom in an old wardrobe. He needed to tell her—thirty-five thousand dollars, cash, for her and the twins if something happened to him.

"Hey, honey," said Jenny as he started bringing in the pickle barrels. "You didn't sleep so good last night. Something on your mind?"

The smell of pancakes clouded his mind for a moment and made him think of the old chicken house when pancakes were a cheap treat against even cheaper cornbread. Happier, if less lucrative, times. "No," he said. "I'm okay." Except that I'm mortally afraid I'm going to die or go to jail any day. It occurred to him that Robert might not *let* him quit even if he wanted to.

Maybe they could move. Maybe they could just disappear. Of course, then, he would have to tell Jenny about the money. That scared him more than Robert.

Ray Bakerman was a big man. "Portly" was his preferred term. His weight was a burden in the heat—*nothing like fifty pounds of butter to keep me toasty in the winter and too hot in the summer*, he thought, smiling to himself. As long as he had an angle on the situation, Ray was a happy man. His brother, Buddy Parker, was thin but they were exactly the same height. In family photographs, Ray liked to stand on Buddy's left. Together, they looked like a misshapen number ten, Buddy being the number one. It tickled Ray to see it. He had never told anybody the joke.

The inhabitants of Buddy's neighborhood invariably referred to it as Ashby in memory of the once-independent township composed of blacks freed by Jeremy. The adjacent town never called Ashby anything but North Ridgeville. After all, it had been annexed in the forties. Right? *Right?* Hispanics, Asians, or any other swarthy demographic wisely decided not to get involved and lived outside of town or in Pilate. Natives lived on the reservation.

Ray lived on the second floor of the Haywood building — which would handsomely pay off as an investment someday — in Ridgeville proper but only a couple of blocks from his old neighborhood. When asked why he chose to live in the white part of town instead in more comfortable and natural Ashby, he laughed and changed the subject. But sometimes, at night with a whisky in his hand, he looked out of the window of his building down on the plank houses around him, each filled with a white family that, at best, gave him no thought at all. At worst they dreamed of white sheets and burning crosses kept at bay solely by the fear of Jeremy.

Then dark thoughts came, diluted only by an image he'd seen when he was briefly stationed in San Francisco on the way to Korea. Wandering the city, he'd found an odd little bookstore filled with strange books about India or Africa or Buddhism. A framed picture arrested him: two teardrops chasing one another in a circle, one black, one white, a drop of white in the black teardrop, and a drop of black in the white teardrop. A *mandala*, said the shop owner. Forces of black and white. Light and dark. Neither is ever pure.

In those moments when he looked down on the houses, he thought of himself as a black grain of sand in a white teardrop oyster. Someday he would make of himself a pearl.

Ray held his brother's face in his mind as he walked the few blocks between his apartment and Buddy's house. Ray never rehearsed ahead of time. Rather, he considered the target person carefully and in-depth to the point that when he finally spoke, he would know exactly what to say.

At least, that was how it was supposed to work.

Ray had that half-dancing motion possessed by some fat men, as light on his feet as a cloud. North on Anderson and right on Price. The sky was unbroken and colorless in the hot sun. Ray felt the sweat pour off him, lubricating his joints and making his clothes and skin one.

In the middle of the road, the street name changed from Price to Garvey, indicating the boundary. Of course, Ray would have known that without any explicit indication. The change was marked by a field of daisies. On the Ashby side of the boundary, the houses were well kept but smaller, with scars and scratches indicating the porches and yards were well used where there weren't already people using them.

Ray waved to people as he passed. Most waved back. One or two laughed and called out to him. One woman gave him a glance she shouldn't have and two others looked away.

The Parker house was two stories tall, surrounded on the north and east sides by a narrow veranda. Buddy was sitting on the front steps. Ray turned up the walk and as he reached his brother, Buddy handed him a beer.

Ray sat down heavily. He tipped up the beer and drained half of it. "Ah." He looked at the label. "Not bad. You couldn't buy an American beer?"

"I like Mexican beer when I'm hot. Sue me." Buddy finished his and pulled another from the six-pack. "What do you want?"

Ray leaned back against the porch and smiled. "Right now? Air conditioning."

Buddy laughed. "The house is an oven. You're better off out here."

"True enough." Ray liked long drawn-out conversations where the actual point was reached at random or by accident. But he knew that would just piss Buddy off. "I'd like you to try to persuade Mister DaFoe to reconsider his position on the road."

Buddy stared at him. "Why would you want that? Oh, right. Used car sales. Real estate. Woolworths."

"Think what you will of my motives. But you know how I can sense trouble."

Buddy watched him suspiciously. "I guess."

Ray sighed. Buddy could be difficult at times. "People counted on this road. Most of them. Some of them have a vested interest in keeping it the narrow track it is. But *most* of them want used car sales, real estate, and Woolworths."

"There are no Woolworths, anymore."

"Wal-Mart, then. They want to join the rest of the world."

Buddy glanced at him. "You should have run for County Commissioner. You could have given Pam a run for her money."

"Possibly."

"I can't change Jeremy's mind."

Ray sighed. "Do you remember the story of the Golden Calf?"

"Yeah. Moses goes up the mountain to talk to God and his people lose faith. Aaron makes a golden calf and they worship it. God gets angry. Moral of the story is not to lose faith, I suppose."

Ray shook his head. "No. You don't understand the story at all. Not at all. God gets angry all right. He's going to dump the Israelites and use Moses' own family instead. It's *Moses* that calms him down. It's *Moses* that persuades him not to abandon his people. The story isn't about us losing faith in God or about God losing faith in us. It's about the *conversation*. Even a mouse can rebuke the king when the king sins. Especially if the mouse is the Eldest."

Buddy looked at him for a long moment. Then, he opened another beer and sipped it. "That's a great story. But Nuthatch County isn't the Israelites. I'm not Moses. And Jeremy DaFoe most certainly isn't God."

"Are you so very certain of that, brother?"

Betty was planting carrots when Pam Small drove up.

It was early Saturday morning before the last week of school in those bare few hours between sunrise and intractable heat. The weather had turned clear and dry and the water table had dropped far enough to let the surface turn from brown gumbo to adobe. Betty imagined the earth rising after Noah's flood transforming the world in the same way: first rock, then mud, then plantable earth.

Betty stood up and stretched her back as Pam approached. Betty was proud of her garden. It was a long strip forty feet wide and a hundred and twenty feet long. She had used the tractor to harrow it into neat rows. Back at the house, she had a hand-drawn map describing the use of each square foot. This twenty-foot section would be Sweet Treat carrots. Good for cooking and salads but they wouldn't keep. Some of it she would use but most would be sold in Sikeston.

"Jeremy's not here. He's planting on the other side of Froley's place," Betty called as Pam came near.

"I'm not here to see Jeremy. I'm here to see you."

Betty watched her for a moment. "You come inside the fence and I'll put you to work."

Pam stopped safely outside the gate. "Fair warning. I didn't bring the right shoes for it."

"Do you *own* the right shoes?"

Pam shook her head. "No."

Betty picked up the hoe and dragged another six feet of furrow. "There you go."

"I need to talk to you about Jeremy."

"What about?"

"The main road."

"He's not known for changing his mind."

Pam leaned on the gate. "He's got to this time."

"Why?" Betty took the package of carrot seeds and poured them into her right hand. She carefully dribbled them into the furrows and eased a bit of dirt over them with her left.

"Because there will be hell to pay if he doesn't."

Betty didn't answer. She finished planting her carrots. She leaned the hoe against the fence and put the remaining seeds back in the packet. "You'll have to explain that to me. Out of the sun. On the porch. With lemonade."

The porch squared the front of the house that looked on Jeremy's fields and part of Betty's garden. It was unsullied by windows or screens. If there were mosquitoes, you got bit. If there was rain, you got wet from the spray. There was a tradition in the County of putting the porch on the portion of the house that faced the road. Jeremy hadn't held with the tradition. When he built the house sixty years ago, he had put the porch in the back where he could see his fields. The part of the house facing the road had only a few windows and a blank door with a roof to keep off the rain. It was difficult to see what was going on in the house from the road, but everything was exposed to the fields. Betty knew this told her something about Jeremy and was still considering what it was.

Ensconced on porch benches and protected from the sun— Betty in dirty jeans and a T-shirt, Pam in trim pants and jacket— Betty poured ice-cold lemonade first into Pam's glass, then her own. She put the pitcher back on the table, drank half her glass, and sat back with a satisfied sigh. Radishes next, she decided. Then, sweet corn and melons. Have to check the weather.

Pam sat in her chair, upright and brittle with frustration.

Betty sighed again, for a different reason this time. "Okay. Explain."

"People got used to the idea of a straight road. They got used to the idea of what it might do for them. Real estate values. New stores. New customers. New jobs. Jeremy stopped all that and it pissed them off."

"People have been pissed off at Jeremy before."

"True." Pam sipped her lemonade. "But these are different people. Nuthatch County isn't isolated like it used to be—

television changed that. They've been told so many times that they're independent Americans that they've come to believe it. Jeremy slapped them down like they were three-year-olds. They don't like it."

"They'll get over it."

"They *won't*. They *haven't*. Remember how I said in the meeting how we're losing two out of every three young people? Why do you think they're leaving?"

"It's a problem for rural areas all over the state. I've read about it."

"More here. Christ, we still have moonshiners!"

"Do you want some?"

"What?"

"Moonshine."

Pam stared at her. "You have some?"

Betty nodded. "Ed Porter drops some off once a year. For Jeremy. We don't drink much. So, we have about ten gallons of eighty percent alcohol down in the basement."

"Ten gallons? When did Ed start doing that?"

"The year Jeremy and I were married."

Pam was quiet for a moment. "Why do you think Ed gave Jeremy moonshine after he married you?"

"You know why." Betty chuckled. "He was trying to get at Jeremy. Our first year was tough and one hundred-sixty proof alcohol can be a good friend." She looked out over the fields. "Jeremy doesn't get drunk. Oh, he can *act* drunk—maybe he even is when he wants to be. But the moment he doesn't want to be he's as sober as Hugh Utterback. I had no illusions about marrying Jeremy. I wanted to marry him for all sorts of reasons. But reality and expectation have a way of being a little different." Betty looked at her out of the corner of her eye. "Not to say shine is a bad thing. It goes well with lemonade."

Pam looked uncomfortable. "Okay."

Betty went inside to the kitchen and pulled out the bottle

from the freezer. She decanted it into a coffee creamer and brought it out to the porch. She gave herself an ounce in her glass and passed the creamer to Pam.

Pam poured an ounce into hers and sipped. "This is quite good. You can barely taste it."

"Yeah. Smooth as grain alcohol."

"Ed should open his own distillery. I bet he could actually make a profit."

"I think to Ed illegal money is better than legal money."

"I can see his point," said Pam, considering. She finished the lemonade. "May I have another?"

"Go easy Madame Commissioner. This is stronger than it tastes."

Pam gave her a narrow look and tapped the glass on the table.

Betty shrugged. She poured the lemonade.

Pam added the moonshine. She drank a bit and put it down. Loosened her collar. "Jeremy keeps this County quiet. All of the conflicts we had a hundred years ago are still here. They've never been fought out and resolved like they have in other places. We're fixed like a butterfly in a collection. There was no anti-slavery movement here because Jeremy freed the County slaves. There was no Civil War here because Jeremy wouldn't stand for it. There was no civil rights movement because Jeremy never allowed segregation. There was no anti-war movement here because there was no Nuthatch County Draft Board. We have a Klan. *Here.* Nobody takes it seriously because Jeremy holds its leash. The road could punch through all that and let in the air of the twenty-first century." She made an awkward jab at the air. Her face was flushed. She spread her hands as if she was trying to hold a basketball. "It could bring us into the real world. It's like Jeremy keeps us on this... this *island.* It's very nice. Everybody has everything they need. Jeremy's island." She giggled. "But it's very small." Pam looked a little cross-eyed for a moment. "Very small." She sat back and closed her eyes. After a moment Betty could hear a faint snore.

"Oh, dearie." Betty picked up the glasses and the lemonade—and the creamer, of course. She poured the moonshine back into the bottle and replaced it in the freezer. Betty never wasted it. One never knew when such a friend might be needed. She made a pot of coffee and drank two cups, one after the other. Then a tall glass of unspiked lemonade.

She opened the front door and the late morning heat rolled into the room. Betty grabbed a hat from the coat tree and went back on the porch.

Pam was lying on her side on the bench, her face sweaty and her hair damp. She had half taken off her jacket and it was hung precariously across the back of the bench and through one arm.

Betty slipped Pam's arm out of the jacket. Pam immediately looked a little cooler.

Betty gently kissed Pam on the side of her head so as not to disturb her. She smiled. Oh, honey. If I were on a different team and unmarried.

Oh, well. Life was filled with unsought opportunities.

Betty went back to her garden where the carrots, like an eager populace, awaited her.

In the Smithsonian American Art Museum in Washington hangs a Catlin hand-painted lithograph entitled simply, "Ball Players." Three magnificently proportioned young Choctaws are holding ancient lacrosse sticks. One is painted a titanium white over his entire body, excepting only his feet, his hands, and the upper part of his face—a pale ghost, slipping unhindered across an imagined field, viewing the world with fierce, unbowed eyes.

Wallace Payton got out of his car and stood, stretching his

back. He looked exactly like one of the Ball Players—save he was unpainted, considerably older, wore a T-shirt and shorts in the early summer heat, and a baseball cap instead of feathers.

He looked up at the family complex of cabins, lean-tos, trailers, and huts where lived Amos Durant was. What would you call it? It bore more of a resemblance to a bombed house than a proper dwelling place. Not at all like Jean Durant's house on the other side of the reservation.

Amos lived in the northeast corner, according to rumor, atop what once might have been an armory. Wallace knew Grandfather Micah Durant had built that. In the thirties, long before Wallace was born, part of the cabin had been reinforced into an above-ground cistern that supplied rainwater to the rest of the complex. In the fifties, when they were both eight, Wallace and Amos' son, Joseph, had helped Amos dig out the foundation and build a fallout shelter.

Now, Amos let him into the rambling house and led him through a maze of interlocking corridors and rooms until they entered a small wood and glass sunroom. Wallace tried to conceal his surprise. This was poor, doomed Claudia's room. Amos' cousin, she'd been as sad and quiet as a deer, both he and Joseph had nurtured silent, unattainable crushes on her all through high school. Mysteriously, she'd left for a year and just as mysteriously returned to build this sunroom as a little tea house. The low tables were built into the wall, and it still had a faint Japanese feel to it. Wallace had heard that this was where Joseph had found her, quiet and sadly dead, her hands gently grasping the bottle containing the Demerol that had killed her.

There were stories that she'd left to have Joseph's baby and give it up. That Joseph had spurned her. Or Joseph had told her of his love and she'd spurned him and died for want of another. Or that it had nothing to do with anyone on the reservation at all. Or that she'd been in an accident while out west and the overdose of painkiller was just a tragic mistake.

Joseph left right after the funeral and didn't return until he married Nadine Prescott. The pattern had been set. He'd come and gone for thirty years.

Wallace had stayed.

Amos sat down in a rickety chair. The room was half glass but still in green shadow as the early summer leaves refused entry to even a single beam of sunlight. The windows were all different shapes. Square. Round. Bits of stained glass were carefully fit between beveled leaded crystal. At first, in the glass and shadowed gloom, Wallace thought they were alone. But then he saw Leonard McFall and Pete Oberly and Amos' brother-in-law, John Blackbird. Jack Teel and Billy Voyd were here, too. With Wallace, that made three Choctaw and three Osage: a mixed meeting. Amos, being the reservation representative to the County, didn't count.

Wallace tried to keep his face calm and unrevealing. What the hell was going on?

"Thanks for coming," Amos said quietly. He reached down and brought up a teapot and then cups and placed them on the low table. He lifted the cover and the sharp smell of sumac filled the room. He poured into the six cups.

End-of-summer tea: County reservation tradition for peaceful discussion. In a room steeped in the sense of death. The old man was pulling out all the stops.

Tradition insisted that the guests have an opportunity to drink the tea before beginning business. Amos waited the bare minimum.

"I've asked you here to talk about the road," he said without preamble. "We are the first meeting of the Secret Bluewater Reservation Road Committee."

"That's a dead issue," said John Blackbird. "Jeremy said no."

Amos nodded. "Indeed, he did. But I've come to the idea that perhaps his point of view might be open to negotiation."

Wallace felt his mouth go dry. "Negotiation" was a nebulous

term.

Jack Teel looked around the solarium. "How do you expect to change his mind?"

"I've kept an ear to the ground," said Amos. "No doubt you've heard the rumblings. People don't *like* Jeremy's decision."

"People don't like getting struck by lightning, either," said Wallace. "The lightning doesn't seem to care."

"Yeah," said Jack. "We all know the story of Faster-Than-Fox."

"I've been hearing about Faster-Than-Fox since *I* was a kid," declared Amos. "And you know how long ago *that* was."

"The feds take DaFoe seriously." John Blackbird leaned on his knees. "Whether the story is true or not."

"Fair enough," admitted Amos.

They looked at one another in sour silence.

"I do not believe," began Amos, "that the County, as one, has ever requested Jeremy change his mind in living memory. John? You're not as old as me but you go back a bit."

John Blackbird looked as if his teeth hurt. "I have no such recollection. Not since Collins Parker."

Amos sipped his tea. "I believe if we can become united behind this request it might be enough to make him change his mind."

"Why?" asked Wallace.

"Because he changed his mind about Collins Parker. Before the slaves asked him for freedom, he was happy to go along with the status quo. He changed his mind about slavery. He can change his mind about this."

"It's a far reach from enslaving a whole people to putting in a new road," said Leonard McFall slowly.

"The road is a symbol," Amos said, holding up his hand. "A symbol of bringing us into the twenty-first century. I think it will happen — too many people want that road — and I want our two great tribes to be a part of it. But that means we must participate and participate together."

Wallace found himself nodding. The old man had a gift for speaking when he wanted to use it.

"What do you want us to do?" asked John quietly.

"We have to make ready. You all have friends and neighbors that you can talk to. We need to pull together a group—maybe more than one—that can present a case at the next tribal meeting. Then, we'll draft something to take to Pam Small."

"Next tribal meeting is in October, just after the fall County meeting. Next County meeting after that is in the spring of next year," John Blackbird pointed out.

"I don't think we'll have to wait that long," Amos said grimly.

As the others filed out, Amos marked Wallace with a glance to stay behind.

Wallace nodded briefly. He walked towards the privy as the others drove away. Once he'd done the necessaries and zipped back up, he returned to the solarium. "What's up?"

"I have an ulterior motive."

"Yeah. Like I didn't know."

"We can use that road to get a casino."

Wallace shook his head. "Even if we got the best road in the world we're still too far off the highway. Nobody will come."

Amos sighed. "That's not how we'll do it. We show that a casino is *feasible*. That opens our land rights. Then, we *trade* those land rights for rights to a smaller site in a better location. That's what tribes are doing all over the country. I want a piece of that pie for us."

Wallace thought for a moment. "Might work."

"It *will* work. But Wallace? The road must be a joint venture. But that casino should be Choctaw."

"Ah. I see." Wallace thought a moment. "How does a Nuthatch County Choctaw change a light bulb?"

Amos gave him a patient, pained expression. "I don't know."

"In the normal way but he keeps doing it until an Osage comes along and tells him to try turning on the switch. Our folks would love to see the money from a Choctaw casino. But they won't risk a dime of their own money to do it."

"I take your point."

Wallace watched Amos a moment. "That's a lot riding on changing Jeremy's mind. What if he doesn't do it?"

Amos shrugged. "We're Choctaw. This wouldn't be the first time we fought for a lost cause."

Joanie kept one small sketch pad and pencil with her at all times. She was always drawing an interesting shadow, a furtive face, a dog lying in a pool of sunlight, a squirrel dead on the road. In this pad were many studies of Carter: asleep, reading, standing, sitting, nude, clothed. It pleased her that Carter didn't mind being drawn. He was unselfconscious that way.

She watched him as he slept, thinking about what Aaron had said. But all she saw was Carter's face: straight nose a bit too long, flat, high cheekbones hinting at the skull underneath, ears close to the head.

Carter's hairline was already receding. He'd be bald at fifty. She giggled and drew him at fifty, first keeping the lines of his jaw intact. Then, puffing them out into jowls. Here was Still-Handsome-at-Fifty Carter. Here was Ruined-at-Fifty Carter. She flipped between them. Which would he be? Would she have a hand in it and, if so, which should she encourage? Still-Handsome was the obvious choice but Still-Handsome was Still-Attractive—and who was to say what *Joanie* would look like at (she did a quick calculation) thirty-six? She could be bowlegged and thick as a truck. A sweet young thing that might sidle up to Still-Handsome wouldn't give Ruined-at-Fifty a second look. There were advantages to letting someone go to seed.

As she looked at his eyes, his mouth, of the drawings, As-He-Was, Still-Handsome, and Ruined-at-Fifty Carter all seemed bothered. Haunted. He had a sort of feral look. She turned the images in different ways. How much of what she saw was there? Was she drawing him or what she saw in him? Did the drawing show who he was or who he would become?

On impulse, she went to the bathroom and drew her own face from the mirror, trying not to see *herself* but just a mere face. Then, she looked at the drawing.

Smiling. A little pixie-like—if you could have a pixie with a nose like that. Not haunted but not easy, either. Not sure what would come next but taking no bets it would be pleasant.

She put a drawing of Carter as he was next to her own portrait. She'd drawn herself looking to her right and Carter looking to his left. Putting them next to one another made them give each other a sidelong glance. Feral meets cynical.

Great.

It was early morning just before dawn.

Jean Blackbird Durant sat in a clearing surrounded by women. Before her burned a carefully made and tended sacred fire. As the brilliance of the sun broke through the slant of the trees, she selected a specific pouch from inside her bag and sprinkled gray powder into her hand. Jean tossed the powder into the fire. Red, green, and blue flames danced.

It was no accident Jean was accompanied by three Osage women and four Choctaw women. The number eight was not coincidence: twice the sacred number four. Four Osage. Four Choctaw. The women themselves were also carefully chosen. On the Choctaw side: Vituria Dillard, Ellie Everidge, Adissie

Finley, and Amos' own sister, Ida Durant. On the Osage side: Charlena Bigheart, Pattie Javine, Louise Moncravie, and, of course, herself. Together, they were the Bluewater Reservation Historical Preservation Society. No one knew they existed.

She'd heard a joke from Louise once—which she thought originated from Wallace Payton. How does a Nuthatch County Osage change a light bulb? He sits in the dark until a Choctaw comes along and changes it for him. There was truth there that was in no way limited to her own tribe.

As the sunlight dimmed the flames, Jean selected another pouch from her bag, deposited the powder into her palm, and tossed it into the fire. A thick gray smoke filled the clearing with a scent of wildflowers and pine. Inside her mind she felt something like a soap bubble popping, breaking down the barriers between within and without. Louise got a dreamy smile on her face. The others grew quiet.

It had been nearly two hundred years since the two tribes had been forced to live together. They had assiduously avoided mingling rituals. Even their creation stories were different. This branch of the Osage believed they had come down from the sky. But the Choctaw had come up from the earth in the far west and worked their way east. Only a few songs had managed to cross the barrier. One was the Morning Song.

Jean began it and the others chimed in. They came to the song as individuals but by the song's end, they were a group with common purpose. The purpose, right then, was to savor the morning silence, the slight buzz from the smoke, and the joining of the Sky People and the Earth People right here in the clearing at first light.

After Jean felt they had spiritually communed long enough, she reached back into her bag and brought out grilled cheese sandwiches and a thermos of coffee. The other women brought out similar foodstuffs and shared them. For half an hour there was no sound in the clearing but the sound of eating.

"There," said Jean, finally. "This meeting is about the road."

Ida snorted. "Right. Like we're going to be able to make Jeremy change his mind."

"Wait a minute," said Louise, uncertainly. "Do we like the road now?"

Jean shook her head. "Not at all. The road symbolizes the modern world which we cast out of our circle."

"Jeremy said no. So, what's the problem?" Ida stretched her legs. She was too old to sit cross-legged for long. One eye remained steadily watching Jean but her other eye wandered, up and down, left and right.

Ida always made Jean feel queasy. After all, Jean *thought* she knew which was the good eye but she could never really remember which one it was. Was it the wandering one checking things out or the steady one? Still, Jean felt sympathy for her. She was having trouble sitting that way herself. Jean gamely tried to look Ida in what Jean thought was Ida's good eye.

"Do you think people in the County don't *want* the road?" Jean asked. "Do you think they're going to take what Jeremy says as the final word? This isn't back when all we had were bows, arrows, and corn. No. This is the twenty-first century."

"Maybe in the twenty-first century we could get cable," muttered Louise.

Jean gave Louise a withering glance but it was lost on her. She turned back to Ida. "Ida. Your own brother is going to attempt to make Jeremy change his mind. Do any of you think he'll be the only one in the County? The only one on the reservation?"

Ida's wandering eye gradually joined her steady one until, hawk-like, they fixed on Jean together. "What are you proposing?" Then, as if caught on a spring, the wandering eye bounced away and looked up and down, left and right.

"We are the Bluewater Reservation Historical Preservation Society," said Jean. "We *preserve*. That means we stop the road."

"What if Jeremy does change his mind?" asked Ellie. "Do we *preserve* against Jeremy?"

Though the question came from Ellie, Jean knew that Ellie was just a front for Ida. It might have been more efficient and just as productive to limit the conversation to the two of them.

"Have you ever known Jeremy to change his mind?" shot Jean back at Ida through Ellie.

"Not recently," murmured Ida, eye wandering up and down, left and right.

It's the *right* eye that wanders, Jean thought. Remember: it's the *right* eye.

"I think," said Louise, channeling Jean just as Ellie had channeled Ida. "That following Jeremy's wishes is the same as preserving the County."

"This time," said Ida in a low voice.

"This time," agreed Jean.

"How?" asked Pattie.

"We defend Jeremy," said Jean. "When discussions come up in favor of the road we weigh in and argue against it. When we hear people disliking the road, we support them. We bring up all of the things that the road would change for the worse and never bring up any good the road might bring. We act as a counterweight."

"A lot of people want that road," commented Ida.

Jean snorted. "We're Natives. We know all about being outnumbered."

Jeremy came home after Pam left.

"You just missed her," Betty said as she pulled the pie out of the oven.

"Just as well." Jeremy sat at the table heavily.

Betty looked up. Jeremy sounded tired. Jeremy never

sounded tired. "What's wrong, honey?"

"Nothing. Only she's going to pester me about the road. Do you know the Pollock boys?"

"Yes."

"They rented Milt Cleary's piece over on County Road 3. Roger Pollock came by while I was plowing over on the west side. Had all sorts of good reasons for me to change my mind."

"Did you?"

Jeremy smiled thinly. "Not so much."

Betty sat down across the table from him. "Is the road so important?"

"Do you want me to change my mind, too?"

"No." Betty shook her head. "I just want to understand."

Jeremy watched her for a long minute and, for a moment, his eyes shifted as if something behind them lifted a shutter and looked out. "I have my reasons."

Betty felt suddenly frightened.

Immediately, Jeremy leaned over the table and took her hand. "You need never be afraid of me."

She smiled at him uncertainly. "I'm not," she said. "Not really. Just startled is all."

Jeremy watched her carefully, gently, and with a face full of love. But at that moment she mistrusted him. Mistrusted his face and voice. Everything seemed mere appearance and form. Substance seemed to drain from the world into him, as if he were claiming the oxygen and the light. As he were the only real thing on earth and she and everyone else were mere shadows.

"I'm going for a drive." She grabbed her purse and was out the back door before she could think. Behind the wheel, down the driveway, and on the road. *Where?*

Buddy. She could always talk to Buddy.

His lights were on and he was sitting in the front room reading a book. She pulled up and parked the car. Turned off the engine and the lights. She held up her hands and watched them tremble. Why was she so frightened? Where had this come from?

"Betty?" Buddy was standing on the porch with a glass of something.

She got out of the car, stumbled, and leaned against the doorway. "I'm okay," she said. Her tone felt forced. "I just need to catch my breath."

Buddy came down the steps and over to her. "Are you all right?"

He was right there. She grabbed him. Felt his wiry body next to her. Smelled him. Right there. Real. Nothing to be afraid of. Nothing mysterious. Nothing hidden. Substance poured back into things. Buddy was not a shadow. Neither was she.

"Whoa, honey," Buddy said. He half supported her, half led her inside, sat her at the table, and put a glass of whisky in front of her.

She shook her head.

Buddy pointed at the glass. "This is good Bourbon whisky. It tastes of wood chips and dirt. Not that paint thinner you're used to. Drink up."

She did and almost choked. That seemed to help.

Buddy sat across from her. "What the devil is the matter with you?"

"I don't know." Betty shook her head. "I was sitting across from Jeremy and I was suddenly *scared* of him. Nothing felt real except for him." She felt embarrassed. Ashamed.

Buddy nodded his head. "I get that, too, sometimes. We forget who he is, don't we? Then, something comes along and reminds us."

"I thought I was *over* that. I haven't felt that way for *years*."

"Yeah. Me, too. That's what I thought when I got back from the war." He tapped the table for emphasis. "I figured damn near getting my head blown away might take the edge off, right? I was *full* of vinegar. He came over to see Dad and I was sitting there across from him—just like you are across from me. He told some joke about a traveling salesman and a milking machine and we were all laughing and I caught a look from him. It all slipped away and I thought I was going to piss myself."

Betty held her glass with both hands. The raw, destructive scent of the bourbon was real. The splinters in Buddy's table were real. There were slight wrinkles on the back of her hands that weren't there ten years ago, subtle reptilian signs of the inevitable advance toward death. They were real.

"I asked him why he didn't want the road and he wouldn't tell me." She looked up at him. "Why do you think he won't let the road go through?"

Buddy shrugged. "I have no idea. Maybe he sees something we don't. Some danger, maybe. Or maybe he thinks we'll be happier without it."

"A lot of people don't think so."

"'Canst thou draw out leviathan with a hook?'"

"Beg pardon?"

"Book of Job, Chapter 41. God talking to Job when Job is pissed off at how God screwed him. Essentially God says who are you to criticize me when I know things you don't?"

"You think Jeremy is God?"

"You're not the first person I've heard today to make that comparison." Buddy sighed. "I don't think he's God."

"What is he, Buddy?" she asked slowly, as if she'd never asked it before of herself or anyone else. As if it was a new consideration. "Deacon Williams thought he was a devil."

"He's not a devil."

Buddy went into the front room and brought back the book he was reading. Betty could see the cover: *National Audubon Society Field Guide to North American Rocks and Minerals*. He flipped through the pages and found a picture of a twisted bit of crystalline rock.

"Here," he said and gave it to her.

She glanced down and back at Buddy. "What's fulgurite?"

"When lightning strikes the ground it can get so hot it fuses the soil underneath. If the soil is sandy enough—or at least has enough quartzite in it—the soil is melted and recrystallizes into fulgurite. The fulgurite follows the route of the lightning through the soil. Some people call it crystallized lightning."

"So?"

He pulled a rock out of his pocket and put in on the table between them.

Betty could see the same crystals and shapes. "Fulgurite?"

Buddy nodded. "I found it poking around Collins' Landing."

"Where Lyle Williams was killed."

"Right outside where the store used to be." He touched the rock meditatively. "Now, I suppose it could have just been any old lightning that struck there. After all, we get a lot of thunderstorms around here. I suppose it could have been just chance that lightning struck down a slaveholder trying to reclaim a runaway slave."

Buddy picked up the rock and considered it in the light. "But I don't think so. Jeremy's not a devil. He's not God. He freed every slave in the County." Buddy turned the rock and Betty saw sparks of color from it. Buddy looked at her. "Collins Parker thought he was an angel."

Atkinson's was open nearly twenty-four hours a day. It opened for the breakfast crowd at four and fed farmers, bus drivers, and late-night party goers until eleven. Shifted to the lunch crowd: the few truck drivers that braved the main road to deliver to County supermarkets and gas stations, bus drivers again after the morning school delivery, and other folks that took lunch at more or less the normal time. At one the bar opened and the early drinkers drifted in. Four P.M. started the dinner crowd. The kitchen stayed open until eleven but table service stopped at seven as bands or DJs rolled in and the joint jumped until two: last call. Nothing left to do but hose the place down, clean out the kitchen, and get ready for the next breakfast crowd.

Both Ed and Robert were morning people and met for breakfast at Atkinson's a couple of times a week. May was turning into June, now. The brief evening respites from the heat were long gone. The only cool weather left was in the brief hour just before dawn. By July even that would disappear.

Ed got there first and caught a booth next to a window. He ordered coffee and breakfast: waffle and bacon for him, ham and eggs for Robert.

Robert arrived a few minutes later. He slid into the booth and drained the coffee without a word.

"Tough night?" Ed refilled his cup.

"Not so much." Robert drank half of the cup and put it down. "Out checking the trailers. Glenn does a good job but I like to keep him on his toes. When I got home Isobel wanted to party so I didn't get much sleep last night." Robert smacked his lips and grinned. "God am I glad I married a Mexican."

Ed sipped his coffee slowly. The Porters had a white heritage—why else did Samuel and Tyson go off to war? It bothered him that Robert had so carelessly tossed that history aside. Ed would have been happy to ignore his brother but was especially bothered when Robert rubbed his nose in it. Which, of course, was why Robert brought it up.

Ed sighed. "Find a place for the new lab yet?"

"Glenn's working it. First site crapped out—turns out it's the old family farm of Grace Cox. Wouldn't do to put a lab on the Sheriff's land." Robert thought for a moment. "Though it would be funny. We need a plan B."

"A new site?"

"A plan B for the road. You don't think the road is finished just because Mister High and Mighty Jeremy DaFoe says it is, do you? It'll come back. Too many people want it. We need a plan B to take care of it when it does."

"Hm." Ed didn't think so but he didn't want to say it. "Let me think about it."

The food came and they didn't speak until finished.

"So," said Robert, lighting a cigarette. "Where do we shoot our illegal spring deer this time?"

"I was thinking up on the north bluffs. Behind your trailer."

Robert's face went cold. "Bad place to be shooting. If we hit the trailer it might explode and then I'd lose one of the Harris sisters."

"Which one?"

"I forget."

"You pick, then."

"Bittersweet. Behind still number four."

Ed gave Robert a feral grin. "All right," he said, calling Robert's bluff. "But we can only shoot north. I don't have just the Harris sisters to lose."

Robert barked a laugh. "How about the crotch? Always a nice doe in the crotch."

Ed liked calling the area where the Bittersweet Ridge and the White Bluffs met the "crotch" but he didn't let on. "Good enough." He paid the tab which indicated it was Robert's turn to drive. Ed took his Marlin and camo jacket out of the back of his Ford and put them down carefully in the back of Robert's Chevy next to Robert's .222. Then, he climbed into the cab.

Robert cracked the window to let the smoke out and started another cigarette.

"Those things will kill you," Ed said mildly.

"Naw. The labs will kill me one way or the other. Tobacco will never get the chance."

Ed laughed.

They passed Harry Carr and a work team putting down patches in the road. Harry waved and Ed waved back before they turned off the main road. As they went up County Road Three, he saw evidence of some clearing. He pointed it out to Robert.

"Yeah. Looks like someone's plowing the old Cleary land." Robert tapped the ash out the window.

"That's a little close, isn't it?"

"Whoever it is would have to go further up the hill and cross over to County Road 11 to get to any of your stills. The trailers are the other way. I think we're safe."

"Maybe." He ought to put up some of those battery-powered security cameras. Might just get a lot of pictures of raccoons and possums. Little Sterling would like the animal pictures. "Seems like it gets a little less wild every year."

Robert shrugged. "According to Small, it's just a matter of time before there's nothing left of the County but us Porters. Hard to square that with plowing new land."

"Yeah." He would have to find out who it was.

Ed and Robert had been hunting (both illegally and legally) since they were kids. Over the years they had evolved a method that gave them the most success. Robert was able to move as silently as a Native so he went off into the woods and drove animals toward Ed. Ed, being the better shot, would wait and nail the animal when it came by. They refined the method based on animal and terrain but the technique remained the same.

At the end of County Road 9, they stopped. Ed pulled on the camo and took out his Marlin. Robert lifted up the .222 but pulled out a different case beneath it. He opened the case and pulled out something new: a lethal black barrel with a long magazine.

"Nice," commented Ed.

Robert pulled it out and held it up. "Heckler and Koch G36." Robert grinned. "I converted it to automatic."

"Well don't spray the damned thing at me when you drive the deer. I'd like to get home in one piece."

Robert eyed him speculatively. "I'd never do that, Ed. You know how careful I am. You're my brother, for Christ's sake."

Something about the tone bothered Ed. "Sorry. Why did you convert it?"

Robert shrugged. "Got to be as well armed as the feds. Just in case." He hefted the gun and leaned it on his shoulder. He waved, stepped into the brush, and disappeared.

Ed looked at the brush. Not a branch stirred. Not a leaf. Not for the first time, Ed wondered how his brother could *do* that.

He found a good spot atop a boulder and made himself comfortable leaning against a tree. Robert could excel at movement but Ed could become as still as death itself. His eyes flicked across the landscape, mind empty, waiting for game to come to him.

Perhaps forty-five minutes passed when he heard a sudden thrashing in the trees.

Slowly, he brought the Marlin to his shoulder and pulled the hammer back, careful to keep his finger off the trigger. The barrel swung as easy and natural towards the sound as a branch in the wind. A moment later a beautiful doe stepped warily past the line of trees. Ed sighted on the doe, checking beyond her to make sure he didn't shoot Robert. *Sixty yards. Allow for drop. No wind.* He squeezed the trigger. The Marlin roared. The doe jumped in the air but was already dead when she hit the ground.

Ed was halfway through dressing the doe when Robert called out to him.

"Yeah?" He had pulled the deer up in the tree with the rope sling and was busy pulling steaming entrails out and leaving them on the ground.

"Found something."

Ed didn't say anything. He carefully cut the entire digestive tract loose from the body, making sure not to contaminate the meat.

Robert was behind him. "I hear some folks say that's the best part."

Ed didn't look up. "You can have all you want."

"Look what I got."

Ed turned.

Robert had a fawn draped over his shoulders, barely thirty pounds of quivering infantile deer flesh. He set it down.

It trembled a moment and then tried to jump away. Robert easily snagged it by an ear. The fawn screamed until he transferred his hold to the neck.

"What are you going to do with it?" The fawn gave Ed a bad feeling.

"I don't know." He rubbed the neck and sides of the fawn. It trembled and watched him. "Maria might like a pet. Isn't veal just young calves? Maybe I can make deer veal."

"You could do that."

"I should have some fun with it first, though." With that, he broke the fawn's hind leg.

The fawn screamed in a kind of desperate bleat.

Robert giggled, looked up at Ed. "We got us a singer." He broke the other leg. The fawn screamed and wouldn't stop.

Ed picked up the Marlin and, holding it one-handed, cocked the trigger and shot the fawn through the skull.

Robert jumped back. "What the hell? You could have shot me!"

"Venison veal." Ed put leaned Marlin back against the tree. "Let me finish up the doe and I'll dress it for you." It was as close as he was going to get to an apology.

Robert sat up. He felt the side of his face. "Hell, I got splatter marks on my cheek."

"Wipes in my pack. Think you might make veal sausage?"

"Venison veal sausage." Robert brightened up. "That might

be good."

Ed didn't say anything. God, he thought. I hope I don't ever have to kill you. I don't know if I'd have a chance.

Luke's position had never really kept him completely busy until now. He had spent a lot of time making up projects to keep himself occupied. As the late John Bitters had told him, the natural granularity of Washington was the desk. The job of keeping Jeremy happy was sufficiently secret to maintain a single desk but had never managed a full desk's worth of work.

Now he had a full-time job.

Keeping Jeremy happy consisted of checking in with him regularly along with the rest of the County and town leaders. He had a regular phone call with each of them about once a week. That had to be maintained to prevent any suspicion. He spent one long Friday call with Pam Small listening to her complain bitterly about how Jeremy was holding back the *whole County*. Luke murmured platitudes: what can you do? After all, he's Jeremy. It's *his* County. Just enough commiseration to keep the home fires burning.

He and Rosen were running four agents. Luke didn't know their names but he knew their parents: USGS, Bureau of Weights and Measures, and the Post Office. Plus, one that DOD worked directly. God, he wished he was working with the FBI or the CIA, or the NSA. USGS? Bureau of Weights and Measures? What was next? The Census Bureau? The DOD was the only organization that made sense. Luke knew that the DOD was legally prohibited from operating on American soil but since that didn't bother Rosen it wasn't going to bother him.

It was like cooking a fine meal. Different elements had to be brought to conclusion at different times. Boiling up or over cooking had to be prevented. The middle of May brought heavy rains that soaked into the farm soil and delayed planting. This kept the farmers at home grousing at the table and annoying their wives, maintaining the proper level of road anxiety. Luke managed to "accidentally" divert a delivery of road construction equipment to Pilate where, of course, they were not accepted. The collection of bulldozers, graders, and asphalt handling machines ended up in a gravel lot half a mile outside of Pilate in full view of the main road. Each day as County residents went to the market, their jobs, or farms they could see bright eager yellow road improvement devices condemned to just lie there and rust in the rain.

As he worked with Rosen, he found out the depth (and resulting impossibility) of keeping Jeremy a secret. The geological anomalies that surrounded Little Mountain had to be erased from LANDSAT and other satellite photographs. There was fractionally more oxygen produced in the County than there should have been and less carbon dioxide. Hydrofluorocarbon production seemed non-existent even though the County residents bought air conditioners and wasp-killer aerosols just like anybody else. Methane production was higher in the County than it should have been. The National Reconnaissance Office normalized everything.

The incidence of gay men and lesbians was a bit lower than normal but, since this usually showed up in adulthood, it wasn't clear this wasn't just the effect of people leaving Nuthatch County for greener pastures. There were significantly more twins born to Nuthatch County mothers than anywhere in the world. A reduced incidence of autism and tooth decay. The polio epidemics had hit the County harder than most places. Despite repeated exposure, there had been no reported cases of the 1918 flu. The average life expectancy was six years more than the national average. The difference in life spans between men and women was next to nothing. The number of centenarians was the highest in the country. Most of those centenarians were bed ridden and/or senile. Incidence of infant mortality was average but the number of miscarriages was much higher. The rate of infertility was higher in Nuthatch County than in any other county in Missouri.

The NSA waved its hands and lo: statistics were brought to heel.

Rosen was right. The days of the Nuthatch County secret were numbered. Five years. Ten on the outside. The secret of Jeremy was like broad-weaved cloth. All it took would be the first cut and then the whole sheet would unravel. He could imagine the press conferences. It would be stark political death to whoever was in power. Given the timeline, that could be *this* administration and they knew it. Luke wondered how high the conspiracy went. Rosen had said Powell was behind it. But had Powell been given tacit permission from Those On High? If so, Luke could understand their motivation even though, like the Porters, he was surprised to find politicians smart enough to see it.

Reports came to them daily. Plans, sub-plans, ideas, plots, and subplots. Rosen brought them in and together they went over schemes executing, schemes planned, schemes being considered. Rummaging through his drawers he found something Deacon had sent him in their early days:

10 things I hate about Jeremy
1. The smell of him. I shipped out from Seattle. While I was there, I went to the old Curiosity Shop. They had this mummified corpse of a man who'd been caught in the desert. There was a beetle-like tang about him. Jeremy smells like that. As if there's nothing inside of him but insects and rot.
2. His body doesn't change. It looks the same now as it was when I was a boy. The rest of us change, grow old, die. Jeremy does not.

3. There's no fear in him. Fear keeps men under control. Fear of failure. Fear of women. Fear of God. There's nothing to protect us from Jeremy.
4. There's no striving in him. Men should improve things. Should leave the world a little bit different than when they came in. Jeremy acts as an anchor to change. He holds us still and in place. He is an impediment to progress.
5. He's nice to dogs, children, and the elderly, like some archaic feudal lord handing out favors. It demeans us.
6. He makes pronouncements that must be followed. And we, like sheep, out of fear, execute his pronouncements. Lest we be struck dead by lightning.
7. He will tell you what he thinks of you. No man should have to know what the unnatural thinks of him.
8. We know nothing of where he came from. Where he's been. Where he's going. At any moment, we could be struck dead by quake or volcano or plague.
9. He's not human. You can tell. He works at being human like an actor works at a role. It is false.
10. He has the same affection we have for dogs. Humans are not dogs.

Some were obviously true. Luke wondered about the rest...
Luke made notes:

Executing: sending letters to the editor discussing the glowing future of the County with the road and its sad fate without. *Note: make sure it's not critical of Jeremy specifically. Also, this will only get to the older population in the County. They're the only ones that read the newspapers. What about the young people? Email? Chat rooms—or whatever has taken the place of chat rooms?*

Maybe talk to Joanie. She might know.

Planned: degrade the road more than usual. Spill some salt in transporting it around the county. Run the dump trucks heavier than code. If it had been winter, they would have adjusted the snow plow to gouge out some bits of the road and then salt the cracks. *Note: is there a way to encourage potholes? Nothing makes people appreciate a prospective new road better than a transmission eaten by the old one.*

Executing: Summer program for kids encouraging independence of thought. Make sure handouts are attractive to parents. Sabotage a gas truck or two. Sabotage the liquor and beer delivery—make sure sabotage is attributable to the condition of the road. Disinformation and fermenting malcontent by individual agents. *Note: hold off on explicit resentment until full summer. Should be more effective if people are hot and angry. Create electrical problems over the summer? Careful, careful. Those hot summers can kill people.*

Proposed: Encourage the vigilante committee to start suggesting violence. The Porter brothers clearly see the road as a threat. *Note: NO! We start general violence and someone will get hurt! Redirect the vigilante committee to non-threatening (or at least non-lethal) means. Possibly against public officials. How to make it clear the true resentment is towards Jeremy without coming out and saying it?*

Luke shook his head. Sometimes he thought his major function in this whole endeavor was to act as a brake to these people.

Chapter 6: Good Neighbors

Every region rotates around a favorite holiday. All holidays, of course, are precious. But some places gravitate towards Halloween. Others towards New Year's Eve. Pick your town or suburb or city and there is usually one day out of the year that the town, suburb, or city subtly claims.

While Nuthatch County observed all of the normal American holidays, it had its own little occasions. "Turkey Day" was not the normal term for Thanksgiving. It was the first day of the spring turkey season. The Porters had a giant barbecue every year on September eleventh to commemorate the tar and feathering of Robert Johnson and the official start of the Whisky Rebellion. Every alcoholic and meth-head in the County was more than welcome. There were more than a few festivals on the Reservation specific to either the Osage or Choctaw community. Both had ritualized the solstices and equinocti. The people of Ashby rented the County Hall every October twenty-first to honor Parker's Day: the day Jeremy freed the slaves of Nuthatch County. There was usually a small quiet party in the woods on the same day attended by those in Ridgeville who didn't think much of Parker's Day. They marked the day with deep drafts of strong drink and spoke of robes and ropes, wood and flames.

County and country met on the Fourth of July where any custom, from alcoholic to teetotaler, Veteran to Draft Dodger, Baptist to Klan, could be paraded in downtown Pilate in front of Jeremy DaFoe and then celebrated in loud, fiery explosions. No one would judge them.

It was like cooking a complex meal, thought Harry Carr. You have to get all the different dishes to come out at the same time.

Whatever tensions and stresses were present in the ingredients of a meal had been introduced long before the cooks ever found them. Nuthatch County was rife with tension: racial, cultural, historical. All held close in quiet desperation by the fear of pissing off Jeremy DaFoe.

So, you cook the stock by inches.

Nate, as telephone line man, and Arnie, as meter reader, encountered people every day. Arnie was a good, likable guy. He managed to throw everything into the perspective of how a new road would make things better. Arnie was the consummate professional. He never let mere facts get in the way of persuasion, be it toppling governments or getting the last corn chip. Nate was a different animal. Nate liked to complain, and that was how he managed to bring up the new road every chance he got: by complaining about the old one. He had never lied to Harry. This would have been a fatal blot on his character as far as Harry was concerned if it had not become clear that, in the line of duty, Nate could lie as well, and for as little reason, as a State Department employee. Under Harry's careful direction, the three of them kept things simmering until the town meeting.

Harry was a municipal official: County Highway Maintenance Specialist. In a larger county, this might not have counted for much. But Nuthatch County was nothing if not small and everybody had an opinion and was willing to share it. Harry liked to appear easygoing. Friendly, even. Once, in Guatemala, he'd conveyed such an open-hearted generosity of spirit that he managed to pull out his nine millimeter and nail his target without either of them losing a smile.

Of the three of them, it was to Harry that people came after the town meeting. Harry would hem and haw and act like he didn't really *want* to talk about Jeremy and the new road but he would ultimately allow himself to be convinced. Sure, they all *wanted* to do what Jeremy said. And, *maybe* he had the best interest of the County in mind. But even Jeremy could be wrong sometimes. And it was getting harder every year to snowplow/resurface/paint/grade that old road.

The important thing was to keep the idea of the road in people's minds as something important and desirable while limiting the very real fear they had of going against what could be a divine being.

Harry grinned to himself. He could tell this operation was being run by amateurs. That little secret DOD agent was a joke. Fine by him. It was much more fun this way.

It took Joanie a while to get up her nerve.

The Brodeur School spring semester was finished by the end of May. There were classes, adult education, and intensive workshops all summer, but Joanie had not signed up to teach any of them. Instead, she packed up sketch pads, pencils, watercolors in one great duffel bag. Her clothes, toiletries, and sundries occupied a backpack. She filled her sketchbooks with different faces, giddy with ideas.

Then, she thought she was acting ridiculous and unpacked everything. The world seemed devoid of inspiration.

Desperately, she went back to the two other surround pieces she'd done before *Marilyn. Exxon Valdez*, where broken shells, oil-soaked rocks, and the corpses of fish and birds suddenly formed into a police portrait of Exxon president, Dan Cornett. And *Flight 232*, where photographs of the survivors, trinkets, torn seatbelts, and lost ticket stubs gelled into the gentle face of the pilot, Dennis Fitch, glancing back over his shoulder.

Why am I always doing portraits from the American past? Why not my own personal history? Why not do a portrait of Grammy Catherine? Luke would like that. Or great uncle John? Or Aaron? Always it's people I don't know.

Then, she repacked it. And found herself drawing children in the park.

My God, she thought. *I'm a wreck.*

By the middle of May, she could put it off no longer. She called Carter.

"Yes?" He sounded tired. He *always* sounded tired.

"It's Joanie."

"Hey, there." His voice turned happy.

That sudden change, as if her mere voice had been enough to push the troubles of the world away, thrilled her. She could learn to live for that. "The term is over in a couple of weeks."

"You can come out more often."

"I can come out for the rest of the summer. Until September." It all came out in a rush. She had planned to hold back, talk about the weather or something. But here she was pounding her stick in the sand with both hands and a rock.

"Ah."

Silence opened up like a great cave. Joanie felt her heart sink. Great, she thought. Well, she could break it off now. Aaron could probably get her some part-time work handling the intro classes. Not much in the way of money but it would keep her occupied. Keeping busy was important as the wound bled for a while, scabbed, bled again, and finally scarred over.

"Joanie?"

"Yes?" Hollow. Everything was hollow. What use was anything? Did whatever she accomplish have any real consequence in the world? Any real good? Was the world any richer for her little surprise sculptures?

"Do you have to wait two weeks?"

For no reason, no reason at all, tears suddenly flooded her cheeks. "Let me see what I can do."

Walter Pollock liked to supervise his sons. Dean and Robert Earl were both cut from the same mold: tall with broad shoulders, blond and blue-eyed. When Walter saw them, he thought of Vikings. They looked as if they would be equally comfortable with overalls or war axes.

Roger was cut from different cloth. His hair was darker. His eyes brown. While just as tall as his brothers, Roger looked more graceful. Almost willowy. Roger was his favorite but it would have taken hot pokers and spikes to get Walter to admit it.

The three of them were working on a float for the parade. The float was simple: a flat expanse of white cloth on which they had built a model of a road, pot holes and all, coming to an abrupt cliff edge. Below the cliff lay a collection of broken cars.

It's a joke, Pa, they had said.

Walter didn't get it. But he was more than willing to help as long as it involved no real work on his part.

They worked quietly, each handing the other tools with barely a word. Three grown men working together so efficiently it was hard to see where one's work began and the other's ended. They farmed like that, too. Never having had much of a work ethic himself, Walter was hard put to understand where it had originated in his sons. Must have inherited it from Jane.

He watched Roger's hands deftly lay out the cloth and staple it down. Roger always made him think of Jane. How he had managed to actually marry her was a mystery to him. She had been beautiful in high school and had only mellowed over time. Walter played the poor bad boy and realized early on that Jane was dating him to spite her father. That was just fine with him. He wasn't all that bright but he was smart enough to realize he'd never do any better. Jane's father had the Shell Oil franchise for the County. After they were married, Walter managed the delivery operation. This mainly involved Walter driving a tank truck over to Cairo to get a load and then run fill-ups all around the County. He was happy with that. Walter had little ambition.

He watched the boys. Sometimes Roger's features bothered him. He had thought about asking Jane about it. Was Roger really his? Or had she played a bit on the side, secure in the knowledge Walter would never stray, or if he did it wouldn't matter much. Walter remembered the old joke about the man with five sons who asked his wife on her death bed about the odd one. Punchline: "He's *your* son."

Maybe it was better not to know.

Still, as he watched the float take shape, he wished he got the joke.

Annie White sat across from Howie and Herbert. Now that they knew about each other, she had put her foot down. No more beating up on each other. *She* decided who did what and with whom, not them. Annie had decided to lay down the law to them here, at Atkinson's, over a fish dinner *they* would pay for. And they would figure out who would pay the check without resorting to violence.

Howie's left eye was closed from the swelling. Well, that

would heal. Herbert was missing a tooth. Annie frowned. She'd have to push Herbert to drive to Sikeston and get a bridge. Or an implant—she'd heard on the radio that invisible implants were the thing.

Both of them watched her, each keeping track of the other. They were like little boys. It gave her a warm glow. But no more punching. That would spoil whatever remained of their good looks.

"Now that we have that out of the way," she said. "What are you to going to do about the Cleary place?"

They looked at her blankly.

"The Cleary place?" she repeated. "Which used to be the Chase farm? Before the Pollocks stole it?" Patience. She needed patience with these two.

"Leave it be?" ventured Howie.

"We didn't have any intention of—" started Herbert.

"Shut up. How the Chase family men came down to you two I'll never know. But old Peter Chase's blood runs in my veins, too. Edward Pollock stole that land and Peter killed him for it. Then, his brother killed Peter and so on and so forth. So that's *our* blood on that land."

"But it's Milt Cleary's land now." Howie spread his hands in confusion.

"Who do you think is plowing it?"

Herbert shrugged and looked at Howie. Howie shrugged back.

Annie closed her eyes for a moment in exasperation. "Walter Pollock's boys."

"Damn," said Howie.

Herbert nodded. "It *is* Milt Cleary's land—"

Annie bristled. "Unfairly! Only because of the travesty of the Great Bare Knuckle Fight of 1903."

"Yes," said Howie solemnly.

They were silent a moment, remembering the story of the

battle royal between Jacob Chase and John Edwards Pollock, Junior, July Fourth, 1903. Jeremy had tired of the Chase and Pollocks shooting at each other over the last fifty years and decided they should fight it out once and for all and left it to the families to work out a non-lethal solution.

Both families were rabid fans of John L. Sullivan. John Edwards Pollock, Senior, had traveled south to Richburg, Mississippi to see Sullivan fight Jake Kilrain in 1899 and had declared it was a spiritual experience and that nothing in his life, including the birth of his first son, could compare with it. Mrs. Pollock's opinion was not solicited.

Both families decided that a good, bare-knuckle fight between the two finest specimens of the families would finally determine the matter. A ring was set up in the park in front of the Courthouse. It was the first event since the incorporation of Missouri that actually drew people away from the Nuthatch County July Fourth parade.

Fourteen grueling rounds later, John Edwards Pollock Junior lay in a crumpled heap, so covered in blood it was difficult to discover the extent of his injuries. Jacob Chase lay next to him, having struck the canvas a scant second later and equally unconscious. In the absence of a clear winner, the Chase family declared Jacob the victor since he had hit the canvas slightly later than John Edwards. The Pollocks cried foul. The only reason John Edwards struck first was that he was *shorter* than Jacob and didn't have as far to go. Victory must be judged based on injury to the opponent. By that measure, John Edwards had inflicted more damage on Jacob. *Not so!* Came from the Chase side of the argument. The degree of injury sustained by Jacob showed he was the *better* warrior. He had lasted longer and with greater spirit.

The rest of the town kept silence in the face of such tremendous entertainment. No one valued their own opinion enough to stop the volleys back and forth between the Pollocks and the Chases.

Finally, the Eldest suggested that this was a draw. Both sides refused to accept such a judgment against their valiant fighters.

Jeremy stepped in and awarded the land to the Cleary family where it had stayed until the present day.

Jacob was never right in the head after that fight. He took to bed, wasting away until he died the following year. John Edwards Pollock Junior lost his eye and the use of his right arm. He left what remained of the Pollock farm and disappeared upon his wife's unexpected pregnancy and birth of his fourth child.

"What can we do, honey?" said Howie plaintively, backed up by vigorous nodding from Herbert. "Jeremy *decided* the Clearys have the land."

Thin-lipped and furious, Annie White looked from one to the other of them. She was sure she'd never looked so good. "I am sick to death of Jeremy DaFoe."

Ed and Robert Porter were orphans, of a sort.

Back in the eighties, Stephen Porter, father of Robert, and Shelby Porter, father of Ed, ran the stills together with only a little opium refining on the side. These were the days before the meth trailers.

About half the moonshine stayed local and never made it north of Saint Louis. The rest was resold to the north. Stephen and Shelby knew the prices were higher in Chicago. Stephen and Shelby decided they were too big for Nuthatch County. They reasoned that northern money was rightfully theirs. They decided to take it to Chicago directly and bypass their regular buyers. In early March, they kissed their wives good-bye, piled into a rented thirty-five-foot truck, and went north carrying five tons of volatile fluids.

Two weeks later the truck was discovered burning cheerily next to Green Bay Road in Evanston. The bodies were found a few days later floating in the Chicago River, stained eerily green since the river had been dyed for Saint Patrick's Day.

Ed's mother, Helen, took Robert's mother, Kathleen, north to claim the bodies. The two women returned to the County, put their husbands in the ground, and took over the stills, all in stoic silence. Ed was thirteen. Robert was eight.

It was Kathleen who started making meth to make ends meet. She taught Robert the craft.

In 1989, Helen told Ed to take over both the stills and Robert. Then she and Kathleen left for parts west. That was the last time the boys ever heard from them. Ed was twenty. Robert was fifteen.

Everyone frequented Atkinson's Road House. But the Road House wasn't the only bar in the County.

Ridgeville supported two bars. Woody's was in Ashby. The Greenwood Tavern was in Ridgeville proper. Both bars were frequented exclusively by the residents of the neighborhood. It was a deep, dark secret that both were owned by Ray Bakerman.

Ray was sitting in Woody's nursing a beer. He was known in Ashby as someone a bit more accessible than his brother and less likely to judge. While everyone in Ashby was proud that Buddy was Eldest, Buddy didn't make the office any more approachable. Ray was a salesman. One of those rare breeds that could sell you anything without taking advantage of you. Ray believed in everything he did and belief is contagious.

Gradually, as the night wore on, the table where Ray sat began to fill. First with one earnest face. Then another. People Ray knew. People that knew Ray.

Ashby was troubled. Torn between what the new road might mean to them and going against Jeremy for the first time.

"I do disagree with him," said Ray at one point. Then: "Mister DaFoe expects our support because we've always given it to him." And: "I know we've always marched together in the parade. We turn and cheer him. That's one of the things we do for him." Finally: "No. I don't think I'm going this year. I think I'll go fishing instead."

Ed woke thinking of Robert, remembering the fawn and Robert's face when Ed killed it. He stared at the ceiling, trying to force sleep to come. But all he could see was the fawn, its screaming cut short in bloody relief by the roar of his rifle.

Rather than disturb Hannah and Sterling, he left and went down to Atkinson's for a dawn breakfast. He sat next to the window and stared into the darkness. It seemed filled with portents and activity he couldn't see.

Ed sopped up a last bit of egg with his toast when Robert sat down across from him. Ed was not surprised. Robert always seemed to know where he was.

What surprised him was when Glenn Waxman and Joseph Durant slipped into the booth.

"Good morning," Ed said cautiously.

"Top of the morning to you," said Robert cheerily. "Glenn has found a site. Joseph is going to supply it."

"Order." Ed waved at them. "Check's on me."

They ordered as Ed watched them.

Ed took in the three of them. Glenn he'd known since the boy came to work for Robert when he was sixteen. For a moment, he fondly remembered Glenn and Jenny's small wedding down at the First Baptist Church, Jenny's bump just beginning to show.

He knew Joseph Durant only peripherally. Nadine Durant's husband. Amos and Jean Durant's only child. Joseph was the son of the reservation representative on the County Commission. Not good. There'd been some rumor that Jean had wanted a girl—that reservation politics would somehow be affected by the sex of their offspring. But he knew little more than that. Ed watched Joseph a moment, noticed his thin face and fine fingers. Noticed the muscles on his arms and the condition of his teeth and skin. Joseph was not a meth head. Or an alcoholic.

"So," Ed thought out loud. "Tell me what you have, Joseph."

"Old lodge just off the southern edge of the reservation," Joseph said softly. "Still in good shape. I'll sell it to you."

Ed looked at Joseph and Glenn. "It's not reservation land."

"No," said Joseph.

"Whose land is it on?"

Joseph shrugged. "Who knows? I've been living there off and on for years. I dug a well. I wired it for a generator. Let you have it for five grand."

"You don't own the land."

"Nope."

Ed looked at Joseph, then back at Robert and Glenn. "What are you selling?"

"The lodge is in a little canyon, fifteen foot deep, no more than a hundred feet long and maybe forty feet wide. Never gets flooded for some reason so there's drainage. Covered over with trees. You can get within fifty yards of it from one of the roads but you'd never know it. You can set it on fire and the smoke would never get out from under the trees. Nobody's ever going to find it from the air or the road unless they know it's there."

"Ah," said Ed. "You're selling me a *location*. If I give you five thousand you give me a place on the map."

"Right."

"Did you build the lodge?"

"Rebuilt it. The original was built by old Tyson Porter to house his Osage honey, Sophie Bigheart."

Ed stared at Joseph. "Tyson Porter had a wife of his own."

Joseph shrugged. "True enough. But he had a little Osage girl he kept on the side."

"That's a damned lie."

Joseph shrugged again. "Think what you like. Like it or not, you have cousins all over the reservation. Tyson only kept it a secret from white people."

Ed looked at Glenn. Glenn's face was expressionless. Ed looked at Robert. Robert was suppressing deep laughter with great difficulty.

"Why come to me now?" Ed asked Joseph.

"There's a storm coming. I'm not going to be here when it hits."

"You're not taking Nadine?"

Joseph shook his head. "She'd never believe me. So: five grand or not?"

"I could kill you where you sit."

"The lodge and your cousins would still be there. It's up to you."

Ed looked out the window. There was now a bare hint of coming light though the stars could still be seen. He turned back to the table. "How long have you known?" he asked Robert quietly.

"My side of the family has chuckled over the Tyson branch for years."

"And now you reveal it in front of strangers."

"Strangers?" Robert laughed. "Joseph might just be one of your cousins. You never know. And Glenn here—" He reached over and pulled Glenn to him to rub his head with his fist. "Glenn is practically family."

Glenn closed his eyes in animal fear.

Ed rubbed the bridge of his nose wearily. The food came.

Joseph added Tabasco to his eggs. Robert munched on his toast. Glenn didn't look hungry.

Ed spoke at last, looking at Robert. "I don't carry that kind of money. Do you have five grand in cash?"

"Yes," mumbled Robert around a mouth full of egg.

"Of *course*, you do."

"Hey. I'm a businessman." Robert handed him the money as if it were the communion wafer.

Ed passed it to Joseph. "Here."

Joseph gave him a slip of paper. "Lat and long. You can use your GPS."

Ed didn't pick up the paper. "I don't have a GPS."

"Sure, you do. There's a Garmin in your truck. Robert has a handheld. What? You wanted me to lead you there? Not happening."

"What if it's a fake?"

"It's not but I take your meaning." Joseph indicated his truck outside the window. "I'm all packed up. I'm leaving after I finish breakfast."

Ed nodded. "Go check it out," Ed said to Robert. "Call me when you do."

Robert protested. "I'm eating here!"

"Take it with you or leave it. Your choice."

Robert grumbled and then grinned. He wolfed down the eggs and drained his coffee. Glenn started to follow him. Robert waved him down. "I got this."

Glenn looked miserable.

Ed felt a twinge of sympathy for Glenn. Ed would never work for Robert. Not in a million years.

Joseph ignored the interchange and applied his interest to his waffles, methodically enjoying each bite.

There was silence for the next twenty minutes. Then, Ed's cell rang.

"Yeah?"

"It's a sweet place. All covered over with forest canopy. Joseph wasn't kidding. If I hadn't known it was here, I'd never have found it. We don't have to pay him for it. I know a perch that overlooks the south road to Sikeston. I can nail him at a thousand yards."

"Okay." Ed hung up and thought a moment. "You done?"

Joseph finished his coffee and nodded.

"Robert says it's a good place. Keep the money. Joseph?"

Joseph looked up.

Ed stared him right in the eye. "Leave the County by the north road. Over the Bittersweet."

Joseph held his gaze for a moment. "Got it." He got up and left.

Ed turned to Glenn. Glenn hadn't spoken since he had sat down. He looked sick.

As well he might, reflected Ed. Now he knew a Porter family secret. That couldn't feel good.

"Go on home, Glenn." Ed waved towards the door. "Go see your wife and kids."

Glenn disappeared like a ghost.

Ed sipped his coffee, thinking about Tyson and some waif of a Native girl, the lodge, his brother, running the conversation over and over through his mind. He suddenly realized how his last words to Glenn might be taken as an indication to get his affairs in order. He chuckled to himself.

Ridgeville's Greenwood Tavern was quiet. Horace was behind the bar. A dozen or so white men—some at the bar, some at the tables—sipped or stared into their beer, either partaking of that particular communion or looking into it to see the future.

Power in Nuthatch County was primarily brokered by white

men—usually white men of Pilate. That was where the bank was. The lawyers. The homes possessed by white men of property. Even the County Commissioner, Pam Small, was viewed more as Pilate White Man than woman.

Ridgeville white men, on the other hand, were the shock troops of Nuthatch County. The rank and file. The proletariat. The men of Pilate controlled money and property. The men of Ridgeville were farmers or served farmers. Gas was sold in Pilate but the majority of car repair shops were in Ridgeville. Furniture was sold in Pilate but re-upholstered in Ridgeville. Tractors were sold in Pilate but the machine shops that kept the farm equipment running were to be found in Ridgeville.

Had this been England or some other European country, the men of Ridgeville and Pilate would have been natural antagonists. Located at opposite ends of the class structure, they would have seen each other as the enemy.

But America has the leavening power of race to mitigate such things. Instead of focusing their envy and rage on Pilate, the men of Ridgeville settled their red-rimmed gaze on the dark men of Ashby.

Lee Thomas nursed his beer at the bar. He was half-lit and whenever he felt that way his mind always came back to Catherine Meyers. Was it sex abuse when you were both twelve?

Lee Thomas could never get clear on the idea. Certainly, he'd been a willing—read *enthusiastic* or *eager*—partner in Catherine Meyers' sexual experimentation. After she'd dropped him as quickly and easily as someone might discard a sock, he had obsessed about her. All through high school. He'd followed her when she went on dates. Spied on her with binoculars he'd purchased with money he'd stolen from his father. Not knowing what else to do with his life, Lee had joined his father's plumbing and electrician business. Digging out ditches to put in sewer lines and replacing septic systems gave him plenty of time to think. It's easy to consider your life while wielding a nine-pound sledge and facing forty feet of limestone to crack.

He watched Catherine play around with all sorts of (to his mind) shady characters. Played with *them* and not *him*. Then, she went off and got herself pregnant. Just like people said she would. Lee would have been perfectly happy to forgive and marry her but she never gave him time to broach the subject. Three years later, she brought home that Prescott fellow and married him.

It was enough to turn a man against women for good.

But he hadn't. Instead, he'd ended up with Sarah. A hard woman who'd been raised in a shack in the close and secret woods below White Bluffs. Sarah did not speak of her childhood but Lee knew that he had stood out as an opportunity to escape. She'd been saved as a Jehovah's Witness while she was pregnant. After the mess of Franklin's birth, she decided Jesus didn't think much of sex and left Lee for the purer salvation of Colorado. Franklin hadn't done much better. He took up with a waitress in Sikeston named Evie and lived with her for nearly a year. A month after the baby was born Franklin came home from the plastics factory to find little Carl screaming his head off, a note taped to the crib that said only "Rent's due on the tenth." Baby Carl in hand, Franklin had come home to Ridgeville on the ninth. Lee had taken him in. There was always room in his plumbing business for his son.

Now, all three of them, Lee, Franklin, and Carl, sat in a line at the bar, drinking Bud and staring at the mirror over the bar. It was Carl's twenty-first birthday and the first time he could be in the Tavern legally. Not that it was much more than a formality. As soon as Carl had been old enough to push a nickel over the counter there'd been a beer next to it.

To a man, they preferred Porter's Piss to this watery brew. But traditions must be observed.

Carl roused himself. "Hey Pop. What's the Klan doing for the parade this year?"

Franklin sipped his beer thoughtfully. "We haven't talked about it."

"How can that be?" Carl stared at him. "It's only a couple of weeks."

"To tell the truth," said Franklin. "None of us had much interest."

"Be a shame to not have a float," Lee mused. "I always sort of liked the flatbed with the cross burning in the back."

"We can't use the flatbed." Franklin shook his head. "Burnt to a crisp last year."

"No!" Lee turned to Franklin. "How'd that happen?"

"Nigras," Franklin said flatly.

"Nigras," echoed Carl. "Fucking nigras."

"Ah," said Lee. "Fucking nigras." Though, privately, he figured it had more to do with drunken Klansmen failing to make sure there weren't any lit embers left behind.

"Atwater was pissed," said Carl. "It was his flatbed."

"I bet." Lee drank a little more Budweiser. This stuff wasn't bad if you sort of squinted and imagined you were somewhere else when you drank it.

"Besides, parading down the street in front of Jeremy." Franklin shook his head. "Didn't have the heart for it."

"How come?" Lee drained his beer and knocked on the counter. Horace brought a refill in his own sweet time.

"The road." Franklin looked uncomfortable. "We could have made money from the road."

"How do you figure?"

"I was talking to Harry Carr," Franklin leaned on the bar, a dim measure of enthusiasm entering his voice. "Harry figured the road was only the beginning. After all, once you've dug up the road bed, why not put in a real sewer system? We could run pipe from Ridgeville all the way to Pilate and tap into their facility."

"Likely overrun it."

"Still be a damned sight better than that old system we have south of town. How many times have you been roused out to repair that old pump? Remember Christmas of eighty-nine?" Franklin shook his head.

Lee closed his eyes and shuddered. The pump had frozen solid, burst its casing, and forty thousand gallons of raw sewage had poured down Bluegill Creek into the Bluewater River and right down to the Mississippi. Right through the middle of the Reservation so the Natives got riled up. Broke all manner of federal regulations—only Luke had stood between the EPA and County bankruptcy.

Covered in frozen shit, the two of them had replaced pipe, valves, and housing. One minute warmed in the decomposing warmth of the water. The next, their clothes stiff with ice from the northern wind. When they'd finally managed to fix the pump and get control of the flow, they came to the same idea at the same moment and stripped, right there on the concrete apron, and hosed themselves off in the freezing wind. They threw their clothes in the dumpster and drove home naked.

"But now there's no road," Franklin said morosely.

"How does that make you want to drop out of the parade?"

Franklin didn't say anything for a moment. "It seemed to us," he said. "When we were talking about it at the meeting that when we walk in front of Jeremy, we're somehow saying we *support* him. We're saying what he does to us is *okay*." He looked up at Lee. "And it's *not*. So, we're just not going to go this year. Let other people walk in front of that damned grandstand and grin at him. We're staying home."

Nadine woke that morning to find Joseph gone.

This came as no surprise. However, being expected was no

protection against a pang she felt in her chest when his side of the bed was determinedly empty in the morning light. Not for the first time—Not the tenth. Not the hundredth—she thought she should just give up on Joseph and find some nice little woman of her own. She dismissed the idea with the ease of long habit. It seemed that the heart wanted what it wanted in spite of logic, loneliness, and sexual orientation.

Nadine was an early riser. The sky was merely a colorless glow in the east when she entered the kitchen. She sat down at the table with breakfast. Coffee: *check*. Toast: *check*. Day planner: *check*. Folder of current projects: *check*.

She opened the folder.

She'd commissioned a survey out of petty cash. Surprisingly, there was a small PR firm in Ridgeville—Bakerman Public Relations—willing to do a quick phone poll. She'd disguised her intention by burying the road question in the middle of other questions about the future of the County. Should we continue to have our own electric company or delegate authority to the SEMO Cooperative? The County bought most of its power from SEMO anyway. Should four new wells be dug on the west side because it was comparatively cheap to do so now even though there was, as yet, no demand for the water? (And might never be, thought Nadine to herself.) Should the County repair the road between Pilate and Ridgeville or build a new one?

The results had been interesting. The Reservation had mixed opinions. Pilate and Ridgeville proper came down solidly on the side of a new road. Ashby came down just as solidly against it but Nadine attributed that to Ashby's undying loyalty to Jeremy. The plan was to take these statistics and bring them up with Pam. The two of them, together, would confront Jeremy.

Nadine had known Jeremy all of her life. Perhaps it was her upbringing in Washington but she had never held any image of Jeremy as just another farmer. Hanging out with Jeremy was like spending time with Jesus. While Nathan Collins had probably known what he was starting when he took in that runaway slave, it had still taken the destruction of Lyle Williams to stir Collins into freeing the slaves. Nadine hoped it wouldn't come to that. But she was prepared for anything.

There was a knock on her front door.

She glanced out the window. The sun was now painting the east in all possible shades of red and purple, limning the higher clouds in gold.

Nadine put down her coffee and walked to the front door. Part of her thought that Joseph wanted back in—he'd locked himself out and forgotten his key. Mindless idiocy in the name of love? *Check.*

It was a young man standing on her doorstep.

She opened the door. "Yes? Can I help you?"

"Hi," he said, holding out his hand. "My name is Glenn Waxman. I need to talk to a lawyer."

"My office hours don't start until nine and my office is in Pilate."

"I can't be seen talking to you."

"Really. Why not?"

"Can we talk inside?"

Nadine looked at him. Waxman was a little man. Nadine thought she could take him. "Okay. Want some coffee?"

"Oh, no," said Glenn as he followed her inside, looking nervously around. "I never take any stimulants."

Great. I've let a kook in my house.

She led him into the kitchen and gestured to the chair opposite hers. Nadine sat down and picked up her coffee. "What can I do for you?"

"Everything I say to you is private? Like talking to a doctor?"

"If you're planning to commit a crime, I'm obliged to report it."

"What about crimes I've already committed?"

"What do you want, Mister Waxman?"

"I work for Robert Porter. I run his... *trailers*."

"Ah." Nadine leaned back in her chair. "I understand your nervousness. But how can I help you?"

"I need *protection*."

"Are you going to turn him in?"

Glenn looked as if he were sucking lemons. "That's the problem. If he even suspects that, I'll end up buried on Bittersweet Ridge."

Nadine nodded. "If we were in Saint Louis. Or even Sikeston. Or Cairo. We could go to the DEA and turn Porter in. It would be dangerous—they'd use you to get evidence." She shrugged. "But we're here in Nuthatch County. The DEA doesn't know this place exists. Now and then the DEA traces something to the Porters. Or the ATF finds a lead on the stills. And then the lead dries up and disappears."

Glenn stared at her. "Jeremy does that?"

Nadine shook her head. "Of course not. I'd be surprised Jeremy was even aware of it. Our *government* does it. I don't *know* that people have been 'disappeared.' But I do know the Feds have a vested interest in maintaining the status quo where Jeremy is concerned. If that means letting a meth lab operate or ignoring a still, they'll do it."

Glenn looked like he wanted to squeak. "What can I *do*?"

"Do you have any money?"

"Some."

"Family?"

"Wife and two kids."

"Take them and run. Porter won't chase you. He knows the score as well as I do. He'll replace you in a week."

Glenn looked miserable. "I have land here."

"You'll have to give it up."

"That's my only choice?"

Nadine tilted her head and looked at him. A germ of an idea

came to her. Certainly, she had told the exact truth to Glenn. She knew the Porters had lived unmolested for over a century. Jeremy didn't bother about them. Jeremy had created the world of Nuthatch County largely by neglect. Whatever vision he had about this place, it accommodated people like the Porters just fine.

Nadine had the statistics on her laptop but she didn't need to look at them. She'd lived with them for years. For whatever reason, the addiction rate in Nuthatch County was much lower than in the rest of the state or the country. The County had essentially unlimited access to meth and moonshine but did not become dependent on it. She had no idea whether this was because of some mystic radiation coming from Jeremy or because the society of the County was so torqued by his presence there was no *room* for addiction. Those were the facts.

That said, Waxman here really represented a larger problem. What did it say about Jeremy that Waxman essentially had to choose between exile and death? Could this be presented to Jeremy as a *moral* problem? What were Jeremy's morals, anyway? She'd seen him in church but that meant nothing out here. Lonely people were desperate for social functions. Bars and churches served the same function. One served alcohol; one didn't—mostly. First Methodist used wine in its communion. First Baptist substituted grape juice.

She drummed her fingers on the tabletop. Waxman could be the thin end of the wedge. Jeremy didn't even have to make a decision himself; he just had to see that such a decision could be made without his authority.

Hm. What would have happened if they hadn't even mentioned the road at County Meeting? If they had just *done* it. Would Jeremy have made a fuss? Here, in the case of Glenn Waxman, why even *involve* Jeremy? Thinking about it: how had the DEA been sidetracked before? They must have checked with the home office in some way. That crossed some threshold to bring the Porters to Washington's attention and they squashed it.

She didn't know how the DEA operated out here but she had contacts back in Washington. They couldn't clear every little thing with the home office. The Porters were a big source of meth but they were nothing compared to any Chicago gang. Nadine didn't think a Porter bust would involve more than a regional office. Yet, it had to have been stopped by someone who knew the score. Someone whose job it was to figure such things out and squash such things.

Nadine had a sudden vision of a vast bureaucracy, its sole purpose to keep Nuthatch County and Jeremy DaFoe quiet.

Thereby putting poor Glenn Waxman in the crosshairs. *Sorry old man. No hard feelings, eh?*

It riled her, and the acid of her anger burned through her brown, waxy life. Wasn't shit like this *why* she became an attorney? Wasn't this the sort of thing she was trying to get back to Washington to *do?* The road was one thing. Trying to get back to Washington was one thing. This *kid* was another. Why the hell had she been out here sitting on her ass all these years?

"You go home," she said. "You tell no one you've spoken to me. Not a soul. Not your wife. Not your kids. Let me think about this. Let me see what I can do."

Nadine knew Waxman might be considered expendable by Higher Powers. Maybe she was, too. But she was, by *God*, the County Clerk here. She was the daughter of Luke Prescott. She was married to the well-known, respected, and failed attempt at peace between the two tribes of the Bluewater Reservation. If they put her in the ground there would be *questions*.

You had to start somewhere. Why not start with Glenn Waxman?

Wallace Payton's farm was on the southern end of the Reservation. He grew mostly subsistence crops such as corn, soybeans, and a broad garden. He and Betty DaFoe sometimes shared a truck going to the Sikeston Market. He kept fifty or so steers and a couple dozen hogs that he sold for cash money. Most of his income came from his equipment: hauling gravel for the County in his dump truck, digging out a septic system with his backhoe, clearing out a pond with his bulldozer. Wallace's father had come back from Korea with contacts in the army. When obsolete heavy equipment was replaced down at Fort Leonard Wood, this Native from Nuthatch County showed up to claim it.

Wallace's earliest boyhood memories were of greasing trucks and filling tanks with hydraulic fluid. Driving past the rusting road equipment next to the road between Ridgeville and Pilate gave him an almost sexual thrill.

He was dropping a load of gravel in Hugh Utterback's driveway when Amos waved at him from the road. Wallace finished emptying his dump truck just as Utterback came out sputtering.

"It was supposed to be *next* to the driveway. Not *on* the driveway."

Wallace glanced at the judge from the cab as he wrote up the delivery ticket. "Be easier to spread this way."

"How am I supposed to get my *car* out?"

Wallace looked around. There was lawn on both sides. "Drive around?"

"That'll hurt the grass."

"The grass'll be okay."

"That's *zoysia* grass. It cost fourteen dollars a square foot! I can't just *drive* over it."

"Ah," said Wallace, finishing his delivery ticket. "Tell you what. I can bring by my spreader tomorrow with a couple of men and finish the driveway if you want."

Hugh stared at him.

Wallace knew what he was thinking. Hugh had planned to call up Harry and get the town to spread it for free. But Harry was going to be busy for the next three days resurfacing County Road 7—Wallace knew this because he was contracted to deliver the gravel. If Hugh wanted the driveway spread out tomorrow, he'd have to actually *pay* for it.

Hugh opened his mouth. Closed it. He waved his hand weakly. "Yeah. Just get somebody over here *early*."

"Sure thing, Judge." He handed Hugh the bill, let the clutch out, and drove down the hill to the road. Amos opened the door and got in.

"Where's your car?" Wallace turned onto the road, turned again, and was on Main Street going towards the main road.

"Leonard dropped me off. He knew you were over here."

"Ah." Wallace wrestled the dump truck around a narrow curve. "I heard a good one. How does Jeremy change a light bulb?"

"I don't know."

"He holds the light bulb and the county turns underneath him."

Amos snorted. "I like that one."

"Need some work tomorrow?"

"I can't handle a spreader."

"I'll handle the spreader. Go on over to John Blackbird's gravel pit and take a load over to County Road 7. Carr is surfacing the road." Wallace tapped the steering wheel. "Take the big truck—number four. Might take three or four trips."

Amos nodded. "First thing."

Wallace glanced at Amos as they turned onto the main road. "So, what do you want?"

"Are you planning to march in the parade?"

"Right next to my old man in the Choctaw section. Just like every year. He's going to wear his uniform even though it's getting pretty tight. I told him to get Sally to let it out some or he's going to fall over on Third Street for lack of oxygen. He said to fuck off. He can hold his breath that long."

"Don't go."

"Why the hell not?"

"I've been talking with other folks in the tribe. We need to send a message to Jeremy that *something is wrong*. If the Choctaw don't show up—or at least not many of us—he'll get the message."

Wallace watched the road equipment as they drove by. What he could do with that *grader!* That *bulldozer!* "Why not have the committee put together a protest float? A big sign that says 'Jeremy! We need the Goddamned Road!'" Wallace held up his hand. "No! Wait! I understand. It's the *Secret* Bluewater Reservation Road Committee."

"If we boycott the parade, we have to do it as the Choctaw Nation, not the Road Committee."

"You mean the Secret Choctaw *Casino* Committee."

Amos smiled thinly at him. "Exactly."

Wallace didn't speak for a moment. "So, you're going to get the whole tribe to stay out of the parade."

"One Choctaw at a time. So: Are you going?"

"Let me talk to the old man."

"Good. Let me off at Atkinson's."

As Amos got out of the truck, Wallace called after him. "If I can persuade him to stay home the one day of the year he can march with the tribe, I'm going to try for *your* job next."

Amos looked up at him. He didn't smile. "You wouldn't like it."

Jean didn't make her living just from telling fortunes and casting spells. Nor did her Womyn Outings bring in much in the way of cash. She did try putting together a seminar on the Kama Sutra once. It created a lot of interest but Jean made the mistake of advertising it openly. She found that while exotic sex generated a lot of curiosity in Nuthatch County, not many were willing to admit it in public. Her position in the Osage tribe gave her many opportunities to attain status and influence, but not so many in the way of generating income.

At one point in the late sixties, an apparently overly ambitious developer named Morris Wilson tried to build a narrow strip mall on the main road at the edge of the reservation. No one ever knew why Wilson had not picked Pilate or Ridgeville or even Atkinson's modest location instead of a flat spot of road five miles from public water and sewer and bordering on Native land. But he poured an acre of asphalt parking lot and raised a bright yellow stretch of garish store fronts. People came for miles to look at it. They parked in the lot and looked at the glass fronts. No one bought anything, of course. There were no stores behind the glass. Wilson disappeared, abandoning a half-million-dollar note on a bank in New Madrid—the bank in Pilate had laughed him out of the office.

The bank in New Madrid tried to recoup its losses but found no buyers. Finally, they put it up for auction and Jean quietly picked it up for pennies on the dollar. No one ever connected her cousin Morris from Mississippi with the bankrupt visionary.

In this crumbling monument to 1960s sensibilities, she put her small shop: *Alternativities*. It blended the two things she thought might sell the best. Alternativities sold organic soaps and oils next to Christmas ornaments and plastic Santas. She picked the herbs herself and renamed them extravagantly. Wooly mullein became Vitality Tea. Yarrow became Sutramin. Various forms of colored water possessed names suggesting amazing properties. King Sexoline. Heartful Infusion. Was there a *Santa Sutra*? she wondered. And could she make a buck out of it?

Jean was creative in her purchasing. Once she had picked up a hundred tubes of camouflage face paint from military surplus. She promptly repackaged it into small vials and marketed it as a night time moisturizer. For years there were women (and some men) who went to sleep looking, and smelling, as if they were on patrol in Viet Nam.

She never accepted anything but cash.

Now and then, whenever someone had more dreams than sense, she'd get a neighbor in one or the other adjacent storefronts. But in recent years the old sixties construction had begun to fall apart. Jean had been thinking carefully about fire insurance policies and lightning strikes. She wondered if Morris was still in business.

This day the shop was filled not with customers but with the members of the Bluewater Reservation Historical Preservation Society sitting around two card tables. The ancient air conditioner clanked and barely moved the flies but did manage to cause condensation to form on every glass, concrete, or tile surface. Jean served iced tea, which was now donating its share of atmospheric water to the tables. She watched a gradual stream from each glass eventually join and fall off the edge in a steady drip, drip, drip. Maybe she should have served coffee.

"Amos is trying to keep every Choctaw out of the parade," announced Vituria Dillard.

Jean fixed her with a glance. "Are *you* going to march?"

Vituria wavered and glanced at Ida.

Ida—one eye moving, one eye fixed—sipped her tea. "It's going to look damned strange if only *Osage* march in the parade."

"Is Amos going to try to get the Osage to back off, too?" Charlena Bigheart seemed to address the question to the room but Jean knew, as ranking Osage in the room, that it was really aimed at her.

"Nobody on the tribal council has said a thing," said Jean. "But while Amos hasn't said anything *publicly*, he hasn't been very secretive, either. He knows just as many Osage want that road as Choctaw. Like Ida says: it's going to feel mighty strange walking down the street with only half of the reservation represented."

"Not even that," said Louise Moncravie. "Everyone wants to be part of the herd. If most of the herd stays home, the rest will follow. Amos knows this."

"Yes," said Jean. "He does."

Ida put her glass down. "If it looks strange with only the Osage showing up, it's going to look *really* strange with only a handful. Or just us." She looked around. Her bad eye seemed to spasm and rolled in a circle.

Jean had to look away. "We have only three options. We try to stop Amos. We don't do anything. We help him."

Ida shook her head. "We don't have to *help* him. We just have to not get in the way. If he's successful, Jeremy will know something's wrong and it won't be our fault. If he's not, we haven't lost anything. I don't think we'll lose, either way."

"All right, then," said Jean. "Are we agreed? We do not oppose him?"

There was a chorus of agreements.

"Okay." Jean looked at all of them, each in turn. "Amos doesn't know about us yet. He thinks his little committee is secret. Ours is. I want to keep it that way."

Ida snorted. "Of course."

John Blackbird, Vice-President of the Secret Bluewater Reservation Road Committee and brother of Jean Blackbird Durant, breathed heavily and rolled on his side.

"Old man sex is like an elephant dancing," he said. "You don't care how well he manages. Just that he *can*."

Ida Durant, Co-Chairman of the Bluewater Reservation Historical Preservation Society and sister to Amos Durant, punched him gently in the side. "Shut up," she said and kissed him.

Chapter 7: The Underlying Purpose of Legitimate Action

For the Fourth of July, the County Commissioner's official duties were limited. The Independence Day Preparations Committee was supposed to take care of everything. In practice, the County Clerk took applications regarding floats up to the deadline (end of March) and passed them on to the Parade Marshall. The Parade Marshall then figured out the order of the floats, the marching bands, the groups, and everything else. For the last twenty years, Jake Withers and Grace Cox had been alternating. This year was Grace's turn.

This left Pam time to concentrate on her real job: managing the County.

She'd given up on the road as a thing. But after talking with Betty, she began to reconsider her position. Not that she didn't want the road—the County *needed* the road—but maybe it didn't have to be done *all at once*. After all, a defeat in battle wasn't the same as losing the war.

Pam was grateful that the state had accidentally left the equipment next to the road. It was going to make her proposals easier to get through.

Start small.

When she looked over the road for pieces that not even Jeremy could argue with, the two ends suggested themselves. One was the old airport road that went to gravel across the White Bluffs and only regained its asphalt next to runway 23. There were also the Bittersweet switchbacks. The gravel was easy; the switchbacks were hard. But the switchbacks would open the road north to Cairo and Cape Girardeau. Open to the hospital. New markets. The *whole* road would make the *whole* County accessible. But the whole County would still benefit from opening up just the road north. The road to the airport would be good. It would shave some time off getting to Sikeston. But without the connector north to the interstate, it was a only minor improvement.

But which one, if either, could she get through the fall meeting?

Probably the Sikeston road, she thought sourly.

Then don't bring it up. Don't mention it. Just lay out the problems with the north road. How many accidents have there been? How many people were forced to get serious care at the clinic when they would be better managed up at Southeast and were kept here by nothing more than a bad road? And how could she show it?

Pam shuffled through her papers. She had admissions to the clinic and discharges. Diagnosis. Severity. Carter would talk about it—he'd talk about nothing else if given half a chance. Carter cared more for the clinic than he cared for his mother. Although it sure looked like Joanie Durant was giving the clinic a run for its money.

Pam chuckled to herself. She didn't begrudge Carter anything. They'd had their brief moment years ago and the memory was sweet. But Pam liked being County Commissioner and Carter loved his clinic. They had knocked heads together too many times over County politics to ever let their guard down long enough to make something work.

But it looked like Joanie had finally gotten under his skin. Much deeper than Pam had ever managed.

Okay. Maybe she begrudged it a *little*.

Short as it had been, that time with Carter had been really fun and it had been a *long* time.

Humming to herself, Pam returned to her work. She'd need a study. It was nearly July. Could she get something to present by August? Wait—wasn't there a study back in the eighties? *Yes.* A whole new road survey. She could use that. She'd need a preliminary estimate—could she get some help from Luke? Maybe get a road crew out here? She had to call him—maybe he could get an answer back to her when she saw him on the Fourth.

Pam pulled out her laptop and started crafting an email to Luke, feeling suddenly lucky to love her job this much.

After ten years Betty had the fourth of July down to a science.

She didn't go in for fashion but she also didn't like getting up on the reviewing bleachers next to Jeremy looking like she just came in out of the field. So: Step One, get a new dress. Step Two, get her hair done. Step Three, plan an evening with Jeremy the night before, because by the end of the fireworks she'd be either too drunk or too tired or both. Planning was necessary.

Step One involved a side trip to Dress Barn after she'd sold all of her produce in the Sikeston market. Which involved a quick change in the truck since she was *not* going to buy a dress while covered in dirt and smelling like manure. Every year, two weeks before the fourth, she gave up one little prayer of thanks for the person who invented waterless hand cleaner and another for whoever thought to package it in large containers. Maybe they were the same person. A double blessing upon them.

Step Two often happened along with step one since Antonio's wasn't far from the Dress Barn.

Step Three required forethought. Not for any scheduling reason but because she wanted a little adventure every year.

Buddy was waiting for her on the bench at her house when she returned from Sikeston.

"Hey there!" she called as she parked the truck. "Give me a hand."

In a moment Buddy was covered with boxes and plastic bags. She opened the door and led him in. "Put it on the sofa. I'll get lemonade."

"Actual lemonade," he said as he set the packages down on the sofa. "Without any… additives."

"You're no fun." She was still excited by the shopping trip. She wondered if the novelty would ever wear off. Imagine getting a new dress every, say, month? She poured lemonade for the two of them and brought the cool glasses back. "It's got to be ninety."

"Ninety-two," Buddy said. "You should get air conditioning."

"What? And give up my very own home sauna? How you talk."

"Yeah."

Betty looked at him for a moment. "What's going on?"

"I think I want to show you something."

"Okay."

"Better change your clothes and bring a bathing suit." He sipped his lemonade again. "This will get messy."

They left the car in the Fox Park lot and half an hour later they were standing at the mouth of the cave below the base of Little Mountain.

"I've been in Fox Cave, Buddy," she said. "It's one of the prime make-out spots in the County." She chuckled "Though I think the attraction palls after you get your own place. Damp clay does not compare to a real bed."

"Yeah," Buddy said absentmindedly. "You'll need this." He gave her a flashlight.

He led her through the narrow entrance into the first gallery. Then, a quick edging through what they'd called the Gate when she was a kid. The last gallery ended in a pool of frigid water.

The room was ghostly. There was graffiti all over the walls but somehow the gray rock walls shone through.

Buddy put down his light and backpack and started taking off his shirt.

"We're going for a swim?" Betty asked.

"That's why I said bring a swim suit."

"Sorry," she said. "I remember this water. It's cold as a witch."

Buddy pulled a plastic bag out of his backpack. "Put your clothes into this."

"Didn't you hear me? I said I'm not—"

"How much do you want to know about Jeremy?"

"What?"

Buddy shook his head. "Strange things are going on in the County right now. I'm getting worried. I have to show somebody a secret. Who am I going to tell? My kids are grown and up in Chicago. My wife is dead."

Betty tried to see his face but it was lost in the gloom. "Your secret is in the pool?"

"Through the hole in the back."

"That's dangerous, Buddy. There was a kid who drowned back there when I was in high school."

"Yeah. I know. Willie Baslim. I remember." He took a deep breath. "He took the wrong passageway. I won't. I've been back there several times. I'm an old man and I can hold my breath for thirty seconds. Surely you can do at least that well."

"I don't want to."

"Betty: it's important. Really."

Betty knew she was going to do it. She shook her head at herself and started taking off her clothes. "You get stuck and I'll leave you."

"I won't get stuck."

The water was even colder than she remembered and when it hit her thighs, she almost stopped breathing. In a fit of anger, she pushed the rest of the way in. Her chest spasmed as if laughing. Buddy didn't say anything. He swam to the far wall and slowly pointed his light down. He took off his pack and held onto it. "Ready?"

Betty took several quick breaths. "Yeah."

Buddy did the same and then he was below the surface pushing the bag in front of him, his light a dimming glow.

Betty followed. The cold of the water made her head ache. She started counting. At thirty she planned to turn back, Buddy or no Buddy.

But Buddy's light started to rise after a few seconds and she broke the surface next to him.

It was a small gallery, barely bigger than the pool but with a small sandy ledge on one side. Buddy crawled up on the ledge, breathing heavily. "I'm too old for this."

Betty pulled herself up next to him. "I'm cold."

Buddy pulled out the plastic bag containing her clothes. "Here. Scrape as much water off as you can with your hand and put these on."

Now that she was sitting on the ledge, she could see the room had several passageways that led away from the pool. "Where are we?"

"About fifteen feet below the base of Little Mountain. We go up from here." Buddy pulled two spools of string from his pack. He handed one to Betty. "Tie it off to one of the stalactites. Make sure it's good and tight. I don't want to get lost here."

"No one knows about this place?"

"There might be a couple of old farts like me that know about this room. I don't think anybody living knows where we're going."

Once they were tied off, he led her into the far passage. He walked without pause past several branches, spooling out the string behind them. When the spools were empty, he put his on the ground and gestured for her to do the same.

"There aren't any more branches. If we find some, we're lost and we come back here. So, if I have a heart attack or a stroke or something you come back here, find the string, and go get help."

"Okay."

Buddy hesitated. "There's some unpleasantness on the way."

She stared at him. "Unpleasantness?"

"There was at least one person that didn't get out."

"There's a *body* in this place?"

"No. Not really. A skeleton. We walk past it." Buddy stopped for a moment. "Well, *most* of a body. The skull and right arm. Somebody put it in an alcove to one side."

"Now you tell me."

"Would you have come if I'd mentioned it?"

"Are you kidding?"

"Exactly." He turned back up the passageway.

"Who was it?"

"I have no idea. He's been here a long time."

The passage stayed roughly man-height but narrowed at times or widened, shortened, and grew tall. At one point Buddy stopped. "Father Fred," he said and pointed with the light.

"You named him?"

Buddy shrugged.

"Fred" had been carefully placed on a pedestal carved out of the rock. His hand, wrist bones, and arm bones were intact and had been fastened together in some way. The upper humerus ended where the shoulder should have been just to the right of the skull. It looked stapled to the wall. The resulting arm hung down in front of the skull and bent up at the wrist as if giving a blessing.

"I get it. 'Father Fred.' You're a ghoul, Buddy."

Buddy led her on until the passage opened into a wide gallery. Buddy held up his light.

Every exposed surface—walls, floor, ceiling—were covered with paintings. Men. Animals. Mountains. Trees.

"Oh, Buddy," she breathed.

"Sit over there. That way you won't step on anything that's not already damaged."

She carefully made her way over to one side and sat down. Buddy sat beside her.

"I forgive you," she said softly. "This was worth the coldest swim of my life."

"Thanks."

Brown shaded into yellow and black as if painted on silk. Reds were bright and vibrant with depth, like the reds of a sunset or a rose. Like most people, Betty had seen pictures of the cave paintings in France and there was a strong resemblance here. Human shapes were stylized—advanced sort of stick figures yet with heft and form—but animals were rendered with careful attention to details. Unlike the French paintings, these animals were all new world. There were a few predators: bobcat, cougar, and wolf. The animal-scape was dominated by deer and elk, leavened by a couple of buffalo.

"How old do you think it is?"

Buddy shrugged. "No telling without tests of some sort. Grandpa Norton thought it was as old as the ones in France but I doubt it. People haven't been in the New World that long." Buddy looked at her shyly. "I saw the caves in Lascaux."

"No!"

"Honest. After the Italian campaign was over, we were stationed in North Italy until the Germans surrendered. Then, we stayed as part of the occupation force. Norton wrote me about them and said if I had the opportunity, I should go see them. He gave me some names. At one point they needed to drive some material over to Paris and I volunteered. Once we dropped off the trucks, I had a little leave. So, I managed to con a jeep out of the motor pool and drove south to Lascaux. The people Norton mentioned helped me out. Met this woman named Genevieve there." Buddy sounded suddenly wistful. "You know, in Europe, they have a completely different take on the color of your skin."

He shook his head. "Anyway, I spent a day or two looking them over before I went back to my outfit." He pointed with his flashlight. "These are a little different. Most of the human figures in France don't have faces. But if you look closely at these there are suggestions of eyes and mouth. And look at that one." He stopped a flashlight on one figure: a man with an animal's head.

"Is that a wolf?"

"I think it's a fox. Look at this one." He stopped a flashlight on another one.

Betty stared at it. "It looks like he has red hair."

"I think that's supposed to be fire."

Betty shone her flashlight across the room. Now that she had noticed the fox-head and fire-head figures she saw them over and over. Here, Fox-head was running. Here he was throwing a spear. Fire-head usually stood nearby. Often, figures crowned with neither fox nor fire gave things to him.

"Look over here," Buddy said softly and pointed his flashlight to one corner of the room.

Fox-head was running but he was on fire. Lightning came down on him. Betty followed the lightning trail back to Fire-head's upstretched hands.

"Oh, my God," she breathed. "It's Jeremy."

Buddy nodded. "Fox's Chimney. Fox Cave. All we have left are the names. Are these pictures a legend they put down? A mythological clash between demi-gods? Actual history? I keep thinking there's a sequence here." He panned his flashlight from one side of the room to the other. "Here is Fox running. Here is Fox hunting. Here Fox and Fire shake hands. Are they friends? Colleagues? Brother deities? Other people dance around them in celebration. Or is it supplication? Notice offerings are made to Fire but not to Fox. Fox is always running with other people or after the animals: a deer, a cougar. Fire waves to him but he always stands off a little by himself except when he's standing with Fox. Is Fox a priest? Then, Fire sends the lightning and Fox doesn't appear after that. Is that bad? Good? A sign of accepted sacrifice or divine punishment?"

Betty stared at the pictures. "What do you think?"

"I think I'm too scared to ask Jeremy what it means."

The conversation with Matt Tibbett was short. Nadine called him up. As soon as he realized who was on the phone, he tried to talk her into coming back to Washington.

"What about the road?" she asked.

"Who cares about the road? We want you back."

"It was *your* idea I finish up the road."

"And it's *my* idea it's not so important that it should keep you in that Podunk place longer than necessary. Finish up and come back to the firm."

Nadine shook her head. Everything changes. "Okay. But I need some names. I need a contact person for the DEA in Saint Louis." She thought a moment. "ATF, too. Someone who doesn't have to beg permission for every little thing."

"Why?"

"It's for a client. I need somebody with muscle. I'm tossing them a shark so they don't go after my little trout."

Matt put her on hold for a moment. "Jonas Cole for the DEA.

Tell him I sent you. The ATF is a bit tougher. It's a woman named Kate Marquis. I don't know her but I'm told she'll hear you out. Does that mean you're done out there?"

"No. I'm staying here for now."

"Why? No road is that important."

"To hell with the road."

When Nadine reached Saint Louis, she drove over to the DEA regional office. Nothing defined this particular office park from any other office space save the DEA logo on the door and the name badge on the receptionist.

"I need to speak to Jonas Cole," Nadine read the nametag again. "Pat."

"What's this regarding?"

"I wish to give information on a crime."

"What sort of information?"

"That is why I'd like to speak with Mister Cole."

Pat watched her a moment. "Take a seat."

Nadine sat down. As she looked around, the office had lush accouterments not normally associated with federal establishments: the DEA's chairs were not threadbare. The carpet was not worn and was still clean. The glass was clear and unscratched. Still, though the voice was muted, the color of the walls, the bland pictures, and a rack of anti-drug pamphlets spoke clearly that your federal government was looking out for *you*. All governmental spaces ultimately looked the same. Maybe all governmental spaces were really one place. Maybe she could pick the right door and walk out of Saint Louis and into the Bostetter Courthouse in Alexandria. The John F Kennedy Building in Boston. The Kluczynski Building in Chicago.

After all those years in Washington sitting in Veterans Affairs, Department of Agriculture, or Health and Human Services offices, this was almost like coming home.

A dark-haired man came into the waiting area. He was

clearly in the post-ingénue phase of his career. No longer the brash young agent, but not yet into the weathered salt stage. "I'm Agent Jonas Cole. You are?"

"Nadine Durant," Nadine said as she rose and put out her hand. "Nuthatch County Clerk."

He took her hand, shook it, let it drop, led her back to his office. He sat her down and watched her for a moment. "And I can help you… how?"

"There's a complex of meth labs down near New Madrid. I can point them out to you. There are also a collection of stills. Have you ever heard of Robert Porter?"

Cole gave her a long look. "Yes."

"I can give him to you. Can you put together a raid by yourself?"

"How big a raid?"

"I know of two labs. There may be a third one but I don't know where it is."

Cole thought for a moment. "I can put together one team."

"We'll have to make a choice. What about the stills?"

"I have friends over at ATF. They're just a couple of blocks from here."

"Ask them about 'Porter's Piss.' That should get their attention."

"Later, maybe. If this pans out."

Nadine shook her head. "That won't work. You need to put together two raids to happen at the same time. One for the stills. One for the labs."

"You let me worry about that. Where are the two labs?"

"Have you got a map?"

"I can do better. I can show you satellite imagery."

Nadine shook her head. "They won't show on the satellite. Just give me a map." She smiled at him.

He scrutinized her closely. Nadine looked back steadily.

Something satisfied him and he reached down into his

drawer and rummaged out until he found a pair of maps. "Can you read a topographic map?"

Years of handling zoning disputes had their worth. "Yes." She pulled out her reading glasses and looked over the North New Madrid sectional. She reached over his desk and grabbed a pen. "Near here and here," she said, marking roughly where she knew Porter's trailers were. "I'll give you details on the day of the raid. Don't try to get permission from higher-ups. You'll have to move quickly or they'll be gone."

"We can move quickly."

The Fourth of July was always hot. Unimaginably, viciously, brutally hot. Everything before had been prologue. Now, summer rolled into Nuthatch County: inexorable, inevitable, and uncaring. Even before the Fourth, temperatures broke into the upper nineties during the day and barely dipped down into the eighties at night. It had been a wet spring and that rain had soaked into the earth. Now, the heat returned it to the air but it stayed low, thickening the air until breathing became conscious labor.

All hot summer days reminded Luke of Catherine. The heat was always worse in Washington, but they weren't in Washington when it happened.

It had been hot. Luke remembered that much outside of the narrow bubble of grief and shock.

The previous year Catherine had been diagnosed with breast cancer. She'd had the mastectomy and chemo and things looked promising. No recurrence—but then, with something like that, what's six months? A year? Five years? That June they'd gone back to the County to ask Jeremy.

Jeremy had smiled and said the cancer would be no problem.

The relief had been palpable. As real and round as a peach.

It had made them giddy. They stayed in the Taverton Hotel in Pilate. Over the next few days, they found new ways to get around Catherine's remaining post-op tenderness and made rampant love—or, at least, as rampant as a couple in their sixties could manage in limited air conditioning. Luke had a recurring thought afterwards when he tried to catch his breath as he held onto her: I never thought it would get *better*.

He woke to Catherine insistently tapping him.

"Yes?" he said, turning on the light and rolling towards her, wondering if he could manage something in the morning. He noticed darkness out the window and corrected himself: something in the middle of the *night*.

But she was quiet, her face panicked on one side, wooden, unseeing, and drooling on the other.

There was, of course, no hospital in the County. Carter Faraday insisted they take the extra time to get to the stroke center in Cape Girardeau rather than the closer general hospital in Sikeston.

"Sikeston will stabilize her. Then they'll send her to Southeast, anyway." Carter shook his head. "It's an hour and a half to Sikeston on the Airport road then it's time at the hospital and another hour and a half to Southeast. It's two and a half hours to Southeast direct. We can call ahead and get an escort. They'll be waiting for her."

"A helicopter?" asked Luke blearily.

"We don't have med flights down here. Not yet, anyway." Carter gave him a pleading look. "I can stabilizer her enough for this. Trust me, Luke."

"If we were home she could go to Wallace Reed. Or Bethesda. Or Johns Hopkins. By helicopter."

Carter sighed. "Yeah. I know. But we're here. What do you want me to do?"

"Let's go to Cape Girardeau."

Jake Withers had his ambulance in front of the Taverton in

ten minutes. Five minutes more and Catherine was in the back, holding Luke's hand with her functioning left and watching him with her good eye.

Jake took the switchbacks faster than Luke thought possible. The ambulance seemed to waddle from one side of the road to the other.

"Did you call Jeremy?" slurred Catherine.

Luke shook his head. "Do you want me to?"

She nodded faintly.

What can Jeremy do? thought Luke. He can't come to the hospital. He's stuck in Nuthatch County. Then, he remembered what Jeremy had said: the cancer would be no problem. Was that Jeremy's idea of a *joke?* He suppressed a sudden rage— Catherine might see. That was the last thing she needed. Maybe Jeremy knew what would happen. Maybe he didn't. Maybe if he did, it was just his way of giving them a brief moment of happiness. With him, who knew?

Luke dutifully pulled out his cell phone. No coverage. There was never any good coverage in Nuthatch County. "I'll do it as soon as I can."

There was a state police car waiting for them as soon as they reached the interstate. It led them all the way north to the hospital. Luke watched the lights spinning. They were so bright it was a wonder Jake could see well enough to drive.

The hospital staff gently but quickly parted them and sped Catherine deep into the hospital. Carter followed in her wake. Luke was left to answer questions and fill out forms. Yes, he had insurance. No, there was no previous history of stroke. Yes, she was on medication for blood pressure. No, she had no history of heart disease. Yes, she's been in the hospital before. Lots of times. She'd had polio, for God's sake. Then, like acolytes opening the gates of the temple, they let him into the ER to sit with her. But she wasn't there. She'd already been taken to the ICU. He followed the signs and found the ICU. But she wasn't there, either. She was in the *cardiopulmonary* ICU.

Lying there, half-conscious, a mask on her face, she roused, recognized him, waved with her good arm, and fell back to sleep.

It wasn't that time seemed to stop. The ICU was always in motion. Doctors moving here. Nurses moving there. Drugs administered. Bloody procedures performed. Curtains sorrowfully closed. The beeps and moans of the machines were continuous and you could always, *always*, hear somebody breathing—a hiss or a wheeze or a rattle or a mechanistic click.

But the motion was repetitive and punctuated by events that were expected. Of course, there was a Code Blue during the night. They were in the ICU. Someone was discharged. Someone was admitted. Visitors came and went. Each individual had a life, family, personality, but all were submerged under the urgent sameness of trying to stay alive.

Finally, he remembered to call Jeremy. Luke knew he had told Jeremy what had happened. He couldn't for the life of him remember what Jeremy said.

At some timeless point, he looked up and Nadine was sitting next to him.

Luke smiled at her. "Hey. Weren't you in D.C.?"

Nadine's face looked brightly polished. She'd been crying but her eyes were now dry. "I got here an hour ago. Did you know you could charter a small plane to fly you here from Logan?"

"No."

"Plane might be an overstatement. It was more like a kite with a propeller. It had four seats but I think that was wishful thinking." She took a deep breath. "I talked with Carter."

"He's still here?"

"Yes. He's talked with you several times. Don't you remember?"

Luke shook his head.

Nadine looked at her mother. Catherine was safely asleep. "We need to find Carter." She stood and left.

Luke looked at Catherine. Her face was waxy yellow around the oxygen mask. Her mouth was open in a way he didn't like.

Carter seemed to appear out of nothing. "Luke?"

"Yes?"

"Come on to the waiting room. We need to talk."

Carter led them to a small green room. It was empty. He insisted they sit. Then, he took a deep breath. "It's a stroke, obviously. A bad one. She's lost pretty much all use of her right side. She can still talk so the speech center is unaffected. You can tell, though, motor control of her mouth is impaired. Swallowing is going to be difficult and dangerous for her. She's stable for the moment so they've scheduled some pictures for later today. After that, we'll know how bad it really is."

"Oh." Luke tried to consider what Carter said but it kept slipping off. He wanted to ask when she would get better and go home but the question felt ridiculous. For some reason or another, he couldn't seem to figure out why that was the case.

"What's the worst it could be?" asked Nadine.

"I don't want to speculate—"

"Come on, Carter." Nadine's voice was stone. "We're in the same big County family. We don't have much in the way of secrets."

Carter nodded. "The good news, first. She's not eighty. She's healthy. She doesn't smoke. She doesn't drink. The bad news: the damage polio did is still there. Her diaphragm isn't as strong as it should be. Lungs are the key, here. We have to keep her from getting sick. Pneumonia kills more people than stroke. If she can regain good lung function and can manage to relearn how to swallow, we might be able to dodge that—it's always a danger in the hospital, what with all these sick people." Carter chuckled. "She's on blood thinners now—I started her on them as soon as we were in the ambulance—so provided she doesn't bleed out and the clot dissolves she might get some function back, provided it *is* a blood clot and not something else. If we can keep her off a ventilator it's a long hard road back to anything at all. If not, it's a long walk off a short pier."

"Would she do better back in the County?" asked Nadine.

Carter stared at her. "You're not serious."

Nadine shrugged. "We know Jeremy's not going to cure her. Jeremy doesn't cure anybody. But he might keep her from getting sicker. If we ask him."

"What are you going to do? Kill a calf on a rock?"

Nadine dropped her eyes to the floor. For a moment, Luke thought she was going to cry but her lip steadied. "No. I'm going to ask him to help in whatever way he can. Just like you do in the clinic. I'll beg him. I'll pray to him. Or kill a calf on a rock, if that's what it takes."

Carter opened his mouth to say something and stopped. He closed it to a thin line. "You're right, of course. Call him. We'll do what we can here to keep her alive. If he can do *anything*, it can't be anything but helpful. But Nadine?" Carter fixed her with his gaze. "He's never done anything when I asked. I hope to hell you have better luck."

Luke tried to make the Fourth every year. Even after he'd fallen out with Jeremy, it seemed that not going was as problematic as going. Certainly, he had to sit in the same reviewing stand as Jeremy and Deacon Williams. Deacon positively *fumed* bad blood in Jeremy's direction. Jeremy just sat there, ignoring them all, holding first Amy's hand and later Betty's, delighting in the marching bands, the floats, the costumes, and just people walking on the street waving.

Despite his and Rosen's ongoing machinations, this year would likely be no different.

For a long time, Luke wondered what Jeremy saw in it. After all, Jeremy had been around for hundreds (thousands, millions) of years. Hadn't he seen it all? Hadn't people done it all for him before? But enjoy it he did, despite the Commissioner's nervousness, Luke's impatience, and Deacon Williams' flat-out hatred.

On the plane from DC, Luke spread out the time in his mind. He and Catherine were married in 1950. Honey Teel had been Commissioner then—little Choctaw woman no bigger than a pencil—not that Luke cared who was Commissioner. County Commissioner was someone you elected every four years. He'd voted for Honey in 1952—the first year he could vote in the County elections. Who came after that? He thought for a minute. Carol Bigheart. He remembered because it was a big deal to have an Osage in office. Though Luke never understood why. Still didn't.

Then, a couple of white men from Pilate. Now, it was Pam Small. He liked Pam. She seemed above a lot of the petty machinations the office always seemed to embrace.

He remembered sitting in the reviewing stand when Nadine had won a prize for the essay she'd written when she was eight. Even then, he had been astounded by how articulate she had been. She must have gotten it all, part and parcel, from her mother.

Luke recalled it had also been a hot day and the three of them—he, Catherine, and little Nadine—sat in a row on the reviewing stand. Amy DaFoe sat sitting next to him and all he could think about was how sexy she was. There was something about her that somehow *breathed* availability. Maybe Marilyn Monroe had it on screen but Amy DaFoe had it on the breeze and she was *right there*. Jeremy didn't notice Luke but Eldest Margaret Allen did and kept giving him dirty looks.

Betty DaFoe had never affected him that way. Of course, he was much older now.

For a moment, past and present were mixed and he was confused. Joanie, he knew, was already in the County. Hanging out with that doctor for the summer.

She hadn't seemed the least bit drunk the last few times he'd seen her. Maybe she wasn't an alcoholic after all. Ain't love grand?

He shook his head. Why think about such things now? County Commissioners dead and gone—wait a minute. The two white guys before Pam Small. Matt Boyd and... Luke couldn't remember the name. Carl something. Were they still alive?

Luke felt suddenly ancient. Remembering old men. Times past. Especially now when things might just be close enough to actually *happen*. As much as he'd disliked Deacon Williams, Luke wished Deacon was here now. To see.

Or not.

The reports they'd had were spotty. The County was in flux—people were angry with Jeremy in a way none of the operatives had ever seen. It was like a sudden upwelling from the depths of a still ocean.

Off the plane and into the rental car. A quick call to Bob Sheffield. Down the Illinois side to the slip and cross the big water on the *New Madrid Fault*. Like he'd done a thousand times before.

"Heard some funny things going on in the County," said Bob.

Here's where I find out that Jeremy DaFoe is known far and wide across the entire Midwest. "Oh?"

"Yeah. Big stink about a new road. Has the whole County riled."

"Oh."

Bob checked the wheel. "Funny place, Nuthatch County. It's like those little country towns where everybody marries their sister. Nobody thinks about anything outside of their borders."

He pointed to himself with his thumb. "I'm from a much bigger place. Over here in Cairo, we have a broader view of the world. More cosmopolitan."

Luke nodded. It wasn't the silliest view he'd ever heard.

He parked downtown and caught lunch in the diner across from the Commissioner's office. The crowds looked thin to him. Sheriff Cox had put out the tape blocking off the usual streets— Luke wondered if the tape was even necessary. The route, down Second Street and up Main, had been fixed since long before Luke had been born. By now it must be written into the County's very DNA.

Luke checked his watch. He paid his tab and walked down Main Street to the reviewing stand. Even here, the crowds were sparse. Listless. People seemed to be talking quietly. Luke remembered vividly a couple of years ago: firecrackers as regular as the explosive ticks of a clock. This year: nothing.

Pam was already in the stand. She sat on one side next to Jeremy. Buddy sat on the other next to Betty. Buddy and Betty were deep in quiet conversation that stopped as Luke walked up the steps. Luke stood up and surveyed the crowd. He saw Sheriff Cox and Jake Withers working their way slowly toward the stand. Across the street he could see the Porters standing quietly, their kids splayed around them.

Luke took his seat. He looked up Main Street. The order of events was as fixed as the route. First came the high school band. Then, a small mob of Ashby residents. Followed by any group that wanted to be seen. *Any* group—the Klan marched here regularly over the years. Followed by the Veterans of Foreign Wars, making a small but effective barrier between the whites and the blacks. He wondered how that came to be. It wasn't tolerance, exactly. No one seemed to like the Klan. They were like unpleasant relatives to be suitably ignored at a family gathering. Or maybe there was something deeper. Maybe the County unconsciously recognized it as dissent. Was it something he and Rosen should have taken advantage of? Too late now.

After the group walk came the floats followed by the police cars. By then it would be late afternoon and the crowd would mill around the square and adjacent streets until the light began to fade. People would move sluggishly over to the ball field to watch the fireworks.

Luke heard the band before he saw them. He glanced over towards the DaFoe. Jeremy was holding Betty's hand, a grin on his face.

The band turned the corner, playing "When the Saints go Marching In." That changed to a jazz version of "Somewhere Over the Rainbow." *Who picks these songs?* thought Luke. The band looked like it was mostly saxophones this year.

The Ashby folk turned the corner behind them. But there weren't many of them—perhaps twenty. Luke sat up. That was a big deal. Usually, the entire town turned out. Men. Women. Children in strollers. Old folks in walkers. This was just a few old men and a couple of children. They looked down at the road as they passed and never glanced up at the reviewing stand. Luke glanced over to Jeremy. He wasn't smiling. He looked surprised.

Then there was nothing. No groups. No Klan. No organization for the emancipation of whatever cause was currently in style. Bits of paper blew in the gap.

A tractor driven by Roger Pollack came around the corner, pulling a float: a great model of a road going up a hill to a cliff, the end broken off raggedly. A pile of small cars at the bottom.

The street was silent save for the steady diesel hammer of Roger's tractor as the float drew along the reviewing stand and then past them. The float turned onto Second Street and was gone. A moment later, a single police car turned onto Main Street, its lights flashing—Luke saw Sergeant Moon's face staring straight ahead—passed the reviewing stand, turned the corner, and disappeared. Two officers followed the car, picking up the tape used to block off the street.

Luke turned towards the people in the stand. Sheriff Cox was expressionless. Jake Withers looked thoughtful while Pam was clearly furious. Betty was holding Jeremy's hand and patting his shoulder. Jeremy looked confused. "Is that it?" he said.

People on the street began to break up, walking away from the center of town. None looked at the reviewing stand. Instead, they looked at the ground, the sky, each other, as if ashamed.

Ashamed, Luke thought suddenly. Not afraid. Not worried. Not wary. Ashamed. As if they had nothing to fear.

Luke felt a deep excitement.

The summer Catherine died, Old Tom Sutter, near death himself but still clear, loaned Luke his empty house south of Pilate. Luke and Nadine cleaned it out and readied the corner cupola into a room filled with light. President George H. W. Bush took time out from his reelection campaign to order a good hospital bed for Catherine. A few nights later, as Catherine fought for her life against pneumonia and Luke sat next to her in the ICU, Nadine accepted delivery of it along with a tall, blond, humorless Marine nurse named Alby Molino. Alby took over, installing one delivered device after another. Eventually, the cupola became indistinguishable from the hospital room save for the windows. Luke wrote a thousand-dollar check to the Bush reelection campaign. He didn't care who Bush would be running against. No Democrat could top this.

By the first of July Catherine still had no perceivable function on her right side and could barely speak above a whisper but she'd recovered sufficiently from the pneumonia to be moved out of ICU. She insisted on returning to Nuthatch County. The ambulance that brought them from Southeast took the switchbacks on the main road carefully. A couple of times the driver got out to check out the road. The contrast between this timidity and Jake's high-speed run made Luke smile.

Alby was waiting for them. "Corporal Alby Molino, ma'am," he said crisply to Catherine and saluted her.

"I've come up in the world," she said softly.

It broke Luke's heart to hear her voice so muted. So slurred. He fancied he could hear every throat scar and lung blemish.

Jeremy called on her the next day.

Luke found himself resenting the visit. Apprehensive. He'd heard all the stories from Catherine and Buddy. When he'd first heard them, he was as amused or comforted as they were. Now, Jeremy seemed like some kind of crow attracted to the nearness of death. What Jeremy had said to them, *the breast cancer would be no problem*, came back to haunt him. The same thoughts circled each other? Was that Jeremy's idea of a *joke?* Was he trying to give them a moment of joy before the inevitable hammer's fall? Was Jeremy just being *inept?*

But Catherine took such obvious pleasure in Jeremy's visits that Luke kept his opinions to himself. If Jeremy knew Luke's feelings, he didn't show it.

Coming back to the County didn't help much. Catherine slowly declined. No matter how hard Alby, Nadine, or Luke worked, how scrupulously they watched and combated every twist and turn of her condition, it inevitably grew a little worse. One day she could sit up. A week later she had trouble. A few days after that she couldn't. The next day she wouldn't try. Luke watched helplessly as Catherine was consumed by gravity.

She didn't get pneumonia again. Catherine thought it was being close to Jeremy. Nadine and Luke thought it was their continuous war on dust and germs. Alby thought it was keeping Catherine at her breathing exercises. No one knew the truth. Though Jeremy visited regularly, the bacteria were kept at bay and Catherine practiced her exercises, the required effort to breathe grew more each day until by the end of July she lay in her bed, eyes shut, the corners of her eyes wrinkled, concentrating on merely getting the breath in and out, in and out.

Finally, on the first of June, she told Luke to sit down. They had to talk.

"Honey?" she said. Then stopped to breathe. "I'm not going to get better." (Breathe.)

"Don't talk like that."

"No one (Breathe.) else is going to. (Breathe.) Not you or Nadine. (Breathe.) Or Alby."

"You'll get better." He felt desperate. He'd never been religious—Righteous had had enough of that as a child and never pushed it onto his own children. Now he wanted to pray to something. Anything. God. Jeremy. President George Herbert Walker Bush.

Catherine shook her head.

Jeremy came that night, standing at the front door and lit from behind by the fireflies. Luke almost sent him away but remembered how Catherine liked having him there. He sat in the room while Jeremy kept her company. Watched Catherine's face as she listened to him. When Jeremy left the room for a moment Luke followed him. He grabbed Jeremy's arm.

Jeremy turned and looked at him, eyes sad and expectant.

Luke bowed his head. "Save her," he said in a low, begging voice. "Please. I'll do anything."

Jeremy took Luke's shoulder. He watched Luke until Luke raised his gaze and they could look each other in the eyes.

"There's nothing to do," Jeremy said.

Carter came by. Jeremy shook his hand. Carter checked on Catherine and then came out to talk to Luke and Nadine. He told Luke and Nadine that the next step to keep her alive was to put her on a ventilator.

"Do it," said Luke harshly.

Carter hesitated. "Luke, you remember—"

"Don't argue with me."

"Dad," began Nadine. "Jeremy said—"

Luke stared at her until she looked away.

She was on the ventilator for six days.

The night of the sixth day Carter came by to check on her. She lay on the bed. The yellow wax pallor Luke had first noticed in the hospital around the oxygen mask had now spread over her whole body. Face, hands, toes, neck: all the same color of old, dried cream. The ventilator click-hiss, click-hiss, seemed to fill the room. Carter looked into her eyes. Checked her hands and feet. Catherine was unresponsive. He gestured to Luke and led him out of the room.

"She's had another stroke," Carter said. "Maybe more than one."

Luke stared at him dully. "I see."

"The only thing keeping her alive is that ventilator." Carter put his hand on Luke's shoulder. "What do you want to do?"

"See her jump out of that bed and take me dancing."

"Yeah." Carter gave him a faint smile. "Think about it. I have to check in to the clinic. Call me there."

Nadine was sitting in the kitchen nursing a glass of something clear. When he came in she poured him a glass and pushed it over.

He sat across from her and sipped it. He recognized Porter's Piss. "Carter said she'd had another stroke."

Nadine nodded. "Alby said the same thing."

"What do we do now?"

Nadine grabbed his hand. "You know what we have to do."

Luke nodded. He did.

Carter came by around midnight. He gave her a shot of morphine to ease anything of her that was left. "Push down this switch and hold it until that light turns red. That will turn off the ventilator. I've turned off the alarms."

Luke saw the pain in Nadine's eyes. "You go on home."

"Dad—"

"Do you really want to bear witness to your mother's last breath? When she's like this? Joseph's home. Go to him. Call Joanie. Get drunk on moonshine. Remember her like she was."

Carter drove her home.

Luke returned to the cupola and sat next to Catherine. For a long time, he just listened to the ventilator. Click-hiss. Click-hiss. For a long moment every good moment he'd ever had with her crowded in at once: meeting her in the water, first sex, seeing her again, getting to know Nadine, being present with her when Joanie was born, holding her as Catherine cried and cried and *cried* for happiness, walking through Washington with her, sitting in their little house in Arlington, Nadine long gone, just the two of them on the same sofa reading, when she suddenly and without warning placing her withered arm on his just to touch him. Tears rolled down his cheeks.

"This is it, honey," he said softly. "Last chance. Stay with me. Please."

But there was only click-hiss. Click-hiss. Of Catherine, there was no sign.

Okay.

He held down the switch until the light turned red. Click-hiss.

For a moment there was nothing in the room but the sound of Catherine's breathing. Then, each breath drew out a little longer. A little deeper. Then came a rattling sound. A long gasp. A wheeze. Then nothing.

For a moment, he saw Catherine's face, whole and alive, smiling at him from the bed. Then, she was gone and there was only the still, yellow wax doll she had become.

Luke stood and looked out the window. He didn't think he'd

ever cry again.

Outside amidst the fireflies was Jeremy. Watching.

Betty held on to Jeremy's arm as he watched, astonished, as the parade (if you could call it that) passed by.

"Is that it?" he asked.

Groups broke apart on the street and went their separate ways. Only the Porters remained, anchored by Robert Porter who stood on the sidewalk watching the reviewing stand. Finally, even the Porters left.

Betty leaned over and whispered in Jeremy's ear. "Come on, honey."

Silently, she led Jeremy over to First Street where she'd parked the car.

Jeremy was silent as she got in. Silent as she pulled out of the spot and silent as she navigated her way out of Pilate. Silent, he watched the scenery pass as they drove towards the farm.

"Honey?" she said quietly. "Are you all right?"

He nodded. Silently.

"It's okay," she said. "It's just a bad year."

"A bad year." Jeremy shook his head. "A bad year." Jeremy started laughing. Hooting. Tears streamed down his cheeks. "*A bad year!* Oh, my goodness. Oh, my." He wiped his eyes. "I didn't think they had it in them. I haven't seen that in—oh, two hundred years maybe?"

"See what?"

"Betty, my love. That was as clear a vote of no confidence as I've ever seen. It's been years—*generations*—since that happened."

Betty felt coldness curl in the pit of her stomach. "No confidence?"

"Abandonment. Disloyalty. Betrayal. Are those words any

better?"

"No."

Jeremy chortled. "I didn't think they had it in them."

"What are you going to do?"

"Do?" He looked at her and back out the window. "You're saying I should *do* something?"

Betty didn't know how to answer that. Suddenly, the cave completely covered by the pictures of Fox and Fire came to her mind. Was that a vote of no confidence?

Jeremy stepped out of the car as she came to a stop next to the house. He stretched out his arms with a grin.

This didn't make Betty any more comfortable.

Inside, Jeremy went to the kitchen and put on the kettle. "Want some coffee?"

"Sure." She followed him slowly, put her purse on the table, and sat down. "Honey?"

"Hm?" Jeremy measured out the coffee into the maker. "What's on your mind? Today?"

"Buddy took me to a cave. The one next to Little Mountain."

"Ah." He turned on the coffee maker, turned, and sat down.

"There are a lot of paintings in there."

Jeremy nodded. "I know. Norton showed me pictures. I've never been in there."

"The man on fire. Is that you?"

"I expect so."

"And the man with the fox's head?"

"Faster-Than-Fox."

"From Fox's Chimney?"

"Yeah."

"Who was Faster-Than-Fox?"

"Now that is an old story." Jeremy leaned back in his chair.

"Osage?"

"Oh, no. The Faster-Than-Fox story was old when the Mississippians were living here."

"Mississippians?"

"The Mound Builders. They were the ones that lived here before the Osage came. Cabeza de Vaca came through and stayed for a little bit. Nice man. Whatever he brought with him wiped them all out. At least the ones around here. Must have been over a hundred-fifty years before the first Osage pushed down into the County. I don't know how they picked up the story but they did. No, Faster-Than-Fox was in one of the first bands that ever made it up here—Clovis point hunters, they're called now. New to me, too. Humans had passed through before but no one ever stayed. I didn't know anything about them." He gestured to himself. "I didn't look like this back then."

The coldness in her stomach seemed to settle there. "What were you?"

"Various things. Cave bears. Buffalo. Elk. Cougars. Giant sloths. Dire wolves. Eagles. Terror birds." He shook his head. "Never had a chance to be a dinosaur—they were all gone when I got here."

"Where did you come from Jeremy?"

He shook his head. "You were asking about Faster-Than-Fox. It's a euphemism. 'Fox' indicates speed, cleverness, and intelligence. Also, deceit. Slyness. A certain moral ambiguity. 'Faster' signified physical speed but also 'ahead of.' 'To the side of.' Faster-Than-Fox was a terrific runner—he could run down an elk given half a start. And that's part of the name. But he was also one step ahead of retribution. Consequences. Penalties. He slept with a little girl—which was not a bad thing back then. Nobody thought twice about a boy or girl of twelve going off into the woods with someone. Young or old it didn't matter. There was no taboo either way. But he picked the wrong girl. High-status girl—daughter of a big warrior and a witch woman. A little *too* young and Faster-Than-Fox was just a little *too* much older."

"I *liked* him, though. I really did. He was a hell of a dancer. And funny. And quick." Jeremy shook his head sadly. "They came to me and said you have to do something. I said, no, I don't. He's your problem. So, they said they were going to kill him and I didn't want that. I said send him away." Jeremy shook his head. "The silly nit said he was *so fast* he could out run anything I could do. He made a *bet* that he could outrun me." Jeremy sighed. "I almost let him get away. I was still new to the whole bound to do what you say thing." He turned the coffee cup on the table. "But I didn't. I stood right there on Bittersweet Ridge and burnt him down right where the stile is." Jeremy picked up his coffee cup, sipped it, and put it back down again.

Betty didn't know how to feel. It was such a mix. Here was Jeremy, her husband, the man she slept with every night, the man who she crawled on top of in the middle of the dark, who made her crazy then, and who, crazy on his own, spent himself inside her. At the same time, here was Jeremy, the ancient thing who had learned human shape solely by imitation. She'd loved Jeremy, her husband, since she was tiny. The ancient thing was a fixture in the County like the sun or the moon or the river, a force to be reckoned with, thought about, considered. She'd thought she'd gotten beyond the ancient part of Jeremy in the ten years they'd been married but look: there it was.

She stood up and went to the window. Outside, the summer sun beat on the trees and gave the leaves a parched look. There was a figure in the field across the road. Someone she knew.

"Jeremy?" she said slowly. "What's Robert Porter doing just standing over there?

Robert had a single favorite spot for the parade. Opposite the reviewing stand where he could watch Jeremy, his wife, the

Commissioner, and other people of power. He spent his time thinking how the world would be a better place without them.

He watched the confusion on their faces as the last police car passed followed by the two officers that gathered up the tape.

"Well, that was a disappointment," said Ed. Sterling was clutching at his father's knees. The boy wasn't crying but he didn't look far from it.

Robert's daughter, Maria, was standing quietly in front of Isobel, their faces genetic mirrors of one another: stoic, watchful, one eye on the street, one eye on Robert. Good. That was the way it should be. A little fear was good in a family.

"Are you kidding?" Robert kept watching the reviewing stand. It looked like Luke was the only one there that understood. "This was the best parade ever."

"Are you nuts?" Ed picked up Sterling and started walking towards the cars. "One marching band. A little bunch of nigras. One float."

"It's true. I did miss watching the Klan glare at the nigras and the nigras glare back. That's always fun." Robert shepherded Isobel and Maria after Ed's wife, Hannah. "Did you see Jeremy's face?"

"No."

"You missed the real show."

Ed looked at him with a worried expression. "I suppose."

Robert thought quietly for a moment. "Look: could you take Isobel and Maria home for me?"

"That's five people for my truck."

"Maria can sit in Isobel's lap. I need to do something. Run an errand."

"On the Fourth?"

"Come on, man."

Ed stopped and watched him for a moment. Then, he turned away. "Okay."

Robert left them in the parking lot and drove off in his truck, alone. He pulled over on the main road next to the rusting road equipment and waited. About ten minutes later, Betty and Jeremy drove past. He gave them a few minutes. After all, he wasn't following them. He knew where they were going. After he judged enough time had passed, he started driving again.

By the time he reached the house, their car was parked and no one was outside. He pulled over and pushed the seat forward. Behind was his new rifle.

The Heckler and Koch G36 is an assault rifle made in Germany. It was built to replace the G3 and was accepted by the *Bundeswehr* in 1997. It has three settings: single shot, burst, and continuous—750 rounds per minute, 12.5 rounds per second. The G36 uses a 5.56mm NATO round—a spitzer-type bullet that yaws when it enters flesh and bounces around doing as much damage as possible. The 5.56 bullet travels about three thousand feet per second. Three thousand feet per second is a bit over two thousand miles an hour. The velocity of three bullets added together is better than lunar escape velocity. Nine bullets added together would get you escape velocity from earth. The famous SR-71 Blackbird, the fastest plane of its day, topped out at nearly twenty-two hundred miles an hour. It was faster than the G36 bullet but not by much.

The 5.56 bullet is just about a quarter inch in diameter. That little bullet leaves the muzzle with a momentum of about 825 pounds. If it were to hit and stop suddenly it would deliver the equivalent of 21,000 pounds/square inch. But, of course, the bullet doesn't remain whole when it strikes flesh. It breaks along the seam and splatters inside the body.

Robert held the gun. He loved its clean, lethal lines. The lightness of it. The choice of black polymer over wood—such a weapon should have no heritage from life. It was committed to destruction.

Robert walked away from the truck, gun in one hand, backpack in the other.

The tensile strength of pine is somewhere around eleven hundred pounds per square inch. The compression strength is less—closer to seven hundred PSI. Clapboard siding and glass were as air to 5.56 bullets.

The day was hot and he stood in direct sun. Heat haze rose from the road between where he stood and the DaFoe house. He pulled out a cylindrical magazine and slipped it in and rummaged further in the bag. One magazine, one hundred rounds. Ten magazines.

He stood, savoring the moment. Grinning. He laughed. Loosened his arms and shoulders. Braced himself.

Opened fire.

The wall exploded in the front room. Glass shattered into dust. The siding opened up as if it were being sawed in half. She felt something hit her and she was suddenly on the ground, on her back, the wind knocked from her lungs, Jeremy on top of her.

"Stay down!" he shouted.

Above her the room filled with dust, broken bits of wood, flakes of paint, pieces of metal. The line of explosions went through the room and tore through the wall sideways. The window frame, cut in half, sagged and the broken glass sheets slid down and crashed. It stopped.

A few seconds passed. "What?"

The wave of explosions came back through the room again. The inside wall came down, then the door frame and the door. Pictures on the wall flew into the air in pieces. Cabinets in the kitchen shattered and came apart. Broken plates, saucers, cups, her mother's platter, suddenly came apart and were tossed into the air like bits of corn.

It stopped.

She was screaming.

It came again, one side to the other, stop for a few seconds, then back.

The table came apart. The inside wall between the kitchen and the front room suddenly parted into three pieces and crashed to the ground.

Again and back.

The other wall, the one separating the bathroom and the kitchen, fell down. The sounds changed from explosions to a *chink chink chink* that Betty thought must be the sink or the toilet or the bath tub. Then back through the kitchen, taking off the top of the gas stove.

With a *whoosh,* fire erupted from the stove. Then, it started raining.

And *back* again. This time lower. It had to hit her. Had to cut her in half just like the walls, the stove, her whole house.

There was a creaking roar and the second story folded over the front half of the house in a crash.

The shooting stopped. A few quick bursts.

"Well, *shit.*" From outside. (How can I be hearing this? Aren't I deaf?)

Robert had made it through six magazines and was putting in the seventh when the front of the house fell over. Now the roof and part of the second story were between him and the rest of the house.

"Well, shit." Where was he supposed to shoot? He fired a couple of bursts but they just seemed to poke through the shingles. No effect. Nothing fun like tearing off the side of the house.

Suddenly, his hair seemed to want to stand on end. His skin felt prickly.

He remembered Lyle Williams.

Time to trot, Bwana. He grabbed the bag and ran to his truck. Tossed the G36 inside.

Flash! Followed instantly by a *Crack!* he felt deep in his body. The force threw him against the truck. Around it. He swung into the driver's seat, started it, and *floored* it.

Flash-Crack! right where the truck had been.

"*Whoo hoo!*" he yelled and took off down the road, the lightning following just behind. *Flash-Crack! Flash-Crack!*

"You too slow, old man!" Robert shouted gleefully, zigging one way on the road, then the other.

Flash-Crack!

The lightning stopped when the house was out of sight but Robert didn't slow down. He tore down the western road, laughing.

Flash! Crack! She felt as if every bone inside her was suddenly shattered. Then another. Then another. She held her ears, screaming, until they stopped.

Silence.

The east outside wall of the kitchen collapsed.

Jeremy picked her up and carried her outside. He ran behind the house. She heard the rattle of the toolbox.

How can I not be deaf?

Deaf, hell. How can I be *alive?*

She staggered back to the house and looked inside. The stove was hissing fire and there was the evil smell of gas. Dust and debris were everywhere. The sink was a fountain. Where the water had fallen the dust had smeared into a thick white paste. Fallen beams, piles of broken glass, paint dust. Betty could hear Jeremy in the back of the house, fumbling with something. The hissing of the gas suddenly stopped but the water went on and on. A moment later she heard the sound of a fire extinguisher.

Betty looked at the white paste that used to be wall paint. When was the house built? 1948? 1955? I wonder if I have lead poisoning now.

In the middle of the kitchen was a perfect circle clear of dust or paint or shattered bits of ceiling. Rivers of white ran through it now as the sink overflowed. Right where Jeremy had been holding her down.

Jeremy appeared in front of her.

Startled, she scrambled back.

"Son of a bitch," he said quietly. He walked away from the house and sat down under the oak. He had something in his hand—a mason jar of Porter's Piss and two coffee cups. He poured and held one out to her. He held it out.

She stumbled over to him and collapsed beneath the oak. "Thought you didn't need that stuff."

"Seemed like the thing to do at the time."

"I'm drinking lead paint."

He shook his head. "Washed them out in the sink."

This struck them both as hilarious and they nearly fell down laughing.

"Almost human, there, DaFoe." She grinned at him.

"Been practicing for twenty thousand years, Thomas." He stretched. "Might have gotten it right by now."

Betty looked back at the house and the grin left her face. She'd lived in this house for ten years, never thinking about it much more than as a dwelling. She'd put pictures on the wall, mopped the floor after tracking in mud from the garden. Vacuumed the floors—made *Jeremy* vacuum the floors—while she cooked dinner. Drank herself silly at the table, secure in the certain knowledge that she was safe here. Safe inside the County. Inside her marriage. Inside her house. *Her house!*

The whole front of the house had collapsed. The second floor sagged down like a fat man's belly, barely held up by the spine of the intact rear. The pictures on the wall were shattered or soaked. Papers—she remembered her pet doctor from school. She had kept his letters automatically, never thinking of them until now. Whatever life she might have shared with him, *this* wouldn't have happened. Her clothes. Her shoes. The bed she had shared with Jeremy for the whole of their marriage. The table. The very walls and windows. *Her house!*

Betty stared at the rubble. She drank off half the cup of moonshine in a quick gulp. She could tell she was feeling grief, rage, smoldering hatred, loss, relief—excitement, too, that she could raze this place to the ground and build something fresh and new on the ruins. But the emotions were distant. Insulated. As unreal as the destruction in front of her. She reached over blindly and took Jeremy's hand, felt the hardness of the palms, the strength of the fingers, the scrape of the calluses. She picked up his hand and kissed it, pressed it against her cheek. It felt like the only thing real in the whole wide world.

"What are you going to do?" she asked.

Jeremy looked over the house, his lips in a thin line. His face was stone but not angry.

"Nothing," he said at last. "Nothing at all."

Part 3

Chapter 8: Summer Dancing

Shooting up Betty and Jeremy's house was the top news in the County in just a few hours. Of course, Nate Guilder's gleeful filming of the entire thing might have helped. It was even worth the bullet fragment in his leg—a small lead piece that glanced off (and shattered) a cow-shaped creamer Betty's grandmother had brought back from a trip to Vermont when she was a girl. Missed the bone. Missed an artery. Nate kept pressure on it with one hand and kept filming with the other.

As much as Nate liked recording acts of destruction (A hobby he shared with several NSA employees back when he worked there. Each of them thought it was a deep secret from all other employees. It wasn't.) it was the aftermath he was waiting for: Jeremy's bloody revenge.

The lightning bolts were a nice touch.

After the second one, it was clear that either Jeremy had very bad aim or he wasn't trying very hard. Perhaps, he was deliberately *missing* Porter.

Nate kept filming after Porter left. Jeremy and Betty sat under a tree and talked. He had hopes of some post-disaster coitus—again, something he pursued as a hobby and kept a deep dark secret from his former employers. It was no more a secret than his little snuff films.

Perplexed, Nate wrapped up his leg and limped the three miles toward town where he'd parked. He managed to drive as far as Harry's before the leg began to really bother him.

Arnie and Harry cleaned out Nate's leg. They had years of field medical experience between them. Nate didn't notice, blissed out on Harry's morphine.

While Nate slept off the morphine, Harry and Arnie went over the film.

"He didn't do anything," said Arnie in disgust.

"No," Harry said thoughtfully. "He did not." Harry repeated the section where Jeremy and Betty drank under the oak. "I wish I knew what they were talking about."

"Planning revenge?" asked Arnie hopefully.

"I don't think so."

"Should we keep it a secret?"

Harry laughed. "No chance of that."

"It's not helpful. Nothing will happen," declared Arnie. "If *Jeremy's* not going to do anything, no one will."

Harry leaned back in his chair, tapping his finger on the table and thinking of all the different constituents of Nuthatch County. "Ever been to Guatemala?"

"No."

"Lovely place."

"What the *fuck* were you thinking?" Ed was white-lipped and furious with rage. Robert had told him to meet at Atkinson's and then dropped his little bombshell. Ed whispered across the table to Robert so that the *whole damned town* wouldn't know it was his cousin *Robert Porter* who shot up Jeremy DaFoe's house.

"That it was time somebody did something." Robert grinned

at him. "You should have seen it. The whole front of the house just *rolled* down." Robert spread his hands. "You see? The place was structurally unsound. After all, you'd think in this day and age a house would be able to stand up to at least a thousand rounds before it—"

"*Shut up!*" snarled Ed. "Was Betty hurt? Was Jeremy? Was there anybody else in the house that *could* be hurt?"

Robert shook his head. "Jeremy? Hurt? This had to be like a tickle to him. As for Betty—as fine a piece of ass as ever walked this good green earth if you want my opinion—"

"I don't."

"I knew DaFoe had taken your heart. I didn't know he had taken your balls as well. I left in a hurry. But I'd guess the lightning indicates at least Jeremy was still breathing—or whatever it is he does. I'd guess the fact that *I'm* still breathing—thanks very much for asking—indicates that Betty is, too. As cold a fish as Jeremy is, I figure blowing away his woman might irritate him a bit."

Ed's hands were fists under the table. They were brothers in all but fact. No one. *No one* had ever made him as angry as Robert. No one had ever managed to so get so consistently under his skin. Was this a feature of all brothers or quasi-brothers? Ed was glad he wasn't carrying a gun. The urge to shoot Robert right then and there—*damn* the consequences—might have been irresistible.

"Calmly, brother bear," Robert said softly. "Remember: Jeremy had me. He could have vaporized me just like he did poor old Lyle Williams. I'm alive because he *chose* to let me live. Now, what do you think that means?" Robert turned his attention to his waffles.

Ed forced his hands to relax. Forced his mind to let go of its single, murderous intent of leaping across the table and strangling Robert. Robert wasn't stupid. Impatient, yes. Intemperate, impulsive, homicidal, and sociopathic, yes. But *not* stupid.

Okay, thought Ed. Jeremy wasn't micromanaging the County. Had he ever, really? That was more the job of the current Commissioner, Eldest, or like official figure. But they had always depended on the unwritten law: Do what Jeremy wanted or *bad* things happened. This was Nuthatch County. Power didn't flow downhill from the feds to the state to the County to the town. It had come directly from Jeremy for generations.

So, either Jeremy *wanted* Robert to shoot up his house (unlikely) or Jeremy had essentially abdicated. Which meant the authority from which the current Commissioner, Eldest, or like official figure derived their power was gone. Which meant they had no power at all.

"Holy shit," breathed Ed.

Robert looked up at him and gave him a predatory grin. "Yeah. 'Do as thou wilt be the whole of the law.'"

Ed stared at him.

Robert waved him away with a forkful of waffle. "Don't look at me that way. I went to college."

"You slept with a college girl for a month."

"Same difference."

The plan was for Luke to use the Fourth to take the temperature of the County. After all, the agents Rosen had assigned to the matter had been hard at work for months. He should have seen *some* response. Luke was briefly excited by the parade but then nothing until he heard the next day about Robert Porter shooting up the DaFoe place. He was on the phone instantly with Rosen.

"Did you hear about—"

"—Robert Porter shooting up the DaFoe farm? Yes. About an

hour after it happened. I have some nice video I can send you. Very graphic."

Luke stopped for a moment. "Why didn't you call yesterday?"

"I wanted to wait and see what would happen."

Luke held out his phone for a moment and then put it back to his ear. He was forcibly reminded that Rosen did *not* work for him. Rosen's allegiances were as mysterious as the workings of the rest of Bush the Younger's administration. Rosen worked directly for the Department of Defense. What were their plans? Did Powell really know what was going on? Did Bush? Colin Powell had known about Jeremy DaFoe from his days in the Pentagon but now Powell was Department of State. DOD was run by Rumsfeld, whom Luke had never met.

Had a Secretary of Defense *ever* attended a Nuthatch County briefing?

Luke thought for a moment. He could not recall a single one. Yet, Rosen had made it clear that DOD had known about Jeremy since World War II.

Luke shook his head. He was an old man. He wasn't cut out for this sort of intrigue.

"What do your agents say is happening now?" he said dully.

"No further reaction from Jeremy. He and Betty are staying with Buddy. You'd think something as powerful and vindictive as Jeremy DaFoe would respond more to an attack on his person. Or on the person of his wife."

"He did nothing at all?"

"Apparently there were a few stray lightning bolts."

"Lightning bolts?"

"A half-hearted attempt at best. He completely missed Porter. And he's done nothing since. This may be a good thing. After all, the whole point of this exercise is to drive a wedge between Jeremy and those he cares about. Porter's actions could be considered symbolic of the County's increasing distance from Jeremy. Jeremy's lack of reaction might indicate his increasing distance from the County."

"Maybe you should come out here and monitor things directly."

"I don't think so. There's no good excuse for me to be out there. I have no… *official* connection to Nuthatch County. On the other hand, *you* have every good reason to be there. It's the Fourth—well, fifth, now. Things are odd. Jeremy's house has been shot up. You're just there to make sure everything works out."

"Yeah." Luke suddenly felt every day of his better than seventy years.

"You're staying at the Taverton as usual, right? Just stay there for a few more days to see what is happening. If Jeremy has become sufficiently separated from the County we can make our offer."

"How will we know?"

"My agents are monitoring him closely. If he's become as distant as we like, we'll know it."

"I can't believe Robert would do that." Buddy shook his head.

The adrenalin had worn off and Betty looked haggard. Buddy was suddenly reminded of the men he fought with in Italy. Not when they went out or were killed or injured in pieces, but when they came back unhurt. People reacted in different ways to getting shot at. Some returned furious. Some returned muttering to themselves in delayed terror. Some could be found just sitting against a tree, eyes sunken, staring into space. Betty looked like she was in this last group.

Jeremy didn't seem bothered for himself but he kept on hand on Betty's shoulder or thigh or hand; he didn't stay out of touching distance. Once he got up to fill their coffee cups and Betty seemed to swim up out of her thick despondency and look around in alarm, only to calm when she saw how close Jeremy was. Buddy looked out the window into the hot midday July day. Somehow it seemed like it should be the dark of night.

"I think Robert was after me," Jeremy said at last.

"He must have known he couldn't hurt you." Buddy poured milk into Betty's coffee the way she liked it. She didn't seem to notice. "Maybe you should go to bed," he said to her gently. "I've been through this sort of thing. You should sleep if you can."

"Maybe," she said.

Jeremy looked thoughtful. "Maybe I should go for a walk for a bit. Make it clear I'm not staying with anybody. I wouldn't want to give him an excuse to come after me here."

Buddy spread his hands. "Can't you just… take care of him?"

Jeremy glanced at Betty, then at Buddy. Suddenly, Buddy knew he was talking to something very, very old. "Not right now."

Buddy dropped his eyes. "You know best, Papa Jeremy."

Jeremy was quiet for a long time. "Not really." He squatted next to Betty. "Honey? I'm going to go off for a bit. You stay here with Buddy."

Betty grabbed his hand suddenly, clenching it to her chest without any change of expression at all.

"I'll stay if you want me to," said Jeremy softly. "But I don't want Porter to follow me here. You decide."

Betty didn't say anything but after a moment her grip loosened.

Jeremy patted her shoulder. "I'll talk to you later," and kissed her on the cheek. Betty didn't respond.

Jeremy waved to Buddy and left out the back door. Buddy waited to hear the gate open or shut but there was only silence.

Betty picked up the coffee and her hand shook. She stared at her hand and after a moment, the shaking stopped and she was able to drink the coffee.

"That's better," said Buddy, feeling inane. What do you say in a time like this?

Betty pursed her lips, thinking. "Buddy," she said at last. "Do you have a gun?"

Annie White drove over to Howie's place first only because it was closer. She called Herbert on the way to meet her there. The brothers were waiting for her in the living room. The mid-afternoon light shone hotly through the window, outlining the day's sweat on their faces.

She didn't say anything to either of them but marched across the room to Howie's gun cabinet and yanked it open. There were three rifles: two Marlins—a 30-30 and 30-06—and a nice semi-automatic .308 Ruger. She pulled out the lever action Marlin and checked the action. Smooth. Herbert took good care of his firearms.

There was a pile of ammunition at the bottom of the gun cabinet. She rummaged around until she found a box of 30-30 shells and began loading the rifle.

"Honey," said Herbert tentatively. "What are you doing?"

"The time has come," she said. The magazine was full now. She levered the rifle to load the chamber, eased the hammer, and put in the last shell. "We're going to take back the Chase land."

Howie reached to calm her but Annie put the 30-06 into his hands. Suitable for elk at a thousand yards. Now *that* ought to do a little damage.

Howie stood, looking at the bolt action in his hand. Annie put the box of shells in his other hand. He hefted one, then the other. "Okay," he said at last.

Annie pulled the Ruger and its ammunition out of the cabinet and handed it to Herbert.

Herbert took the rifle reluctantly. He popped the clip and started loading it. "Handguns are in the drawer.

Annie nodded in approval, opened it up, and smiled. Two oiled and lethal 45s and a sweet little 9 millimeter. "Howie, I didn't know you had it in you."

"Hey," said Herbert. "I got guns, too."

"I know, dear," Annie said soothingly. "We'll go by your place on the way."

Herbert looked up from the clip. "What about Jeremy?"

"To Hell with Jeremy," Annie said decisively. "He doesn't count anymore."

Walter was in his habitual chair in front of the den television where he'd happily been yelling back at the evening news when he heard the commotion down stairs in the rec room. The first thing he thought of was that float—what a giant load of crap *that* turned out to be. At the end of the parade, he'd felt like telling the boys what for but when he said something and they turned towards him, all three expressionless faces waiting dutifully to hear him since he was their father but with no more intent to listen than they'd give to a goat, he found he couldn't speak.

"Yeah, Dad?" prompted Robert Earl.

"Nothing." And he remembered the joke again, like he'd remembered it daily since Roger had been born. Roger, his favorite though he'd never admit it. *Whose is Roger?* From Jane would come the answer: He's *your* child.

He turned off the television, got up from the chair, and made his way over to the downstairs door. Rested his hand on the knob. If he went down there, would he be able to ask? Did he care? Was it really important?

Since the parade, things were different. First the parade itself. Then the shooting up of Jeremy's place. Every sound. Every commotion was different, too. The world was completely new. Everything in it looked exactly the same but had been born just seconds ago. Strange thoughts kept echoing in his mind. If the world had been created whole and entire a moment ago, would he feel differently? Would he feel fifty-six or would he somehow know he was newly formed?

He opened the door and walked downstairs. Jane was there, sitting at the table, a pile of clips in front of her, methodically filling each with cartridges. The boys had taken apart their rifles and were inspecting them, cleaning and oiling each component, and then gently putting them back together. Jane and the boys fit together as well as the guns. Each precisely machined into close tolerance to work with one another. There was little talking. As Jane finished filling a clip, she passed it without asking to whoever had the correct gun for it. Roger took the clip for the 7mm magnum. Dean the .223. Robert Earl the 7.62. Jane had her own rifle out, a sweet .22 hornet she'd asked for on her birthday years before. For killing coyotes.

He must have made as sound for they stopped and turned towards him. Each watching him. Measuring him.

Walter cleared his throat. "What's going on?"

The boys looked at Jane. Jane smiled at him. "Some varmints on the parcel where the boys are farming. Nothing important."

"Ah." Walter looked at her and the boys. "Looks like you're going to war." Nothing changed in their expression but suddenly the room felt colder. He tried to laugh. "Won't be much left of those varmints."

"No, honey," Jane said. "Not a thing."

"Okay," he said hurriedly, backing out of the rec room. "I'll just leave you to it."

Whose boy was Roger's? Or Dean? Or Robert Earl? The

answer was obvious.

They were Jane's.

The idea originated, as such ideas do, from the inspirational powers of alcohol.

The Thomas generations—Lee, Franklin, and Carl—were afternoon drinking in the Greenwood again. Carl preferred to drink in a bar. Lee considered it an affectation of youth. When Carl was old enough, he'd discover the joys of drinking at home where if you fell down and pissed your pants no one would throw you out in the snow. Not that there was much snow in July. It was the principle of the thing.

With considerable experimentation, the three of them had discovered that Budweiser became palatable if mixed with whisky. As time progressed, they decided the beer was superfluous.

"We should burn a cross in his yard," said Carl suddenly. "That's what the Klan does, right? Burn a cross in someone's yard."

Mike Atwater was sitting down the bar from them. "Beats setting fire to a truck."

"It does," said Lee, sagely. "But whose yard?"

The bar fell quiet. No one had burned a cross anywhere but at meetings or in the July parade for generations.

"*His,*" insisted Carl.

"We need a name, son," said Franklin.

"Buddy Parker."

"Uh oh," said Mike. "You want to burn a cross in the yard of the Eldest?"

"Eldest *nigra.*" Carl slapped the counter for emphasis.

Silence fell in the bar as they considered the possibility.

"We could be like Lester Maddox," Lee said in a hushed

voice.

"Lester Maddox is dead." Franklin shook his head. "We could be like George Wallace."

"George Wallace fucking *repented*," Carl said scornfully. "Also, he's dead. Screw them. We could be the fucking Ku Klux *Klan* instead of some Fourth of July wannabes."

"Yeah," breathed Lee.

"Yeah!" cried Franklin and was echoed around the bar.

"But what about Jeremy?" Mike said.

The tavern fell silent, eyes on Lee.

Lee looked around the bar slowly. "Fuck Jeremy."

Glenn jerked open the door of the trailer and ran up the steps. Jenny was cooking something and the twins were watching TV. He turned off the stove and took her hands.

"You have to go," he said.

"What's wrong?" Jenny searched his face.

"Did you know I've been working for Robert Porter?"

Jenny stared at him. "Yes."

"Okay. Well, the feds are raiding his trailers tonight and I don't want you here when he figures out I told them where to find him."

Jenny stared into his eyes for a long moment. "You are coming with me. We'll drive to Kansas City. I know some people there. They can—"

"I got to help the feds," Glenn said gently. "You go to Kansas City. Call me when you get there and tell me where you are. I'll find you—"

"*You can't stay,* Glenn. That crazy son-of-a-bitch will kill you. He'll shoot you dead like a dog. I won't have it!"

Glenn took her in his arms.

The twins came over from the television and watched the

two of them, mouths open.

"Honey," Glenn said gently. "Minutes count. He'll shoot *all* of us. Go get some things. Just enough to get by and I'll meet you at the truck."

He ran outside and into the old house: *second floor cupola, false bottom in an old wardrobe*. Glenn reached inside and pulled out a box. In the box, neatly bound with duct tape were bundles of bills. Forty thousand now. He ran back outside. Jenny was convincing the recalcitrant twins to get in the back seat.

"Here," he said, handing her the money. "That should get things going in Kansas City. I'll be there in a couple of days."

She hefted it, turned, and put it in the car on the front seat. Then, she came back to him and grabbed him and planted a kiss on him the likes of which he hadn't known since their honeymoon.

"Don't you get killed," she said fiercely. "Don't you even *think* about getting killed."

Then, she got in the car, started it, and drove off.

Wow, he thought. What a woman I married!

Then, he realized she had taken their only car.

Mary Jo Pedersen picked up her baby and held it. Little Edwina was a gift. She'd never had the possibility of a child. Now, every time she picked her up, she felt the pull of the Caesarian in her ample belly. A reminder of that unexpected trip to the clinic back in February.

It was no miraculous virgin birth but as far as Mary Jo was concerned it could have been.

She sat and played quietly with the baby in her lap. Sid had found a job as a night guard in Sikeston and was sleeping until his shift. What with ninety minutes one way, Mary Jo didn't want to wake him until she had to.

Sid had taken to the baby as strongly as if Edwina were his own. And who was to say she wasn't? Babies were mysterious things.

Mary Jo stared into space for a moment. She picked Edwina up and went outside to the porch. The sun was setting, a hot blinding golden sphere. Something. Something.

Mary Jo went back in and shook Sid. "Honey?"

"Yeah. I'm awake. Time for my shift already?" He sat up and looked outside the thick curtains. "It's still light."

"Time to go now," she said with determination. "Me and the baby will come with you tonight."

"I don't know —"

"Don't argue with me. Just get dressed."

Mary Jo was waiting in the car when Sid came outside. He slid into the driver's seat. "You going to tell me what's going on?"

"Never mind."

They drove west towards Sikeston as helpless people in the County had always fled just before a great murderous catastrophe.

Chapter 9: Things Fall Apart

Nadine stood in the afternoon sun cursing Glenn under her breath. ATF and DEA were going to meet her here, next to the abandoned government road equipment, and she'd intended Glenn to take credit for it. But the son-of-a-bitch hadn't shown up.

Four black Suburbans rolled onto the gravel from the direction of Pilate, pulled up next to her car, and stopped. The windows were so darkly tinted Nadine couldn't see who was driving.

The driver's side door opened and Jonas Cole stepped out. Nadine felt cold air pour out of the open door and cool her ankles. A moment later Kate Marquis came out from around the other side. No other doors opened. The Suburbans could have been populated by the dead for all Nadine could tell.

Cole shook her hand. "Where's your client?"

"Not here," Nadine said thinly.

Cole sighed. "It would be better for him if he were. We could vouch that he helped us."

"I'll vouch for him."

"You know where these sites are by yourself?"

"Yes. Any knowledge I have is due entirely to Glenn

Waxman." Nadine enunciated her words clearly enough to be understood in a court of law.

Jonas rubbed his forehead. "Yeah. I get it. Glenn Waxman can't be here today because he's otherwise occupied. But he's responsible for the information you're giving us."

Marquis brought out two topographic maps of Nuthatch County and spread them out over the hood of Nadine's Buick. "Show us where they are."

Nadine looked over the map and made sure they were correct as far as she could tell. Maps of Nuthatch County had a bad habit of being oddly wrong. She put her finger down on a notch in the west end of the Bittersweet Ridge. "You'll find a still back up in this hollow off County Road 3. Another is on the other side of the bluff but you'll have to take the road around it. You can't go over the bluff on foot." Marquis marked the spots.

Nadine ran her finger to the south west. "Here is one of the trailers. The other one is off County Road 7—here. They're all hidden from the road but there's a dirt path wide enough for a four-wheel to get up there. Probably how they got them up there in the first place."

"Okay," said Marquis, taking one of the topographic maps. "Let's go."

Cole nodded and started walking over to one of the other Suburbans.

"Wait," called Nadine. "I want to come with you. To protect the interests of my client."

"We'll manage."

"I insist."

Cole looked her full in the face. He turned to the open Suburban. "Cofetti?"

A tall man came out of the Suburban. "Yes, sir."

"Let the air out of all of her tires."

"What?" Nadine shouted. "You can't—"

"Shut up," said Cole. "You've done your best for your client.

We're not going to shoot anybody unless they shoot first. If they do, and your client's on their side, hopefully he'll keep his head down because I'll sure as hell blow his head off if he opens fire on me. But I am not taking a civilian into what is almost certainly going to be a firefight. You wait here. Or, better yet, walk back into town and have a beer or something until we get back. I have your phone number. I'll call you when it's over."

Cofetti was working on the second tire when Cole finished.

"Oh, for Christ's sake." Cole walked over to her car and walked around, shooting a hole in each tire, carefully aiming away from the Suburbans. He handed Cofetti the map and pointed him to the passenger side. "I'll drive. You navigate." As he closed the door, he looked at Nadine. "You can send me the invoice for the tires."

Marquis, watching them both, now got into her Suburban and the convoy drove out onto the road as one.

Nadine watched them recede in the distance.

She went over to her car and ineffectually kicked one of the torn tires. What was she going to do now? Call AAA? She sat on the tread of a backhoe, contemplating her situation.

A truck filled with men pulled in from the direction of Pilate next to the road grader. The men piled out carrying, Nadine suddenly realized, various rifles and shotguns. The driver came over and looked her over belligerently.

"Who are you?" he asked.

"Nadine Durant, County Clerk," she snapped back.

He stepped back. "I'm Bill Keller, president of the Organization for Nuthatch Country Progress. We're here to take possession of the government road equipment for the greater good of Nuthatch County."

Nadine started to protest, drawing on the mantle County Clerk like a comforter. Then, she stopped. "Okay. You do that. Can I get a ride back to Pilate?"

Bill looked uncertain. "I don't know—"

A second truck rolled onto the gravel from the direction of Ridgeville. One of the men in the back of that truck stood up in the bed and declared, "We take possession of this road equipment in the name of the Nuthatch County Self Actualization Committee."

"You can't do that," shouted Bill. "We did that."

An ominous growl came from the Organization, answered by the Committee.

Oh, Lord. She looked at the two groups, looked at their guns.

Nadine managed to crawl deep into the bucket of the back hoe just as the shooting started.

Years ago, Buddy had boxed up all the Jeremy photographs and papers Grandpa Norton had left him. The sun was just closing down for the day when he found that box up in the attic and brought it down to the kitchen. He placed each scrap carefully on the table, trying to make sense of things. Norton had taken some nice pictures of the cave paintings—how had Norton gotten that old camera and flash under the water?

Buddy shook his head. It was funny how the mind worked. Buddy had been fifty-five when Grandpa Norton had died at the ripe old age of eighty-seven. He'd known that man for fifty-five years, from when Norton was a young man, through the weakening middle years and into dark old age when Norton, riddled with bone cancer, had taken to a particular chair and refused to get up. You'd think Buddy would remember the whole span of that time but instead, he always thought of him just before he got sick at the end, white-haired, shuffling instead of walking, voice weak and high instead of booming. Buddy's first thought when he saw those cave pictures was how had that old man managed to get under the water. Buddy had managed—but, of course, that was not how it was at all. Clearly, the pictures must have been taken years earlier. When Norton had been a young man.

Norton spoke little about Jeremy until death started to lay a secure claim to him. Then it all came tumbling out. Thoughts and conclusions made over decades of study. Buddy looked over the books, pictures, drawings, and maps, with a kind of awe. Norton had made Jeremy his life's study. Buddy had never been so thorough, so completely scientific, about Jeremy. Here were drawings made from the photographs covered with annotations. One read, "Connection to Mayans?" with a line to the stylized lightning bolt. "Action at a distance outside of the County?" read another. Some symbols on the walls of the cave were marked "Anasazi." Some "Aborigine." One set of notes suggested Norse runes—"A visit or a communication?" Some were marked "Unknown???" Some of Norton's notes dealt with the unknowns. Were they unknown North American civilizations? Communications from civilizations outside the County? Non-human cultures? Norton had underlined his conclusion: "Who could know?"

Buddy had gone through this box before, but the trip to the cave with Betty had given him a new perspective. He saw these things through *her* eyes. New and wholly remarkable.

The pounding on his doorway finally caught his attention. He answered the door.

Ray was standing outside. "They're coming."

"Who?"

"The Klan."

Buddy stared at his brother. "You've got to be kidding. Jeremy—"

"If we put our faith in Jeremy, we're liable to get killed." He gestured for Buddy to come outside. "We've got to make a stand."

Betty came downstairs, drying her hair. "What's going on?"

Buddy turned to her. "Ray says the Klan is coming here."

"Oh." Betty ran back up the stairs and came back with the .45 Buddy had given her. "I'm ready."

Ray nodded. "Let's go."

"Hold *on*." Buddy turned to Betty. "You get in your damned car and you drive over to Pam Small's house and you get her and Cox to come over here."

"Buddy—"

"You go *now*. Out the back way quick. So, I don't have to worry about you."

Outside, in front of Buddy's porch, stood perhaps twenty men with guns. Hunting guns mostly, though there were a few pistols and military-looking hardware Buddy could not identify. "Jesus."

"We put our faith in *him* and we're just as liable to get killed," Ray said quietly. He pointed to the crowd. "You're the Eldest. You're supposed to lead. So, lead."

"Lead what?"

"Lead us against the enemy." Ray put his hands on his brother's shoulder. "It is time." He turned Buddy to face the crowd.

The men of Ashby gave him a subdued cheer. In the gathering evening gloom, Buddy could recognize few faces through his cataracts.

"What are we going to do, Eldest?"

"I guess I'll go talk to them." Buddy stepped down from the porch. The crowd parted before him and closed after him, followed him across his yard (*going to have to reseed the grass after this*) and down Garvey towards the border between Ridgeville and Ashby. He stopped where the streets changed names. Ray stood next to him on his left. A few hundred feet away a group of perhaps twenty men wearing sheets and carrying torches walked slowly toward Ashby. Several of them were puffing as they carried an eight-foot cross nailed hastily together from four-by-fours.

The white-sheeted men stopped short of the border. A half dozen of them set down the cross with a grateful wheeze.

Buddy was surprised at how menacing they looked with only their eyes visible through ragged holes. He couldn't identify a single one of them.

"Stand aside, Eldest," boomed the Klansman standing nearest Buddy. He held up the torch signifying he was the leader.

Buddy knew the voice. "Come on, Carl. This has gone far enough."

"Eldest," Carl said. "We aim to burn a cross in your yard. We aim to show you once and for all who's the boss around here."

Buddy shook his head. "Look. Nothing's happened we can't manage. Nobody's hurt. You just head on back home and I'll tell Jeremy it was all a misunderstanding."

Carl leaned forward almost in Buddy's face. "The only thing protecting you niggers in the County has been Jeremy." Carl swung a meaty fist and hit Buddy on the side of the head.

Buddy went down in a heap, stunned. The first thing that ran through his mind: *Oh, please God let me not break a hip.*

Carl leaned over him. "Fuck Jeremy."

Ray stepped forward and shoved Carl away. "Fuck you," he said and brought up his ancient revolver and fired it in Carl's face.

The shot and angry whine of the bullet startled everybody including Ray and Carl, who both expected Carl's face to explode into bloody ruin. Instead, Carl stood, eyes tightly shut, powder burns all over the hood.

"Huh," said Ray in surprise.

Carl opened one eye, saw the gun, closed it again.

Ray dropped the pistol to Carl's chest and fired again, this time with expected results as Carl's chest caved into a crater of bloody and bone.

"Shit," said Buddy as both sides opened fire.

Pam Small's mother had died of pancreatic cancer when both she and Peggy had been in college. Pam's father had been killed in Viet Nam when they were kids so there was no one else. Pam, being the oldest, decided it was her job to provide whatever passed as a home and family for her and her sister, Peggy. Once they became adults, they fell into a monthly dinner. Both of them said publicly they were doing it for the other sister. Privately, both would have felt lost without regularly seeing each other.

It was Pam's turn to cook. Pam lived in their mother's house on the outskirts of Pilate. She had only her cat, Rupert, for company. Peggy preferred to live in an apartment over the Pileggi Market, a block's walk to the clinic.

Pam drained the pasta into the sink, holding it in the colander with a wooden spoon. "I swear, Peggy. We should both get out of this town. You could get a job up at Southeast. Or even Barnes in Saint Louis." She tapped the wooden spoon against her lips meditatively. "I bet I could get a job as city manager in one of the county towns up that way. Hell, it couldn't be any harder than this."

Peggy smiled indulgently, swirled the wine in her glass, and sipped it slowly. A little was okay. She wasn't on call *officially*. But only she and Olivia Thomas regularly worked at the clinic so the odds were good she could be called at any given moment. "You love it here."

"I don't know. It's all gone to crap. The parade. Shooting up Jeremy's house—"

"That really happened? I thought it was just a story."

"Robert Porter shot it to pieces." Pam shook her head. "I had no idea a firearm could *do* that."

"I heard Jeremy didn't do anything."

"Not a blessed thing. Some people claim they heard thunder

so he might have thrown lightning. But it's pretty clear Robert got clean away with it. If Jeremy threw lightning at something I don't think he'd miss so I don't put much stock in that part of the story." She put the pasta back in the pot and added the white sauce she'd made, and then gently stirred in bits of catfish she'd sautéed on the stove. Rupert stood at her feet and complained loudly that those fish were *his*. Pam ignored him. "They're staying over at Buddy's."

Peggy considered her wine. "Well, I guess you can say that's pretty strange. But leave the County over it? Come on, Pam. You've weathered worse than this."

Pam shook her head as she served up bowls of steaming goodness. "I don't know."

There was a pounding on the front door. Pam and Peggy looked at one another, put down the bowls, and went into the front room to open the door.

"Buddy sent me," said Betty. "The Klan is attacking Ashby. He said to get Grace and get over there."

Peggy picked up her purse. "Drop me off at the clinic."

Betty nodded and looked thoughtful for a moment. "Hold on." She took Buddy's .45 out of her purse and handed it to Pam. "You take this. You might need it more than me."

Pam stared at the pistol in her hand like it was a live rat. "I don't know anything about guns."

Betty laughed shortly. "It's loaded and set. Safety is off. Just draw the hammer back and pull the trigger. A pistol like this kicks like a mule so don't let it hit you in the face. And aim each time."

"What if you need it?"

"I won't need it."

Pam looked from Betty to Peggy, not quite able the change gears that fast. She shrugged, put the gun in her purse, and followed them out the door.

As the door closed, Rupert leaped on the table and began to

feed.

The Taverton Hotel was constructed in a brief moment of prosperity between World War I and the crash of 1929. The well-to-do of Pilate became mysteriously convinced a new railroad line would pass through the County on its way from New Madrid to Saint Louis. Wealth would fall like rain. They were disappointed. The new line never materialized. The only trains for miles continued to run on the Illinois side of the river, tantalizingly out of reach.

The hotel was built on contradictions. Gilt edge scroll work on the door frames of rooms not much bigger than the occupying double bed. Stained glass sealing windows that could not be opened before the age of air conditioning. A broad kitchen capable of feeding a mighty army of transient businessmen that served a dining room where half a dozen would have to rub elbows to fit.

Luke had eaten dinner alone. He was the sole visitor in the hotel. The rest were permanent residents and chose to use hot plates in their rooms rather than pay the prices charged by the kitchen. Luke, depressed over the lack of action after the parade and the shooting, had considered having his meal sent to his room. But the Taverton cook had to be monitored. Once Luke had gotten a hamburger with a lit cigarette under the bun. Another time he'd been served a gasping catfish, eyes still rolling. He'd been outraged and yelled at Bess to come out and *deal* with this. Bess had come out and crushed its head with a mallet. "Will that do?" she said, imperturbable as stone, cigarette dangling from her lips.

Coping with her from the dining room was much easier than hauling a steak burnt hard as cork down the stairs to the basement kitchen.

Back in his room, leaden pasta weighed him down in the room's single chair. He stared out the window.

Nothing had happened.

Depressed again, Luke called the front desk and ordered a bottle of whisky and some soda. It arrived a few minutes later. Luke swore it was delivered by the same ancient relative of Bess that had served the Taverton since Luke had become liaison. God. That was forty *years* ago. When had Bess become master of the kitchen? When had this homunculus started at the front desk? Luke couldn't remember anyone else here. Was he senile? He tipped the old man generously and closed the door.

He poured himself a generous drink and sipped it, pressed the icy glass against his forehead.

This was it, he thought. He'd tried with the backing of the entire Department of Defense. And what had happened? A single sociopathic criminal revolutionary aimed at Jeremy and missed.

Hell, what had Luke expected? The County to rise up and cast Jeremy out? After thousands of years?

Luke wondered what Jeremy had been like without human beings around. Had he taken the form of bears or buffalo? Cougars? Birds? Luke couldn't imagine Jeremy as anything other than a human being. Or, at least, wearing a human skin. He remembered a word he'd heard years ago: *Skinwalker*. Where? Some airport novel? That's what Jeremy must be, wearing the *skin* of bear, buffalo, or man, something unnatural living beneath.

Luke poured another drink. He felt a little better. Alcohol had been a good friend to his family. Tried and true in times of hardship.

The Taverton had central air these days but it made the room atmosphere cold and heavy. Luke had picked this room on purpose. It was the room he and Catherine had always asked for. The room they'd stayed at when he first returned from DC as liaison. The room he and Catherine had occupied the summer she died. Before the stroke, when they were lying there pooling in sweat, the closed window had become intolerable. Luke had taken a jackknife, cut through archeological layers of paint, and pounded the recalcitrant window open.

Now, after years of his repeated pounding, he was able to open it without too many bruises. Luke leaned outside, breathing in thick, heavy air. The window wasn't far above the sidewalk. He could look up and down the silent and empty street. Inside the air was like breathing cold mercury. Outside the air was like breathing steaming milk. It wasn't clear which was better.

The Sheriff's car tore down the street, lights blazing but silent. As it passed, Luke recognized Grace Cox driving and Pam Small beside her. In the back were two men he couldn't see clearly. Officer Price? Sergeant Moon? He couldn't tell.

"Huh," he said.

A moment later four more cars raced passed, each filled with men. Luke could see the turgid menace of rifles held vertically.

Okay, he thought. *That's* interesting.

The street fell silent again.

Luke felt hopeful that something was happening. He shook his head. No. This was a lost cause. Jeremy would be here forever. Luke would die. Nadine would die. Joanie would die. Jeremy would go on and on.

The sun set and darkness filled the streets. The streetlights came on.

Luke heard shooting in the distance.

"Huh," he said. He came back inside the room, poured himself another drink, and brought the bottle to the window. Luke tried to remember the last time he heard gunshots in Pilate. Shooting flotsam in the river? Hunting season? He couldn't recall.

There was a crack up the street and a piece of brick shattered in the wall next to him, brushing his face with fragments. He stared at the wall for a moment and then felt wetness on his cheek. He touched it, brought his hand into the light. Blood.

"Huh," he said for a moment.

Then, it hit him and he jerked back into the room, ran around the bed into the bathroom. Where to hide? There was a stand-up shower. He got in that and looked back at the tiny bathroom. There was only a small window on the other side. The rest of the bathroom was tiled white. He closed the shower curtain.

"Well, that's stupid," came a voice.

Cautiously, Luke drew back the curtain.

A balding middle-aged man with a bad comb-over stood in the doorway wearing a Nuthatch County Municipal Services shirt.

"Do I know you?" said Luke.

"Harry Carr." Harry pulled a towel off the rack and tossed it to Luke. "Clean yourself up."

Luke wet the towel and washed off the blood. It was a slight cut. He could have been hit in the eye. Luke shuddered, thinking about it. "Did somebody shoot at me?"

"Don't flatter yourself. It was an argument gone bad up the street. Weapons were used. I came here to protect you."

"I'm gratified the Nuthatch County Municipal Services is interested in my welfare."

"Sorry." He pulled out a badge. "Harry Carr, Bureau of Weights and Measures."

"Bureau of Weights and Measures?"

"Don't start. Rosen sent me to make sure you got out all right when the shit hit the fan."

Luke stopped dabbing at his cheek. "What's happened?"

"What's *not* happened? The Ridgeville Klan is in a firefight with the Ashby blacks. The Chase-Pollock feud has started up again out on the Cleary land. Old arguments and bad blood are surfacing here in Pilate." Harry spread his hands and laughed.

"It's everything you ever wanted."

"I didn't want any violence."

"Hey. This is America. You take the lid off; you get violence."

Luke put down the towel. "Because Jeremy isn't doing anything."

Harry made a gun with his finger and thumb and pointed it at Luke. "Bang on. Now we've got to get you out of here."

"Not without my daughter. And my grand-daughter."

Harry rubbed his face. "You're not making this easy. I don't know where Nadine Durant is. But I can bet Joan Durant is at the clinic with her boyfriend."

"Let's go there."

Harry tapped his chin. "There's a bar brawl turned into a firefight on A Street. Somebody set a fire on River Road. We can drive towards the main road and cut north and back again to get to the clinic."

"We could just walk. It's not far."

"We'll drive. When we get there, you can tell me how much you would have preferred walking."

While Amos and Jean didn't live together anymore, they still jointly owned the old house at the County reservation border. Amos arrived there as the moon was coming up. Jean was on the front porch, dressed in beads and paint and not much else. Amos looked at her body, ravaged by age, and remembered when they were first married.

"You heard?" he said.

"Jeremy giving up and the County going to hell? I heard." She watched the moon come up.

"There's talk on my side to join in. Go after the Osage once and for all."

"I hear the same. The Choctaw time is done. Let us rise up."

He joined her on the porch and stared at the moon, rising and full, wreathed in clouds. It was just as majestic and silent as if there were nothing happening in the County at all. "What do you say?"

"I say there's no good reason for any Native to get between two white men shooting at each other."

"Couldn't have said it better myself. I'll tell mine. You'll tell yours?"

"Yes."

Amos stepped down from the porch and looked back up at her. Damn. She still looked great. He licked his lips. "Might come back here after."

Jean looked down and smiled at him. "I might be here."

He grinned and jogged over to his car. Ruined him, she did. Just *ruined* him for any other woman.

Harry led Luke to a Nuthatch County Highway Department truck. He pointed to the driver's side. "Passenger side door doesn't work."

Luke climbed up and scootched over to the passenger's side. Harry followed him and sat down, fastening his seatbelt. Luke saw this and decided the better part of valor was fastening his own.

Harry started the truck and played with the pedal, raced the engine, then tweaked something under the dashboard and tweaked under the dash again. Each time the engine sounded throatier. Meaner.

Harry grinned. "Nitrous. You never know when you're going to need an extra bit of power."

With that, he floored it and popped the clutch. The truck bounced down the road.

"Skitters like a roach on a griddle, don't she?" Harry

chuckled. He caught Luke staring at him and laughed. "I've been here *way* too long."

The truck roared down A Street and turned west on Broadway on two wheels, something Luke had never seen outside of a movie and would have sworn right up to that moment was entirely due to special effects. Luke almost threw up.

"Roll down your window," yelled Harry. "And get down."

Luke got down first and rolled down the window from a crouch. He saw now that Harry was driving with his left hand, his right occupied with the largest pistol Luke had ever seen.

"1911 Colt 45. Philippine model. Knock a man down no matter where you hit him."

"I didn't ask!" shouted Luke. "Mind the road!"

"Ah, this? I could do this in my sleep. Guatemala City? Now there's a challenge." Harry brought up the gun and fired without seeming to aim. The roar filled the truck, followed a moment later by a scream. "Molotov cocktails. *That's* why you have to knock them down."

Luke tried to bury himself in the seat well. He covered his head with his hands.

Harry began to sing.

The game was played on Sunday. It was played in the Devil's back yard.

Another turn, this time to the left, and a bump that nearly tossed Luke up from the foot well and out the window.

"Shit!" yelled Harry. "Road block." He turned in his seat quickly and fired back behind the truck. Another scream. "Fucker won't do that again. Will you?" He started singing again.

Jesus playing quarterback. Moses playing guard.
The score was six to nothing. The boys from hell were ahead.
Jesus scored a touchdown and this is what they said.

The truck screeched on the brakes for longer than Luke

thought possible. Surely the tires would catch fire. Burn down to the steel. The steel itself would melt. Something seemed to catch the front end and spun the truck around, once, twice, three times.

Stay with God! Stay with God!

Rock 'em, Moses! Sock 'em, Jesus!

Stay with God!

The truck stopped, rocked sickeningly from side to side, and finally became still.

"Here we are," said Harry. "The clinic. Carter Faraday's here. And, since your granddaughter is fucking him, it's more than likely she is, too."

I'd kill him if I were thirty years younger, Luke thought as he clawed his way over the seat and worked his way down. *Twenty years younger.* He knelt on the ground and kissed the sweet asphalt. *Ten years.*

When Joanie awoke that morning, Carter was already gone. He'd left a note he'd be leaving the clinic at six. Joanie found herself smiling. Resolutely decided against it. Smiled again.

Carter lived in half a mill house made of honest brick from when Nuthatch County had a brickyard, reflecting a time when Nuthatch County had a mill. Both brickyard and mill had burned down and been abandoned, the ruins razed and covered with gravel. The old site was currently occupied by abandoned highway equipment.

She decided to make Carter dinner. To that end, she walked to Pileggi's, bought pasta, mushrooms, a sweet-looking collection of crawfish, and spices. Returning to his house (she had her own *key!*) Joanie put all ingredients away, made a quick lunch to take with her, and pulled out a medium-sized pad and her tin of watercolors. It wasn't even nine yet. There were seven miles of river bank on the east side of Pilate and she planned to put it all to use.

The July sun changed the colors drastically from sun to shadow, from morning to afternoon, from dirt bluff to Mississippi River. At one moment, a log would be a shadow beneath the water, lit only by mysterious accident. The next, the same log would be as illuminated as the Book of Kells. Upstream barges rolled and thrust against the current for every mile and downstream barges drifted in post-coital bliss.

Much of the bank was scoured down to bare earth by the continuous current and dropped straight down to the water. Often in bad weather, these bluffs would calve into the river like glaciers, leaving behind a mud shelf just under the water. Sometimes, the falling earth would be big enough to resist the force of the river and make a breakwater against the current. If it lasted long enough, grass and trees would take hold and stabilize it, holding it down. Small lagoons and islands would form creating. temporary, still, places.

Other bluffs, stabilized by trees, ruled over a small slice of geologic time as the river carved down their sides, exposing bare rock, caves, and the cross-sectional remains of sinkholes.

Some landscapes cry out for a particular medium and technique. The mixture of river, earth, and trees denied sketching and sculpture and insisted on watercolors. Joanie did not consider herself a watercolorist but bowed to the inevitable.

She shared her lunch with a companionable crow, bald with age. As long as she was willing to toss the old crow bits of bread and bologna, he was willing to sit and let her first sketch and then paint him. At one point she was able to get him to perch heavily on her arm as she fed him potato chips. He seemed fearless, certain in his knowledge that he could blind her long before she could hurt him.

Feeling far too exposed, she set him carefully on a tree branch. "You wouldn't do that, would you?"

The crow watched her with one eye, then the other. Then, suddenly he exploded in a great *caw!* and rose in a rush of wings. She wondered what that meant. Laughter? Defiance? Frustration? More food?

She started working her way back towards Pilate to get to the clinic by six. Joanie found herself smiling again.

The sound of the gunshots stopped her while she was threading a chancy section of trail. Joanie looked up. Heard some more. This time, she heard the tumbling scream of a bullet after it struck brick. It sounded like it was coming from Pilate.

Joanie stopped. The clinic's main entrance bordered A Street but it sounded like that's where the shots were coming from. Instead, she walked up D Street to get to the clinic by the back way. As she walked up the hill, she heard more shots, some to the west, some to the south, but all of them safely *not* on D Street.

The hearse was in the loading area and next to it, two pickup trucks. She glanced at the closest truck as she walked toward the loading entrance. Stopped. Returned and looked again. There was blood in the bed, sticky and drying.

Inside, a crowd of people ran up and down the short corridors. She recognized Peggy Small and Jake Withers. Grace Cox lay on a gurney as she was pushed by a nurse she didn't know. Pam Small ran next to her, holding up an IV bag.

Joanie followed Pam more by reflex than by design. Now that she was closer, she could see Grace was conscious and calmly holding a plastic trash bag to her chest. They pulled Grace into an exam room just as Carter rounded a corner. He closed the door without ever seeing Joanie. She was left standing outside.

Clearly not a good time.

Joanie started walking towards the front of the clinic. Surely, she could be of some use.

Carter saw Pam, pointed to the trash bag. "Hold that down." He pulled Grace's hand to one side. Olivia started pulling equipment out from under the table.

Pam pressed the bag and felt a hole beneath her hand. Grace responded with a gasp. She felt the gasp pull at the plastic. Now she knew what "sucking chest wound" meant.

Olivia took the moment to pull an oxygen mask over Grace's face. Then she and Carter took a good hold of the sheet under Grace. "On three," he said. On the count, they slipped her off the gurney onto the table. Grace stifled a moan. Carter injected something into the catheter attached to the IV bag Pam was holding. Pam looked ashen.

A moment later, Grace sagged on the table.

Carter moved to the cabinet and began pulling down instruments. The nurse cut the cloth from around Grace's wound, deftly leaving Pam's hand in place. Pam stood there, holding the IV bag with the other hand until Carter took it from her and hung it on the rack over the table.

He looked at Pam. "I'm going to take over pressing the bag."

Pam held down the bag until she felt his hand and then stepped out of the way. She washed the blood from her hands and then, not knowing what else to do, sat down next to the door.

Carter and Olivia blocked her view. Everything sounded tense and abrupt, urgent. Life and death.

"What happened?" Carter called over his shoulder.

Pam shook her head. "Betty came over to tell us there was some race war going on in Ashby so Grace pulled together some volunteers to see if we could calm things down. I went, too." Pam shook her head. "It was madness. Everybody was shooting at everybody else. Grace went down just as she got out of his car. The rest just scattered. I pulled her back into the car. Then, the windshield exploded. I couldn't see anybody that came with us. I drove her here. I didn't know what else to do." Pam started to cry.

The activity stopped. Carter listened to Grace's chest with the stethoscope and then took her blood pressure. "She's stable. Stay with her. Come find me if anything gets worse. Like her breathing starts to slow or she sounds like she's gagging." He turned to Olivia. "Let's go." The two of them bolted out the door.

Pam stood up and took a paper towel to dry her face. She stood next to Grace. "I always liked you, Grace," she said quietly. "I hope you can hear that."

She pulled the chair near the table and sat there and held Grace's limp hand. Pam listened to Grace breathe. It was the most important sound in the world.

There was no let up.

Every few minutes or so someone else would be brought in through the door. Some were carried. Some were driven. Some walked in from the street under their own power. Peggy had Joanie divide them into three groups. Those pumping visible blood or unconscious were brought into the working area — sometimes just to be settled on the floor. But close to where Carter could get to them. They were Group 1. Group 2 contained those who had significant wounds that could be managed in the waiting area. They were watched unless they took a turn for the worse. Group 3 had to wait outside on the concrete apron until they were either seen or transitioned into Group 1 or Group 2.

It fell to Joanie to make the rounds of Group 2 or Group 3 to see if any had been promoted. Some Group 1's were demoted back to Groups 2 or 3. Some of Group 3 wandered down the street to a bar to have a smoke, something they couldn't do on the clinic grounds. To them, even imminent death took a back seat to a nicotine fit.

She didn't see Carter. He never managed to get out of the working area. She did see Group 1 people disappear into an office and come out bandaged up and brought out to Group 2. Jake Withers showed up and turned out to be astonishingly good at a lot of the work required to keep members of Groups 3 and 2 from being promoted to Group 1. Joanie was surprised there was that much overlap between being a nurse and being a mortician.

By midnight the rush seemed to abate a little. Jake sent her to the kitchenette to make some coffee.

She heard Carter's voice. "I can't talk to you now."

"Where's Joanie?" That was Granddad.

"Back at my house as far as I know."

At that point Joanie realized Carter had been so busy he'd never seen her there.

"I called and there was no answer!"

"You think I didn't do the same? But in case you haven't noticed there's something like a war going on in the County. At the moment I'm the only doctor."

Joanie followed the voices to a half open door. Inside was an office. She stopped, listening.

"Just a moment, Doc." This was from a voice she didn't know. "Do you know who I am?"

"You're Harry Carr. Nuthatch Highway Department." Carter sounded tired.

"Try again, Doc."

There was a long pause. "You're Harry Carr, Weights and Measures agent in Nuthatch County."

"Yeah." There was another pause. "Mister Prescott, may I introduce Carter Faraday the Department of Defense agent in Nuthatch County and implementer of your policy. Doctor

Faraday, let me introduce Luke Prescott, liaison between the Federal Government and Jeremy DaFoe and architect of the mess going on outside."

Joanie pushed the door the rest of the way open. They all looked at her: Harry, smiling. Luke, surprised. Carter, ashamed.

Harry clicked on the safety of his pistol and secreted it back on his person. The rest of them, startled by the click, stared at him. "That's the thing about a gun," he said cheerfully. "Everybody pays attention."

Joanie looked at her grandfather. "You..." She faltered for words. "*Designed* this?"

"Not exactly," Luke said. "I planned disaffection. I didn't plan war."

She looked at Carter. "You made it happen?"

Joanie saw a stream of expressions cross Carter's face: self-justification, explanation, regret, acceptance. "Yes," he said finally. "Harry had a bigger hand than he's letting on but the final decisions were mine."

Joanie looked at Harry. His eyes were cold though his face never lost its jovial expression. For a moment, she achieved clarity of vision she'd not known was possible. She saw Harry's whole life. The only happiness Harry had ever known was the act of executing chaos. She looked at her grandfather and saw the history of pain that had brought him here. Joanie turned to Carter and saw how he felt trapped by some choice he'd made long ago that had inevitably led to this moment. Any of them could easily justify every step along their path to right now.

She looked at herself, in love, blind to anything but that, nothing visible around her except through that shimmering, joyful lens. Until right now, at this moment, when she at last saw clearly.

Joanie turned and closed the door behind her, hurried down the hall and out the front entrance. Outside, there was bloody violence and death but it was better than what she left behind.

Robert Porter liked to check on both trailers once a day—plus one more, once the lodge was made useful. Hell, this could get to be a full-time job.

The sun was just setting as he pulled the truck up the dirt road and slowly made his way over the ruts. He remembered hauling those trailers over this road. By the time he'd had them on blocks and stable both axles were broken. Robert patted the dashboard of his truck like he'd pet the flank of a horse. *Good girl.*

He pulled up to the side of the trailer. The air was filled with the sharp stink of acid, a bit of sulfur, and something that smelled coppery. Robert had never been able to identify it.

Regardless, that meant Delmar (or was it Katie? He was never able to tell the Harris sisters apart. That both answered to either name didn't help matters.) was in the middle of a batch. Robert knew better than to disturb a meth chemist. That's how they had lost trailer number three.

He sat on the trailer steps. The trees draped over him like a great quilt, holding in the humidity but keeping back the worst of the heat of the day. The earth was warm through his shoes. It was quiet, the time between the afternoon stillness and the night chorus. Time for hawks to settle in for the night, insects to ready themselves on the sides of trees, and bats to wake and contemplate the coming dark.

Robert reached behind the seat of the truck and pulled out a cool, but no longer cold, six-pack of Coors. He cracked one open—punctuation in the stillness.

It wasn't a sound exactly. It was the feeling of a sound. The slight wave front of something that could have been a sound had he the ears of a fox or a cat. He put down the beer as if unconcerned and reached behind the seat again—nothing important. Nothing untoward. Just potato chips, maybe. Or a sandwich. And felt nonchalantly for the stock of the G36.

"DEA," came a shout. "Come out—"

That was all they had time for. Robert was already firing as he pulled the gun out, a swathe of automatic fire as he ran from the trailer back towards the truck. *Explosive rounds*, he thought as he rounded the truck. *I should have loaded up with explosive rounds.* He was getting soft.

The DEA opened fire on the truck. *Heh.* Lined the bed with steel years ago. Ed called me *paranoid*. Yeah. Right. It's never paranoid when they really are out to get you. He opened the door from the other side and grabbed the extra magazines.

The steel in the bed sounded a giant's slap every time it was hit. Robert brought his feet up on the running board so he wouldn't get shot in the foot.

Wait for it. Every firefight had a pause. A moment to return fire. Otherwise, there could be no advance. No regroup. He listened to the firing. It sounded like one set of shooters was at ten o'clock. Another at noon. Maybe a third at two o'clock. He closed his eyes, visualizing where they might be. *Wait for it.*

A pause. Robert was up in a heartbeat, ripping a burst at ten, noon, two, then back down before they could return fire. He was back behind the truck when he heard two screams.

The covered trailer window came up and two sets of guns came out and opened fire on the DEA. "Goddamn revenuers!" yelled one of the sisters.

"Go girl," came the other.

Distraction! Up again, blasting at a run. They opened fire a moment after he made it behind the trailer.

Bless the Harris sisters, he thought as he ran through the woods. Who the hell thought they'd *both* be there? Bless their family which had been fighting revenuers since before he was born. Bless them for distracting the long arm of the law long enough for him to get away.

Ed Porter pulled off just before County Road 3 to check on the progress of the Pollocks clearing the Cleary land. Robert Earl waved him on with a rifle. Obligingly, Ed had moved up the road and pulled over behind some trees to see what was going on. He was in a perfect position to observe two black Suburbans roar up the road.

Black Suburbans meant DEA or ATF—ATF, if they were properly informed, since Robert's trailers were on the other road. But DEA would have been bad enough. Ed sighed wistfully. No amount of bribery, chicanery or firepower would stop them—or persuade Ed give up his life for 160 proof alcohol. The stills were disposable.

He drove home. If they knew who he was, they'd be waiting for him, but the idea of leaving Hannah and Sterling was intolerable—though, truth be told, Hannah was more than capable of taking care of herself.

Ed drove down to the main road and turned right. Past Atkinson's—where there was some sort of altercation in the parking lot—past Ridgeville and up County Road 4.

Hannah wasn't there.

Ed allowed himself a few minutes of uncharitable thoughts—was she the one that turned him in? (If it was him and not Robert.) Could she be talking to ATF *even as he was thinking about it?* Every man has a paranoid moment once in a while. Robert had them continuously.

The more he thought about it, the more he thought Robert had brought this on them. Pushing the envelope with one trailer after another. The DEA had a sort of attention deficit disorder for different kinds of drugs but there were a few that consistently held their attention. Heroin, cocaine and meth. Other drugs may take center stage for a bit, like ingénues getting their bite at the apple. But the old standards were guaranteed to get them off their ass.

Ed had always known his Nuthatch County immunity couldn't hold forever. Eventually it would fail. The important thing was to keep enough aside that when the axe finally fell, it missed and there was enough left over to find a new line of work.

Ed shook his head at his paranoia. The day Hannah said one damned thing to the federal government it would rain frogs, the seas would fill with blood, and there would be a black president. Better, a *woman* black president. A *lesbian* woman black president.

He took the time to pack up the Bronco with anything they might need, planning as he packed. Try to get out of the County entirely or hole up? There were only two roads in and out of the County—maybe three if you counted on that old ferry between Cairo and Pilate. It wouldn't take but a small team to block both. There might be a couple of trails they could pack out on. Maybe one he could force the Bronco over. For the first time in thirty years, he wished he still had that old VW Bug. He could take that thing anywhere. Old stream beds. Mountain trails. Mud. Water. Anything. But it was long gone.

It was dark when Hannah turned into the driveway. Sterling was in the passenger's seat. Ed was ready to rip into her for not keeping Sterling safely in the back seat when she opened the door, ran around the car and hugged him.

Surprised, he hugged her back. "What's going on?"

"I was visiting Anna in Ridgeville," she said. "The Klan marched on Ashby. It was a riot. You could hear the gunfire all the way to my sister's."

Ed held her. It probably would have been safer to stay with Anna but they were here now. Safe. "Come on and get in the Bronco. We're leaving."

"Why?"

"ATF."

She nodded. Hannah led Sterling out of the car and into the Bronco.

"It's time for animaniacs," he complained.

"Later, honey." Hannah looked at Ed.

"We're going on a camping trip, Big Guy." He picked Sterling up and hugged him, then ensconced him safely in the back seat.

"Where are we going?"

"A place Robert and I picked up a while back. No one knows where it is. We can wait it out there until we can figure out a better place to go."

The roads were just too chancy. Better to find a place to go to ground. No one knew about the lodge except Joseph, Robert, Glenn and Ed. Ed sat bolt upright. It was Glenn who had dropped the dime on Robert. Probably informed on Ed, too. Once the feds realized what they had with Robert, they'd scrape Glenn clean to see what else he might know. DEA could be waiting for him. ATF could be waiting for him.

But there wasn't any place else. The Reservation was off limits—the Natives would shoot them dead for thinking about it. The stills were in the Bittersweet Range and the trailers in the White Bluffs. Both places were going to be Open Season for Porters. The lodge was the best of a bad lot. If Glenn had turned it over, Ed was caught—but he was caught *anyway*.

Ed turned off the lights. He'd driven these roads in the dark so many times he could tell where he was by the feel of the tires on the pavement. He didn't slow down until he turned off the road and put in the lat/long for the lodge. Up the dirt road laughably called County Track 2B—not enough to be maintained. He worked his way up the road and stopped.

Ed got out with a flashlight, looking for the turnout spot Joseph had mentioned, found it and got back in. Once he had the truck stashed, he felt a little easier.

"Okay," he said. "You wait here while I check this place out."

"Bullshit," she said as she rummaged in the glove box for a second flashlight. "Not today. Come on, Sterling."

"Okay," he said. That meant no firefight. Thoughtfully, he slipped his pistol under the seat. If the ATF was waiting the pistol could only get them all killed. If they weren't, he could come back for it.

The trail was grown over with new maples. More than once he had to backtrack to find his way. Then there was a rise. He shone his light over the edge.

Glenn was sitting in front of the lodge. "Evening, Ed. Mrs. Porter. Sterling."

"Evening, Glenn." Ed waved the light over the hollow. He didn't see anybody else. "I'm unarmed. Anybody waiting for me?"

Glenn held up his pistol. "Just me. I figured you and Robert would come here when things went bad. You better come down, first. Something here you should see."

"Wait here," he said quietly to Hannah.

After a moment, he managed to work his way down to the lodge. Ed could hear something strange. A stuttering sound like an interrupted breath.

Glenn was sitting in front of the entrance. "Shine your light over here."

Ed did so. Lying on the ground in a pool of blood was Robert, eyes closed, each breath shallow and straining. Two wounds in his chest, one deep and pulsing, the other half closed.

"He knew it was me," Glenn said conversationally. "I knew he would. I waited here. Missed him with a head shot but I got him in the lung. He didn't die. I tried to shoot him in the head but the bullets kept missing." Glenn shook his head. "I sat here for an hour trying to figure out what to do and damned if he didn't start to heal. I shot him again when he sat up. Damned if he's not healing again." Glenn looked up at Ed. "He'll kill me. He'll kill Jenny. He'll kill the kids. He won't rest until he does.

You know that's true, Ed."

Ed stared at the gasping body of his brother. He could see the second gaping wound beginning to lose, drawing together bits of button, cloth, a piece of the jacket's zipper—healing around it. Robert watched them both with animal hatred.

"I know it." He sat next to Ed. "Hannah?" He called. "Go around to the other side."

"What am I going to do?" Glenn asked.

"Damned if I know."

The fireflies came out and lit the night.

Betty watched Peggy and Pam leave. She felt lighter without the gun. Better. Easier. Having that ancient pistol meant she might have to use it. She was just as happy not having that choice.

She knew Pam was going to drop Peggy off. Betty had a different destination in mind. The events in Ashby had left her with no illusions as to what might happen. For all she knew, Buddy was dead. The thought gave her a hollow feeling right over her heart and she resolutely pushed it away.

Instead, she concentrated on her driving.

Nobody really knew Jeremy. How could any human being with a tiny finite human lifespan make any real claim to know what went on inside him? That said, no one knew Jeremy better than she did. Betty had been Jeremy's wife for better than ten years and she *knew* he had shown her aspects of himself he had never shown any living person—emphasis on the "living" part. Who knew what he had exposed to his dead wives? The idea shook her a little. Betty realized suddenly that for all that had happened, for all that Jeremy was or might be, she still loved him and didn't regret marrying him one little bit. *Staying* married to him, however, was still up in the air.

Huh, she thought. The heart really does want what it wants.

So, she thought. If I were Jeremy (*Ha!*) where would I end up?

The answer was obvious: Little Mountain.

As she left the car it wasn't lost on her that she'd been right here in this same Fox Park lot just a few days ago with Buddy. She wasn't going to the cave. Jeremy knew exactly what each image in the cave meant but he wouldn't be there today. He'd be above ground where he could see. He'd be up on Table Rock.

The fireflies came out as she walked the trail up the base of Little Mountain. They lit the dark switchbacks until she reached the flat ledge. There, she found Jeremy.

He saw her and gestured for her to come over. "Have a seat."

She sat next to him. Table Rock was quite a ways above the trees. She could see the dark hulk of the Bittersweet Ridge march away to the west. Pilate was a collection of small lights. The darkness of the river curved away from them to the south and beyond the river she could see the lights of the Illinois and Kentucky towns. All through the trees, fireflies winked on and off, like tiny stars coming into brief existence and then lost forever.

"They're fighting the Klan in Ashby," she said.

"Yeah. I saw that." He reached to his side in the darkness. "Have a drink."

Betty took the bottle from him. She could smell the acrid sweetness of Porter's Piss. By the faint light she saw the bottle was half empty. "You've had a good shot at it already."

"Think of it as fulfilling the human experience. Didn't you say I was getting almost human?"

A feeling like getting punched in the stomach. She didn't say anything.

"I'm glad you're here," he said softly. "Bad stuff's happening all over."

"You've got to do something."

He shook his head in the gloom. "No, Betty. I don't."

"Why not?" She sipped the bottle, not knowing what else to do.

Jeremy took the bottle back from her. He held it up and looked through the glass at the stars. "It's time for all this to happen," he said. "The County has gone on like it has for as long as it could. I don't have a better explanation for you than that. So," he brought down the bottle and sipped it. "You can sit here with me and watch it happen or you can go back down into it. It's up to you."

She took back the bottle and took a long swig. "I'll stay."

"Good. I like your company."

Betty looked around. She'd been here before but now she noticed how odd Table Rock was. The ledge was a flat oval, carved out from the limestone. A flat spot with a shady overhang. "What is this place?"

"Worn out mud deposit," Jeremy said. He pointed up. "Back in the Jurassic when all of this was underwater and flat, a big boulder got cemented in place. Mountain building pushed it up about forty million years ago. Watched it all happen. The mud was fossilized, of course, but soft. When it was exposed, it washed away and eventually the boulder fell about forty feet into the river. The Mississippi wore it away so there's nothing left." He looked down. "We're higher now. Below the boulder were flat layers of limestone. Once the mud stone washed away there was this spot. Nice, isn't it?"

"You sound like you want a compliment."

Jeremy surveyed the space. "Well, it's possible I did give the boulder a little push. Think of it as a porch with a view."

They were quiet for a little while, passing the bottle back and forth. The night filled with crickets and cicadas, bullfrogs and the distant concussions of gunfire.

"So," he said at last. "Do you want a divorce?"

Again, a feeling like being punched. "I don't know."

"I've never been divorced before." He laughed shortly and sipped the bottle. "Fulfilling the human experience."

Betty took the bottle from him and cradled it in her lap, suddenly ready to weep. For her. For her marriage. For the County. For the passage of time. "People are going to get killed."

"No," he said so quietly she wasn't sure at first she'd heard him correctly. "They're not. I made a promise that when this day came no one would die."

"To who?"

"Faster-Than-Fox."

Grace's breathing changed. Pam sat up immediately. But this sounded better, not worse. Deeper. Stronger.

She stood over her just as her eyes opened. "You're alive," Pam said.

Grace looked up at her for minute. She coughed. Shook her head. Coughed again, turned her head and spit something gelid on the table's paper. "I shouldn't be." She tried to sit up.

"Oh, for God's sake." Pam tried to push her down.

"No." She shook his head. "I feel… I don't know. Weird." She poked at her chest. Winced. "Pull the bandage off."

"Are you *crazy*?"

"I don't think so." The bandage was taped down. Grace pulled up a corner and glanced down. "Look."

Pam leaned over and pulled the bandage back. The wound was sealed tight. Maybe even healed a little around the staples. "It looks better than I thought."

"Better than it ought to. Old Thomas shot me with a 30-06 from twenty feet away. It should have blown me in half. Help me up."

She struggled to sit up. Coughed again and spit out blood.

"That feels better." Experimentally, she sat up straight. "I want to stand."

"You fall and you're going to die on the floor."

"I'll take that chance."

Pam helped her stand up.

Grace tried to breathe deeply. Winced. "I think I only got one lung."

"That's better than you deserve."

"Where's my shirt?"

"They cut it off you."

"Figures." Grace felt at her side. "Where's my weapon?"

Pam shrugged. "Back in Ashby?"

"Yeah." Grace walked around the room a little. Turned her shoulders this way and that. "Feels like stuff is pulling inside but nothing terrible. Like a weak leg." She stood still for a long moment. "How long have I been here?"

"It's after midnight," Pam said. "Six hours more or less?"

"Okay." There was a soiled clothing hamper. Grace opened it and found a Johnny without much blood on it. "This'll do."

"Do for *what?*"

Grace turned to Pam, her eyes pointed. Dark. Determined. "There's shit going on out there. I'm the Sheriff. You're County Commissioner. Who else is going to stop it?"

Pam looked at her. *I'm seeing her for the first time.* "There isn't anyone else," Pam said. "Not in Nuthatch County."

"Let's go."

Joanie didn't know where to go. Back to Carter's house? Unthinkable. She didn't have a car—it wasn't clear it was safe, anyway. At least on foot she had freedom of movement. Between houses. In back yards. Through sections of wood.

She saw no one. She *heard* guns go off nearby, across a park heavy with fireflies, down the street, in the next block. But never the people. As if they were all hunkered down in their houses hoping this would all go away.

Joanie knew just how they felt.

Or maybe they were sitting in the dark, a window open, a rifle at ready, just to take pot shots at anyone walking by.

She kept to the shadows.

Eventually, she managed to make it past the edge of town. It was deep night now—"half way to morning" as Grandma Catherine used to say. If there had been a moon it was long gone. The night was hot and filled with the electric roar of cicadas and the brittle song of crickets and katydids. Bullfrogs grunted a rhythm to the chorus. The dentist drill whine of mosquitoes hung in her ears. All punctuated by the fireworks irregularity of gunfire.

Madness.

The fireflies were everywhere. Thousands of them. They flew in front of her, landed on her hair, her shoulders, as gentle as the gift of grace.

She made it as far as the abandoned road equipment and rested on the running board of a road grader.

Carter was behind this? Her grandfather? The County abandoned by Jeremy? She felt suddenly bereft, a body and mind wrapped around a sudden absence. A hole inside of here where there used to be visceral substance. She was hollow. If she turned just *so* the wind would blow right through her.

Joanie heard labored breathing nearby. For a moment, she sat there, trying to ignore it. But she remembered the people hurt at the clinic. This could be one more.

"Is anyone there?"

The breathing stopped. Then a single inhalation to back a man's loud whisper. "Over here. For God's sake be quiet. He might hear you."

She crawled over the gravel in the direction of the voice,

found a leg. "Where are you hit?"

"In my belly," he whispered. "Head shots don't work but gut shots sure do."

"Earl?" came a call behind a bulldozer. "Come on out, now. There's no shame in handing over this patch of ground to the Organization for Nuthatch Country Progress. Let's not play last man standing."

"Son-of-a-bitch," muttered Earl. He clawed at his side and dropped something heavy and metal, picked it up again.

A flashlight beamed on the two of them. "There you are, Earl."

"I'll kill you, Keller."

"You've tried that once or twice already," Keller said. "Me, too." He gestured with his pistol. "Looks you'll get another chance."

In the light, Joanie looked at Earl. The wound had closed, drawing in bits of shirt and belt. She stood up and stepped away from the two of them. Keller didn't even glance at her but held his gun at his side.

Someone grabbed Joanie from behind and clapped a hand over her mouth. She started to fight but a voice came from next to her ear. "Come on. We have to get away from this."

It was her mother.

Joanie backed away just as Earl brought up his gun. Keller matched him and shot him again in the gut. Earl shot lower. Keller collapsed in a whistling scream.

"There are half a dozen of them scattered around," said Nadine as she led Joanie between a front loader and the backhoe. "They shoot each other, fall down, an hour later they get up and do it again. They all ought to be dead."

"He said head shots don't work."

"Yeah. Maybe a splattered brain is something even Jeremy can't fix."

Joanie stopped and looked at the shadow that was her

mother. "You think he's fixing people?"

"Not very well. Come on. We have to climb into the front loader. The back hoe bucket only protects from three sides. I learned that the hard way."

Joanie realized her mother was limping. "Did you get hit?"

"Yeah," Nadine whispered through her teeth. "Right in the kneecap. If I don't walk just right it just slips backwards. Then, it takes forty minutes for it to pull itself together. Not a good forty minutes, either." She reached up and grabbed the lip of the front loader bucket. "We'll have to help each other up."

A car drove up from the west, turned onto the gravel and shone the light directly on them. Joanie looked down at her mother's leg: a half-healed hole where the kneecap used to be. She wanted to throw up.

Footsteps crunching on gravel. Joseph grabbed Nadine and draped her arm around his shoulder. "Come on. Both of you. Get in the car. We've got to get out of here."

"Joseph," said Nadine shakily. "I thought you were gone."

"Yeah. Changed my mind." He helped her to the passenger side of the car.

Joanie jumped in the back seat. "I'm in."

Joseph closed Nadine's door and ran to the driver's side.

Earl had turned on his side and pointed the pistol in Joseph's general direction. "Are you Organization or Committee?"

Joseph stopped. "Neither. I'm Native."

Earl lowered his gun. "All right, then."

Joseph spun the car around, showering gravel over the men. "Son-of-a-bitch," yelled Earl.

Down the road now, fast enough the car swayed side to side as if the road were scalloped.

Joseph slowed down as they passed Atkinson's on the left.

It was on fire.

Joanie, Nadine and Joseph ended up at Amos and Jean's house. Nadine's knee had improved markedly. She said it didn't really hurt. It made her walk in an odd way that really bothered Joanie but she couldn't say why.

Cooped inside, they didn't know how to occupy their time. Playing cards or watching television while the County outside the Reservation was grinding itself into chutney seemed the wrong thing to do.

After a while, Jean excused herself and went upstairs. Amos made a pot of tea and left it with them, pleading age and fatigué. A few minutes after he disappeared upstairs there was the unmistakable sound of bedsprings moving and giggles.

Nadine and Joseph looked at one another.

Joanie thought: *Don't you dare!*

But they both went upstairs anyway. In a few moments, the house vibrated with a sort of asymmetric counterpoint.

Joanie couldn't stand it. She found a bottle and took it out on the front porch. That was still too close. She found a picnic table a hundred feet from the house. As far as she was concerned, she'd have to be deaf drunk to go back inside there.

"The next week is going to be tough on you." Jeremy was sitting across from her.

"*Jesus Christ!*" She jumped back, slipped on the damp earth and started to fall just as Jeremy reached over the table and grabbed her hand. He held it as she straightened herself and got back to the table. "You scared the piss out of me."

"Not quite." Jeremy chuckled.

"Very funny." She gestured to everything: the house, the night, her ruined love life, the destruction of the County. "This is all your fault."

"Yeah. I know." He drummed his fingers on the table. "Things should settle down by noon or so. You get your parents and grandparents up and come to Little Mountain. We all have to meet together."

"We'll see. I'm not going to stop any animal noises."

"I want you there, too."

She suddenly felt the need to swallow past the great lump in her throat. "Me?" she squeaked. "Why me?"

"I like your work." He grinned at her wickedly. "I think you really should do my portrait."

And he was gone. One minute there. The next not even close. No sound. No flash.

She waved her hand where he had been. Nothing.

"Okay," she said to the air. "But I want to be hung over for a meeting like that."

Luke tried to chase after Joanie but Harry stopped him at the door.

"It's too dangerous outside," he said, smiling. His grip on Luke's arm was iron.

"She's my granddaughter!"

"Who *chose* to go outside into a war zone rather than be here with you or her lover boy."

Luke stopped, looked out the doors. She was already gone. He had no idea which way.

Luke shrugged off Harry's arm and looked around. The lobby was filled with people with different levels of wounds. Two men in the corner were playing cards, bare-chested save for bandages over chest and abdomen. A woman lay next to them, neck and shoulder swathed in cotton, her left arm ending in a stump. Others had lesser wounds—arm bandages, leg bandages. Luke recognized Hugh Utterback leaned back against the wall, one eye uncovered but closed; the other suspiciously bandaged, suggesting an empty socket.

"I never meant any of *this*," Luke said in a low voice.

"Yeah." Harry looked around the lobby. "That's what my case worker said back in Guatemala. Nobody ever sees the big picture."

"We have to find Jeremy," breathed Luke. "He can stop it."

Harry shook his head. "No can do. That's the same as going after the girl. I've been tasked to keep you safe. If you want to get out of here, I figure the best way is the ferry—"

"I'm not leaving."

Harry shrugged. "We can stay here. The clinic is defensible."

What could he do? He reached for his cell—nothing. He must have left it in the hotel. He almost asked to go back there but stopped. Harry would nix that, too. "Do you know how to get in contact with Rosen?"

Harry looked at him blankly. "Rosen?"

Damn! "Let's find Carter."

They had to wait outside of the tiny OR until Carter stabilized someone's neck wound. They pushed their way in while he was washing up.

"What now?" he said wearily.

"Can you get in touch with Rosen?"

Carter gave Luke the same blank look Harry had given him.

"Your contact in Washington," Luke said impatiently.

Carter didn't answer immediately. He dried his hands. "You know they're healing?"

"What?"

"Grace Cox had a sucking chest wound—some large caliber round tore a hole into her left lung and blew an even larger hole out the back. She should have died." Carter turned around from the sink and leaned against it. "The hole filled in after a few hours. She and Pam left a little while ago to see if they could stop what's going on—minus most of Grace's lung. She *healed* but she didn't regenerate anything. That's going on all through the clinic. Probably all over the County."

Luke stared at him. "Jeremy?"

"Know any other source of miracles? Also, I've been hearing that head shots don't work. Guns miss or don't fire at all."

"I overheard that," said Harry. "I figured it was just because they were amateurs."

"No head wound has come through the door. Chest wounds. Belly shots. Shattered limbs. But no head wounds and no deaths. I haven't lost a single patient."

Harry chuckled. "I guess brains are something even Jeremy can't fix."

"I told you we needed to find him," Luke said to Harry.

"And *I* told *you:* no fucking way."

Luke looked at Carter. "Your contact in Washington?"

Carter pulled his cell phone out, pulled up a contact and handed it to Luke. "Just press send."

It seemed the phone rang forever. Then an artificial voice answered. "What do you want, Faraday?"

"It's Luke Prescott."

Pause. Then came Rosen's voice: "What's going on?"

"Riot. Mayhem. Bloody war," said Luke. "The County is tearing itself apart."

"That's according to plan."

"I didn't plan for a clinic full of wannabe corpses! The plan was to disaffect Jeremy from the County, not destroy the County in the process."

"I have a squad of the Missouri National Guard on ready in Perryville. They can come down and pacify the County."

"Pacify," Luke said, tasting the word. "Like they'll keep this a secret."

"This squad has been specially trained."

"Specially trained?"

"Yes, sir."

"You've been *expecting* this?"

Pause. "We're prepared for every contingency."

"Why the Guard? Why not the whole damned *army?*"

"That would be illegal, sir," said Rosen stiffly.

Let us keep our trivialities in perspective. "Who is 'we'?"

Another pause. As if he could read minds, Luke knew Rosen

was considering carefully what he could and could not reveal to Luke. No wonder he'd never seen a Secretary of Defense at a briefing. If the Joint Chiefs had known about Jeremy, no doubt the Secretary knew, too. But kept his distance to keep his own machinations secret.

Luke closed his eyes. He had no idea of the scale of plots within plots. What plots included him? Jeremy? Nuthatch County? What plots didn't? Did McNamara's Viet Nam include contingency plans involving Jeremy? Did McElroy's plans for the Soviet Union under Eisenhower? Did Marshall's plans for the Korean War?

"The Department of Defense, sir. Of course," said Rosen at last. "What should we do?"

Luke rubbed his forehead. Could this make things *any* worse? "Call out the Guard. Bring this to a close."

"Right away, sir."

Luke handed the phone back to Carter. He sat down. No doubt Rosen was already setting things in motion. He was so very efficient. The Guard would be spreading through the County before dawn, enforced order in their wake.

What if Harry hadn't stopped Luke? What if they had found Jeremy, what would he have asked him? Make it right? Fix everything he, Luke Prescott, his liaison, had screwed up? What would Jeremy have done? Snapped his fingers and turned back the clock? Or say, in Jeremy's dry voice: *It's your County now. You fix it.*

Chapter 10: Things To Be Determined

It's amazing how quickly things can be settled if your guns are big enough.

An hour before dawn, twin Chinook helicopters descended on the flat ground across from the road equipment. Minutes after landing, a hundred men in half a dozen vehicles shot up and down the main road, following carefully planned routes. The remaining conscious members of the Nuthatch County Self Actualization Committee and Organization for Nuthatch Country Progress watched dully.

Though the County citizens were more than willing to blow the crap out of each other, they were reluctant to fire on American uniforms. The Guard met little resistance.

By the time the Guard found the ATF, the stills had been destroyed and the agents were frustrated and angry after a night's wandering through the mosquito and poison ivy infested woods without finding a single person to hold responsible. The Guard was a welcome distraction. Kate Marquis was taken into custody after knocking cold a sergeant who questioned her female ability to lead an all-male squad. When the sergeant woke up, he sought her out and moved in with her the following Christmas.

The DEA team was unable to rush the trailer through the hail of bullets visited upon them by the Harris sisters. Cole's team was overtaken by the Guard in the early morning. In recognition of the increasing fire power, Delmar, always the more sensible of the two, decided to live another day after all. She and Katie slipped out the back through a cellar hole and tunnel, leaving six sticks of dynamite as a going away present.

The explosion could be heard as far away as the charred ruins of Atkinson's but neither the agents nor the Guard were injured.

The Pollocks and the Chases very nearly buried the hatchet in each other. Both families were crack shots but slightly better at concealment—the product of years of deer hunting. Though there were more than a few close calls, neither side actually managed to nail the other. Eventually, the four Pollocks (the three sons and their mother) managed to get the drop on the Chases (Howie, Herbert and Annie White.) The final solution was interrupted by the Guard.

The war in Ashby did not end so nicely. While Jeremy kept anybody from getting actually killed, most of the men in both towns were crippled. There was no fight left in them when the Guard came.

One Klansman took dead aim at Buddy's heart with a 7 millimeter. Ray pushed him out of the way and took the bullet. The fall broke Buddy's arm but Ray was badly hurt. To Buddy, getting Ray to the clinic intact was the hardest and best thing Buddy had ever done.

By noon the Guard was holding down Pilate. Captain James Parnall, the CO of the operation, came directly to the clinic to find Luke.

"That's me," said Luke when the Captain finally was brought

to him. Luke had decided to make himself useful and had taken Joanie's place when she'd run off into the night. Right then he was changing the urine bag attached to the catheter which, itself, was attached to a sleeping Bob Sheffield, shot in the abdomen trying while trying to dock his ferry. He had come over to see what was going on.

Luke looked up at the Captain. "Did you find Nadine or Joanie Durant?"

Captain Parnall consulted a notebook. "Not yet. But so far, we've been able to calm things down with a minimum of bloodshed. No casualties on either side."

"What a surprise," said Luke dryly. After all, there had been no *casualties* all night long. But the Captain would not know that.

"We've been told to take you wherever you need to go."

"Hold this," Luke said to the Captain and handed him the full urine bag. He replaced it with an empty one and took the full one back. He deposited it in the hazardous waste pail and washed his hands without ever noticing the grimace of distaste on the Captain's face or the speed with which Parnall washed his hands afterwards.

Luke had to find Jeremy. All night he'd been thinking about where Jeremy had to be.

Harry was mopping up a blood spill in the lobby, working carefully between sleeping wounded. It was like some picture out of the Civil War: people lined up on the floor next to one another, being checked on by Peggy, Olivia or Carter.

But it was different, thought Luke savagely. Very different. All night he'd been seeing people gradually get better. It was like watching the hands of a clock, so slow as to be imperceptible. Luke had forced himself to watch. Amputations—like Jake Withers eye—showed no sign of growing back. But he could see flesh and bone knit together. Bloody wounds stanched themselves, scabbed over, the skin knit together. Like watching bamboo grow. Or kudzu. Each one a dull ache inside of him. *I did this.*

"Good news," said Luke. "The National Guard has everything under control. We're free to go. Captain Percival here—"

"Parnall, sir."

"—is happy to take us anywhere. I think I know where Jeremy is."

"Okay." Harry nodded and leaned the mop against the wall. "I'm ready."

Buddy stood up when Carter came into the lobby. He'd refused to take any pain medication. Not today. Not when things were happening and he had to be sharp. But his broken right arm hurt badly and it scared him. He'd seen people his age waste away when they broke a bone. Any bone. He tried to console himself that it could have been worse. The idea of lying in Ashby with a broken hip while being shot at made him shudder.

But Ray had it so much worse.

"Buddy?" said Carter. "Looks like Ray's going to live." Carter laughed shortly.

"Yeah," said Buddy, snorting. *Everybody* was going to live through this night. That had become obvious. The question was what they were going to have to live with. "How bad is it?"

Carter sighed. "Ray lost most of his liver. All of his spleen and about half his pancreas—he's going to have to lose a lot of weight to keep from getting diabetes. But that's for later. He's lost his entire left lung. I couldn't save any of it. It was one of those hunting bullets and just exploded in there. I was picking out pieces for an hour." Carter stopped and closed his eyes, swayed on his feet.

Buddy started to steady him with his right arm, thought better of it, and reached out with his left. "Are you okay?"

"No." Carter shook his head as if to clear something out. "Fortunately, he didn't sustain any damage to his digestive system. I was worried about peritonitis but the pieces missed the stomach."

Peggy Small came up next to him. "Doctor Faraday?"

"Yes?"

"We haven't had any new patients for an hour."

Carter looked at her blearily, trying to understand what she said.

She took his hand and look into his eyes to get his attention. "You can rest for a bit."

Carter looked at her, then at Buddy. "No new cases."

"For the moment, Ray is as good as he's going to get," said Buddy. "She's right. You ought to rest."

Carter stared at him. "We need another doctor."

There was an open couch behind him. Buddy and Peggy guided him to that. When the back of his legs touched the cushion, he sat down heavily.

"Yeah," said Buddy. "I expect we do."

Carter looked from one of them to the other, his eyes looking sunken, fighting sleep like an errant three-year-old. The lids closed and he slumped to his side.

"Yeah," said Buddy, cradling his arm. "Can I look in on Ray?" he said to Peggy.

"Sure."

Peggy led him down the hall to what served as a recovery room. Ray's dark skin had an ashy character. IV tubes led into him and a few large tubes led from under the sheet to bulbs.

"Drainage tubes," Peggy said when she saw where he was looking. "We don't want too much edema."

Buddy nodded, not taking his eyes off his younger brother. Deep in his heart he knew that this had to be his fault. He wasn't cut out to be Eldest. He was incompetent. If he'd been able to see what was coming, he would have been able to head it off.

He felt Papa Jeremy's hand on his shoulder. "Things can happen that aren't your fault."

"What?" Buddy looked for him and there was nobody there.

"Did you say something, Buddy?" asked Peggy.

"No." He looked at his brother, turned and left the room.

Carter caught up with him as he was leaving by the front entrance. "Hold on," he said.

"I thought you were asleep. You must be exhausted."

"Internship. You learn to cope. Where are you going?"

"To find Jeremy."

"Wait." He pulled off his white coat and tossed it in a bin. "I'll come with you."

It was after dawn when Betty woke up, snuggled next to someone. "Jeremy?" she said and opened her eyes.

Buddy smiled down at her, his right arm in a sling. "You sleep well?"

Her head hurt and her teeth felt fuzzy. "Well enough." She sat up. Jeremy was leaning against the back wall. Carter was sitting next to him. Neither was speaking but Carter was holding the empty bottle.

Betty touched Buddy's arm gently. "You're hurt."

"Ray fell on me," he said. "Broke my arm."

"Was he hurt?"

"As much as anyone. Nobody's died so far."

Betty nodded toward Jeremy. "He said nobody would die."

"That part I figured out."

"This is all his fault."

Buddy inclined his head towards her. "Yes," he said, drawing out the sound thoughtfully. "And no. Jeremy didn't fire a single gun. He kept everybody alive. We did it to ourselves." He rubbed his knee. "I've been thinking about this all night. It's come to me that it's not Jeremy's job to protect us. To make us special. It's our job to humanize Jeremy."

"What does *that* mean?"

Buddy grinned at her. "I wish I knew."

Luke and Harry reached the park in a Humvee. Luke didn't like it. The Humvee bounced and jittered like a bug burnt by a magnifying glass. It followed every dent and ridge of the road religiously and didn't glide over them like a proper automobile.

Parnall parked the Humvee and consulted his notes. "Jeremy DaFoe is here?"

"Yeah," said Luke shortly.

He called someone named "Lead Tiger" on his radio and reported their position. A moment of silence and the voice at the other end said to wait there. "Lead Tiger" would be meeting them.

"Screw this," Luke said and got out of the Humvee. He'd be damned if he were going to wait inside. At least he'd have honest earth under his feet.

The dawn sky was an electric blue, burnt white at the edge where the sun was rising.

Harry got out with him and stretched. "Going to be hot."

"Yeah," Luke said. In the distance, he could hear the deep tubercular sound of diesel engines. A troop carrier came around the bend and slid to a stop next to them, splashing them with dust.

Captain Rosen stepped out of the cab.

"Needed to see things in person?" Luke said.

"Of course." He turned back to the cab of the truck. "Deploy and secure the area but don't go up the mountain. We'll be going up there ourselves."

Luke could hear another car coming. "Hold on."

A moment later Joseph's car turned the bend and swerved to avoid the troop carrier. It almost ended up in the ditch but stopped just in time.

Joanie got out. "That's the stupidest place to park I've ever seen."

Luke hugged her, a great burden suddenly washed away. "You smell like you've been drinking."

"Truth in advertising."

"Is Nadine all right?"

"God knows. She and Joseph were squeaking the bed all night. Amos and Jean, too. I sure wasn't going to wake them up no matter what Jeremy said. I left a note."

"Ah," said Rosen. "Perhaps it's time for me to meet Jeremy DaFoe."

Joanie followed in the rear, behind Luke and Harry, behind Captain Rosen. When the trail emptied onto the ledge, she saw Jeremy sitting with his back to the rear wall of the ledge. Carter was standing a little way off, staring out to the west. She wondered what Carter was thinking about. The clinic? His machinations? Joanie Durant?

Sitting on the edge, their legs dangling over the five feet of air to the next ledge down and about seventy feet to the one after that, were Buddy and Betty sitting next to one another.

Jeremy looked bad. He looked unkempt and dirty. His clothes were stained and he sat watching them with open hostility.

Nobody wanted to approach him. They seemed to mill near him without actually engaging his attention.

Finally, Rosen stepped forward. "I'm Captain Joel Rosen, US

Army." He stuck out his hand.

Jeremy stared at him for a moment. "I know who you all are." He stood up, slipped and leaned against the wall, drank what was left of the bottle, and threw it off the ledge. A moment later they heard a thump and shattering glass.

My God! Joanie thought. Was Jeremy drunk? Could Jeremy *get* drunk?

"You could hurt somebody doing that," said Rosen mildly. "That's my men down there."

Jeremy shook his head. "No. I missed Corporal Gresch. And they're not *you're* men. They are the men of Captain James Parnall of Poplar Bluff. Twenty-eight. Unmarried but a father— though he doesn't know that yet." Jeremy leaned over the ledge. "You hear that, Captain Parnall? Julie's goddamned pregnant. And she's yours so don't even bother thinking about it."

He turned back to them. "I know you all." He pointed at Luke. "This was Deacon Williams' idea first. I liked him. He hated my guts, of course. There's always somebody like Deacon." He pointed at Luke. "Then, you got your feelings hurt and threw in with him. There's always somebody like you, too. Somebody to come along and get on the train when it comes by. They never *start* the train. They just get on." Jeremy turned to Rosen. "There's always somebody like you, too, Joel. Somebody who sees an opportunity and jumps on board. Deacon thought it up. Luke picked up the ball. But *you* carried it through. You and your little agents, Harry, Arnie, and Nate. And Carter." He turned to Carter. "There's always somebody like you, Carter. Somebody who does the dirty work against his better judgment."

Joanie watched them. Rosen was unmoved. Luke was seething. Carter stared at the ground.

Jeremy looked to the west. "Ed? Yeah. I'm talking to you. Throw me that bottle. Just throw the fucking thing. Yeah. It's all over. Thanks." Jeremy reached up and there was a bottle in the air as he caught it. "Every last Porter *ever* was a pissant. But man can they make alcohol."

He unscrewed the top and drank deeply. "Sixty-six million, two hundred and forty-six thousand, five hundred and two years I've been on this miserable rock. You have no idea. No idea about *anything*. This fucking place was burnt down to limestone. Sterilized. Between the firestorm, blast wave, and steam there was nothing alive. It was a thousand years before this place had a sprig of grass—well, it wasn't grass. But it was green. No real forests for forty thousand years after that. No fauna to speak of for half a million years but dying insects and birds blown off course." He wiggled his fingers at the dirt. "First came these little rodent things. No respectable animals at all. I had to wait another sixty-four million, seven hundred and thirty-two thousand, eight hundred and eighty-nine years for some intelligent conversation. Not that you provide *terribly* intelligent conversation, mind you. But there are words in a string. Concepts. Sentences. And now you've come to boot me out of here. I predate your species. I predate your fucking taxonomic *order*. Who the *fuck* are you to tell me to leave? I can melt this goddamn *state*—"

"Shut up." Luke stepped up to him. "Could you have saved Catherine?"

Jeremy shook his head wearily. "Of course, I—"

Joanie saw Luke swing up from his hip. Swing like a prizefighter. Swing with everything he had. Every muscle and bone taut and directed to this one strike. He hit Jeremy on the side of his jaw with a fist like a ham, like a boulder, like a cannonball at the end of his arm.

Jeremy was lifted clear off his feet over the edge.

Betty screamed but no one moved.

Jeremy started to fall over the ledge then landed on his feet, standing horizontally on the vertical rock.

Luke watched Jeremy for a long minute. "Son-of-a-bitch." Luke turned away and walked to the other side of the Table Rock.

The rest just stared at Jeremy.

Finally, Joanie walked over and looked down.

Jeremy was standing horizontal from the cliff face, rubbing his jaw. It seemed misshapen but as he pushed and prodded, it came back into alignment. "Didn't think he had that punch in him. That's the thing about human beings. Watch them for half a million years and they can *still* surprise you." He reached up to Joanie. "Give us a hand, would you?"

Joanie grabbed his hand and helped him walk over the edge back to vertical.

Jeremy leaned over and took a few deep breaths. "Where'd that bottle get to?"

Joanie looked around and saw it on its side, half empty. She picked it up and handed it to him.

Jeremy stood up and took the bottle. He now looked completely sober. He sighed and screwed the cap on. "You win, Captain Joel Rosen. You planned on disaffecting me from the County. It worked like a charm. My wife will divorce me. My liaison tried to break my jaw. Everybody else just stood and watched. You don't get much more disaffected than that. *Fine.* My connection with the mammalian world will come to an end." He pointed to the flat rock. "Bring some jackhammers up here—funny thing, that. You brought in and abandoned all the equipment you should need."

Rosen nodded. "I hoped so."

"Dig it up right here. It's just limestone."

Rosen thought for a minute. "What about the diamonds? The files said there were diamonds here. Kimberlite pipes and such."

"Diamonds?" said Harry.

Jeremy smiled sourly. "Diamonds. Everybody likes

diamonds. The kimberlite surrounds it — it would be hard to get to it from the side. From here, though, it's just soft limestone all the way down."

"What is it?"

Jeremy didn't speak for a moment. "Call it my counterpart."

"It'll be too heavy to move. The mass indicators —"

Jeremy gave him a withering look. "With everything that's gone on you think a little thing like mass will be a problem? You won't have any trouble. Trust me. It wants to go." Jeremy looked around. He seemed at a sudden loss. "You'll need two cars. One for it. One for me. We can't be a lot closer than we are right now. You'll have to get it off Earth. That means the shuttle — I guess we can put it at one end and me at the other. Think you can do that, sport? If you get us into low earth orbit we can take it from there —"

"*No!*" Betty came over to Jeremy. She took his hand. "Don't you dare leave me." She drew a ragged breath.

"Honey," he said gently. "You don't have to do this."

"I said 'until death do us part' and I *meant* it. I knew what I was getting into."

Buddy stepped forward. "Stay. That way you can get as drunk and bitter as any of us."

Jeremy looked at them helplessly, then at Rosen. "What happens if I stay?"

"War," said Rosen instantly. "The secret will come out. The Russians already think there's something strange going on. What do you think they'll do when they find out about you? Then there's our own country. The Pentagon is already split about you and they are people who know something about you. Imagine what the rest of the country will do. Eventually — sooner rather than later — there will be war over you."

"Yeah." Jeremy turned to Betty and Buddy. "War if I don't go."

Joanie felt someone take her hand. She looked up. It was

Carter.

"I'm sorry," Carter said.

Joanie could tell he had gone through all of the explanations and justifications and discarded them. She didn't know if she could forgive him but right now, facing war and destruction or Jeremy's disappearance, she didn't think it was important.

Buddy looked thoughtful. "Can you and your... counterpart be separated?"

Jeremy nodded. "*I* can't send it away. But that doesn't mean it can't be moved."

Luke snorted. "That doesn't make any sense."

"Rules," said Jeremy. "All civilized people have rules."

Buddy pointed at Jeremy. "What would happen to you if the counterpart were removed?"

Jeremy watched him levelly. "I'd grow old and die."

Rosen turned his attention from one to the other. "What about your, ah, special abilities?"

"Diminished." Jeremy pointed down to the limestone. "It does the heavy lifting. I'm just one parlor trick doing parlor tricks."

Buddy turned to Rosen. "Take the damned thing. Shoot it up into space. Leave Jeremy here with us. In twenty or forty years there won't be any problem at all."

Rosen considered them. "Jeremy can't be in charge anymore."

Buddy exploded. "Did it look like he was in charge last night? Does he look like he's in charge right now?"

Rosen didn't say anything for a long time. "I'll have to make calls but I think I can sell this."

"*No*," cried Luke. He lunged forward, hands open to throttle Jeremy.

Luke would have killed Jeremy. He was ready. He was able. The loss of his brother, his nephew, *Catherine*, moved him forwards, opened his hands, made him reach towards Jeremy —

Jeremy looked up at him.

Around Luke there was a vast wasteland, choking with dust. Everything burned and long dead. The wind scouring the earth was the only sound. The sky was dark gray smoke.

He stopped.

"This is because of me." Jeremy looked around. "I allowed this to happen." He looked up at Luke, eyes filled with tears. "You're right, Luke. There is such a thing as an accounting. Such a thing as sin and retribution. Such a thing as justice. It is the mark of all civilized people."

Jeremy unfolded himself. Burning brightly, he towered over Luke, his smile huge, kind, sad. Luke looked up into the light and it seemed to burn comfortably through him, leaving nothing left of him but pleasant ash.

"Thank you," Luke said as the last of him burned away.

Joanie tried to reach Luke before he messed everything up.

But Luke stopped suddenly, his hands dropping. He seemed to shake himself, give Joanie a quizzical glance. Then, he sat down in a lump, staring ahead sightlessly.

"Grampy?" she rushed to his side.

Luke looked up at her, his eyes an old man's limpid blue. He shook his head. Stared at her.

"What did you do to him?" Joanie whispered to Jeremy.

Jeremy didn't say anything but patted her shoulder reassuringly

Harry stepped past Luke over to Rosen. "Say," said Harry. "I was wondering if I could be part of the excavation crew."

Ed watched Robert breathe in and breathe out. On occasion, Robert opened his eyes, closed them.

Glenn sat across from Ed. Hannah and Sterling stayed in the lodge. They'd built a fire and cooked dinner but Hannah refused to even see Robert much less subject little Sterling to the dubious honor of a deathwatch for his uncle.

But Robert continued to knit through the night. Come dawn he was awake but without the breath to speak.

Robert's eyes were bright and shiny as the shell of a beetle and reflected no more human warmth than an iguana's.

Ed watched when Robert saw Glenn, saw him measure Glenn carefully, then look away, satisfied. Ed had no doubt Glenn was a dead man.

By the time the eastern light was coming through the trees, Robert could mutter between inhalations. He motioned Ed to come closer.

"Didn't think I would make it, did you?" Robert whispered.

"You were pretty shot up."

"Little Glenn did that. You take care of him until I get better." Robert gave Ed a wolf's grin. Coughed and spit out a little blood. "Then *I'll* take care of him."

Ed nodded.

"We'll take care of all of them," Robert said in a low monotone. "Bigger trailers. Better labs. We'll sell as far north as Chicago. West to Los Angeles. East to New York. South to Miami. *Nothing* will stop us. Not after what we've faced." He reached out and grabbed Ed's hand. "You and me."

Ed patted Robert's arm. "You have to rest and get your strength back." He leaned forward next to Robert and said softly. "I couldn't find Isobel and Maria."

"They *left*," Robert said fiercely. "After I shot up Jeremy's house. She screamed at me and I slapped her. Went out to the shed to clean the G36. Came back she was gone and the house was empty. Back to Mexico. Texas. Louisiana. I never figured out where the hell she came from." Robert grinned, grimaced, grinned again. "Hell of a piece of tail, though. Kill them if I see them again."

"Even Maria?"

"Girl ought to stay and look out for her daddy." Robert glanced up into Ed's face and squinted. "Okay, softie. I'll be nice. I won't go looking for them. Only if I see them. That satisfy you?"

"Sure." Ed looked into Robert's eyes. "I need a drink. I have some bottles stashed in the truck."

"Did you find my G36?"

"Yeah. It's in your truck."

"Bring it back. Feel better with it next to me."

Ed came at the truck from the side. It was still hidden under the trees and he didn't see any government agents lurking around. He opened the door and pulled out a bottle of Porter's Piss.

"Ed?"

He looked up. Jeremy was standing not twenty feet away. "Holy shit."

Jeremy grinned at him. "Yeah. I'm talking to you. Throw me that bottle."

Ed looked at Jeremy, then back at the bottle.

Jeremy shook his head. "Just throw the fucking thing."

Jeremy looked like he'd been up all night. Stubble on his face. There was something about him—then Ed caught it. Jeremy looked as if were just like anybody else. All these years, Jeremy had *tried* to look like normal people. But now he did.

"Are you..." Ed tried to think of the right word. "Mortal?"

"Yeah."

"Then you're done with us? Done with the County?"

"It's all over."

"Take it with my thanks." Ed tossed the bottle to Jeremy. "It's been good knowing you."

"Thanks."

And Jeremy was gone.

Ed went over to Robert's truck. It was locked but he had the key. They'd always shared keys. He found the G36 behind the seat and pulled it out, looked over the action. The chamber was loaded. The gun was set to automatic—Robert's favorite setting.

He walked back to the lodge, climbed down into the wash, and around to the front of the lodge.

Robert was trying to sit up. Vitality coming back every minute. Eyes wide with madness and glee. It was amazing that Ed saw it now when for so many years he'd ignored it.

Glenn watched him, watched Robert, watched him again, as fascinated and enslaved as a bird by a snake.

Robert caught sight of the G36. "There she is," he crowed.

Ed lifted it, pointed it directly at Robert's head, and held down the trigger until the clip was completely empty.

Joanie was able to get Luke to stand by talking to him gently and pulling him up until he responded. It took a while to get him down to the parking lot. He would walk for a few steps and stop until Joanie, cooing and gently pulling, got him started again. The two of them formed the head of a small procession.

Once they reached the parking lot, there was a sudden flurry of activity. Men were dispatched. Rosen barked orders.

Joanie paid no attention. Buddy helped her lead Luke over to Joseph's car and sit him down on the passenger's side. When he sat down, staring and unmoving, something broke inside of her and Joanie began to cry in great wracking sobs. She buried her face in Carter's chest.

When she was able to speak without crying, she looked up at

Carter. "What's wrong with him?"

"He's been struck," came a woman's voice from nearby.

Joseph and Nadine were standing there, holding hands, Amos and Jean next to them. Jean came forward and turned Luke's face up to hers, peered deep into his eyes. She turned and spoke to Amos. "Do you agree?"

"I could see it from here."

"Struck?" Joanie said.

"He has seen more than a man can stand and remain unchanged." Amos watched Luke, a sad and wistful expression on his face.

"Will he get better, Grandfather Amos?" Joanie stood straight. Stood formally, as one should before someone worthy of great respect.

Amos came forward. He squatted and took Luke's face in his hands. Luke's gaze moved around, left and right, up and down, until it finally settled on Amos. Luke put out a hand on Amos' shoulder. Amos patted his hand and stood. "He's strong. He will recover." He looked at Jean with stern pride. "We will care for him."

Jean nodded.

The ATF and DEA investigated the destroyed two trailers and four stills and found no one and arrested nobody. Following venerated and noble government tradition, they declared victory and left the field. Jonas Cole decided right then and there that he was done with police work. He graduated with a degree in Divinity from Harvard University and ended up helming a church in Oklahoma.

Annie took a shine to Robert Earl and dropped the Chase brothers like a pair of dead rats. The Chase brothers took it in sour good grace as they had always thought Annie was out of their league anyway and got blind drunk at the White/Chase wedding. In a fit of generosity (and more than a little fear of reprisal) Milt Cleary threw in the disputed parcel as a wedding present. After a hundred years, the Chase-Pollock feud was finally at an end.

The Harris sisters escaped and, as both Porter families had disappeared, took over the making of Porter's Piss. They proved to be as good at distilling as they had been at recreational chemistry. The meth industry never recovered.

Glenn Weatherwax never said one word about where any of the Porters had gone. He took his money and rebuilt his grandfather's house, fitting it (finally) with running water and indoor plumbing. He became one of Grace's deputies and would have been happy to stay there until retirement. But when Nuthatch County became part of Mississippi County, all deputies were subject to background checks. Glenn, Jenny, their young boys, and a tiny baby daughter sold the old house and left Nuthatch County to work at Bully Boy Distillers, in Boston, Massachusetts. Eventually, he rose to the position of master distiller.

Ray healed minus spleen, lung, and other assorted organs. But it did not stop him from opening *Wooley Worthington's Department Store* right on the empty property between Ridgeville and Ashby, two years after the war. At Ray's forceful insistence, Buddy Parker and Lee Thomas were both there to cut the opening ribbon.

Mary Jo Pedersen and Sidney Robinson and their little girl Edwina never returned to Nuthatch County. They moved from Sikeston to Cape Girardeau where Sidney got a job as a night guard at Southeast Hospital. He remained there for thirty years, a father, then a grandfather, then a great-grandfather. After he retired, he and Mary Jo traveled, seeing things they had never, *ever*, considered when they lived in the County. Sid died in Barcelona, sitting next to Mary Jo on the balcony, as the sun set.

Mary Jo, not realizing it, died a few minutes later, exactly as she would have wished.

But all of this happened later.

Few things can be done instantly and excavating the core of Little Mountain from Table Rock took a few days.

In the meantime, it became well known that once the excavation was complete Jeremy's power would be gone. Nuthatch County was like a man leaning on a crutch his whole life being told he could now walk on his own. The County lurched and drunkenly stumbled but there was no violence. One night had been enough.

Surprisingly, few resented Jeremy. After the Night of the War, as it became known, no one seemed disposed to throw any stones. Instead, they seemed to welcome him into the County as if he were coming to live with them for the first time. It was a new place, they seemed to say. A new start.

Let's do this together.

The mid-August heat wound around Nuthatch County like a hot wire. People moved slowly. Some didn't move at all but sat on porches fortified by an endless supply of ice-cold lemonade and thanking God himself for the invention of the refrigerator. And lemons. And ice.

Joanie drove down the county road and turned into Jeremy's driveway. The remains of the front of the house had been torn away and stuffed in a dumpster nearby. A new structure was taking shape on the foundation. Its form was suggested by a maze of two-by-fours. Betty was enthusiastically nailing a scaffolding together—though how anyone could do anything enthusiastically in this heat was beyond Joanie.

"Hey," Joanie said.

"Hey!" shouted Betty. She found her way through the wood and jumped down to the grass. She hugged Joanie. "How are you doing?"

"Good."

"And Luke?"

Joanie shrugged, suddenly sad. "Amos says he's getting better. I can't see it."

Betty smiled sadly. "Why don't you ask Jeremy about it?"

"I don't want to talk to him."

"Then why are you here?" Betty smiled. "To see me?"

Joanie smiled in return. "As much as I like you, Pam asked me to come over."

"Why?"

Joanie looked down, kicked at a piece of dirt. "Jeremy asked her to. Apparently, this was after he asked Buddy, Carter, and Ray."

"How's Pam? I haven't seen her lately."

Joanie laughed. "Secretive. But I saw flowers on the mantle with a card. I recognized Grace's handwriting."

Jeremy came around the edge of the house, wiping something off his hands. Joanie was startled. His hair had gone gray and his face had gained that odd slackness of skin marking people past forty. Joanie realized that he had always *looked* a little old but had never actually *been* old. Now, that was changing.

Jeremy saw Joanie and smiled and came over, started to stick his hand out, thought better of it. "I've been working on the plumbing."

"Yeah." *Just as well*, she thought. *I don't want to shake your hand anyway.*

"I'm getting back to work." Betty kissed Jeremy and walked

back into the stud forest.

Jeremy checked his watch.

Odd, she thought. I never saw him with a watch before.

"Thanks for coming out," he said.

Joanie shrugged. "What do you want?"

"Right now, some lemonade. How about you?"

Reluctantly, Joanie followed him into the shade of the oak. He opened the cooler and pulled out a bottle of lemonade.

Joanie saw beer past the lemonade and was about to ask for it when Jeremy picked up a bottle and handed it to her. She opened it, took a long drink of the crisp mix of hops and alcohol—the perfect drink in this heat. For a moment, she just let it flow down her throat, in her, through her. "That's good."

Jeremy nodded and sat in the grass. He checked his watch again.

Joanie sat across from him. "Now: what do you want?"

"I need someone to represent me in Washington."

Joanie choked on her beer. "Right. Pull the other one. You're just a private citizen now."

Jeremy pointed to his gray hair. "Not quite yet. You couldn't have missed what's happening to me."

"I didn't." Politeness kept her from smirking.

"There's going to be all sorts of transitions. There are going to be town councils and mayors. We're not big enough to be a county on our own so we'll probably be annexed into Mississippi County."

"Pam's going to love that."

"All sorts of transitions. We need to get as much as we can from Washington while it lasts. Once I'm gone, that's it."

Joanie sipped her beer. "You really think they're going to give us anything now?"

"I do. There are still a few parlor tricks that I can manage."

"You want me to talk to the President for you."

"That's right."

"I wouldn't know where to start."

Jeremy laughed. "That's exactly what Luke said."

A coldness shook her. "All right. I'll do it. If you bring Luke back. That's my only condition."

Jeremy shook his head. "I can't. He has to find his own way back."

"Why?"

"It's the nature of you mammals."

She stared at him hard to see if he was making fun of her but his face was solemn. "Explain."

Jeremy thought for a moment. "Every experience you have isn't just recorded. It's parsed, taken apart, analyzed, and pigeonholed all over—it's the process by which you take something of the outside world and make it part of your very biology. I can't take that away from him."

"He's a vegetable."

"Is that what Amos says?"

Joanie looked away. "No. Amos says he'll come back better than before."

"He's exactly right. Luke will come back. Luke will be better than ever. I can promise you that." He checked his watch again.

It irritated Joanie. "What's so damned important about the time?"

"Wait." He watched it and counted down. Finally: "Three. Two. One. Lift off."

For a moment, Joanie felt nothing. Then, there was an odd feeling of something pulling at her. Something strong for a brief instant—like the pull of a close magnet. Then, it faded quickly until there remained only an odd sensation like the after-effects of an electric shock. She looked at Jeremy.

"It's not the distance so much," Jeremy said. "After all, it's been a thousand miles away for weeks. But escaping the gravity well has an effect."

"Did everybody in the County feel that? Or was it just me?"

"Most felt something. You were closer to it. Or, more accurately, it was closer to you."

"Your… counterpart? That's what Buddy called it."

"STS-105. Remember this day: August 10, 2001. Four-ten in the afternoon." Jeremy checked his watch. "Just dropped the boosters. It's on its way to the space station. Of course, it will never get there. They'll open the bay and push it outside."

"Will it just stay up there floating along?"

Jeremy gave her a sidelong glance. "Of course not. It'll go where I tell it."

"What?" It came to her as a brilliant flash. "You bastard. You *planned* this. You planned the whole thing."

"No." Jeremy licked his lips. "Joanie, I knew all of the people who got hurt since they were born. I knew their parents. Their grandparents. Do you *really* think I would engineer a night like that? If I could have stopped it, I would have. Nuthatch County was a spring that had to be unwound."

Joanie looked away from him. He sounded like a querulous old man. "Maybe you could have taken longer to let it happen."

"The way it happened wasn't my idea, Joanie. It was Luke's."

She turned back to him. "Couldn't you have stopped him? You are the All Powerful Jeremy DaFoe."

Jeremy sipped his beer. "Yeah. You're right. There's no excuse."

"Grace is missing a lung."

"Ray's missing more than that. Keller needed an entire bowel resection. I tried to make it as painless as possible but this was the best I could do. I couldn't free myself. It was a rule."

"All civilized people have rules."

"My people more than most." He leaned forward earnestly.

Joanie stared at him. "What the hell are you, Jeremy?"

Jeremy laughed shortly. "Nobody ever likes my answer."

"That's because you never say!"

"It's a rule."

"All civilized people have rules." Jean sighed. "Give me something or I won't do it."

Jeremy looked out across the fields. "I was sent here to negotiate a truce between two great beings. I failed and for that reason I was trapped here." He looked back at Jean. "Now that I'm free I may just get a second chance."

"So, you're free. Go see the President yourself."

Jeremy shook his head. "And scare them into thinking I might be the same as I ever was? No. It's better that you go. As a favor to an old and dying man who might have enough tricks up his sleeve that could make them listen." He looked haunted. "They should listen."

Joanie bit her lip. "Grampy will be okay?"

"You have my word. Have I ever lied to you?"

"Only about the most important things."

"Except for that."

Joanie heard Betty singing to herself in the house. "Does she know?"

Jeremy shook his head. "You're the only one. You and Luke. Amos has suspicions. Besides, I couldn't deprive Betty of a lifelong dream. She's going to grow old with me and die."

"Why would you do that?"

"I love her," Jeremy said simply. "I never married anyone I didn't love."

Joanie watched him for a moment. "How about the rest of us?"

"Heh," he said. "You're all sad and broken children. What's not to love?"

"You could say that about anybody."

He nodded. "I could."

"You could say that about chimps."

"Chimps are great."

It came to her she was perhaps being played. "And puppies."

"There's always love for puppies." Jeremy gave her a sly,

feral grin she could take to her heart. "Unless, of course, you're going to eat them."

Joanie laughed and then looked at him. *Really* looked at this human wannabe. Every time in her life when she had beheld him, she had made him human. With that face, those eyes, that mouth, what else could she do? But this time, for once, she tried to see him without putting a man's face on him. Looked at him as if he were a piece of art, admiring the brush strokes, watching for the effects, as if he were no different from the trees, the sky, or the earth. What did she see but a splash of brown and gray, split by a slash of rose and a pair of blue splashes? Something that she knew? Something that she could trust?

Who knew?

"Okay," she said.

"Good." He drained the lemonade and threw the empty back in the cooler. "You'll need to get back to Washington before the end of the month."

She stood up. "I'll need an enormous expense budget. I'm flying back here to see Carter anytime I damned well please."

"Of course. And you'll have to get that plasma cutter you've been wanting. I want to see my portrait."

The President's secretary never actually looked at her. She radiated disapproval—after all, what would such a slip of a girl need with the President?

Joanie understood exactly how she felt. How the hell did people survive Washington in a suit? Two days after Labor Day and it was still hot as hell. *Summer wool my ass.* She sighed. Quicker done was quicker back to Baltimore and the visiting Carter.

Finally, Major Rosen opened the door and motioned her to come in.

They were all there: Cheney pushing his jaw forward like a pit bull. Powell leaning forward with his elbows resting on his knees. Bush giving her a half-grin that looked more like a smirk every time she saw it. Just as well he was born again, she thought. He would have needed something overpowering to rein him in.

"What can I do for you, Ms. Durant," said the President.

"I'm here at the request of Jeremy DaFoe," she said. *Don't be nervous*, she thought. *You represent something older and more powerful than any of them.* "A gesture of good faith."

"What would that be?"

She looked around. "Can we open up one of these windows? Or maybe the door to the terrace?"

Cheney shook his head. "What the hell is this? These windows don't open."

"Okay." *It's just a parlor trick. Remember that.* "He said to do this." She made wide motions with her hands as if she were turning a large and recalcitrant crank.

With a sudden pop, the windows began to open.

"Shit," said Cheney. "Aren't they fastened shut?"

"Do they even have hinges?" asked Powell quietly.

"Ms. Durant. Please stop."

She looked up. Rosen had a pistol aimed at her.

"Oh, please," she said. "After what happened in the County do you think that's going to do any good?"

The pistol wavered.

"Look," she said, still cranking. The window was almost completely open. "He just doesn't want the windows broken. He's being polite. This is a symbolic gesture."

"Major," said Powell. "I thought you said he was powerless."

"I didn't say that, sir." Rosen holstered the pistol. "I said the majority of his power was gone. Nothing left but parlor tricks."

"Nice trick," said Powell dryly.

At that moment a bald eagle flew through the window,

circled the room, and landed heavily on the desk.

They were frozen, staring at it.

It stank. There were bits of meat in its claws and beak. It towered over them from the splintering desk. The eagle lowered his head and swept them with his gaze and screamed.

A moment later, they found themselves at the far end of the room, huddled as far away from the shrieking thing as possible.

Joanie forced herself to walk over to it. Jeremy wouldn't let it hurt her, would he?

It glowered at them.

"Jeremy realizes he lives in the United States," she said by rote. There was no way she could say this without memorizing it. "It is a great nation and has been a good home for him. But he's been here longer than you. With or without his powers he knows things. He understands things." She took a deep breath. "He can't do much anymore, but he has a long history. Perhaps he can be of use."

The eagle screamed. It flew around the room and back out the window. The windows were suddenly closed as if they had never been opened. Were it not for the claw marks on the desk and the stink of fish there might never have been an eagle at all.

The President and his staff gaped at the closed window.

Jeremy had said something was coming. Joanie had no idea what Jeremy knew. He would say only that it was important. Only that whatever it was would define this man, this *President*, for the rest of his life. She felt a sudden pity for George W. Bush. She gave him her brightest smile in consolation. Like Jeremy said: get in while the getting's good.

"Jeremy was hoping for help in straightening the main road."

Epilogue

Betty stood facing the toilet tank. On top, there was an oddly shaped cylinder. There was a tiny window on one side with the symbols "+" and "-" printed on it. Neither symbol was highlighted.

There was no room to pace in the bathroom so she rearranged the medicine cabinet. Nothing much was in there: a small box of band-aids, some pain pills from years ago when Betty broke her leg. Aspirin. Acetaminophen. Ibuprofen. She wondered if Jeremy would now have pills of his own. Were there blood pressure pills, heart medication, and stool softener in their future?

The medicine cabinet was too small to take much time. When she was done there was still no highlighted "+" or "-" showing.

She cleaned under the sink. Behind the trash can, scrub brush, and Draino, there were different mounds of items lost to time. Things left down there that dampness and age had turned nameless and unrecognizable.

When Betty finished she stood and went back to the toilet tank.

There, glowing a bright pink and drawing in all light in the room, was a "+" sign.

She was pregnant.

Betty felt dizzy. Everything seemed a little gray. She sat down on the toilet lid. Betty had spent *years* reminding herself that there was *no* possibility of this ever happening. None. Put your impulses and desires into other things—other people's children at the school. Her garden. The farm market. Rebuilding this house—all worthwhile things to be sure. Things she likely would have done regardless. But companioned with the certain knowledge that whatever she did had to compensate for what she had given up to be with Jeremy.

She went to the door and stepped out into the front room. Between the harvest and the school year, they hadn't finished yet. The floor was bare plywood and the walls, though sealed, showed studs and raw siding.

Betty passed through the kitchen. She could hear the television in the bedroom. Something tense. She opened the door to the bedroom slowly.

"Jeremy," she said. How to begin? "I have some news. I have something to tell you."

Jeremy was sitting on the bed, his head in his hands. On the television, there was a picture of a building spewing smoke.

"Honey," she said hesitantly.

Jeremy said nothing.

"Honey? What's wrong?"

Acknowledgments

Like everything else, this book had a team behind it.

Wendy, who has been completely behind me from day one. Ben, who has been right behind her. Jennifer Stevenson, who beta read and copy edited it, and has been insistent it get out ever since.

The Cambridge SF Workshop was there for me as well. Their help, as always, was completely essential.

For all of these people, and for those I've not mentioned explicitly, from deep in my heart, thank you.

Credits

Nuthatch County
Steven Popkes

Published by Walking Rock Publications in association with
Book View Café Publishing Cooperative
ISBN: 978-1-63632-170-7

Production Team:
Cover Design: Wendy Zimmerman
Proofreader: Steven Popkes
Copyeditor: Jennifer Stevenson
Beta Reader: Jennifer Stevenson
Formatter: Steven Popkes

About the Author

Steven Popkes lives in Massachusetts on two acres where he and his wife raise bananas, persimmons, and turtles.

He works in aerospace making sure rockets continue to go where they are pointed. He insists he is not a rocket scientist.

He is a rocket engineer.

For updates, notional entries, subscription to newsletters, blog, and all-around interesting things, look on the website:

www.stevenpopkes.com

About Book View Café

Book View Café Publishing Cooperative (BVC) is an author-owned cooperative of over fifty professional writers, publishing in a variety of genres such as fantasy, romance, mystery, and science fiction.

BVC authors include New York Times and USA Today bestsellers; Nebula, Hugo, and Philip K. Dick Award winners; World Fantasy Award, Campbell Award, and RITA Award nominees; and winners and nominees of many other publishing awards.

Since its debut in 2008, BVC has gained a reputation for producing high-quality ebooks, and is now bringing that same quality to its print editions.

www.bookviewcafe.com

Book View Café Publishing Cooperative